ZIP & MILLY

BIG WATER

DR. ALEX VALENTINE

CONTENTS

THE FAMILY SECRET

— DUCKLINGBURG, SOUTH DUCK,
SUMMER 2017

My Human, the Old Lady, has a small computer with a picture of an apple, which I tried to bite once when I was just a puppy.

The Bitten Apple Computer is a good machine, even though it is getting old. Its power button gets stuck sometimes, which is why Old Lady finally resorted to never turning the computer off for the night.

Great by me: when she is asleep, I use the Bitten Apple Computer to type my Diary of a Spaniel.

Forgot the introductions. I am Zip the Spaniel.

Most Humans believe that Spaniels are bird hunting dogs.

But my Old Lady does not hunt.

She is a scientist, very famous in her academic field.

Very, very famous. I did not catch for certain if she was awarded the Nobel Prize or nominated. Or just rumored to be nominated.

Must investigate.

What I did see for myself was her visa to America. First Preference EB-1. Which means she's an extraordinary scientist and that America was ecstatic to import her outstanding brains. She did not even need an offer of employment to be imported into the U.S.A.

And there is more. There was a large free space on Old Lady's visa form for her to write in anybody she wanted to bring with. She could invite whomever else she wanted —write in any name. But she chose to bring me, "one pure-bred black and roan English Springer Spaniel, tail docked, shots current." Me! Make what you want of it.

Also, she brought Milly, my younger sister.

Because Old Lady does not hunt, I classify myself as a guarding dog. My sister Milly helps. We are quite skilled.

We guard our Human from all unpleasantness— small, medium and large ones. And especially from that one unpleasantness that we never talk about. That one is our family secret.

It is a tricky unpleasantness because, on one paw, it's so hush-hush that I should not even share it with my diary. On the other paw, I have not quite gotten to the bottom of it enough to understand.

Must secretly investigate.

❧

When we lived in Paris, Old Lady mostly worked on research of illnesses caused by broken genes. Old Lady was very busy, and only seldom found time to walk me in the Luxembourg garden.

But then things changed.

The customs agents at Kaliningrad Airport seized 20,000 blood samples—test tubes with bio-material intended for her genetic research. Almost 250 kilos of undeclared cargo went down the drain.

That caused quite some dust-up!

We had to quick skedaddle somewhere safer.

From Paris to Waterloo. That's in Belgium.

In Belgium, more horrid threats befell us. That's when Old Lady finalized her other research.

Here's what I understand about it.

Although most proteins in human genes are common to all Humans, there are some proteins that are unique depending on the Human's country, race or even region. Old Lady isolated those unique proteins and found a way —a tiny molecule—that worked on those unique proteins.

Once those unique proteins and the molecules Old Lady found fit like lock and key, we thought we hit the jackpot.

But, that's when Old Lady's friends who subsidized that research, announced that they were cashing out. Selling the research . . . and us. Old Lady's friends had put for sale everything—all the instruments and test tubes, the lab equipment, the journal entries, every last lab rat, all the lab hands and withal my Old Lady and her outstanding abilities. And naturally, me.

That was real trouble.

Old Lady quick booked a trip to America with brief stop in Germany so that we could buy Milly. Milly and I have the same parents, it's just that she is from a much later litter. Mom Phoebe acts young, but she is up in age already. Milly was in mother Phoebe's last litter, there will be no more puppies. Most definitely. Old Lady said that it was lucky—and reasonable for only five hundred euros.

Privately, I thought Old Lady bought a second dog to get off scent those "friends" who tried to sell us. They put out a search for a "Lady with a dog," not with two dogs.

So that's how we touched down in New York, America. The entry visa, like I said, was no problem.

In America, Old Lady declared she's retired.

We settled in the South, a quiet Southern town called Ducklingburg.

I like the new life. Old Lady's very busy with retire-

ment. I write my diary and guard her. And I keep our family secret: that we are all much younger than our calendar years.

I have not dug to the bottom of that secret yet.

But in time, I will ferret out the truth, I am sure.

If need be, I'm not above asking for help.

Old Lady's best pupil, Professor Fedya Arrnoff works not far from here, in Oklahoma.

Right now, Professor Arrnoff is very busy. He's looking for a molecule to fix his own genes so he only needs three hours of sleep each day. But when he finds that fix and changes his sleeping genes, he'll, of course, have lots more time.

In short, even though I've been sold by my Old Lady's friends, they will not find us here. I'm optimistic on this front.

Other than that, our life here in the American South is dreamy. We even made friends with the locals.

We dogs befriended Theodore, the alpha male Fox controlling the abutting forest.

Old Lady drinks tea with her friend Lariska, the seamstress from Avossia. Sometimes they speak Russian, other times they practice their English. Myself, I understand English pretty well, but I miss a lot when they speak Russian real fast.

Each day here is bathed in sunshine. The ever-bril-

liant camellias and magnolias give shade in our yard. There's lots of fascinating smells—dirt, jasmine, roses, chipmunks.

But enough about our new home in the South.

The sky above the forest's getting lighter.

I don't have much time. It's morning soon.

Back to my guarding duties.

❧

Thing is, Old Lady's email account gets lots of junk mail overnight. It is my guarding duty to clean it.

Old Lady used to be upset with junk.

"SnoreBGone remedies," she groaned, hitting the delete button peevishly, "I don't snore. How do they even know if I snore?! Are they listening?!" For such a smart person, Old Lady is clueless about some things.

It used to hurt me to hear Old Lady so riled first thing in the morning.

Can't say I blamed her, though: all that junk! What don't they promise, those spammers!

Flatten your belly! Remove crowfeet from your face! Lengthen your life! Enlarge! Reduce!

Like that ad for "hair growth remedy"—that came up every night for a while. Our Old Lady does not need that either. Her fur is short and naturally silky, just like mine and Milly's, only Old Lady is more on the Summer-cloud colored side. Milly and I are more on the spotted side. I am black with tan. Simply speaking, I have blazing orange spots. Milly is red roan, which stands for red and gold. And truthfully, my sister Milly snores much louder than the Old Lady, even though Milly is not even two years old and otherwise acts like a puppy.

But now that Old Lady stopped slamming down the laptop lid for the night, I get her mailbox cleaned up for her. My Human is eighty-four years old—in the best part of her eighties, as she likes to say. She has no time to spare to be upset with junk.

To do my cleaning job properly, I've got to read all of Old Lady's emails.

My sister Milly says I'm nosy, but that's not true. I do Old Lady a service.

With my paw, I can only push one key at a time, like those humans who type on little keyboards that only work with thumbs. Also, I am extremely careful to keep all the important e-mails. I can tell the junk from the important post: my mind is well-developed, even if I look young: nobody thinks me more than two years old.

Weather updates are important where we live.

Coupons for dog treats—those are important anywhere.

Plus, one has to be careful not to forget to re-order dog food. Last time, Old Lady and her friend Lariska were gone for a full day and forgot to even leave us those tasteless dry food pellets.

Now, by the time Old Lady wakes up in the morning, her computer mail box is nice and clean, and the important emails are all on top. I heard her boast that she stopped getting junk.

"Magic," she said, "I complained, and all the junk stopped coming."

No idea it's all thanks to me.

But I do not need her gratitude. I am her guarding dog and it's my job to make her happy.

— DIARY OF ZIP, THE SPANIEL DOG.

1

FOX SLINKING 101

In the dark cool hour when the Moon had just gone off her nightly duty and the Sun's shift had not yet started, Fox Theo licked his lips, and left for breakfast.

In stark contrast with his closest friends, sibling Spaniels Zip and Milly, Fox Theo lived in wild woods and got to choose his own menu daily. Zip and Milly lived in Old Lady's house, and had no say about what Old Lady cooked them for breakfast.

On days when hunting did not pan out, Theo's back-up plan was to call on the Human settlement across the Ravine. That's how he made the acquaintance of the Spaniel Siblings Family. Actually, he had only seen Old Lady from a safe distance, but

Spaniels Zip and Milly were always good for sharing some food.

But Fox's breakfast today was pre-planned since last yester-night and Theo did not envision depending on the hospitable generosity of Zip and Milly.

❧

Quail cafe, as the Fox privately dubbed the set-up, was a row of cages belonging to a large and loud human community—The Scared Hare Country Club.

The lands of the Scared Hare started a few dozen jumps down Sneaky Creek, immediately beyond the bridge that carried Old Dandelion Road's traffic across the Sneaky Creek.

Early that Summer, the Club's Head Chief had demanded quail eggs. A new wife of one of the sustaining members objected to the plight of chicken —and so *Quail Egg Omelet with Garden-Fresh Greens* promptly appeared on the Club's breakfast menu and—Theo hoped—on his menu too.

Quail Cafe had been under Theo's careful surveillance for some time, right from the first scent of the newly-installed quail coop. Theo was a careful and wise fox, not one to rush in recklessly before adequate reconnaissance and planning.

The coop stood almost a hundred yards away from the Caretakers' Cabin. Not a dog or a cat in sight. Not even a noisy chicken or duck to clack CLUCKAAAAAWK and spoil the hunt by sounding an alarm. Just a coop-full of soft-gray, spotted, warm, exquisite, succulent quail who, in the wild, could protect themselves by the natural camouflage that made them blend undetectably into the underbrush. However, no protective underbrush here.

❧

As always happens, the weakest link was the Club's own Caretakers. Theo knew that the youngest, Robbie—never locked the coop's door, just closed it. And that previous evening, Robbie left last.

Light as shadow on soft paws, using care to touch nothing with the bright-white tip of his luxurious red tail, Theo slinked toward the coop.

The Fox stretched out his body, covering the last step without moving his paws from the ground, then gently raised his head and sniffed the air.

Not for any trappings of safe life with Humans,

like his buddies Zip and Milly would Theo trade this exhilarating moment—the amalgam of curbed impatience, caution, concentration of all his skill and might! No, he, Fox Theo was not in the least bit envious of the safe and measured life of domesticated animals in service of a human. Forswear the ardor of the hunt? Not for anything! In moments like this one, Fox Theo refused to comprehend the motives driving wildlife from his woods to accept Human friendship. How could one give up this excitement, this passion, the urgent imperatives of an empty stomach that knows not exactly how it will next be filled?

Oh, the pleasure of the hunt!

Little Robbie's slipshod closure of the heavy latch would not stand up against the pressure of a determined tug from his proficient paw.

Theo wedged one claw into the crack, then pulled, wedged in the whole paw, pressed with the shoulder and his tail, gray in the morning twilight, cushioned the door behind to silence the thump.

The way was clear for the grand opening of Quail Cafe.

Theo had dealings with sloppy quail coops before. The quails dropped eggs wherever the spirit moved them.

The Fox moved quickly and efficiently.

No eggs by the first group of sleepy quail.

Two deliciously tempting eggs in the corner across from the door. Then, a little further in, one more.

He grabbed tiny quail eggs quickly, pressed with tongue against his palate, and swallowed the insides, jamming the thin soft eggshells inside his cheek. On and on until his mouth was so crammed with soft eggshells that not even one more of the tiniest, daintiest slippery, most deliciously yolk-smelling eggs could fit in.

What a sumptuous breakfast! Light and nutritious, and good for fox longevity.

Theo was about to take leave, when he was tempted again. A young quail hen sensed movement and sleepily turned around the corner to investigate.

Seeing Theo, she fluttered to the side, and Theo could not explain how, but he quickly herded the little quail through the door, out of the coop.

But Theo was a clever fox, and he was not about to jump headlong after his catch like a pirate, especially with a mouthful of eggshells.

The quail was also no fool and made for the house, where the quail custodians were still dead to the world in morning sleep.

First, Theo must discreetly get rid of the damning evidence—spit out the shells that were interfering with his pursuit of the quail.

Robbie was careless about securing the door but he was no simpleton; if he'd find a chewed-up ball of eggshells by the coop, he'll put two and two together. Little Human was a fan of fresh quail eggs himself, swallowing them still warm and, true enough, throwing a clutter of eggshells all over the place. But his eggshells are not chewed up in one big ball. Human children don't hurry, don't suck out the yolk. Oh, that tasty, incomparable to anything in wild Theo's ration taste of warm egg . . . runny white . . . soft yolk. Theo enjoyed the aftertaste.

Theo was no longer hungry. And did not like to over-eat. But quail for dinner was an enticing thought.

The Fox crossed a small glade and aimed for the overgrowth tangled in kudzu—incredibly quick growth, up to a foot a day. Best place for hiding.

Naturally, navigating into snarled, tangled kudzu growth was not an item on any fox's bucket list. But wait half an hour and the pernicious vines will grow back together so tightly that his entrance could not be used twice and will not betray that anything has passed that way.

Ideal hiding place for the blue-gray slippery ball.

❧

The kudzu usage as a hiding place was Theo's recent discovery, as was the wall of kudzu itself—an entirely new addition to the Forest landscape, something that sprung up since the longtime owner of the Foxes' Forest died and willed the land to his least favorite Nephew.

Under the late Uncle's ownership, the Forest was kept fastidiously clean; aggressive vegetation was held back, the underbrush cleaned out; even dead and sick trees were helped along. The Uncle was a proud, conscientious Forest owner.

When Uncle died, the Forest under conservation was quite the only thing that his nephew—a middle-aged loser by the name of Steve-the-Builder—had received for inheritance.

It was a nasty joke, that inheritance. Instead of long-anticipated seed capital to finance Steve's ambitions, he got only this land.

An albatross around his neck, land that would not bring him any income or profit. Yet, there were taxes to be paid to the City, and upkeep to be done to please the neighbors and to uphold the family name.

Thus far, his long-awaited inheritance turned out to be Steve's largest liability.

Yes, the opening of Uncle's will was the worst day in Steve's bland life, a slap in Steve's ruddy, slightly puffy face.

The residents of Theo's Forest all remembered the day when Steve inherited the land. As usual, the owls were first to spread the news:

"Cheap Steve! Stiffed Steve! Steve—the heir without a lair. What's for dinner, Steve?" The Mockingbirds embroidered on the news, singing all day and evening, "Can't build, must clean!" and as the season progressed, "Steve won't clean! Cheap Steve!"

The schadenfreude of the forest dwellers was in no way dampened by Steve's blatant cutbacks of his ownership duties.

The Forest was being quickly overtaken by ugly weeds and kudzu.

The Uncle kept the Forest prettier, but no cloud without a silver lining, thought Theo. Kudzu served its purpose: No better hiding place.

And so cool and shady. One would not find a spot as cool anywhere in Zip and Milly's yard.

Making a purposeful effort, Theo clutched his strong jaws and slowly sucked the last drop of egg gloop. There was no hurry, he decided.

Watered down with saliva, the last drop of quail egg juice softly hugged his mouth dissolving in the last gulp.

Theo coughed up small mountain of eggshells that was jamming his cheeks and twisted his head to shake out the last, stubborn particles.

Like sand on the tongue.

He sneezed.

Looked around.

Listened with ears cocked. Nothing suspicious presented itself.

What a lovely breakfast! And now so sleepy! . . .

He stretched out lazily on the ground. Sniffed. The scent of quail coop was tickling his nostrils. The warm little hen quail was all by herself, strolling all alone . . . And he dozed off.

His nap was cut short.

Jerked awake by a loud "BOOM" sounding through his head. A danger signal. But there was no danger.

Theo shook off the unwelcome feeling, came

fully awake, and began to concentrate on that dainty quail fluttering around. . . *Warm. Helpless. And it won't even cackle like the chicken hen, which spoils the hunt with ungodly noise. Oh no! The quail was too dignified to flap around and squawk like a hen in the coop.*

Quail had natural dignity, as if they lived in a royal palace, and not in a coop.

An excellent dinner material.

Fox stretched and climbed out of his hiding place, damning the tenacious embrace of the kudzu fuzz and the Human who was shirking his obligation to keep the Forest underbrush under control.

❧

Steve was a loudmouth braggart, but for all his ambitious posturing, and all the struggle to impress his friends and family—The Forest Owner he now entitled himself!—Steve in reality did not have the money even for seasonal clean-ups.

"Cheap Steve," growled Theo, getting irritated about the clinging kudzu fuzz. Theo was a fop at heart, and took pride in his orange fur. Shaking vigorously to free the precious coat from the last remnants of kudzu crud, he plodded back toward the coop.

But the quail must have hatched under a lucky star. When Fox returned to the coop, the Caretaker Lilly was already covering the quail, catching it under a butterfly net.

"My little fool," she cooed, pressing the plump, gray little bird and stroking its head with a finger, "Let's get you home, it's not safe out here."

Dinner's a bust, admitted Theo, but, on the other hand, breakfast was quite excellent. All organic, no chemical additives.

❧

Theo yawned, stretched, and—BOOM-BZZT!—something burst in Theo's head and swelled, roaring to the tip of Theo's tail, pulsating like a warning siren. He rose up to hind paws and sucked the air in, testing it nervously. Something had changed in the wind, changed ominously.

Did he imagine?

Theo's head buzzed with the noise again, and now he felt a jolting jab of pain—so strong that his eyes shut and mind went black he knew not for how long.

When, finally, Theo pried open his eyes, the day turned tingly, numb and dark. All he could see was the darkness . . . except for . . . maybe . . . *was that real?*

Far ahead . . . one solitary spot of orange light that felt like it was not completely there, like an illusion, an oasis formed by his overwhelmed mind. But the orange light grew solid, acquired depth, as it formed into a windy, inviting passage, just narrow enough for a fox to squeeze to safety.

Theo gasped for air, and could not pull it in his lungs.

The air engulfing him grew dense, constricting, unbreathable. In the sudden pitch-darkness of the day around him, *he knew: he had to run*. The air was different inside that orange passage—friendly, fresh and beckoning. He could breathe there, see there—if only he could reach it.

The black, constricting density was pressing Theo's body harder, fighting him for each breath. There were not many breathes left for the fox. *He had to . . . he must . . . escape into the place where he could see and breathe. He had to reach the orange passage. Quickly!*

And so Theo pushed all his strength together—and he ran.

2

FRIENDS

Ducklinburg's dreadful Summer got scorching hot that year. Zip's tongue drooped out as soon as he pushed through the front door on his way out for morning business. By the time Zip skipped halfway down the length of stone stairway of Old Lady's house, aimed for the perfect patch of grass in the front yard, he could smell his paws charring black. Zip briefly dipped his front paws into the fountain with tepid running water before scooting back inside.

"Hot! Had to do my business in nanoseconds, know what I mean," Zip complained to his sister, who was already waiting in the kitchen, spread-eagle on the marble tiles that no longer cooled her sweltering belly.

"So hot," agreed Milly dreamily, turning over to the stream of cold air coming from the floor air-conditioner grill.

"I wonder how the wildlife is managing the heat without air-conditioning. Fox Theo, for example. That royal red tail!" Milly practically drooled, "white-tipped and so fluffy, so darling! So lavish coat of fur . . . a problem in hot weather."

That's my sister Milly for you, thought Zip. Kindest heart. Always worried about all of our friends. Always a little in love for everything hairy, even the most dodgy and dangerous.

Mentally listing all the noble qualities of his younger sister, Zip plopped by her side and tried unsuccessfully to wedge his hind paws, scorched by the morning walk outside, into the stream of cool air. That's when his mind adopted a more critical bend.

Milly rarely cares about the feelings of those closest to her.

Case in point: Milly's silky golden-colored butt nearly plugged the kitchen cold air vent, and what was left of the desirable flow got trapped in her cascading Spaniel dog ears. The kitchen air was rapidly heating up and starting to smell like wet Spaniel dog.

"Quit hogging all the cold air, Milly," softly barked Zip under his breath, but Milly did not even twitch her light-brown nose in response to him.

"Let's ask Theo for sleepover tonight. The Old Lady'll never notice." Milly's silky golden butt only budged a bit, the better to cool another side.

"No, Milly. It's his job to live in the woods. Theo's wildlife. "

"But, Zip, hospitality—"

"Drop it, Milly."

"But Zip, his tail!" Milly hid her blushing nose between her paws and murmured, "It makes my heart excited! Oh, Theo!"

❧

Theo's full name was Theodore, which was appropriate for a red fox with elegantly thin black paws and a splendid imperial white-tipped tail—naturally bushy, never trimmed. "European style tail," Milly called it.

The long, airy red guard-hairs encircled the upper part of Theo's head, his cheeks, and ears. They rose over his neck in an airy golden mane which gave him an aura of strong and majestic masculinity, an almost lion-like effect.

Theo had made his first foray to the backyard home of Spaniel Siblings at mid-day, around Christmastime last year, when the unusually thick snowfall made it harder to hunt.

Theo dropped by unannounced, and immediately charmed impressionable young Milly. And angered Zip. Bigmouth and a moocher, thought Zip.

And was not wrong.

The Fox's agenda was really just to gossip and to scavenge.

"So," started Theo without standing upon ceremony, his black boots dancing on the hardened snow by the fire-pit, prancing back and forth, to better sniff the air above the Spaniels.

Milly stepped in to sniff Theo's face. Zip considered making new acquaintances by mutual butt-sniffing, but Theo was not going to stoop to that method.

"You new here? Must be from out of town? Your Human bought this?"

Some animals, thought Zip irritably, manage to act snooty and superior even when they are bumming leftover food and spreading rumors.

Theo jerked his nose in the direction of their elegantly grandiose home—and without pausing for either Spaniel to confirm, leaned in to confide a juicy rumor:

"Thought they'd never unload this." Red pointy nose, white whiskers curiously pointed frontward, stretched out again in the direction of the house. The implied insult hung awkwardly in the air.

"Grrrr," warned Zip, and sniffed Fox's shallow paw print in the snow ominously, as if to demonstrate he had the Fox's number.

Realizing that his confidence came out sounding like condescension, Theo attempted a backpedal, "Your Human must've got it for a song . . . good for you!"

Zip's back hairs bristled and steam streamed above gaping jaws, teeth bared. He'd never before been insulted so slyly.

Irate, he spread all four paws in a wide, steady stance, set to bark the fox out of his backyard, to ban this ill-mannered intruder forever. This would have put an abrupt end to a barely budded friendship, if it were not for Milly.

Milly interjected with a soft query:

"Why was our mansi— . . . the house especially hard to sell?" asked Milly innocently.

Zip froze in place, staring down the brazenly gossiping guest.

Zip did remember hearing Old Lady exclaim that their new house—mansion really—was unusually reasonably priced, but he had never questioned what he assumed was just their good luck.

It paid to investigate, decided Zip. He could always chase off the red-haired rascal later.

"Yes, why?" barked Zip, his whole posture showing clearly that Fox Theo better answer if he knew what was good for himself.

"You don't know?!" the Fox tried to stall, but when Zip made to advance on him belligerently, spat out: "The previous owner was a criminal. They jailed him. Everybody knows," he added with an air of defensiveness.

"What's that to do with our house?" pushed Zip, getting seriously upset.

The Fox saw that his attempt at friendly outreach was a flub, and being a smart animal, did not wish to respond. So, instead of clamming up, Fox Theo started talking up a verbal snowstorm of uninformative gibberish.

Zip lost track in under forty seconds. After about two minutes, Zip had to fight his own eyelids to stay awake.

Fox talked about "bad history," or maybe "bad aura." Fox used long words like "foreclosure," and "unexpected landscape," and "quite a shock." Zip was impressed at wilding Fox's vocabulary and dropped his guard for long enough for Fox to depart backwards, talking nonstop as his figure disappeared into the shrubbery.

Zip growled after their unwanted guest, then turned to Milly to see what she'd learned from the encounter.

Predictably, his sister was no help. Her eyes glistening, Milly whispered hotly, "That splendid tail! Why don't we have gorgeous tails like him, Zip?"

That's all she cared for.

❧

That year, Milly even tore up a few wrappings under the tree to see if Santa brought her furs for Christmas. Which, of course, he hadn't. Milly spent most of the holiday sulking by the mirror and trying to catch her own stub of tail.

"Why did Old Lady have to dock us so short," Milly griped about their Human, "Theo's tail is so bushy and warm!" Milly wagged her whole butt and snarled again: "barely a stub. Barely."

"Docked is the breed standard for Spaniels, Milly," assured her brother.

"Inelegant," returned Milly, reversing her spinning circle from clockwise to counterclockwise.

"Functional," retorted Zip, nipping Milly's ear just in time to ward off her collision with the Christmas tree. A bright yellow glass ball on top of the tree hesitated after the resulting bump, but dutifully kept its place.

"Theo looked at our tails funny," persisted Milly, twisting her neck to the butt and wagging the tail to one side, "What if he asks why my tail's so short?"

"He won't. Manners."

"Why did I let them? I should have told them no," growled Milly.

"You were weeks old."

"I don't remember. Do you?"

Zip shook his whole body noncommittally: actually, he did remember.

Back at the time, the two of them—Zip and Old Lady lived in Paris. Old Lady worked a lot, and Zip took walks with housekeeper Michelle. Michelle talked quickly and sweetly. First thing he learned was "Arreter tu!" The menace of Michelle's rr-s was almost indecipherable, especially compared to the Russian rr-s of their previous lives, "Rrazboinik, dzhokerrr."

From Paris, Old Lady went to Germany, the Institute of Molecular Genetics. The business there was no success at all, but for one thing: Old Lady bought Milly from Frau and Herr Boing. Old Lady said it was great luck: Milly was Zip's own sister, only much, much younger. Now Michelle walked them both—him and Milly. That was more fun. Still, Old Lady was busy all the time, worked a lot. Got tired and nervous. After that, they moved to Belgium, a tiny town called Waterloo. Old Lady worked even more, two jobs. First job was her favorite, but it ate up all her money. Zip did not understand how a job can eat money. The second job was easy and paid well, but made their lives complicated. The housekeeper now spoke Flemish, which at first neither Zip nor Milly understood. But after a few days, Zip mastered all commands. That's when the scandal broke. The culprit was that second job, the one that was easy and paid well. Actually, the second job was no more because the customs of Kaliningrad Airport seized 250 kilos of test tubes with blood. That was reliable information. Zip heard it himself:

Two hundred fifty kilos, twenty thousand samples . . . down the drain—literally.

Zip'd never seen those tubes. Anyway, he couldn't have counted this high.

He remembered green scrubs, a fidgety doctor who spoke to him in Flemish.

That's when Zip and Milly's tails got chopped and they all boarded Lufthansa for America.

Zip was not going to muddle Milly's little head with that old rubbish and, noticing his sister's petulant expression, gave Old Lady's justification,

"A docked tail is the working gun-dog standard in America. If anyone should ask, just tell them. That ought to put a muzzle on any impertinent nosiness."

But nobody ever did ask.

Eventually Milly took solace in the fact that her ears were much longer and silkier that Theo's.

Secure in the thought that her silky ears were more than a match to Theo's tail-fluffiness, Milly was pleased to play the genial hostess and, as the months flew by, Theo's sporadic visits had gotten more frequent.

By Summer, Theo's visits were as sure as rain.

❧

The Spaniels whiled away the hot August morning, jockeying for position near their favorite kitchen air-conditioner vent.

Sweet Milly, albeit not even in Zip's weight category, kept winning the battles for position, and corking all the coveted coolness with her own butt.

The dogs agreed that Fox Theo needed reinforcement, and pooled half a toast and almost a whole strip of bacon for his late breakfast. But Theo did not show up that morning. Nor was he there for lunch. Milly blamed Zip's lack of hospitality, which, naturally, added to her moral right to enjoy cold air.

By early afternoon, even Zip grew slightly concerned and went to the window to investigate. There was no sign of Theo's now-familiar fox-tailed shadow by the fire-pit.

But something else captured the dogs' attention.

The tree-tops started moving. Without any warning, the cool North-West Wind blew in from Canada and, in mere minutes, all the Ducklingburg heat dissipated, disappeared completely. Somewhere, hundreds of miles away from Zip's fireplace, the Atlantic Ocean was surging and billowing, and sending wind in Zip's direction.

Old Lady, coffee cup in hand, stepped outside. The leaves on the neighbors' dogwood rustled restlessly.

"It's going to rain," predicted Old Lady, and explained "late August is the storm season here in Ducklingburg, even sometimes tornados." Old Lady's soft gentle fingers touched Zip's back as she warned, "You two stay here, in case there's a windstorm."

Paying no attention to the warning, Zip and Milly silently crept around behind the Old Lady's back and toward the front door. The front door creaked softly and the two dogs streaked toward their favorite outdoor resting place, the fire pit.

❧

"Fresh wind, it's so sweet to breathe," waxed Milly poetically, trotting alongside Zip and kicking up a few specks of sand that landed on her brother's nose. Finally, she hurled herself onto her favorite place by the fire pit.

"Zip, dear, let's not fight over who gets to lie

down where. You can have the coldest place on the floor tonight. I yield my turn."

Feeling that he was the adult, Zip agreed amiably. Why quarrel? Especially since the weather had cooled down anyway and there was no further need for the air conditioner.

"Thanks, Milly, I already yielded my turn to Old Lady, but thanks anyway."

"You are so thoughtful, my Zippy," said Milly sweetly, and started digging a hole in the safety sandbox—the best place by the fire-pit.

"Wonder what happened to Theo?" she asked for umpteenth time, and muttered to herself "darling black-booted paws, simply gorgeous fluffy tail."

"I do not know," agreed Zip, edging into the sand by his sister, "Wasn't here for lunch."

"Or breakfast," echoed Milly. "Very strange."

3

THE WORRY

"I've already had breakfast," said the familiar voice, and Theo strolled in quickly from the downwind side.

"We'd been waiting and wondering," Milly turned her head, inviting Theo into conversation. It was the first time in quite a while that Theo had missed both lunch and breakfast.

"Sorry that it's a wrong time for dinner leftovers," noted Milly with regret.

Zip noticed that Theo's manner did not show hunger, but his muzzle wrinkled with lines of suppressed tension.

"Top of the morning to you, Theodore," Zip said softly, acting as if nothing was out-of-the-ordinary.

One had to watch the tone of one's bark when

communicating with Wildlife. Plus, it was better to not attract Old Lady into coming to see what was going on.

Zip would not dream of asking The Fox directly what he wanted or addressing him by the informal Theo. One had to maintain decorum.

"Greetings, Zip. Don't worry, Milly," responded Theo, "I had a brilliant morning—light breakfast but nutritious."

Robbed the Country Club's quail coop, Zip figured, and, diplomatically, did not ask any more questions. Zip's view on Theo's piracy at the Country Club was this: What I do not know, I will not be honor-bound to report as part of my guarding dog duty.

Milly's glittering eyes moved from Zip to Theo, two creatures who managed to maintain a friendship despite profound differences in their outlooks on life.

She knew that Theo considered his independent way of life the only way worth living. Conversely, Zip looked down on Theo's scavenging and, as for Theo's hunting—that was perfidious piracy according to Zip. Robber, brigand!

But both friends kept quiet about their difference of opinions. Indeed, their differences only made their friendship stronger, which saved Milly from unnecessary upset. She loved them both.

❧

"I've already had breakfast," repeated Theo uneasily, "that's not why I'm here."

Theo hesitated, considering how best to approach the subject; then he decided to be blunt. It was, after all, a matter of safety.

How does one explain all that to spaniels, with their conditioned air—cool in the Summer, warm in the Winter? How does one that Air itself gets dense and oppressive? How does one explain hostile elements at all to a Spaniel, a coddled creature whose life is spent relaxing on soft sofas, a creature whose food appears reliably without lifting a paw to procure it?

Theo was hard pressed to put into words what happened to him just after his mild and nutritious breakfast.

How would one go about wording it?

That feeling . . . the air itself grew dense and bitterly cold, engulfing and constricting his whole body, encircling the fox tighter and tighter in the suffocating, gelid whirl. The air itself brought

Worry, made Theo's body tremble; that's why the fox set off and run, chased on, driven by the bitterly cold, hostile air. The air was gaining on him, pushing him on.

Despairing to put this episode into words, Theo only mumbled,

"You and Milly, you should be fine. You're under human protection—"

"—Protection from what?" interjected Milly.

"—There's bad news though. And ... one very unpleasant piece of news affecting you," went on Theo. He dithered some more, then plunged in.

"Big Water is coming."

"The National Weather Service made no warning," Zip retorted politely, taking advantage of the pause. The Fox never hurried his sentences. "How do you know?"

"I just know," insisted Theodore. Both dogs looked at him incredulously, and he resolved to spell it out: "Worry came."

"What did it look like, Worry?" asked Milly innocently.

"Can't describe. It does not come to human-near dwellers, you do not need Worry. The Human figures out your problems in advance and solves them for you as they happen. We, wildlife, don't have your kind of protection. In order to survive, we need to be tuned in to Worry."

"Describe it," Zip asked. It's not that Zip doubted Theo, but he was honestly curious. Zip was always eager to learn something new.

"Worry," Fox shut his eyes tight and wrinkled his whole face, "It crawls under the fur and pulses in the head. Like fear," he shook his head, and corrected himself, "not like fear, actually. Fear settles inside, it's very hard to get rid of it. Fear makes me cold inside, and wet and sticky outside."

"Happens to Humans," agreed Zip, "they shiver from fear and they have this expression, covered in cold sweat."

"Zip, dear," interjected Milly gently, "Old Lady never shivers or gets sweaty."

"I read it on the internet," explained Zip calmly, "Research."

Zip paused, deep in thought.

"Happens when a wild creature meets a human with a gun," added Theo.

Milly and Zip shook their heads in unison.

We are not afraid of a gun. Old Lady has one in her nightstand, and one in her purse. Once there was a rattle downstairs in the night, and she took it out to protect us. Turned out to be a raccoon, but still.

We are on friendly terms with the gun. Maybe we could even be on friendly terms with the Worry, the dogs wondered.

The Worry seemed sillier by the minute. But the Spaniels did not want to be rude. Zip was trying to think up something nice to say, to calm Theo down, but Milly almost blew it.

"Theo, maybe there really is no Worry? If nobody's seen her. And you can't describe her."

"You Human-Dwellers just don't get it!" The now-annoyed Fox's tail fluffed out, like a fire flame, and the dogs were abruptly reminded that they were addressing a Wild Thing,

"You never take responsibility, you—" Fox rattled something under his breath, and Milly later swore that he used some curse words and even nastier words like "irresponsible human-near dwellers," "welfare" and "public assistance moochers."

Zip stepped in, trying to divert the conversation from a touchy debate over the existence or not of the Worry.

"What do you mean by Big Water, anyway?"

"Right," echoed Milly, "How big? And where?"

The Fox was cooling off, and Zip explained, "We get a rush of water almost every rain, it even floods up to the back porch."

"One-hundred year big. Happens once in a hundred years." Theodore regained his air of importance, "So big that no animal alive has ever seen this much big.

"A lot of water will come," added Fox, with simple sadness.

"So, what will happen?" the dogs asked in chorus.

"It's hard to know exactly what or exactly why," responded Fox.

Means that nobody knows, thought Milly.

"But there are circumstances," Fox added, then paused and sniffed the air suspiciously. This time, the dogs did not dare interrupt, waiting intently for Fox Theo's pompous pronouncement: "there's been some change of circumstances."

The Change of Circumstances began as soon as the Forest changed its ownership—the night when Uncle's will was read and all the Forest creatures learned that the woodland where they live now had a new Human Owner. They were the Wildlife of Cheap Steve. Inexplicably, they all felt Change.

And it's not like Wild Community was even all that miffed about lack of the Forest cleaning. No, that was not it. The issue was much deeper. The Wildlife understood immediately, with the same instinctive certainty that let them know of the comings of storms or goings of the predators: there was trouble brewing. Their new Human, Steve, was trouble.

The Wildlife pricked up. They all felt danger. Some panicked and began stockpiling berries; others turned to loud swaggering, designed to prove it to themselves that they were not afraid. There even were a few who talked migrating. Whatever the plan, nobody was left untouched by the ominous change.

The perpetrator of the coming "change," this Theo could sense with certainty, was the new Human Owner of the Forest—Steve. But Fox did not want to finger Steve out loud because such an accusation would diminish Fox in the eyes of his friends, might be deemed a breach of propriety. Human Steve did not exactly inspire the affection of the wildlife community. That's on one paw. On the other paw, Fox Theodore was of the mind that Tradition made it his responsibility to be deferential to his landowner, if not loyal. And most importantly, the danger that emanated from Steve casted its vague shadow onto Fox himself, and his numerous family. As yet himself unable to understand the particulars of the looming threat, Fox did not dare to claim too much detail in his warnings to others.

Steve was planning some nasty change. What

change? Fox Theo did not yet know, and hesitated for fear of making a fool of himself by passing on what might turn out to be misleadingly elaborate warnings.

Both dogs stared, waiting. The pause was getting awkward.

Milly broke the silence first.

"What change and where?" asked Milly, only because hospitality meant she was expected to show interest regardless of whether she could understand a word of what their friend was talking about.

The Fox did not answer right away, then squeezed out the response, "Circumstances under the Bridge."

"The Bridge?"

"The Bridge across the Sneaky Creak. The Bridge where I … we … Where I found Milly when she was lost that once."

Milly made a step backwards and growled irritably. She hated the Bridge and did not like to be reminded of the story.

4

THE BRIDGE

Milly was always way too gullible and social. She only saw the best in every animal, and always made new friends. No matter what the creature, it was "my new friend," "my buddy," "my BFF."

She'd dragged in all manner of buddies, from birds to reptiles. A neighbor's rabbit, a turtle from the creek, a possum stealing scraps at night—anybody who so much as smiled at Milly would get invited to munch on the Spaniels' food.

Zip was not really greedy, but he did not much like to share. The Old Lady paid good money for Spaniel food. Zip reasoned that, if she'd wanted to throw it out in the Forest, she would have done so.

Besides, this entire zoo was prone to help themselves to the water from the dogs' dishes. And, believe it or not, some of Milly's "friends" were so unmannerly as to step into the dish from which they were drinking. Or worse.

Unsanitary. Even disgusting, concluded Zip.

And also stupid, especially since there is a perfectly clean water in the Spring a few steps away.

But carrying hospitality to a naïve extreme was not the worst of Milly's habits. The worst was her propensity to stray. The instant her brother Zip was not watching, Milly somehow floated into the neighbor's yard.

The neighboring humans all already know her. The plastic surgeon was quick to install her back home. The banker had two small kids who liked to pull long Spaniel ears but Milly claimed that was friendship, that the children were "only playing" affectionately.

The latest in Milly's streak of girlfriends was a young coyote adolescent, almost a pup. Curious, free-spirited and full of joy, the pup coyote persuaded Milly to explore the world.

"Think outside your yard," were her exact words. The particular exploration that the coyote touted led away from all human yards, down into the ravine, all the way to the place where Sneaky Creek flowed noisily under the Bridge.

According to the Pup Coyote, the water noise under the bridge was water-music.

"Music, Milly, tinkling music!" enthused the Pup, "You have to be tuned in to hear! It is a real concert. My older brothers taught me to appreciate it. They are extremely cultured!"

Milly did not want to seem uncultured, and agreed to go listen to the concert.

"My brothers were planning to come too," said Coyote Pup, "would that be OK?"

Milly did not want to seem a prude, and said yes.

And in no time at all, Milly's BFF Coyote pup was making introductions to her brothers—a whole pack of much older, larger, gnarly-looking Coyote brothers. A frisky pack of young coyote ne'er-do-wells.

Theo arrived just in time, and plunged quickly into negotiations.

Meanwhile, it took Zip a little while to rouse the Old Lady, and by the time they had reached the scene, Negotiations were in full force. There were two burly coyote brothers on each side of Theo, and the rest of the rugged pack was busy pushing Milly further into one of the dark, damp, scary tunnels, deep under the Bridge.

Were we to come a moment later, thought Zip, I do not like to think what would've happened.

Of course, Old Lady had packed what she called "heat" in her little clutch bag.

As soon as she grumbled, "Milly, do you know these boys?" and went into her purse, all of the Coyote Brothers disappeared, like they were never ever there.

❧

"Under the Bridge," whispered Milly, "Yeah, I know the Bridge, Theo."

"Surprised you were not grounded for a month," grinned Theo.

"Old Lady would've," admitted Milly, "but she got sidetracked."

That was true: Milly got lucky.

Zip had earned himself many a much harsher talking-to from the Old Lady for much lesser misdeeds. Milly would likewise have gotten a strong comeuppance, but the Old Lady now had a bigger target in her crosshairs: her quarrel was with the Bridge itself.

The Bridge—a concrete mammoth just downstream from Old Lady's land—was part of the Old Dandelion Road, one of the busiest drags in town that ran from business district to the South Side. The four-lane, two-way expressway adorned with ten-feet median of manicured grass and flowers swooshing with speeding traffic, it was framed on either side with matching stretches of bright-green lawn, to buffer speeding cars from a rare daredevil cyclist or pedestrian.

Along the edges of the Bridge, a row of twenty-feet-high towering evergreen American Holly, were employed to cover up the precipitous, untidy and permanently littered ravine that served as the bed of Sneaky Creek.

The hollies protected the aesthetic sensibilities of the travelers with their whitish flowers in the spring, and dark red berries in the fall.

All this splendor was supported by five monolithic concrete walls which formed four tunnels of gigantic width, length and height. The bed of the Creek inside the tunnels was likewise fortified in concrete.

The Bridge was a powerfully sullen construction designed to direct Sneaky Creek's passage through the tunnels under Old Dandelion Road.

But when it rained, Sneaky Creek filled up the whole ravine, rising quicker than self-rising pizza batter. And lately, the batter of the Creek was getting too big for its pan. When it rained, even Fox Theo did not dare jump across the ravine, and had to edge along the shoulder of the bridge, along the hollies.

But now the Bridge tunnels were being shrunk. Somebody deft, ill-meaning and cunning kept sneaking in and pouring concrete under the bridge and behind the bridge, downstream on both banks of the ravine. With skillful concrete pouring, the bed level under the bridge rose higher, the tunnels shrank—the pathway for the Creek behind the bridge kept getting squeezed narrower and narrower-- until the whole construction began resembling a dam more than a bridge.

Which made Old Lady furious.

"They pour concrete inside the tunnels," she hissed, "The Bridge's a bottleneck!"

Then she reached in her clutch, and both dogs cringed, wondering if Old Lady planned to shoot the offending tunnels under the Bridge and free Sneaky Creak.

That was a stupid thought, of course, but Milly had gotten everybody all panicked, so nobody was thinking straight.

Old Lady rummaged for her phone, and started snapping pictures behind the bridge where in the piles of concrete were visible in all their ugliness, blocking the egress from under the bridge. She even jumped with the Spaniels from one side to the other. Zip liked the game, and the concrete surfaces were good for jumping: no sticky seeds got caught in the fur between the paw pads.

But Old Lady refused to enjoy the jumps. She muttered about the negodniks who poured concrete in the Bridge's tunnels and banks, thus plugging the Sneaky Creek's pathway so much so that it no longer could escape downstream. Now she understood why lately, after the lightest rain, water filled the ravine to the brim, spilled over, gathered into a make-shift swamp, spreading treacherously toward Old Lady's yard. Now it was clear why, what change of circumstances was responsible.

Old Lady attentively examined every bit of under-bridge terrain, shaking her head.

"Just wait, you wretched rascal. Nothing lasts forever and this outrage will eventually end. Someday, a house on this upstream side of the Bridge will be bought by someone influential. What we want is somebody with money. Or connections with the City or Department of Transportation. Or lots of time on their hands and a local press connection. Or a smart, ballsy trial lawyer.

Old Lady spent a long time climbing under the bridge, clambering up the right bank, and up the left, retreated to the depth of the ravine and making selfies with the bridge from every angle.

By the end, Old Lady got so worked up and exhausted that Milly and her wayward wanderlust were forgotten.

"We know about the Bridge," said Milly.

❧

"Theo," repeated Milly defiantly, "We thank you for your bravery—you saved my life, of course—but Old Lady knows all about the Bridge. Besides, I'm not afraid of a little creek water. I've jumped over and into Sneaky Creek. No problem. Old Lady jumped too, and made pictures."

Milly shook her hind paws, remembering the jump but glossing over the fact that the "into the Creek" part had been a bit unintentional, even embarrassing at the time. It was that time she went to listen to the music with coyotes: her front paws had cleared the water easily, but she forgot about the back paws, and, even more lamentably, forgot that the hind paws were attached to her furry plump bottom. That had shifted her balance, and sent Milly rolling down the cement bank towards the watery frog habitat at the bottom,

"Old Lady asked me to come shower in her tub a little. Lots of dirty sand washed out of the ears and from between the toes. That's all." Milly shook her whole body, proud that she got to share the bathtub with Old Lady, and added, "Not afraid of a little water."

"Big Water," corrected Theo.

The Spaniels chorused, "So what? We get BIG shower?"

"Big Water will invade, come into Old Lady's house. That's what Worry is telling me," announced the Fox with solemn sadness, "and then—"

"—Water never comes inside the house," protested Milly, "It's not even near the kitchen on the bottom floor. Certainly not even close to the bedroom—that's on the second floor, waaaay up," Milly jerked her head up in the air, then shifted her gaze down toward the back entrance, "The water always stops a few steps from the ground floor, leaves just a little puddle. It will not dare—"

"It will," Theodore delivered his prophecy, "and then—"

"Old Lady will not let it," insisted Milly, "Old Lady knows all about the water."

"Old Lady knows?" Theo was clearly taken aback, "Worry spoke to Humans? No way. Besides, as I said, there was a change of circumstances. The Bridge," frowned Theodore, "has swallowed too much of Sneaky Creek's path. Now the path is much too narrow for Big Water, much narrower than that day when Old Lady saw it."

"Why?"

"I saw them yesterday, pouring more concrete into the tunnels, deep under the Bridge. Again."

"Them—who?"

"Humans. I do not know them. But the real question," Fox inhaled deeply and went silent.

Zip and Milly held their breath.

"The real question is—" Theo cut himself off again, and bit his upper lip so hard that the bristly dark hairs of his vibrissae stood up on ends. What Theo did not dare say was: the question was Who caused the pouring—gave the orders which for all wildlife were so calamitous?

As a matter of fact, the massive pouring started in earnest just after the death of Uncle was announced, and Steve inherited title to the Forest.

And Theo did receive intelligence, and it did

come from very certain sources . . . Still, Theo did not want to think that Steve was giving orders to plug the Sneaky Creek. Besides, Theo told himself reassuringly, Steve's cheap, he does not have the money for this nonsense.

But Cheap Steve or not, the bottleneck of Bridge's tunnels was poured with concrete on both sides of the ravine downstream and was pinching Sneaky Creak narrower and narrower.

No sooner did it start to rain, the water quickly collected upstream of the Bridge and rose sharply, filling up the whole ravine.

Even on the days when it just drizzled, the deer did not dare to cross the ravine in front of the bridge for their daily trip into the Humans' backyards to pluck fresh rosebuds or whatever other tender plants were on the Deer Menu du Jour. The pluckiest of rabbits only crossed along the bridge; the sickly ones declared that they'd rather do a cleansing-weight-loss diet of rain water.

On days when it poured, the water spread on both sides of the ravine—both right and left. The horrifyingly fast rust-colored stream almost reached Old Lady's back door. On the other side of the Creek, it set off for Theo's Forest. It flooded burrows and killed off the dwellers. It littered the Forest with flotsam trash—old plastic bottles and buckets, old boots and mattresses, dried brunches and the whole trees taken out with roots.

No way, decided Theo. Cheap Steve can't even afford to clean the Forest. What motive would he have to litter it deliberately? Besides, Cheap Steve was Theo's Human. Better to be loyal. At least deferential unless there was evidence that clearly discharged the wildlife from duty toward their landowner.

The Fox jumped up to a low-hanging branch of giant Magnolia Tree and started whipping the air with the white tuft of his tail. He was moving the tuft in the shape of a figure eight, which he only did when severely confused.

Zip and Milly are friends. Old Lady is a friend. The scraps that he so often scavenged did come from Old Lady's table.

And Theo did have information—a rumor really —that Old Lady's furry family could maybe use.

Theodore's head filled with jumping, swirling thoughts and questions. His Human's reputation versus preserving the food supply. A dilemma.

The practical approach won. After all, good food was not just a matter of survival. There was also the matter of his pride. Theo was a family man, and providing for the kits elevated Theo in the eyes of the kits' Mother. To be a strong, wise, caring provider for his family . . . the practical approach won.

"I can tell you," Theo made up his mind, and now spoke quickly, spurting out what he'd heard, even though he only half-believed. "I'll tell you, but—"

"But?" encouraged Milly.

"I do not know who is pouring, and it does not matter," said Fox, slowing down again, "But I have an inkling as to who's ordering the pouring. It's just a guess. OK, it's more than just a guess. I heard. Alas. I know for sure. Yes. It's the t-truth," Theo stuttered momentarily, then added firmly:

"My Human landowner, Steve. Yes. I am sure. Steve is the one who's leading this horrific effort, to fashion a dam in place of Bridge. It's Steve. That's the bitter truth, bitter for the me, and for you, and for our whole Forest."

The Fox was finished and expected an uproar. But both dogs just sat there, staring, stunned. Finally, Zip broke the awkward silence.

"How do you know all that?" Zip asked bravely, because that's what Old Lady always asked when she did not like whatever news she just heard.

"Yes, who told you," echoed Milly.

"I'd rather not disclose my sour—"

"I know. The Worry told him," mocked Milly, "the invisible Worry." Sometimes when Milly got nervous, she tended to forget her manners. Everybody knew that about her, and Theo was not even noticeably offended.

Silence fell upon the trio once more. Fox Theo could not believe it! After all the courage he had to summon, after all the hesitance, after he'd betrayed his own Human, these silly canines were going to heedlessly dismiss him. They did not believe him!

"OK, I'll tell you," Fox looked around warily, even though there was nobody in the yard except for the trio.

"My source is Freckle," declared Theo proudly, and looked at his friends as though he had said that his source was The New York Times.

But the bewildered dogs were looking askance again.

"What's Freckle?" said Milly finally.

"Not what. Who. Freckle is my youngest, from the last Spring litter—"

"You called your pup Freckle?" interrupted Milly.

"Not me, I would not … that's what her Human calls her, at work."

"Work?"

"OK, so I'm not exactly proud of the pup's choice of career."

Fox Theo jumped up, arched his back and plummeted, paws down, tail straight, as though he was trying to fall through the ground. The ground did not take him, but he swallowed a mouse that fortuitously lost its way under the tree roots. Theo hoped, in vain, that the touchy topic of Freckle's "work" had been sufficiently diverted,

"Like I was saying, Freckle is an honest source, and her information is reliable."

"How does Freckle know," Zip asked, "Who told her?"

"Nobody told her, she eavesdropped," retorted Theo honestly, "that's what she does."

"Eavesdropped where? Hiding in the kudzu forest," scoffed Milly.

She really needs to work on her self-restraint and tact, thought Zip.

"No kudzu," Theo still did not take offense. "Freckle works at the Humans' golf club."

"Works?" the dogs almost forgot about their troubles, "Works for Humans?"

"Sure. Tricks with golf clubs. For treats. Like I said, my daughter's chosen career is not a source of fatherly pride."

Theo lowered his nose and pretended to scrutinize the red bug that was playing dead on the side of the fire pit. Zip was trying to wrap his mind around Theo's unlikely claims.

Big Water. Golf Club. Proud wildlife Theo had a kid who worked for Humans. Tricks with golf clubs? Theo's Human littering his own land.

"Your kit does tricks with golf clubs?" Milly blurted out tactlessly.

"That bit just slipped out. I really did not mean to share anything about tricks," an embarrassed Theo admitted. He then jumped up abruptly and trotted out of the Spaniels' yard without any parting niceties.

Zip could just barely hear Theo mumbling, "Freckle makes me worry. Worry, Big Worry, the Worry makes me thirsty, I'm going to drink at the Spring. Spaniels' water is no good, it may be clean but smells like chlorine . . ."

Milly and Zip watched the fox disappear into the underbrush along the Creek.

They sat down side by side and pondered what Theo had just claimed.

"He is exaggerating," whispered Milly, and tried to lick Zip's nose.

"Zip," Milly was pushing her side against Zip's for

confidence.

"What?"

"Zip, I think I can begin to feel Theo's Worry in my fur."

"Nonsense," Zip told her, even though he could feel it too. But then he remembered that he was a Spaniel dog, and not some hysterical Pomeranian, so he figured he'd be logical about it.

"You checked the weather reports?" enquired Milly.

Of course, Zip had checked the weather, finding nary a drop of rain in the predictions.

"Every day checked. There's no National Weather Service hazardous weather conditions alert this week."

"It seems to me," said Milly, sounding pacified, "that the whole hysterics is trumped up. Theodore could not even describe what this Worry looks like. Maybe, there is no such thing as Worry. Have you checked inside the ravine?"

"Not yet," barked Zip and they both ran down to the edge of the ravine. Deep down, Sneaky Creek was barely visible. No threats there. The water murmured lightly, and looked completely harmless. The whole scare was slowly dissipating.

When they got back into the house, Old Lady had already turned off her TV, and it was time for bed.

And both Spaniels returned to their daily chores. One had to take care when going to bed because doing it properly is not as easy as it looks. The challenge was to settle in Old Lady's bed without attracting her attention. The jump must be perfectly calibrated. The bed was high, but one could not accelerate too much. Must make a soft, two-point jump: front paws go first, then push up and bring in hind paws. Then one had to noiselessly snuggle into a place by Old Lady's legs. The important thing was to shoo away overly arousing dreams, so as not to get agitated and end up instinctively seeking solace by creeping up onto Old Lady's pillow.

Old Lady hated it when there was a dog sleeping on her pillow. She might even . . . horror . . . push.

Zip could not abide being pushed off the bed. Nothing worse than waking up in the middle of an unplanned landing on the hard floor and then having to pretend all morning that this entire embarrassing incident pertained to someone else . . . No, thanks, sighed Zip.

Both dogs settled in by Old Lady's knees and Zip whispered to Milly that, maybe by next morning, this whole day will turn out to be just a bad dream.

5

THE BIG WATER

"Boo-oo-m!"

"Bo-aa-m!"

The noise that woke up Zip was deafeningly loud, louder than anything he'd ever heard before. It shook the whole house, and echoed inside Zip's ears.

Still sleepy, the spaniel braced for the fall—thought he'd chanced onto the Old Lady's pillow again, and gotten shoved off.

But he was not falling; he was still on the bed. Opened one eye—dark. Stretched—hot. Sniffed—and his heart started racing zero to ninety. In the putrid heat of August, Zip smelled it—it was like bushels of dead frogs were steeped in a smoothie of their own poop, and topped with a bucket of last Autumn's compost. Gross!

The smell was close by, definitely within the house, probably something hiding just behind the bedroom door, ready to pounce! Which was odd. It would be hard for anyone to creep into Old Lady's house after dusk.

The Old Lady was fastidious about home security.

Every evening, around nine o'clock, Old Lady locked and bolted all the doors. Then, around ten o'clock, she always asked,

"Zip, did we lock the doors? Let's go check." And all three of them would troop downstairs and make sure the bolts had not moved, were in their proper nighttime places.

Still, the smell and the noise somehow did creep in.

"Intruder! Rrrwr!" Zip barked, and his trusty sidekick Milly woke up and helped out with the barking, not necessarily in that order.

Milly and Zip had perfected their "intruder alert" bark over time, responding diligently to the daily deluge of different threats. Zip was to bark the low-pitch part, setting the tone and harmony, while Milly filled in with the higher-pitch soprano howl and growl.

The resulting bark uproar was powerful and

moving, a far more formidable deterrent than any clanging security alarm. Together, the Siblings were undefeated against every deadly threat that had the temerity to make a move against their family. The neighbors' dogs would never presume to pee on the grass patch in front of Old Lady's house. The phone guy once found himself stuck high up on the pole pretending to tinker with some wires. Even the mailman knew to bring dog cookies as peace offerings.

Together, Zip and Milly were awe-inspiring guard dogs, and they knew it!

After the barking racket penetrated the bedroom walls and spread over the house, Zip felt good about his prompt pushback against whatever they were fighting.

But only for a few seconds. The barking was well-executed, but despite all the effort of growling and barking, the putrid smell was creeping even closer.

Zip's bark slipped into a cough; Milly squeaked softly. Without looking at each other, the Siblings escalated to the second step of their well-tested Intruder Resistance Protocol. Chasing each other, they scattered off the bed and, two pairs of long silky ears swinging wildly, paws pattering with urgency, wheeled around and streaked to shelter, scrambling under the bed, twisting into their trusty Safety Zone. From underneath the bed, two muzzles then poked out carefully, and two pairs of unblinking eyes watched Old Lady's bare feet jump off the bed. In a split second, both noses twitched, recognizing the familiar and comforting smell: Old Lady's pistol was coming out of the bed stand.

"Way to be a guard dog," boasted Milly, "We alerted. The Intruder will be shot."

Alerting is a big part of a guard dog job, and the Spaniels did it masterfully: Old Lady's bare heels were covering the bedroom in zig-zags. Shuffle to the door; pause; rush back to the windows.

"She'll shoot from up here, through the window," whispered Milly, and started making her way out from under the bed, "Get ready; we'll fetch it when she shoots it."

But instead of shooting, Our Old Lady yelped,

"Oh My God, the car! The car is sinking! POTOP!"

"What's potop?" whispered Milly, backing in under the bed again.

Communicating with Our Old Lady was not always straightforward. Old Lady spoke a few languages, mostly all at the same time.

When she spoke English, Milly and Zip understood her perfectly. Zip started out knowing about a thousand words, and kept learning. Reading definitions and asking Google on Old Lady's computer helped a lot.

But when Old Lady did not speak English, it became a lot harder to understand her, although they were learning, thanks in part to Google Translate.

Plus, both Spaniels read Human faces, smell, and voices better than Israeli airport security profilers—they knew when a Human was upset, or happy, or lying. Or in pain. And obviously, whatever that *potop* thing was, it obviously was up to no good.

On her part, Old Lady understood perfectly everything Milly and Zip had to say. The minute the siblings even conceive a thought that was not appropriate for a well-bred Spaniel—somehow, she already knew, and would spring on them out of nowhere to hold her outstretched index finger to the snout and order: "Don't do that! Fu!"

Old Lady must have read the dogs' thoughts, because her face appeared sideways under the bed, and she gave them their orders.

"Stay! *Mesto!*" which meant *place*; the Spaniels

learned that command a long time ago. "It's dangerous. *Potop!*"

Milly and Zip exchanged a knowing look. They understood their mission. They were entrusted with guarding the place under the bed. On her end, The Old Lady would shoot *The Potop* and save their Car.

❧

Because Zip and Milly were ordered by Old Lady to stay, the duo felt protected and decided to get out from under the bed and investigate.

The bedroom windows had a good view of the back yard, if one jumped up on the large white leather chair. Of course, there were prohibitions against that jump, but surely those restrictions were lifted in such a dire emergency as this.

The back yards of Old Lady's neighbors stretched out all the way back to the Sneaky Creek, but Old Lady's land stretched beyond Sneaky Creek and bordered with the Forest because the Creek whimsically turned onto, looped on Old Lady's land, then straightened, following the border with the Forest.

Normally, Sneaky Creek made its daily trip to the Bridge by flowing in a single stream until it reached the tunnels, then splitting into three streams to pass under the Bridge and emerge from the tunnels as a twinkling rivulet, playful and tame on the emerald fields of the next development—the Scared Hare Country Club.

In fair weather, the Creek was not much of a menace on the Spaniels' land. There was usually not more than a foot of water in it, and it was very narrow—one Fox's jump. Until it rained, one could not even spot Sneaky Creek from the house windows.

When it rained, though, Sneaky Creek could rise to ten feet, and that's when the Spaniels could see the top of water from the bedroom window. It was an entertaining sight. Floating tree branches swished by, and occasionally a duck would take a ride on one.

Sneaky Creek separated the White Goose Lane neighborhood from the Forest, the home to Fox Theodore and his family. But even though the foxes lived not very far, just on the other side, it was not easy to get across.

In fair weather, one had to slide down into the ravine, jumping carefully over all the frogs who hid under large boulders along the narrow stream; then it was a job to climb the opposite, much higher, bank of Sneaky Creek. And that's in fair weather. When it rained, even Fox Theo preferred to look for a detour. Of course, both Spaniels were strictly prohibited from approaching the edge of Sneaky Creek's ravine.

"Let's check if we can see Sneaky Creek from here," said Milly.

Zip and Milly jumped up on the chair, pressed noses to the window, and then their jaws slacked a little in confusion. They sure could see the Sneaky Creek, but—

"Where's everything?" Milly wondered.

It was an excellent question because everything was gone. The fountain—the pride of the neighbor to the left—had vanished. There was no toy house that belonged to the daughters of the surgeon to the right. There was no trace of the flowerbeds. The tall trees in the forest behind the ravine had transformed into short bushes.

There were no landmarks left. Nothing but water. Lots of water, dark, rust-colord, moving water. The sky was dark gray too, and rainwater was falling down like a wall, dark and dismaying.

Just like Theodore had told them, there was Big Water.

"Look," barked Milly, "What happened to Old Lady?"

All the dogs could see was the top part of Old Lady—it was wading though the water, towards their garage, hands flailing fiercely just above the water.

"Is she waving us to come down?" worried Milly, "She is maybe telling us to come save her, is she?"

"No, she's balancing," squinted Zip through the window, "Hands are for steering, she has no tail, remember?"

But as Zip looked closer, he was not sure that Old Lady could manage without them. The Big Water was aggressively attacking, trying to push Old Lady out.

"Zip," whispered Milly softly, "I think the Worry came. What if Old Lady lost her balance? Can Humans swim at all?"

"All Humans are excellent swimmers, I'm sure," answered Zip quickly. Zip was bluffing. He was not actually sure. Why would Humans send Spaniel dogs to fetch downed ducks, and never so much as tread water alongside? Why stay on shore if they could swim?

Zip shook his whole body, trying to get a well-reasoned thought out of it. But it was his job to keep Milly from panicking. Besides, Old Lady knew how to shoot, so it seemed right that she'd learn how to swim, which was, after all, more natural.

"What happens to us if she can't swim?" whimpered Milly.

"Stop panicking. Look!"

Old Lady had finally made it into the garage and Spaniels could see a dull yellow light inside. Zip thought he made out the taillights of their car.

"The Car's moving!" Milly was excited. Both Spaniels understood Old Lady's Plan now.

"Old Lady is saving the Car so we can escape!"

Zip thought about an adventure, and his paws started to dance. He remembered fondly his forays in the Car with his snout firmly wedged in a slightly opened window, a rush of outside air thrilling his nostrils.

Indeed, the Car backed out from the garage, creeped back a few feet of driveway invisible under water, then halted. The Car's back end floated up lightly, picked up by the current, like a bad egg in boiling water.

"Big Water's rising!" whined Milly.

"The motor drowned," Zip agreed, feeling the hope draining out of his body.

But down in the water, Our Old Lady did not lose hope. She climbed out of the Car, swung around to the hood, leaned on it, and gave a hearty push. The car jerked momentarily in her desired direction but, alas, then twisted and started moving into deeper water. Big Water kept coming, and there was less and less left of Old Lady's top half.

"Come back to us," whimpered Milly, then switched to a howl-and-bark, "Swi-ii-im ba-aaa-ck!"

"Shoot it, shoot Big water!" barked Zip, then decided it was time for action,

"Milly, we should help her."

"Louder bark?" said Milly quickly.

"No, let's run downstairs."

"That's not the protocol. We stay undercover," Milly said timidly.

"She needs us!" glared Zip, "Now's not the time for protocol. Don't be a coward!"

In retrospect, Zip should have listened. He'd later blame himself for all that happened. After all, hiding under the bed was the protocol. On the other paw, Old Lady was in trouble. And, truth be told, Zip was scared; it did not seem at all safe under the bed, away from his Old Lady.

"Big Water is coming for us, Milly. We need to be with Our Old Lady," he decided.

The dogs twisted their backs in unison. Quick shake, then run.

Out of the bedroom, Zip in the lead, bounding down the stairs, they skidded into the great hall, leaped past the front door, still locked and bolted, slid around the curved hall wall and past the darkened, empty kitchen, and panting, the dogs reached the spiral staircase which twisted down to the ground floor with exit to back yard.

As Zip's paw stepped on the spiral stairway, which was now three steps shorter on the bottom, the putrid stench slammed into his nose.

"Danger," he barked, "Old Lady is in danger!" and headed down.

The step where Zip had planted his front paw was covered under stinky foaming water. He raised his right paw, and gave the Big Water a good smack. Splash … the paw went straight through the shifty assailant, nearly taking Zip out of balance. Big Water sniggered and sprang up another up half a step towards the dog . . . Zip shoved back again, then bit it as hard as he could, and then he gave Big Water his most intimidating snarl—the one with enough growl to scare off even the neighbor's Golden Retriever Sam. Big Water momentarily seem to hesitate, but then regrouped, spat in the dog's face, and made another creeping move, slithering farther up the stairs.

Zip could not later explain what was his motive at that moment, except he speculated that his hunting instincts had kicked in.

"Old Lady needs our help!' exclaimed Zip, threw himself off the stairs, into the water, and paddled madly, maneuvering to avoid collision with the red plastic bucket floating on his left, a wheeled flower stand on his right, and a rush of objects that bumped straight onto his nose. It was surprising how many things could swim.

❧

Milly, the whiny, unreliable Milly, was paddling by his elbow.

"Zip, look!" Milly gave a side look to their right, "the back door can swim too! Look out!'

Zip followed Milly's eyes and with a jolt of surprise, saw the heavy shadow in the water. Milly was right—the door had somehow made its way inside.

Now we know what made the BOOM, concluded

Zip. The stream of water slammed the fortified back door down onto the concrete floor.

"Milly, look out!" A giant flowerpot with blooming rose was headed squarely at Milly's nose.

"Zip, we are all right, the exit's open!" panted Milly, clearing the pot.

Zip twisted to avoid collision with the drifting massage table, which careened in the water, headrest bobbing separately, aimed at the dogs at an alarming speed.

Now, both dogs were only a foot away from the exit, paddling madly with all their might, straining to keep their place against the rapid current of Big Water, rushing at them, intent on invading the house through the yawning, gaping, suddenly scary threshold.

"Zippy," Milly was screaming at Zip's shoulder, "Old Lady's outside! Right . . . there—" he heard Milly choke her words as a surge of water smacked against her muzzle.

Gasping, snorting and sneezing, Zip reached the outside first. But instead of fresh air, the whizzing wind slammed a bucket-full of rain into Zip's muzzle, plugging his nose and throat, clouding his eyes.

And that was the last thing Zip remembered.

6

SPANIEL CURIOSITY

When Zip came back to his senses, he was in his Old Lady's bathtub, which is where he always got his wash, although usually he stood up straight on all four paws. This time, though, he was lying flat on his belly. Zip tried willing his right hind paw to move, but there was no use: he could feel none of his paws. None of his extremities could be moved.

"If only I wouldn't have docked your tails so short," lamented the Old Lady, "you would have been easier to catch in the water."

That explained the dull ache around Zip's tail. Zip tried to wag it, but it did not move either.

"You got lucky, Zip" grumbled Old Lady.

"If you had followed your curiosity another

couple of feet, the Creek current would have swept you away . . . who knows where. . . . Under the bridge . . . sucked into the tunnels, best case—" Zip thought he heard Old Lady sniffle. Must have gotten some of that dirty water in her nose.

Zip was irate! His Old Lady apparently thought that he plunged into the flood water out of *curiosity.*

Bollocks! It was bravery! It was instinct: centuries of breeding to plunge unhesitantly into the water, and duck-in-teeth, return to one's owner's feet. Old Lady, of course, is heavier than a duck, even heavier than a goose, but she was in trouble, and Zip selflessly rushed off to save and protect her. He was a Spaniel dog: that's what they do.

"No dog can swim through this much flood water," muttered Old Lady, "not even a Newfoundland! As soon as flooding water gets more than a few inches-deep, the force of the stream will knock you off your paws. A foot and a half, and it washes away even a Subaru Outback and no amount of panicky dogpaddling will save you . . .. What were you thinking?!"

Zip tried to remember what he was thinking but, right at that moment, his thinker didn't seem to be working much better than his all-but-useless extremities.

He knew he had hit Big Water with his paw, then

lost balance . . . and that's when things must have gone horribly wrong.

Zip closed his eyes and tried to gain account of what exactly happened. But it only made his head spin. As hard as he tried, all he could remember clearly was the nauseating smell, and the unstoppable assault of rust-colored, dirty water.

The current had slapped and covered Zip, then dragged and submerged him, hitting him against the wall of the house. Or maybe he first hit against the wall, then slipped, sank and got covered—Zip could not say for sure.

Does not rightly matter, he thought dimly to himself, *because when you meet a wave of water with your nose, it feels like getting smacked hard by a big stone.*

The cladding around the first floor of the house was done in jagged natural stones, so hitting against the wall was, in fact, like being hit with—well, big stones. So it was getting smacked, then stoned. Or stoned, then smacked. Zip wasn't sure which it was, nor was he sure that he ever wanted to remember it accurately. Either way, Zip personally did not see any *luck* in this turn of events, at least not at first. From the dull pain in his rear, Zip figured that Old Lady did catch him by the tail.

"I told you both to *stay,*" scolded on his Old Lady,

"I would expect this from your sister, but you . . . *YOU*?!"

All the while, Old Lady was giving Zip a good, vigorous washing.

"Your decontamination bath. Inside and outside, Young Man," she said, "there are *pathogens* in the water. Bad move gulping it by the gallon."

Zip wanted to object that he surely did not gulp the pathogens on purpose, that all this water pumped inside by itself.

And it certainly was less than a gallon.

But Old Lady was not listening.

The scrubbing outside took time.

Then there was the cleaning on the inside. And that was mean! An odd tasting pill was stuck into his mouth, and Old Lady held his jaws shut until he swallowed it. He chose not to bite back.

Old Lady washed the floor afterwards and all that time Zip heard her muttering unflattering words about Spaniels in general and the *Spaniel Curiosity* in particular.

Pummeled by the water, exhausted and embarrassed by the scrubbing, daring not to object or disagree with his Old Lady, Zip fell asleep.

Zip woke up again in the dead of the night, his muzzle resting on Old Lady's lap. She was sliding her hand down his still slightly damp fur.

Zip had never felt Old Lady's hands shake before. She'd always been extremely firm with the pen and the hammer and her pistol. But now her fingers shook, petting his long silky ears.

She muttered "Zippy."

That was odd. Old Lady was not one for big emotional displays of affection.

Without lifting his head, Zip opened one eye, sucked in the air. Hot and humid. Like in the shower by the end of the wash.

Not knowing why, Zip remembered something Old Lady said before.

"Why did you choose the South?" asked her friend Lariska. "New York has more to offer . . . Shows . . . Broadway."

Old Lady had answered quickly then, "So that nobody could find us," then added, as though in justification, "My work. I'm at a critical juncture when I must avoid excitement and physical stress. The farther from my colleagues and science-related much-a-do—"

Zip was a fan of quiet life. But now Old Lady's hands were quivering. Zip felt a tickling in his nose: *he will not allow! Nobody dares!* . . . Zip lifted his head. There was no sign of anyone else around.

There was no light anywhere either, he was not even sure where the window was. No neighbor's floodlights, no streetlights.

Zip licked her hand. She did not say "Stop licking," as she usually would have.

Odd again.

Instead, she said, "What have we done, Zippy? What are we going to do?!"

Zip sniffed around Old Lady, and now he could smell it: Big Grief had come.

He barked inquiringly, "What?"

But Old Lady did not say.

"Who? What?" Zip barked again, and his bark echoed around the house.

"Milly," Zip called demandingly, "did you sleep through Big Grief? What Who Wrrr? . . . Milly?! Where did you wander off to?"

Zip's ears popped up, and before he could stop them, his paws jumped off Old Lady's knees, and his nose activated his very best Searching Mode.

"Milly??!"

The house reeked of Stinky Water Smell, and the

sensitive Spaniel nose could not sniff Milly's scent through all the stench. So Zip scurried off to search the Human way—with his eyes.

Zip made the rounds of all Milly's favorite hangouts. Dashed by the cold air vent, but found nothing —not even any cold air. Bolted upstairs and scrambled under the bed, but the hiding place was empty. Checked Milly's food bowl, then mentally clapped a paw to his forehead and checked his own food bowl. There was still plenty of food left in it, but Zip's stomach was turning topsy-turvy, and treats were the last thing on his mind. No Milly, no trace at all.

From the kitchen, his heart somersaulting in his throat, Zip scurried back and flung himself up into Old Lady's lap, sniffing her hands vigorously.

"Millyyyy," Zip whined quietly. Then louder. "Mi—"

Old Lady's hand was on his muzzle, hushing him gently. But he would not hush. He barked and carried on, but in his heart, he knew what had happened before Old Lady said it out-loud.

"Zip," she said, "Zippy. It is just the two of us now. Milly's gone."

7

THE CANOE

The sunrise was so soaked with water that nobody could rightly tell when the night had oozed away. The day was in no hurry to start on its unpleasant task of sorting out all the damage and destruction that had been cloaked by night's shroud.

The Spaniel Dog and his Old Lady fell asleep on the couch and slept through the morning, leaning on each other. It took a long time for Old Lady's hands to finally quit trembling, but eventually she calmed down. When the gray light of late morning struggled through the still-falling drizzle, Old Lady's hands were resting heavily on the dog's silky ears. Both the Old Lady and the dog were twitching restlessly in their sleep, dreaming of frantically seeking out their missing Milly in the perilous and stinky currents of the raging Sneaky Creek.

Zip woke up first, felt the warm reassurance of Old Lady's hands on his head, wagged his tail tentatively, and gratefully sniffed in her familiar scent. But then, the hot putrid smell of standing water hit his nose and the memories of the wretched night came crashing back. B*ig Water . . . Stink . . . Booooom . . . Whoosh . . . his body hurt and something really bad happened . . .*

Milly!!!!

I LOST MILLY!

Wishing that he never woke up, Zip was about to re-close his eyes when, from under the eyelids, he spotted some movement outside the window. There was an indistinct reflection in the window pane.

As quietly as he could, so as to not rouse up his Old Lady, Zip slid off the couch and crossed the floor.

He set off for the kitchen where a small chair by the bay window gave a good vantage point of the back yard. As he was scrambling up the chair, he thought that he saw it again—a hazy silhouette of something floating across the yard. But when he was up on the chair and pushed his paws against the windowsill, the backyard was empty of anything except muddy water. Zip could have sworn that he had glimpsed ripples on the water while he was jumping up the chair, but now that he had a full view of the back yard, the water surface was so impenetrably still, so desolate, that it looked like a slab of brown-tinted concrete. Zip let out a tiny whine and bent his hind paws a little on the chair, astonished by what he saw.

The late morning was filled with light. Golden. The sky above now shimmered bright blue without a hint of cloudiness. The land below was an appalling sight. From edge to edge, and beyond the ravine, all the way to the Forest where Fox Theodore lived, everything was under the water. The fresh morning sky reflected dimly in the water's muddy-red surface. The world was desolate. The forest and the sky were hushed, as though Big Water had bound and gagged everything alive.

Not a bird aloft, not a chipmunk below, not even a snoopy squirrel.

"The water has not gone down? Never seen anything like this," whispered Old Lady, who had shuffled lightly into the kitchen and came to hug her dog from behind. She did not even mention his trespass on the forbidden chair. Zip and Old Lady stood entranced, afraid to move, taking in the eerie grandeur of the watery landscape. Zip wondered if everybody had died, if he and the Old Lady were now truly alone. It was not clear what that meant for grocery shopping. Was that as bad a thing as it seemed? What about Fox Theo's family? He had kits again . . . and can fox kits swim? *The Worry probably helped Fox find a safe place for his family,* Zip hoped, gazing around to try and find where a safe place would possibly be. But all he could see, anywhere he looked, was water and more water. Stinky water.

Zip shook his head, to try and clear it of bad thoughts, accidentally spraying a little drool on the window glass. Old Lady usually knew exactly what he was thinking, and he did not want to upset her with his headful of gloomy feelings.

But just as Zip was shaking out bad thoughts, his eyes half-closed, the momentary glimpse from before had reappeared. He froze, mid-shake, afraid that his eyes were playing tricks. But no. There was, indeed, something in the yard. Long and green, the floating object appeared from its hiding place behind the roof of Old Lady's half-flooded detached garage and glided noiselessly through the murky water, sliding straight towards the two watchers in the window.

"Look," said Old Lady, putting her hand under

Zip's nose and moving it in the direction of the intruder, "A CANOE. Floating in our back yard. Never thought we'd live to see that, did you?"

Since Old Lady had already spotted the intruder, there was not really any point in barking. Instead, Zip just let out a little whine of acknowledgement and the companions stood together, watching the green canoe as it was easing into full sight.

"Is this nextdoor Dick?" said Old Lady, squinting and rubbing the window glass with a bit of paper towel she'd pulled out of her pocket. She was right. Dick—a neighbor from three houses upstream—had his canoe course set straight for their kitchen window and was paddling lazily but purposefully.

"I think he is waving at us?" mumbled The Old Lady, "You think he's in trouble?"

Zip let out a low growl. Saying that Dick was not their favorite neighbor was putting it mildly. They disliked Dick—a long-standing neighborly dislike that started after one mid-sized rain.

The offense was still fresh in Zip's memory.

Dick had stopped by the Old Lady's yard (on foot that time, without the canoe), kicked around in the deep puddles with his yellow-and green rubber boots and commented with glee how glad he was that *his* own yard stayed dry.

"You must have wicked flood insurance premiums," he said, giving a long gaze to the far side of the yard that was, at that very moment, shining with the mud and littered with soft drinks cans which Creepy Creek had been floating on its travels downstream and carelessly abandoned in its hurried retreat.

Old Lady was always eager to discuss the water issue.

"The bridge's plugged up," she explained hastily, pointing down the Sneaky Creek, towards the bridge, "Somebody's been pouring concrete." She was about to ask Neighbor Dick if he wanted to join her and petition the City to clean up the problem, when Dick showed his real colors.

"Boy, I'm glad your yard is designed to collect our flood water," he said, flicking a candy wrapper right in the middle of one of the puddles that had settled by Old Lady's the fire pit.

"Designed?!!" snarled Zip, "What did you just say?!"

It was true that White Goose Lane made a two-foot dip right where it ran into Old Lady's property line.

It was also true that, adding to the insult of its lowland location on the front, the back of Old Lady's property was plagued with another terrain misfortune. The Sneaky Creek, which framed obediently the rear of the neighbors' emerald-green lawns, keeping a respectable distance from the houses on White Goose Lane, did something odd when reaching Old Lady's house. It sprang into a sharp, capricious turn aimed directly for the Old Lady's house, and set off across the back yard. Only steps from the fire-pit, the wayward water took ahold of itself, rounded back, and took its leave downstream. When Sneaky Creek rose after a heavy rain, bowl-shaped set of the land combined with the location of the stream created a watery invasion: the better part of Old Lady's backyard was covered under water and the Creek crept close to the back porch.

Yes, it was true that Sneaky Creek liked to take advantage of heavy rainstorms by playing in Old Lady's yard before making its way back down into its proper bed and eventually draining through the tunnels of the Bridge.

Everybody on the Street could plainly see that, of course.

But well-mannered neighbors had the decency to act embarrassed when their dogs' balls or lost flower pots took off in the rain and ended up stranded in Old Lady's fire pit.

The terrain of Old Lady's land was a *misfortune*.

But to say that Old Lady was somehow "designed" to suffer this misfortune, as though she did something to deserve it? And to gleefully gloat?!

Old Lady's generosity was all that saved Dick from a good Spaniel biting. From that day forward, taking their daily walks, Old Lady and the Spaniel Siblings crossed to the other side of the street, and never even put a paw on Dick's sidewalk. If Dick was out, pottering in his yard, Old Lady would barely nod and the Spaniels trotted by as quickly as they could.

I short, Neighbor Dick was the not their friend in any weather, and certainly not the face they wished to see in a disaster.

"What does he want with us *now*?" Zip growled and twisted his chin around and up examining Old Lady's face, "Did he come to gloat some more?"

"We better find out, Zip," Old Lady leaned in and twisted the handle of the window latch.

The glass pane edged ajar.

Dick's oar was dipping right - left - right - left.

"Should we ask him, Zippy?"

"Rrrrr," suggested Zip, catching Old Lady's ambivalent expression out of a sidelong glance from his glistening brown eyes.

"You think we shut the window and turn our backs?"

Old Lady was ambivalent. If only Dick and other neighbors on White Goose Lane would've supported her when she tried to get the City to unplug the cement cork under the Bridge! Today's disaster might not have happened at all. To heck with Dick.

On the other hand, Dick might be in trouble.

Old Lady believed in a moral obligation to help neighbors in need. She turned away from the window, crossed the kitchen floor, her face changing from contempt to concern. And back again.

Finally, she strode off to the door with no deliberate expression at all, hoping that her mind would make up itself. Zip trotted in front of her, and nearly smashed his nose on her shoe, because he kept twisting his head back, trying to read Old Lady's face for proper cues of his own approach to Dick. Zip noticed that Old Lady did not reach for her pistol, but her lips were pursed in one thin, grim line. By the time Old Lady jerked the front door open, Zip was pretty sure that she was going to slam it back right in the Dick's face quicker than Zip could bark "GET OUT TRRR-RAITOR!"

Having rounded the house, the green canoe made

to dock, at the top stair of Old Lady's front entrance because the rest of stairs were submerged.

Old Lady was about to say something, when Zip saw her whole body relax and give out happy vibrations,

"MILLY!!! My girl!" Old Lady gasped.

At first, Zip did not understand Old Lady's meaning, but then it hit him.

Neighbor Dick was clumsily attempting to balance his canoe, as he was pulling from under the seat a shapeless glob of red, limp, smelly, sopping wet . . ..

"Doggie here," explained Dick, "was clinging to the high branch of the old magnolia, down the stream." He nodded downstream with his chin, both his arms busy with passing a soaked, forlorn-looking dog into Old Lady's eagerly outstretched hands.

"Thanks for your trouble," was all the response that the flustered Old Lady could muster before turning on her heel and dashing up the stairs with Milly cradled in her arms.

8

THE PAPARAZZI

Zip let out a very muted whine.

After being whisked upstairs, the limp, grubby, shapeless, bunch of smelly golden-colored Spaniel fur formerly known as Zip's sister Milly was promptly spread out in Old Lady's huge bathtub. Zip became a wide-eyed witness to the process which he already knew that Old Lady called the *inside and outside decontamination wash and scrubbing.*

Now that Zip could see precisely what was involved, it made him doubly grateful that he had passed out, that his blackout had spared him any memories of most of his own scrubbing experience last night.

Old Lady let him stay in the bathroom, and he

watched, sometimes moaning very quietly, "Millyyyyy…."

Little by little, though, the lifeless red smudge limply sprawled on the bathtub floor developed signs of awareness. First it twitched its tail, and then it sniffed in and opened its eyes blankly.

The cleaning was followed by a good warming rub with dry towels and, finally, topped off by a wrapping with a well-worn woolen throw. In surprisingly little time, there were encouraging signs that Milly as he knew her was back. For now, though, she barely had the strength to lick a little Half&Half with yolk and honey in a saucer that Old Lady was holding for her. Hearteningly, Milly braved it and licked the saucer clean.

It was late afternoon by the time the sofa in front of the cold fireplace was finally occupied by Old Lady, sitting in the middle with Zip and Milly on either side, both drooling on her lap.

Their whole family was back together.

Nobody had the energy to do a happy jig, but everybody's hearts were quietly dancing. Although they all were a little sad, too.

To ease the smell of flood, Old Lady lit an enormous candle in amber-colored glass with letters AMBRE *34 Boulevard Saint Germain*, a location somewhere beyond the streets where Zip and Milly had been allowed when they lived in Paris.

"Saving it in case of important guests," smiled to herself Old Lady, as she was fumbling to extract a wooden match from an odd-looking matchbox, "but now I think that my most important guests are already all here."

She momentarily let go of the matchbox to fluff the Spaniels' fur, then pluck out a red-tipped match and flicked it against the matchbox side with a practiced move. Old Lady's face was illuminated in the newly struck match's light, and then the Guest Candle flared up and enfolded the reunited family in its aroma. Zip wrinkled his nose at the strange smell, and threw a questioning glance at Old Lady.

"*Tonka bean*," Old Lady explained nonchalantly. "Don't nitpick, Zip. Would you prefer the smell of sticky floodwater?"

Zip made himself comfortable on the couch, nose tucked under Old Lady's right hand, and the trio settled in to forget all worries the for a spell. Old Lady in the middle, a Spaniel flanking each of her sides, Old Lady's now-calm fingers resting on the long Spaniel ears . . . all three watching the flickering flame of the festive Guest Candle.

We don't need guests to enjoy ourselves, thought Zip.

This comfortable thought (to the extent one can think comfortably in a house surrounded by water on all sides) repelled the tidal waves of worry.

At last, the candle flickered and burned out. The Old Lady and two dogs were already fast asleep on the sofa.

❧

The insistent knocking on the front door came in what felt like minutes later, but there was already twilight in the window. The fast and forceful rapping sounded as though the flood-ravaged water spirits felt lonely and were bidding to come in and seek the solace of the companionship of living creatures.

"Back door is clean off its hinges, standing wide open," smirked Old Lady, "but still these geniuses are hammering on the front door like Big Water is after them. Want to see who?"

Zip wagged his tail lethargically and forced a lazy yawn that unmistakably relayed: *no, I do not want any more company*. But his Old Lady had already shaken sleepy Spaniel muzzles off her lap, crossed the foyer and was unlocking the brass safety hinges on the front door.

"Ducklingburg Fire Department," young forceful voices cut through the thick wooden doors and ruptured the stillness of the house.

Zip scooted off his warm place on the couch, threw a sideway glance at his sister, whispered, "I just better go make sure," and bravely joined his Old Lady in the doorway.

"*Fire* Department, are you?" Old Lady's left eyebrow shot up mockingly. Her usual self-assurance was back.

In yellow and black waders, two firefighters had already treaded through the hip-high water in the front yard and were mounting the entrance steps. Their third teammate sat watchfully and at-the-ready in a rubber rescue craft powered by a small outboard motor.

"You really think we're in solid danger of a *fire* here?" Old Lady mocked.

"Welfare check-up, Ma'am. Evacuation option, Ma'am. Evacuate you to dry land?" The firemen made synchronic sweeping gestures towards the far end of White Goose Lane where *dry land* could indeed be seen. The would-be heroes puffed up their chests and flexed their limbs, eagerly anticipating the chance of whisking the Old Lady into their rescue boat and off to a refuge that the Big Water had not invaded.

"What's that happening over there?" The Old Lady pointed her finger at half a dozen figures swarming at the Dry End of the White Goose Lane.

"Oh, *that*," the lead Firefighter turned pink, "That's the Ducklingburg crew from Channel 9. To capture video of the *evacuation*." The hero in the making stretched his mighty hand invitingly towards Old Lady, obviously in hopes that the cameras were already rolling and properly zoomed in on the dramatic rescue-to-be.

"It's absurd," refused the Old Lady forcefully, "We are not going anywhere."

"No pressure, Ma'am," the Firefighter backed off. "You maybe in need of supplies? Some bottled water? Medication? Food?"

"Now that you mention, don't mind if I do. These two," Old Lady pointed down, "would like two bowls of chicken soup, and we could all share a pizza. They prefer with extra cheese." Zip was surprised to see Milly, just now arrived by his side and already standing pretty steady on her paws.

The youngest Firefighter slapped two fingers to his temple in a half-mocking salute. Old Lady sure was excellent at giving orders.

"Cuties don't want to evacuate?" coaxed the firefighter in the boat, switching to baby-talk and reaching for Milly's nose, "Nice boat-ride, doggie? Go for a nice walk?" He managed to say his wheedling lines while keeping his face appropriately framed for a zoom-lens shot by the dry-land bound press.

Zip cocked his head and sniffed the air. Actually, it *would* be nice to stretch his paws, and maybe do his business on dry land. The newspaper bits that Old Lady had spread in the basin of the guest bathroom were, frankly, a little embarrassing. But, alas, Old Lady wedged her sharp knee in front of the front-most firefighter and gave the Spaniels a hearty shove inside the house, so only their curious wet noses were now flaring nostrils from behind her ankles.

"No boat rides, thanks." There was no way Old Lady would leave her house. Abandon her books and documents, paintings, her furniture, all her stuff? NO WAY at all.

Old Lady was just about to pull the front door closed when the leader of the fireman trio wedged his humongous hand in the opening and, dropping the fake Superman attitude, took a distinctly different tone of appeal.

"Ma'am," he jerked his head conspiratorially towards the rigid-looking figures waiting down the

Lane where dry land started. "Ma'am . . . Ducklingburg Firefighting Association could use your cooperation today. Chanel 9 is here. Ducklingburg Firefighters would benefit from favorable exposure."

Zip imagined himself gracing the Channel 9 Evening News enfolded in the arms of a strapping firefighter, and that did not seem half bad.

"Woof," squeezing his nose through Old Lady's knees, Zip voiced a single vigorous bark, indicating that he'd be up for the job of the Old Lady family spokesdog.

"We are *not* getting evacuated," cut off Old Lady gruffly, "Go evacuate somebody else."

But, just as Old Lady was finishing her retort, two more vessels docked opposite the firefighters' rescue boat, berthing by the balustrade of Old Lady's top stair.

One of the boats sat heavy in the water under the weight of a good-sized TV camera and nondescript boxes—battery power-packs or equipment cases. Inside that boat, a Human was holding up a stick with a fluffy duster-shaped microphone that immediately made both Spaniels feel like TV stars. The second boat only carried one bouncy young Newsbabe with no props except those that a bountiful Nature had fortunately provided to her.

The press had arrived.

The Newsbabe exuded enthusiasm and daredevil spirit. The viewers of Channel 9 Ducklingburg News were in for a treat today.

Her pre-planned script had every necessary element. The role of the *villain* was played by raging, raving Mother Nature. The *victims* were an elderly Old Lady and two exceptionally well-groomed, adorably cutesy Spaniels. And, of course, the Newsbabe herself was a treat to watch, especially to male eyes. On a watercraft, cordless mike in hand, tightly fitting jeans hugging her hips, surrounded by water as far as eye could see, Newsbaber reveled in her starring role. Her pink-colored top threw a warm glow on the professionally made-up face. The blond tresses were topped today by a rain-cap, chosen for its eye-appeal rather than its water-resistance.

But there was more!

This relatively mundane news segment had an unexpected sizzle: the victimized structure—7 White Goose Lane—was itself a notorious landmark in the City's recent history.

The Newsbabe cut to it straightaway.

"The people of Ducklingburg still vividly remember this address—7 White Goose Lane." The cameraman in the companion boat panned from a wide-angle shot of the flood-surrounded house to a zoomed shot of the bronze address plaque affixed to the front of the house.

Newsbabe pressed on.

"Two years ago, the Ducklingburg community watched in shock as we reported from this very spot. A mastermind criminal, hiding in our very midst, right here, at this very same address, on this very same exclusive street. Illegal multimillion-dollar deals—" intoned Newsbabe.

Back at the studio, the producer clicked his fingers, and a window opened in the right-top corner of the TV screens. A shaky shot of 7 White Goose Lane, its gleaming two-sided polished wood doors flung open, revealing the grandeur inside as a dozen federal agents in marked vests swarmed in and out.

Newsbabe's voice was soaring now. "Chanel 9 reported then on the surrender of one of Ducklingburg's most notorious criminals—"

The window in the corner of TVs now displayed the perp walk. Four agents preening on camera around a short, kind-faced man, who shuffled obediently un-handcuffed down the grandeur of his stairs, past his fountain, and into the agents' awaiting van.

Newsbabe kept on.

"—Depraved and lavish . . . brought to justice at long last . . . right here, in this very house—"

The video of last year's perp walk in the TV corners above Newsbabe froze to a still shot, as Newsbabe turned her attention today's news.

"Today, we approached the new residents of 7 White Goose Lane to find out how they are braving this natural disaster."

Newsbabe's calculations were on point. With the prior house owner serving untold years deep in the federal system, Ducklingburgers had to know: W*hat sort of people took over the notorious 7 White Goose Lane?*

Newsbabe gestured at her cameraman to capture the Disaster. The water—surreal-looking, brown-colored, specked with floating litter.

"With twelve inches of rain falling in the span of just a few hours, we are on site of the biggest natural disaster ever seen on the banks of Sneaky Creek. This is what the experts have termed a five-hundred-year flood." Shamelessly, Newsbabe invented a historical weather report and fictitious experts who had rendered the report.

Meanwhile, the camera panned out to showcase the extent of 7 White Goose Lane's devastation.

Certainly, the House was no tasteless McMansion.

Its architect, imported from Northern Europe, gave skyward movement to his Cathedral-like design. A touch of Gothic Grandeur was softened by the warmness of the colors. The house was tied to the uneven elevation of the lot, its front entrance soaring ten feet off the ground, while the ground floor back entrance was concealed behind the ornate airiness of natural stone columns.

Even bedraggled in this darker hour, the architect's creation stood proud of its harmony and beauty. From the back, the water crept half-way up along its stone-covered ground floor, giving the house a bizarre resemblance to a docked cruise ship, the darker colors of the stone forming a hefty hull under the airy deckhouse of apricot pastel stucco above. The deep-coral red metal roof was defiantly aglow, undamaged except for a scattering of windswept leaves torn from the foliage of the Forest where Theo lived.

The proportions of 7 White Goose Lane were calculated shrewdly with an eye to the fabled golden ratio and integrated masterfully into the difficult landscape. It all worked perfectly. The only bit that the famous Northern Architect and his notorious

Ducklingburg client failed adequately to anticipate was the capricious nature of the Sneaky Creek.

Once in five hundred years, repeated the Newsbabe.

Most people don't plan that far ahead.

9

THE EVENING NEWS

The Newsbabe arranged her face to elicit maximum sympathy for the new owners.

How are they braving the terrible disaster?

How high had the Big Water climbed?

How much of their home—that proud citadel concealed behind high walls until destruction opened it to public prying eye—had succumbed to stinky destruction?

The Newsbabe was about to do her darndest to delight her audience with answers to all these intriguing questions. Predictably, the late news watchers would draw their own dry sheets higher to their necks and mumble self-congratulatorily to the Universe: "Buying a house where it's designed to flood? What silliness! Must be from out-of-town, Bless their innocent hearts!"

Behind Old Lady's knees, Zip took one tentative step forward. Milly cocked her ears. "I think I've seen this TV crew doing live coverage of a dog show once," whispered Zip to Milly. "They were reporting about Ducklingburg entries in the purebred competition."

Participating in a purebred dog competition was a longtime cherished dream of both Spaniels, a dream that Old Lady kept stubbornly resisting. Zip had subscribed Old Lady to the DPC (Ducklingburg Purebred Competition) email list a long time ago, and he also kept flagging their electronic invitations as urgent—but Old Lady refused to take the hint.

"Competition?" Milly's eyes glistened with pride, "We *are* purebreds, and—" Milly was about to launch into a recitation of their distinguished bloodline, when—

"Jump in, doggies," urged the Newsbabe, patting a vacant spot in her boat, and cooing at Zip, "Such lush, long ears, such attractive Spaniel looks! You are a water dog, aren't you, you sweet little doggie? For sure, you aren't afraid of boats, are you?"

Before Zip could make a well-considered, rational decision about the matter, his paws sprang in response to an instinct-driven, involuntary impulse. With one short leap, he soared into the air, and landed inside the boat, mere inches from his new acquaintance with the blonde fur. The Newsbabe, who turned out to be not quite without props after all, adjusted her mike and pushed it into Zip's muzzle.

"What's your name, sweet doggy?" she asked inanely, and without waiting for Zip to respond, went on with a slew of other stupid questions. Very shortly, Zip understood that Newsbabe didn't really expect her show guests to answer her at all; rather, this was just her technique of asking questions which implied their own answers.

"You survived the disaster?

"Were you scared??

"Did these nice Firefighters come her to try and save you???"

Any idiot would know that the answer had to be "yes" every time.

The Newsbabe petted Zip's chin and nudged his muzzle closer towards the camera.

The questions were stupid, but the camera's positioning made perfect sense. Zip figured which way to face for his best shot in order to look like a heroic celebrity and got in character right away. The viewers of Ducklingburg were bound to agree that he was a purebred dog possessed of the lushest ears, straightest back line, and the most graceful spring in his step.

"Let's get a shot of both doggies," ordered the Newsbabe, suddenly dropping her sweet hostess tone for a more authoritative one.

"Here now, young man, do you mind handing me that other doggie?" she asked the Firefighter who seemed to be in charge. He was still loitering around, wading through the shallow water in the front, irritably waiting for a chance to make his superiors happy with his own shot of on-camera fame.

But Milly took a step backward and uncooperatively planted her silky butt onto the stone floor of the landing.

"Thank you very much but I've already had my boat ride today," she signaled with a shake of her head, politely but firmly declining her grand opportunity to appear on-camera.

Zip wished his sister were in the boat, on camera with him to share their moment of pure-bred glory, but he understood her reluctance. Milly had had more than her share of bobbing in the water, and the comforting firmness of the front steps was quite enjoyable enough. Milly' rear was now firmly glued to the land, not to be uprooted by any promises of mere media fame.

The Newsbabe turned to Old Lady, almost bowing obsequiously.

"We're minutes to evening news. We'd like to have you on live, on the air. Just a brief statement, to reassure our viewers and demonstrate your terrific courage in the face of adversity."

Old Lady was about to tell off this pushy intruder who shoved cameras in dog's noses and called them "victims," but something had occurred to her. A shadow of impish irreverence glided across her face, and she winked at Zip.

"Glad to." Old Lady raised her index finger, "just give me two minutes to smarten myself up." Wondering what she was up to, Zip saw Old Lady scurry inside the house and disappear up the stairs.

She was back before Zip could wiggle himself out of the Newsbabe's grasp. Old Lady had dressed up in proper public appearance clothes, including even her signature amber brooch and holding something in a paper folder.

"Ready," she rasped, and by the sound of Old Lady's voice, Zip suspected that Newsbabe would soon quit petting him so calmly and happily.

In the end, Old Lady's maverick nature prevailed over her resolve to wait out this portion of their lives in a safe harbor, away from notoriety and the stardom of the world.

"I always knew it; my Human has a plucky character!" whispered Zip proudly. Admiration and delight were swelling in his chest. *Oh, to be famous! Glory was such a good feeling!* Zip felt the welcome light of the camera lovingly gliding over his nose. Old Lady had, he thought, overreacted in abandoning the benefits of fame and fortune in exchange for greater security in their lives. If giving this interview was a sign that Old Lady had changed her mind about a reclusive life, then Zip was all in favor.

"How are you doing, doggie? She is shivering with fear," the Newsbabe rapped out two lies, and Zip wasn't sure which falsehood was more insulting.

"I am NOT shivering," barked Zip, working hard to control his upper lip, while still keeping his photogenic pose. "It is ninety degrees outside! I am *not* afraid, and I am most certainly NOT a SHE!" It crossed Zip's mind to do the male dog territory-marking thing, but he thought better of it.

Newsbabe was paying no attention to anything except playing out the script already formulated in her head. She had launched into a spirited story about the perils of high flood water, widening her eyes in demonstration of alarm, even though, apart from possible career advancement, the dirty water had no effect at all on her well-being. She then lauded the Ducklingburg firefighters' bravery, intimating that these strapping fellows (the camera jumped to smiling open faces of the Firemen) had risked life and limb to save Zip from deadly peril.

Zip gave out a soft howl in the direction of Old Lady, but she only shrugged apathetically: he had brought this on himself. Zip was learning that celebrity lives are notoriously filled with barefaced lies and baseless rumors.

". . . A few questions to the victim," the Newsbabe forged ahead relentlessly with her on-air spot.

"I really hate it that she keeps calling us *victims,*" thought Zip, scrambling to put an end to his interview the only way that he knew how, by jumping out of the Newsbabe's boat. Unfortunately, by now the front steps were too far for a single jump, and Zip had no wish of mixing up with the foul-smelling water.

Besides, his Old Lady was now on-camera.

While Old Lady had briefly gone inside the house, she threw on a navy-blue linen sundress and a yellowish pearl choker, And, of course, she pinned on the amber brooch, a trademark of all her outfits. Nothing like those disheveled disaster victims they sometimes show on TV!

Old Lady was clutching a small green folder that looked like it could not have more than a few leaves of paper inside.

Puppy pictures, predicted Zip. *She always shows my puppy pictures.*

"Is everybody safe in your household, Ma'am?"

"Oh, yes," Old Lady's smile held no trace of panic, "and I would like to thank my neighbor Dick for saving my Spaniel Milly."

The videographer thoughtfully lowered his camera shot, and a close-up of Milly's gold and red-ochre ears, dry and fluffy now, filled the TV sets of the entire Channel 9 viewing area. All over the city of Ducklingburg, the women pressed their hands into their bosoms and moaned "Ahhhh, doggie!" and the kids screamed "I want one just like that."

"You did not wish to evacuate," announced Newsbabe peppily. "Unyielding in the face of a horrific, Ducklingburg record storm. You survived the wrath of God! A brave hero!"

"No," Old Lady said tartly.

"No, you do not see yourself as a hero? All alone, with the dogs. . ." flattered the Newsbabe.

And all over Ducklingburg, the wives turned to hug their husbands and murmur: "George! This old gal lived through *the wrath of God,* all *alone*! So darling. We will grow old *together,* won't we, George?"

"Yes," responded husbands, eyeing the screen. "And that old bird is still elegant."

"NO, it was NOT God'd work," Old Lady quickly added. And before Newsbabe could see what was coming and head it off, Old Lady said perfectly clearly despite the heaviness of her foreign accent:

"*God* had nothing to do with it, dear."

The camera zoomed to a close-up of Old Lady's face. Old Lady paused and took the tone she customarily saved for her sensational deliveries at European scientific symposiums. It was a speaking style which, as many years of experience had proven, kept audiences all over the world spellbound and on edge.

"Don't finger God for this. It was—" she paused again, "—a MAN-MADE disaster."

"*Man-made*?!"

The camera-man made the mistake of panning the shot to include Newsbabe, who had trouble erasing the look of shock off her face. The usually so predictable disaster coverage was developing an unexpected and, by all indications, a political bent.

Old Lady was already holding up the green file folder that Zip had forgotten about.

"Kindly zoom in, young man." The cameraman meekly complied.

Now the green folder opened, revealing, just like Zip expected, a stack of photos printed to fill the pages. But, disappointingly, they were not his puppy pictures.

"This is the Bridge just downstream from here," Old Lady was holding up the photo. "Zoom here, young man." And young man zoomed, entranced.

Old Lady was no conventional beauty but there was an unusual attractiveness to her. Her demeanor commanded attention, whether one ended up loving or hating her.

She knew that, and used the effect to her advantage.

The cameraman looked to Newsbabe for instructions, but his only clue was a helpless shrug. He kept on rolling.

"The space under the Bridge . . . Four tunnels." Old Lady paused and separated certain words while her well-tended finger counted,

"One-two-three-four. *Wide* tunnels. I took this photo when I moved in."

Old Lady shuffled and produced another photograph.

"This one, I took later."

Another shuffle.

"And *this* was photographed just last month."

Old Lady's voice, calm as though reciting a basic fact of science, summarized: "You can see what happened, plainly. Instead of four wide tunnels, there are now only two narrow ones left. So, when storm water rushes down Sneaky Creek, the Bridge becomes a bottleneck, a dam that makes the water pile up and flood the land. The resultant devastation," Old Lady nodded at the rusty water, "is what you see all around you right now."

Newsbabe briefly wondered whether she should celebrate her first triumphant scoop as an investigative journalist or surreptitiously signal *cut*.

Ambition won. The camera continued to roll and, likewise, Old Lady's on-air exposé proceeded.

"Who is responsible for this scandal? Who benefits from this dangerous destruction?" Old Lady paused before answering her own question with a question:

"*What* is downstream?"

And now the answer leaped to the lips of raptured TV viewers.

"The Golf Club! The Scared Hare Country Club," whispered the Ducklingburg Wives.

At the sound of that name, the Ducklingburg husbands looked up at their TV sets and asked their wives, "Honey, what did she just say?"

Old Lady pushed on.

"The flood water now cannot drain quickly enough through the tunnels. Not like before," continued The Old Lady with certainty.

"Because the Bridge is now in effect a dam, the upstream land is now a storm-water catch basin while the downstream land of the Club gets only a trickle of rainwater, a trickle that Sneaky Creek can carry away harmlessly."

The camera followed Old Lady's hands as the now famous Green Folder accepted snapshots of the Bridge, and was pressed into the passive hands of the unwitting Investigative Journalist.

"Here you go. Uncork the Bridge—and for your next Big Water victims, you will be interviewing the Board of Scared Hare Country Club."

By that time, the viewership of Chanel 9 Live News had spiked, the twitter buzzed with snapshots of Green Folder, and Ducklingburg husbands started making phone calls.

"Uncork. That's all you have to do," Old Lady finished, her voice assured and somewhat triumphant. Still betraying no trace of smile, she turned to Zip,

"C'mon, Young Celebrity! Home!"

The Spaniels' "15 minutes of fame" were over.

Zip felt a firm grip and was lifted into the air, pressed to the rubbery-rough jacket of a burly Fire-fighter. Milly barked softly "me too," but remained staunchly unwilling to uproot her bottom from the safe, dry landing.

Old Lady shoved the dogs inside one by one and, once they stopped panting, the house fell back into its silence. The uproar outside was muted out. The stink remained in the air, however—as repulsive as ever.

Half an hour later, all three TV stars were lying peacefully upstairs, in Old Lady's bedroom.

"You think that autograph-seekers will ask for our pawprints now?" murmured Milly.

"You wish. Ducklingburgers would not pay much attention to a small thing like this on the news," yawned Zip.

"No, I think they'll notice," said Milly optimistically, and rolled over on her back to air out her slightly overheated stomach. "Too bad Old Lady did not pick me up. She would have looked even better holding me!"

"I bet you my turn bringing back the tennis ball, that nobody'll remember," grumbled Zip.

❧

The Spaniels did not find this out for some time, but even by the time they licked each other's noses to seal the bet, Milly had already won it.

At that precise moment, one of the most ambitious businessmen of Ducklingburg was placing a call to one of Ducklingburg's scariest lawyers.

"It's Steve," said the ambitions businessman. "You watched the news today? Whatchugonna do about *that*?"

The scary lawyer on the other line cleared his throat with disdain.

"Steve, you done lost your mind if you're thinking I'll want to mix up with this."

Uneasy businessman Steve and lawyer Paul nevertheless agreed to meet immediately to ponder *taking steps.*

Before two furry TV stars were soundly asleep, their adventure with Big Water was very much the focus of a worried debate on the financial side of town where neither of the two Spaniels had ever even set a paw.

10

BURNING MYSTERY

"Zippy, you sleeping?"

"What do you want, Milly?"

"Why do you think I want something?"

"'Cause you called me Zippi-ee. Why aren't you asleep?"

"Zippy, I think Old Lady did not like seeing herself on the News today," breathed Milly, and added in a frightened whisper, "Maybe it's because she did not have enough time to do her make-up?"

Zip opened his left eye half-wide, and said thoughtfully,

"No. She always looks good to me. The way she pins that brooch . . and pearls . . . Just like Elizabeth the Second."

"Who?"

"The British Queen."

"Are we relatives?"

"No. Queen has corgis. Stupid dogs. Ears twice the size their heads, perked up all the time. No harmony of form."

"Then what?"

"To be honest," Zip paused meaningfully, "I still can't believe she even ventured onto TV. It seems to me," Zip paused again, and now his ears showed he was quite awake, "she's been avoiding all publicity since we moved to Ducklingburg."

"Why? Did she do something wrong?" Milly's breathing hastened, as she added, "You're right, she does not let us—"

"Yes," agreed Zip, finishing his sister's thought, "She does not let us do *anything*. We asked to be enrolled in pure-bred competitions; she would not take us. We wanted dog collars with our names: she refused."

"Totally!" Milly's voice trailed up in poorly repressed resentment, "Sam has two shiny metal tags, right on his collar! A dog biscuit shaped inlay has his phone number, to call home if he is lost. The round tag says SAM, in all caps, and the last name of his Human in small letters. The tags jingle together so gloriously! Ding-dong, ting-aling. The quicker he runs, the louder the clatter he makes,"

Milly closed her eyes and listened, in her imagination, to the coveted metallic *clinking* of Sam's tags. Her eyes reopened wide in fear, having confronted a terrible possibility.

"Zippy, did we do something wrong? Is she ashamed of us?"

Zip growled irritably.

"Zippy, I was thinking about collars. That white-collar who lived in our house before us, the criminal. Is he our relative? You sure he misbehaved? What did he do, Zippy? Why was white-collar guy so bad?"

Zip did not have a good response to that, but Milly was already miles away, muttering about her favorite subject.

"Old Lady always wears a brooch pinned under her collar. That's pretty. Yellow or golden. Theo has such a majestic white collar. White ruff even—"

Zip thought of biting his sister to stop the all-too familiar refrain about all the neighborhood attractions—*trinkets, majestic ruffs, bushy tails* when Milly turned clumsily, and bumped her paw into Zip's side. "I . . . Zippy, I love your cobalt black fur too, and all your yellow spots, too."

"Thanks," Zip softened, and added after a long

pause, "There's no way the Criminal in white collar is our relative."

"Then why do we live in his house? . . . What's wrong with this house, Zip?" added Milly dolefully, "What you think?"

"I think we must quit guessing and investigate."

"How? *In-ves-tigate*?" Milly exclaimed quietly.

Zip leaned into her ear and passionately explained his plan. And inexplicably, Zip's passion worked. Milly, the waggish and wistful Milly, was on board immediately, out-of-her-fur with delight, and suggested even to steal the stub that was left of Old Lady's festive candle.

"To throw some light on this," she said.

Mindful not to clink their claw tips noisily on the wooden stairs, the siblings set off up the staircase, headed for the Secret Room.

The door creaked.

"We will not need the candle, after all," declared Zip, "Old Lady stocks a fallback flashlight here. Eternal battery!" And muttering something under his nose, Zip foisted into Milly's paws a short red cylinder lettered on one side

ENERGIZER

and on another side:

WeatherReady

"Spin the handle, and it will light up," instructed Zip over his shoulder, as he scurried around the room perimeter, searching.

It did not take Zip long to locate the box marked in blue sharpie, *House Closing Documents*.

"Time is of the essence," muttered Zip, and spilled the entire box onto the floor.

His spaniel dog nature kicked in, and he lounged into the search.

"Light this spot," commanded Zip, "Spin the handle. Spin harder!"

Property Tax Bill . . .

Address . . .

Parcel number . . .

Zip was moving his lips as he was pawing through the papers.

"I do not know these words," Milly was embarrassed to admit.

Zip did not react to his sister's complaint and kept sorting out unnecessary sheets.

"Offer of Purchase and Contract . . . Milly, light this spot, don't slack!"

"Your ear is in my way," defended Milly. "Found it yet? Zippy, what are we searching for?"

"Light here, and don't talk so loudly. We are not *searching,* we are *investigating,*" said Zip, and added, in response to Milly's baffled look, "We're reading the whole ball of wax indiscriminately."

He went back to whispering to himself as he read, pointing to particular lines of the documents with the sharp claw of his left paw.

"First line . . . *Buyer's Name'* . . . Old Lady. We knew that.

. . . .

"Price . . . We don't care; we paid it already.

. . . .

"Aha! *Seller's Name*!"

"That's the *Criminal!?*" exhaled Milly.

"Just an illegible signature," whispered Zip regretfully.

"Settlement Statement," Zip read on, "Move the light here, Milly. Very small letters."

Zip pushed his nose so close to the papers that he could have been sniffing them diagnostically.

"Aha! Found it!

Name and Address of the Seller

"He does not have an address," interjected Milly, "He is in prison."

"*Ian Sider*," read Zip loudly. "*Mr. Ian—*"

"—Do we know *him*?" asked Milly.

"First time hearing," shot back Zip.

Milly sighed, relieved.

"Means we are not related, for certain."

"After that, it's all hand-written. Milly, spin the handle harder. This is from some lawyer to our Old Lady!"

BY FACSIMILE

Dear Old Lady, Flood Insurance is Mandatory for your new ho—

"—Zip, must we investigate the whole pile?" injected Milly, ". . . Turning this handle . . . My right paw's killing me."

Zip tore himself away from the paper, and barked with irritation, "Then use your *left* paw, Milly. I found what we need! Here!"

"About *the Criminal*?" asked Milly almost lethargically. She was losing interest.

"About our *House*," corrected Zip. "It was in the newspapers, the whole story."

"Zip, that's lots of letters. You'll tell me later, right? Just the essential parts. You got it all, though?"

Zip read for a long time, breaking occasionally to ponder, and frequently returning to the beginning of the paragraph. Milly spun the handle dutifully but with increasing signs of fatigue, asking at decreasing intervals,

"You got it yet?"

"Mostly. I only do not get why our Old Lady would buy this House sight unseen. That's just not her. You've seen her shop at Farmers' Market. She'll check every apple. On *all* sides. She taps the watermelon front *and back*. She close-sniffs the fish."

Zip scooped up all the sheets between his paws and muzzle, and was shoving them back into the box when his eye caught on something new.

A thick, glossy page torn out haphazardly from a magazine was almost entirely taken up by the gigantic photo of a bald, mustached man dressed in a boring suit and tie. The mustache was straggly, its upside-down corners giving the owner a perpetually sullen look.

The caption under the photo announced the mustache to be growing on the face of *the supervisory Federal Attorney on the case. Paul . . .* Zip's curiosity satisfied by knowing the mustache-man's function in the cast of characters, he skipped over the details of the man's last name and education and jumped to the article's lead.

> *White Goose Lane Magazine reports from the Courthouse.*
>
> *After snatching victory in this High-Profile matter, the Supervising Federal Attorney sat down with us—*

"It's an interview," whispered Milly, whose interest was perked up by the glossy paper and the pictures. "Mustache unkempt like on a stray, but the hair on his head looks very carefully licked down."

Zip read out-loud.

QUESTION: *Paul, you were the federal prosecutor leading the investigation in this high-profile—*

Zip skipped a few lines

QUESTION: *We understand that the Department of Justice initially intended to leverage your investigation to take down even bigger . . . Can you comment?*

Zip skipped a line.

QUESTION: *Is it true that you were unable to*

persuade Mr. Ian Sider to cooperate? Sources quote Mr. Ian Sider saying he would rather 'serve a jail sentence than be a rat.' Can you disclose who were the upper echelon criminals commanding such loyalty from Mr. Sider? Should they have been your real target?

Zip skipped a few lines, muttering under his breath,

"This mustached Paul . . . Federal Paul . . . Federal Mustache worked under high pressure and won . . . subpo— subpe—

"I don't know how to pronounce this word, Milly. Or what it means."

"Skip to the end," suggested Milly.

Zip tore ahead to the bottom of the page, and found it filled with puffery.

> *A brilliant career awaits Federal . . . Paul . . . our own local hero. . . .*
>
> *Rumored to be on the short list for the recently vacant post of Director of FBI or . . . a high-level post in the Department of Justice.*
>
> *The White House is reported to have called to personally congratulate—*
>
> *Also, our sources report that several large law firms are already wooing the rising young lawyer away from federal service and into private practice.*

Promises of a partnership with a seven-figure annual paycheck—

Zip unglued his nose from the page, and summarized, somewhat shakily:

"Federal Mustache Paul caught our House Criminal."

"So what?" Milly forgot to spin the handle, and the room gradually settled into semi-darkness. Zip did not respond immediately, too busy processing what he had just read.

"Federal . . . Paul . . . got promoted because he caught our House Criminal, Mr. Ian Sider. Our Criminal must be . . . vicious. ... *Big payoffs,*" whispered Zip under his nose, trying to penetrate the meaning of such unfamiliar matters, "Seven figures."

"What figures?" asked Milly looking around, suddenly worried. "Where? Here? Don't talk about figures. It is dark."

"Means money, by far more money than I know how to count. Every year. Milly. This Paul promoted because of our important Criminal. Spin me a little more light here," ordered Zip, "Let's find out where—"

But at that moment, they heard quick footing on the stairs, and the mocking voice of Old Lady.

"Who nipped the festive candle?" demanded Old Lady. "Bad enough we nearly drowned, you want to torch the place as well?"

"NOPE!" barked Zip loudly and rolled the safe red emergency Energizer cylinder towards Old Lady's feet. "We did not burn!"

"Out! *Marsh otsyuda*," commanded Old Lady in Russian. "The whole town is asleep; you are the only ones still skulking around."

Old Lady was mistaken. Not everyone in town was asleep that night.

Steve the businessman was awake and very worried that the Department of Transportation could easily uncover who spilled concrete under the bridge. And pin on him the crime of unlawful "diversion." Which might well facilitate Steve's making a personal acquaintanceship with the prior owner of that goddamn House.

Steve's friend Paul the lawyer was also sleepless, tossing and turning in his bed. Paul had not yet received the lucky ticket on the non-stop train from the boonies of Ducklingburg to a prestigious office at Main Justice, a hop, skip and a jump from the

White House. Nor did he yet have that offer of a seven-figure law partnership in hand.

Now, Steve was very much concerned that the sneaky, covert game of his buddy Steve could become overt, publicized in the worst possible ways. Considering the sensationalist climate of the times, plugging a bridge with concrete might even be characterized as "domestic terrorism."

Worse yet, Paul's well-known close friendship with Steve would possibly result in internet-driven suspicions of collusion: *What did Steve's best buddy Paul know about the concrete, and when did he know it?* That the truth might be uncovered about the answer to that question was what Paul feared most.

In short, the fallout from this mess, this Concrete-gate expose, might nip Paul's magnificent career in the bud.

Heavy thoughts, anxieties that, in at least two guilt-ridden brains, kept at bay the solace of sleep.

11

ROSIE'S BETRAYAL

The roiled, rusty-colored water lingered on. It settled on the ground floor and refused to seep away for two days and three nights.

Old Lady talked to herself in hushed undertones. Did not read even a single page of her favorite *Anna Karenina,* nor *Gone With The Wind.* The only thing she read was a thick stack of small print titled *Flood Insurance Policy*. From the first line to the last line, and then over and over again, her finger hovering over the page, lips whispering the legalese. Later, that careful study came in very handy.

The Firefighters ferried in the food.

Tea was boiled on the gas stove, each time Old Lady murmuring, "Thank God they did not turn off the gas."

It was all not so bad, Zip and Milly decided. They all slept clustered unusually close together; that way, the strange smells and splashes were less scary. The dogs were permitted to settle almost by Old Lady's pillow. They were pleased with this new closeness. Life was not too bad at all.

The only distasteful thing for everyone was that spaniels had to do their business inside the house, on paper bags from the supermarket. Zip and Milly were embarrassed.

And, naturally, no walks. On either side of the street.

❧

At long last, the water subsided, leaving behind the stench—sharp, nasty. Everything around turned out to be covered in yellow-red-dirty powder—every bush, every blade of the grass, the flowers, the walls outside the house and the garage.

Every evening wash, this powder-dirt and unidentifiable scuzzy lumps had to be scrubbed off the Spaniels' paws, bellies and long ears. Old Lady grumbled and made half-hearted threats to shave them clean. Even before the flood, Old Lady was displeased that Zip and Milly swept the ground's dirt with their ears. But what were they supposed to do? Not like they could walk around with their noses sticking up. They would not see anything except for the sky. And Fox Theodore would deem them intolerably snobbish.

In short, everything around was covered with a patina of mud, mold, mildew, each of which made its own loathsome contribution to the medley of unpleasant smells. It smelled horrible everywhere. Hot, damp, stinky.

Electricity returned eventually, but the air conditioner refused to start. The engine had died under the water.

As the water receded, the neighbors started social activity.

The first to come to life was neighbor Suzy, the one who lived across the street and owned half a cat. Right from the get-go, instead of her usual drawling "How y'all dooooin'," Suzy commenced lamenting her misfortunes. Her children lived too far, the air conditioner kicked the bucket, but most of all, she was upset about her half-owned cat Rosie. How could this furry scoundrel have abandoned her in this dark hour?!

Zip and Milly itched to correct: Rosie did not

abandon anybody. She left to see her real legal owners. Suzy said she *owned* half of Rosie, but Rosie was actually a *timeshare.* Not Rosie's fault that her real legal owners were out making money most of the days and therefor the neglected Rosie spent her time with Suzy.

Eventually, Suzy realized that talking exclusively about herself was impolite and tried to make amends by changing the subject.

"Your house was on the news. So handsome under its striking red roof. Tea-rose white walls . . . such a flattering contrast with the water. Like a handsome ship. The news said you'all House was the epicenter of the flood."

Zip and Milly prepared to growl at Suzy's undiplomatic "rubbing it in" remark, but Suzy realized her blunder and abruptly took leave, whimpering unintelligibly.

The Spaniels decided not to see her off across the street. Too stinky.

Fox Theo was right. Big Water brought a lot of worry.

12

THE AGENT

From the start, Zip and Milly saw eye-to-eye with the Insurance Agent on one point. Best place for negotiations was on the landing, outside the front door.

The ground floor, after the disaster cleaning crew had pumped out the water, was still wet and stinky.

The main floor was clean and smelled like Pine floorwash . . . but still unbearably hot. Also, the air was stinky if one took a deeper sniff. The flood smell wafted up from the ground floor below.

The third floor was Old Lady bedroom. Besides, it was also hot and stuffy.

Above that was the restricted access floor with

Old Lady's secret room where nobody at all was allowed, anyway.

Long story short: since the air conditioner's motor drowned, anywhere one tried inside the house was hot, stuffy and smelly.

The yard was equally unsuitable.

The fire pit, the path leading to it, and everything around was still covered under a thick layer of something that had been sticky at first and then dried into a dusty, dirty, rusty colored sediment which smelled strongly of sewage.

But the stair landing at the front door was like an island. Almost untouched by the invasion of Big Water, the landing and one step under it remained its pre-flood color. By a process of elimination, that had to be the site where business would be conducted.

The Insurance Agent twisted his neck around and sat down to the right, upwind.

Zip and Milly appreciated his savvy later. Old Lady sat down next to him, feet parked one step down, on the only clean step.

On Old Lady's lap, the Spaniels spied a folder with the Flood Insurance Policy. Zip knew that for sure, because he remembered that Old Lady had been reading the policy almost the whole time since Big Water came until The Agent arrived.

Zip and Milly settled closer to the entrance door, and could see and hear clearly, just as clearly as if they might've been allowed to lie on top of the negotiation table in pre-flood times.

"I," began the Insurance Agent, "represent FEMA. You know FEMA?"

Old Lady nodded.

The Agent smiled. Unzipping a fake-leather folder with a multitude of pockets, he liberated a stack of pristinely clean pre-printed forms with bright blue stickers that directed:

SIGN HERE

"I will give you a check for $10,000 today.

"All we do is fill out these forms. I'll fill them out myself, later," he offered hastily, "It's quicker that way. You need not worry, FEMA will pay for everything." The Agent was all smiles now. He tried to give Old Lady a pat on the back, but she dodged with an agility that he did not expect.

Zip and Milly exchanged quick looks, both simply in disbelief that somebody would be so stupid. It's a known fact that if your *insurance company* offers $10,000 bucks without even looking at the damage, then the true damage must be much more. "I'll fill the forms myself" means he'll fill them out in the manner that best benefits this FEMA. "FEMA will pay for everything" defines "everything" as "as little as FEMA can get away with paying." Realistically, this FEMA has no intention of unnecessarily throwing money into Big Water.

What kind of naïve yokel did this Agent take our Old Lady for?

It's not that Zip and Milly disliked the FEMA Agent. But he smelled . . . not good, as if he had lingered too long and absorbed too much of the pungent perfume of a flood. Which, in fact, he obviously had.

The Agent knew about his odiferous handicap and, taking it into account, diplomatically chose his location somewhat away from the sensitive noses. Zip and Milly enjoyed upwind and stayed as far as possible. Old Lady was obliged to sit closer, but she wisely held a fat folder between her nose and the Agent.

"Well," Old Lady immediately mounted an attack, "I simply cannot wrap my mind around this. How do I not spend your ten thousand in one place? Replacing the air conditioner alone comes to twelve thousand. Disaster cleaning post-flood is another twenty-five thousand.

The Agent had been around the block, and parried swiftly.

"Sure, I know that. Everything will be paid for. Let's just get the ball rolling here and sign those forms," he urged as he stretched his face in an even brighter smile and patted one of the folder's pockets, "I have the check here."

Old Lady's eyes did not follow his patting hand, instead staying glued suspiciously to the stack of forms.

"Don't worry, I'll help you with those," said the Agent, misinterpreting Old Lady's interest, "I'm here to help the insured . . . you."

"Let me see the paperwork," Old Lady replied.

"Don't trouble yourself, I'll fill it out for you," the Agent insisted, his hand poised over the papers. "It's quicker if I do it. You just sign and you get *your check*."

Schooled by considerable experience in these negotiations, the Agent placed well-calculated emphasis on the words *your check*.

His approach was shameless and well-practiced. He was reading questions off the forms already:

FIRST QUESTION:

What was the level of flood water in your basement?

Zip and Milly gave each other a dark look. The Spaniels had seen his sort of folk before, sycophantic and patronizing at the same time. The kind of folk that asked Old Lady to "just sign," figuring that she would not or could not read the clouds of small print above her signature line. That sort of folk did not do well when confronted by Old Lady.

It was not for nothing that Old Lady read her insurance policy for days, as if she were enthralled by the characters or the romantic turns of the plot. She had studied and mastered every jot and tittle of the policy.

Zip raised his fireball-colored brows, signaling: *wait for it . . .*

"Basement?! I don't think so," Old Lady snorted. "I'm very well aware," Old Lady countered quickly, "that FEMA does not pay for *basements*. It clearly says so in the Contract. More importantly, though, I'm also very well aware that my *ground floor* does not fall within the policy's definition of a basement. I do not *have* a *basement*, so let's not waste our time talking about the exclusion of coverage for *basements*."

Milly let out a short, satisfied growl: *and there you are!*

The Agent knew his stuff as well, and retorted: "I would not risk calling it a . . . The house sits on a steep slope. Almost thirty degrees."

"Right here," Old Lady quickly whipped out a few pieces of paper, "It says that the slope is irrelevant. "*A basement must descend from the street, from the entrance, leading down,* and what I have is just the opposite. That floor has two bedrooms with closets, a bathroom, a fireplace and six windows. Everything is heated and air-conditioned. I will not sign the form if you check the box 'basement'."

"In my opinion, it's a 'basement'," pressed Agent softly.

"In my opinion, it's definitely 'not basement'. Or else sign that paperwork yourself," snapped the Old Lady.

It is not that Old Lady had no manners. She did say 'hello,' and 'please,' and she never did say any words that one is not supposed to say in front of small children or purebred dogs. But the thing about Old Lady was that she said exactly what she thought, and what she thought was not always flattering.

Agent just opened his mouth to add something, but at that moment, his cell phone rang. He launched into a lengthy conversation with somebody, explaining that he would do his best to be on time, but that he did not know when he would be finished here.

The Agent looked harassed and worn, and it was obvious that he did not particularly like Old Lady and the Spaniels. Zip and Milly smiled at each other and stretched out on the landing, their hind paws in the frog position, prepared for what was certain to happen next.

The Agent would later—almost a year later—testify in Federal Court that he "felt right off: Old Lady was a troublesome customer." An Agent speak for not easily duped.

The Agent finished with the phone call. The dogs and Old Lady waited to hear what he'd say, but Agent kept gazing into the faraway yonder, and his expression clearly said that he was fed up with the "*basement-no basement*" squabble. And even more fed up with himself, his job, and unending worry that the stink would never leave his skin and clothes.

Old Lady was not a bad negotiator, so long as she did not lose her cool and become too impatient.

Zip and Milly waited.

A fresh breeze picked up, again not towards the dogs. The Agent kept looking above their heads, and his expression clearly betrayed that he was thinking of the futility of further wrangling with Old Lady. His supervisor would order him to call white black anyway.

Old Lady broke the dull silence and spoke first.

"Here's my suggestion. You write 'basement' on this form, and you sign it as representing your decision. First thing tomorrow, I will petition Federal Court, and we'll figure it out there."

Agent surrendered. "You win. Let's make it 'the ground floor'."

He moved his finger down the Form.

NEXT QUESTION:

How high did the water rise?

"One foot? Two feet? What do you think?"

"I don't have to *think*. I have photos. When the water receded, it left traces on all the walls. I put a measuring tape against it and took photos. Add them to your report as exhibit, as Photos 1, 2, etc. . . ."

Agent ceased resistance.

It became clear that filling out the forms with descriptions, photograph, and Exhibits #1, #2 , #3 would take hours. Zip and Milly had by now lost interest; their side was clearly prevailing in the form-filling effort. So, the Spaniels set off to see what was going on with the neighbors.

Old Lady called out to their backs “Milly, not one paw off White Goose Lane. Zip, watch her!”

Zip barked assent. Milly had to be watched all the time; she was way social and not especially discriminating, and oft-times acted against her own interests. Got caught up with the Coyotes, recklessly followed them into the forest. Never would’ve found her if it were not for Fox Theo. Then she had a puppy crush on red Sam, three times her size, and an old Labrador to boot. Labrador’s Human had to shoo Milly away, it almost came to kicks. Disgraceful.

Milly immediately set sail for the neighbors on the left.

“Stay close,” commanded Zip.

At the neighbors’ house, a cleaning crew was removing from the garage all the belongings that had gotten flooded and piling them together outside. All goods looked like they had been freshly painted with ochre paint. Both Spaniels were fascinated by the array of what the neighbors had in stock. They’d never seen things heaped up like that: the bike, kids’ blankets, boots, garden implements—all in the same disorderly pile.

The cleaning crew worked very fast. When they were done, the neighbor—he was a Manager from the Bank of South Duck—came out with a piece of white kids' chalk and chalked the outline of the pile.

"Why did he draw the chalk line on the ground?" was puzzled Milly, "Does not look like hopscotch. Who could jump over this pile? I do not know. A kangaroo maybe."

"It's not Australia, Milly," refuted Zip. "Maybe it's so that nobody steals anything," he ventured a bold hypothesis.

"Fi," Milly twitched her tail stub, "Who'd want this junk. We have plenty of our own. Old Lady said that Water brought infection. Hepatitis and other illness. It's all very dirty. And diseased-infected."

"Still, what'd be the purpose of the line? On TV, they talked about crossing red lines. But this one's white. Can't wrap my head around it."

"Me neither."

"Maybe Suzy knows? There she is, with the other neighbor from across the street."

Suzy and the neighbor might well have known the purpose of the line, but they were busy with accounting and gossip related to whose cars had drowned in the neighborhood.

Suzy was in a good mood today. Cat Rosie

returned and was showing her love and devotion by dragging to the back porch all the by-now partially decomposed dead mice, moles, chipmunks, and other critters that had been flushed out by Big Water. Suzy was burying them by the dozen.

"Before the Water rose too high, Dick managed to drive his Mercedes to safety at his son's and sailed his canoe instead."

"Patrick's cars both drowned. They don't even have a garage."

"The surgeon and anesthesiologist get to work by sharing an ambulance that tiptoes close enough through the water to fetch them. Means both families lost their cars too."

"Old Lady had the worst of it. She does not even have car insurance."

"How come? How does she drive without?"

"Just the liability, in case she drives into somebody. Decided that if somebody drives into her, the guilty party's insurance will pay."

"That's true, they'd pay. Eventually."

"But flood is not covered by insurance. Poor Old Lady. She's all alone. She has nobody. Poor sweet, frail old thing."

Zip and Milly were outraged by the "frail old thing" label. Suzy herself and that neighbor from across the street, they neither were of cheerleading age.

"Let's go home," Zip whispered to Milly.

❧

Old Lady and the Agent were still sitting on the landing where Spaniels left them. But suddenly the Agent made a better impression now than when he first arrived. The forms-filling business now behind them, it seemed that Agent and Old Lady had become buddies. They were sitting side to side, chatting amiably. Old Lady's folder with the Flood Insurance Policy and Agent's unzipped leather portfolio were stacked peacefully on the landing behind their backs, covered under untidy stack of finished forms.

Turned out, Agent also lived alone and also had a dog. When off on travel, he hired a neighbor's son to watch the dog, for modest compensation.

Agent was saying wearily that "Nobody has ever sued FEMA in our district. At least, I never heard of it."

"How come?" asked Old Lady.

The Agent shrugged and launched into spirited stories about lawsuits against other, non-FEMA insurance companies. Turned out, during his lengthy work life, this Agent was employed by all sorts of insurance companies—small and big, regional and international, home, auto, and even reinsurers. Each of them got sued on daily basis. It seemed that every Tom Dick and Harry sued every insurance company. And each time, the Agent got roped to testify in court as a witness. *Spent more time in court than out of court,* he complained.

"Was cross-examined on damages to property, naturally, you'd expect that. But the talk was about all sort of unexpected matters—mental and emotional distress to the policy holders, unreasonable denial, low settlement offers, punitive damages five times the actual damages—"

The Agent shivered. "Hate court. Everybody stressed. Ladies—nervy; men—incensed. Excuse my non-political correctness."

Agent shook his head and shrugged the shoulders, "Nothing like that with FEMA. Of course, there's law suits in big disasters, somewhere. But never homeowners like you. Nobody sues FEMA single-handedly, no never."

It was already late at night when the Agent finally rose to depart, leaving in Old Lady's hand the $10,000 check, as promised, adding tiredly,

"Your demands . . ." Agent held a dramatic pause, "in short, in my experience, FEMA never had—"

Old Lady gestured him to stop talking.

"I understand your meaning, young man. I'll have my attorney look into this."

And, without shaking hands, they parted.

❧

For the night, Zip and Milly settled by the front door. It did not smell any less here, but the marble floor was slightly cooler. And here, the dogs could discuss, without fear of waking Old Lady, the question of *attorney*. They've never heard about such before.

"Zip," Milly moved in closer to Zip, then moved away. Zip's ears, and everything below the top of his back smelled horrible. Nor did the smell disappear when Milly crawled away a little farther.

"Milly," growled Zip, "why are you fidgeting?"

"You smell bad," said Milly, embarrassed.

"So do you. We did not get a wash today. Old Lady was upset and tired."

"Zip," Milly moved closer again, "I did not understand about the attorney. She said '*my attorney.*' Do we know him?"

"Not sure." Zip pondered. "Suzy across the street . . . Her father was an attorney, but Suzy does not work anywhere."

"Lariska maybe," offered Milly, "she and Old Lady drink tea and talk. What do they talk about?"

"Lariska for sure is *not* an attorney," concluded Zip, "But I remember: they talked about attorneys."

"What did they say?"

"Lariska talked. She could not find a good attorney, and that's why she can't divorce her husband."

"So?"

"I was not much paying attention," fessed up Zip honestly, "The only thing I remember is that Old Lady thought that they should investigate the *legal market.*"

"How's that, Zippy? I don't get it."

"Internet research. Read what they say on the webpages. About the lawyers."

"Did you read it?"

"No. But I have a plan, I can read what Old Lady read. I'll check her search history; she never clears it. Then we'll know who 'our attorney' is."

"Are you sure?"

"Positive."

"Zippy," Milly shuffled and moved away again, "I think that if we sleep separately, it will smell twice less. Only from me."

13

THE SAUSAGE

The sunset blazed with orange fire, and in the sun's last rays, the crust of ugly, rust-colored dust that covered fountains, walls, fences, mailboxes—everything—took on the deceptive appearance of a deliciously-colored chocolate coating. Behind the ravine, where the flood did not touch the trees, the greenery was bright and fresh, without the stinky crust.

Big Water left, and Spaniels' old friend Fox Theodore paid a visit.

Theo could have said "I told you so," but he had too much class.

After a few respectful "how do you do's," Zip bided his time waiting to see what his guest had to say.

Fox Theo looked nervous, as though Big Water had not gone away.

"I was . . . worried," the Fox high-sniffed the air and spat into the fire-pit, "but I knew you'd be all right." Both dogs nodded in unison.

There was a pause.

The Spaniels wanted to tell the Fox that the Worry was over, and that it was time to celebrate reunion with their friends. But everybody knows that saying "don't worry" never helps against a worry.

So, instead of empty reassurances, the dogs waited for the Fox to talk.

Theo cocked his head to one side and vibrated slightly from the tip of his nose to the tip of his tail, then froze and waited distastefully watching the ochre-orange cloud of dust that he had stirred up settle all around him. Then he got up and moved to a new place. The only clean spot left on the concrete was the imprint under where Theo had just sat.

"Sorry," the Fox grumbled. "The forest stinks to high heaven, can't hunt a thing!" The Fox licked his nose, hinting that now would be a good time for a little gesture of hospitality.

"May I offer a chicken paw? Fresh from Old

Lady's kitchen garbage, never once gnawed," ceremoniously bowed Zip.

"Means the chicken breast is finished up already," sighed Fox "Is chicken on your menu every day?"

"No," injected Milly defensively. "Sometimes Old Lady eats out, with Lariska. Then we get these pills from big bags with a photoshopped picture of Clumber Spaniels. Edible. But only after a long while, when you are hungry enough.

"According to small print on the bag, they *are full of vitamins and nutrition,*" said Zip derisively.

"I don't fancy them either," nodded Fox.

"Do you fancy a fresh sausage instead, Theodore?" Milly gave her tail an enthusiastic wag.

Zip had not even noticed when Milly darted to the house and returned, a sausage clutched between her jaws. Milly dropped the sausage down on the clean imprint where the Fox had just sat, and all three animals stared at it.

"Did you ask Old Lady?" Zip enquired, although he was pretty sure that he knew the answer.

"No. But . . . the duty of hospitality . . . Old Lady loves our friends."

"Looks new," Theodore was reaching for the sausage with his paw.

"Where did you get it?" Zip demanded, pressing

his own paw preventively on top of the sausage. “What is Old Lady doing?” growled Zip disapprovingly.

“Sitting by her empty plate; probably thinks she already ate the sausage,” reported Milly calmly.

Fox licked his upper lip. The sausage glistened mouthwateringly, so plump, bursting with juice and sweet aroma.

But he was a guest here.

The Fox tried to look the other way. He liked the sausage far better than the bony chicken paw, but there was something else that really troubled him. *Should he tell them?*

An awkward pause ensued again while Theo sought to resolve an inner debate between his sense of moral obligation and his primal programming as a wild hunter.

Sausage, thought Theo, *looks so soft and juicy.* And, driven by instinct, the fox inched closer. The wild animal inside him whispered, *Hunt! Grab the sausage! Make a run for the forest!!* But then the bonds of friendship intervened with a hefty tug in the opposite direction: *Isn’t it wrong to steal from friends?*

Friendship won.

Theo screwed up his face, shaking with suppressed temptation, and pulled away his nose,

"The chicken paw will do lovely. Especially since it's new, never once gnawed at."

❧

When the chicken paw was eaten, Fox did not stretch out, as he would usually after feeding, front paws extended to support his muzzle, ready to nap to the backdrop of whatever chatter was in progress. Instead, he just stood there silently, constantly shifting from paw to paw, looking around restlessly.

"Theodore," Milly still stayed in character of hospitable mistress, "perhaps you'd like to move into the shady center of the flowerbed? It is warm in the sun. August is not the best season in Ducklingburg."

Fox shook his head.

"It's not so bad around the fire pit. The concrete is pretty cooling. And then again, the flowers: they throw shade and add a certain seclusion to the ambiance."

But he did not look like he enjoyed the ambiance.

"I'm . . . was . . . worried—" the Fox started haltingly.

"—It's all behind us," shot back lackadaisical Milly.

Zip could not help getting a bit irritated. The Fox's doom and gloom was overboard. Big Water was all gone. Time to stop the whining.

Milly giggled, but the Fox kept gazing around, as the invisible Worry was sending him secret signals. Then he said, "I'm still worried. I don't like that your Old Lady thinks that she ate the sausage herself."

That was Zip's thinking precisely, and he added quickly: "I was also thinking, it's not good to steal from the table. You need to kick that habit, Milly."

Both stared at Milly expectantly.

The sausage, still displayed on the clean patch of concrete, still smelled heavenly.

"What do you want me to do, boys," Milly snapped. "Take it back?"

"Yes," nodded Fox.

"Exactly," agreed Zip, surprised. He was pained to deprive Theo of a tasty treat, but family came first.

"Old Lady is not going to eat a slobbered sausage," protested Milly.

"True. But she will know that she can remember what she ate and what she did not," insisted Fox.

"What's the point? The sausage is ours now!" Milly tried to take a bite, but Zip snapped at her and she backed off.

Fox was watching Milly, at the same time taking

stock of his surroundings, as though he heard a signal of upcoming Worry.

"There's still Worry," sighed the Fox, as if to himself, and tried hard to not think about the sausage.

"Now what? A *drought*?" Zip tried to joke.

But Fox did not smile back. He sighed deeply and blurted out hastily.

"Freckle told me that *if* Old Lady loses her memory, they could use medical experts to . . . *re-home* her. Your House will be auctioned by the City. There is a buyer already. Actually, two buyers, and that leads to lots of disagreements."

"I don't quite understand," admitted Zip, then turned his head to Milly,

"Drag back the sausage. Now!"

Milly seized the sausage gingerly between her teeth and licked off the juice,

"And don't even think of accidentally swallowing it," Zip instructed Milly's behind as she reluctantly trotted away. She returned shortly, looking innocent and unconcerned.

"Freckle. She told me—" Theo stopped himself before he indiscreetly spilled too much, but the Spaniels were not paying attention anyway.

Fox swallowed a mouthful of drool, bid goodbye

to the forlorn hope of a square meal, and suddenly was overcome by melancholy.

Soft, mellow twilight was descending upon the flood-ravished backyard of Old Lady and cloaking it with an aura of peace, embellishing the properties of her neighbors to the left and to the right on White Goose Lane.

Neither Fox nor Zip nor Milly wanted to break the quiet, to spoil the attractive illusion created by Nature's artifice.

I should tell them, thought Theodore, *and make sure that at least Zip pays proper attention. After all, Freckle risked her life to get this news!*

And so the Fox broke the silence.

"It's a long story," Fox started, gazing wistfully towards the green tops of the trees, and shuffled his hind paws in preparation for the storytelling, "The Humans in the golf club downstream—"

"Freckle eavesdropped again?" Zip interrupted, still lightheartedly. "She's certainly smart and enterprising beyond her years."

"Fox years are different," Theodore seemed easily sidetracked, or maybe just glad to change the subject. Considering the circumstances, it seemed appropriate to share personal things, so Theo muttered on. "Fox kits are not walked around on a leash. Most grow up and have their own families by the next Summer."

"Lots of hassle, that," Zip encouraged the change in topic.

Hope he does not start again, thought Zip, *enough already with omens and augury.*

"In the woods, foxes only live a few years, gotta make a move on it. Longer lifespan if one joins a zoo. But I'm not sure it's better to sit for twenty years behind the bars or three years of hunting at sunrise . . . raising the family . . . what can be more romantic than Spring courtship . . ."

Theo closed his eyes, and softly howled, "My first vixen, her snow-white chemisette, and such elegant narrow face. This young lighthearted creature turned out to be such a caring mother to my kits. Would not give up that year for a hundred years of human food! Not for any eating . . ."

Pro-wild-woods lifestyle propaganda's getting laid on real thick again, Zip thought, but had no energy to argue. *Freedom, woods, wild life.* On any other day, Zip would have risen to the bait and provided push-back, defended his own domestic lifestyle. But today, Zip just said:

"Your youngest must, indeed be brilliant. She feeds as well as in the zoo, so she'll live long. And she is not trapped in a cage. Plus, her social life is only rivaled by that of O'Malley."

Theodore stared quizzically.

"The Fox News broadcaster. Got himself fired for living like the whole year is Spring courtship and every female is in season," explained Zip.

Fox considered and zeroed in on the favorable facts.

"You said the news channel is called Fox?"

"Yes. That's what I said. *Fox*."

"See? It all comes out in favor of my youngest's theory."

"What?"

"She said the Scared Hare County Club will soon be renamed into Fox Golf Club."

"Well-well," Zip twitched his cheek distrustfully.

"Freckle's been doing her best to boost the renaming of the Golf Club where she works. Fox Golf, that would sound good, don't you think?"

Zip was a little dubious about the benefit of the name change, but he only twitched his cheek and did not answer. Observant Fox noticed and backpedaled a little, "But like I said, I'm not that proud of the kit's career. Still, she risked her life to get that job."

"She risked her life?"

"There's lots of useful things can be learned, eavesdropping," said Theo, ignoring the question.

"Why did she risk her life?"

"She is a valid informant, an honest gal and not just one of those anonymous sources," added Theo impatiently. "We would do well to listen to her."

Theo noiselessly sprang to his paws and, without bidding goodbye, set out for the ravine.

Zip followed him.

Without speaking to each other, the two friends trotted side by side. Distracted by the beauty of the fading, low-in-the-sky sunlight, Fox Theodore resolved to postpone telling his friend how the Humans from downstream had already prepared their attack on Zip's Old Lady. Deadly hunt, on many fronts, like a pack of wild animals surrounding their prey in Theo's forest. *Best not to speak of it today.*

They stopped above the no longer raging Sneaky Creek, now a misleadingly harmless-looking stream. Theodore the Fox and Zip the Spaniel, side by side, their backs to Old Lady's house, surveying their peaceful world—Zip and his wild friend, two equals in that moment, each putting off until another day their inevitable confrontation with the approach of a new, horrifying Worry.

14

THE MONEY

When the Big Water that comes once in five hundred years left, Old Lady's house began attracting all manner of Contractors and Sub-Contractors and even Contractors who for some reason called themselves *Generals*.

As much as these different intruders they all differed in sizes, sounds, smells, and hair colors, they were all the same when it came to the pitch of their speeches: the pitch was always *well-rehearsed*.

The Spaniels could tell that those pitches had been tried and repeated for years before Old Lady called them. The sales pitches were well-tested on lots of other ladies. Older ladies . . . younger ladies . . . and ladies of all sorts of ages in between. And pushing these Contractors to go off pitch was nearly impossible.

First wave of Contractors all called themselves Generals.

Generals smelled self-assured and never stuttered. They knew the answers to all Old Lady's questions before she even asked. Every one of them of them addressed Old Lady *"Y'ALL"* and referred to himself as *"WE,"* implying a bigger Company. Milly cocked her right ear and snickered. Zip wrinkled his nose. The dogs already learned the meaning of that "*we*" puffery. And so did Old Lady.

"Who is going to supervise the repair?" Old Lady interrupted unceremoniously, cutting short the protracted flow of sales propaganda.

"You mean?"

"I mean, who will hear my complaints in case I don't like the job *they* do?" Who will be in contact with me?" pried Old Lady.

"Why?"

"'Cause *they* do not speak any English. Nor will they understand any French or Russian, my only other languages."

All of the contractors and sub-contractors were well-mannered and turned a deaf ear to such political incorrectness. But Old Lady did not drop the subject until she was assured that the owner of the company would be on hand to supervise. Only then did she get to business.

As for the business, Old Lady posed the exact same business question for every Contractor:

How much to return the House to its pre-flood state?
Beginning with reinstalling my back door?

And although each of the Contractors had studied the exact same *South Duck Builders' Code* and was licensed by the exact same *Ducklingburg Building Board,*—and although each proclaimed identically that *quality was paramount,* the amounts they quoted for the same back door were vastly different.

The very first General Contractor to be invited to Old Lady's House had the prettiest website of them all. On his website, everything sparkled, photos flew into the pages, bounced, faded or even grew and shimmered.

Milly did not like General Contractor Number One. Before he even knocked, the Spaniel sensitive nose caught an off-putting stench of vainglory.

General Contractor Number One started not with an inspection but with a self-important warning.

"I doubt if you can afford me," he declared.

The dogs could clearly see that Old Lady was offended, but swallowed it politely. Contractor's next statements continued the belittling assault on Old Lady's house.

"Your stucco is not hard. Synthetic."

"I know *that,*" confirmed Old Lady.

"One of the chimneys has faux stone way up, at the top."

"I'm not repairing the *chimney-top,*" parried Old Lady.

General did not seize his insults of the House. He found some fault wherever he looked. Then, he moved into the next phase of offense.

"No free estimates. My hour costs $250. Preparing the estimate will take me five hours, and at my rate—"

But before he could finish, Milly intervened. Approaching from the General's rear, she moved in intimately and took close sniff of the seat of his jeans, moving her jaws with an expression of concern.

"Milly, stay back," ordered Old Lady, and changed the subject:

"Do you like dogs?"

The General beat retreat and without waiting for

response, Old Lady rendered a quick dismissal. "I'll call you when I come to my decision."

Contractor Number Two was also first, but first from the other end of the pretentiousness list, first from the bottom.

Contractor Number Two was no General. He was bald and fat and kept wiping sweat off his face with the outside of his palm.

"FREE ESTIMATE!" was his main and sole sales pitch.

At the lower, flood-ravished, floor, he shuffled around what used to be Bedroom #1, then around former Bedroom #2. Then stared wistfully in the direction of what remained of the bathroom.

Old Lady proffered a copy of the FEMA estimate:

"Here's what my insurance will pay—"

Bald Head flicked a drop of sweat from his nose and was all of a sudden in a hurry, promising he'd "call later."

That was the last the dogs heard of Contractor Number Two.

Then came the visits from Contractors and Sub-Contractors from the middle of the List.

Old Lady kept foraging for someone to do repairs *cheap, quick* and *well.* Or at least quick and well. Or cheap and well. Or at least repair the back door. The one that by force of Big Water was taken BOOM! off the hinges.

Eventually, Old Lady called in the whole List. *Bid it! Bring in your estimates!*

Contractors shuffled in and out and soon after, emails started buzzing in.

Free estimates!

And even though every Contractor estimated referencing the same South Duck Building Code and the same materials, the resulting bids splattered all over a bewildering range of many thousands.

Still, to reinstall the back door, even the cheapest on the Contractors' List wanted many times as much as what FEMA had offered to pay.

Which was "not more than $50."

❧

Every night, while Old Lady and Milly were asleep, Zip re-read Old Lady's email exchange with many-many Humans who all signed off as FEMA:

FEMA's Insurance Agent

FEMA's Junior Adjustor
FEMA's Senior Adjustor
FEMA Most Senior Adjustor

and Humans without any titles at all, who just signed off as:

FEMA

But whatever name or title they called themselves, their answers were unswervingly the same:

"FEMA will not pay for any damage incurred *above the waterline.*"

"FEMA will not pay without separate receipt for labor and materials."

That's when the process stalled.

The entire cohort of Contractors, independently from each other but nonetheless uniformly, refused to reveal the carefully guarded industry secret: what part of their door replacement estimate was actually for the door, and what part was to install it on the hinges.

That simply was not a question to be asked in a polite Contractor company.

Eventually, a hairy guy with hedgehog-like cover

of black prickly fur all over patted Old Lady on the back and offered conspiratorially,

"No worries, Lady, I understand completely. I'll set you up for $50. Got spare door in my shed. It's old but still sturdy. Can't cut though with a bullet. Metal. Labor included. For small extra, my nephew can even clean off the rust."

"$50 is a good price," coaxed Hedgehog. "Cash, naturally. I don't work for check."

Old Lady and the FEMA Humans were at impasse, that much was clear to Zip. FEMA Humans were greedy and mean-spirited, that was also clear. He was not worried about them. What worried Zip was his Old Lady. What motivated her? Did she regard the argument with FEMA as a game. Or—and Zip's heart pounded and froze at the thought, *were they too poor to afford the door?*

❧

The days flew by. Then weeks.

The Spaniels and Old Lady got by without the back door. At first, the lack of a door was slightly scary. But the weather was warm and they got used to it. Besides, there was no cause for alarm.

It's not like there was a place for bad guy to hide inside on the ground floor: all the partitions between the bedrooms and the bathroom were ripped out, so an intruder would be in plain sight at a glance.

Secure enough.

Besides, not like bad guys could get from ground level into the House, anyway.

Before Big Water, the House used to be accessible from ground level via a staircase. Of that, now only half remained, and hung, suspended shakily exactly 59 inches in midair. The lower, wooden, stinky, part of the staircase that got submerged under flood water had been sawed off by a trio of frightening Cleaning Humans wearing identical black boots, blue overalls, with faces covered under identically scary masks. *Disaster Clean-Up Crew.*

For intruders there was no way from the ground floor inside the house. Unless one was really good at vertical jumping.

One week followed another.

Entire list of Ducklingburg Contractors delivered their estimates. Still, none of them betrayed profession by revealing how much of their estimates was labor and how much materials.

According to Contractors, it was "all together" because "labor and materials are all together, that's how it's done, ma'am." On its part, FEMA with iron resolve refused to pay anything at all for "alltogether estimates." Not even for the lowest of estimates.

"Again, an impasse," summarized Old Lady.

Old Lady and the dogs kept on living without the back door, optimistic that nobody would come jumping up from the ground floor.

"Humans," assured Fox Theo authoritatively, "definitely cannot jump that high. Especially since there is no good run-up space.

"A fox could . . .. But think about it, Zip: What cause would any self-respecting fox have to go jumping at night into Human houses? When your Houses doesn't even have any hens? Or rabbits! or pigeons! And—pardon me—has two spaniels. I don't see the point. For what?"

"Before Winter comes, we have to re-install it," Zip was thinking out loud, "or else a lot of critters will try to seek shelter in bad weather."

"Good dry location," nodded Fox; then added doubtfully, "except on days when there's a strong rain."

"You're right. I fear Old Lady could get sick from this chagrin."

"No getting sick for her. Freckle's orders," Fox howled suddenly.

"What else is Freckle saying?" asked Milly.

"She said to watch the Money. That everything is a matter of money. How is Old Lady? Money-wise?" asked Fox.

Zip reached his right hind paw to scratch just below his right ear and sighed, "I can't make it out. I am not that gifted mathematically."

The friends sat silent.

Each thought his own thoughts.

Fox Theo was thinking that the Forest post-flood was full of the expired mice, rats and rabbits. Dead. *Excellent feeding—for now. Foxes were getting fat. But present mice fatalities will lead to dwindling of mice families and consequently to diminishing production of newborn mice. Everything speaks to that. Which means that Winter feeding will be substandard, and Spring feeding will be downright inferior. That all follows from simple arithmetic,* thought Fox Theo.

Zip was thinking about the passwords. Without the passwords, he could not hack into Old Lady's bank accounts, and see if she had money and how much. Without concrete information of their financial liquidity, it was hard to predict the outcome of the Old Lady-FEMA battle and, consequently, of the future of his family. *In a war of attrition,* thought Zip, *Old Lady's staying power is critical. Financially speaking.*

"I'm excellent at counting my kits. Last litter, we had five," Theo returned to the subject at hand.

"Five is a lucky number," Zip jovially jumped back into the fading conversation, "The Disaster Cleaners want twenty-five."

"No way? Twenty-five!" Theo took alarm, "That's outrageous! *Five plus five plus five, plus five, plus five, plus—*"

"I know," said Zip. "I practiced on the air conditioners. Cost us *five plus five plus two*."

Milly could not count at all, but very much wanted to be a part of the discussion.

"Old Lady said that FEMA only paid half the air-conditioner," she said, interrupting Zip.

Milly sat back on her hind paws, and prepared to pontificate.

"The air conditioner consists of two parts, one on the ground outside. The side that neighbors with the cardio-surgeon," Milly let out a bark to indicate direction. "The second part is in the attic, under the roof. The entrance there is just off the Secret Room," she added lowering her voice confidentially.

"One part—drowned. The motor does not start. Second—is dry. FEMA is not going to pay for dry half, no matter what. It's up there on top floor, above the water level," Milly gazed upward. That's even higher than the magnolia branch where I was saved from Big Water."

"We still have to throw out dry half and buy a new one," said Zip, shaking a drool ribbon away dismissively, "AirConditioner Technician said so. I heard. Guy with mustache and panama hat."

"Why'd you have to throw out the dry one?" asked Fox to be polite.

"It's like I said," explained Zip patiently, "One and another half! First half and second half are the two halves of one machine. Can't make one half work right without its matching second half. Mustach-Panama-Guy said it won't work."

"Yes," approved Milly. "Mustache-Panama. He'd do two halves or none at all. Threatened to quit. And if he did not change it at all . . . very hot in the Summer, and in the Winter . . . actually, I have good fur for the Winter. Zip too. And it doesn't get all that cold here in Ducklingburg."

"She's right," agreed Zip again, "if you get half a vacuum cleaner or half a lawn mower, it would not work either. Agent said to take what FEMA gives and be happy, though. Even if it's only one . . . half. But, like I said, I have not investigated for certain yet how Old Lady got money for the other half. Or how much she has left now."

"Mind if I ask," said Fox trying hard not to sound offensive, "You think Old Lady maybe bought only *half* of the insurance?"

"No. Whole thing," Milly bit her lip. "Old Lady never pinches penny where it matters."

"I heard her say it cost her five—" started Zip.

"Why do you need insurance in that case," mumbled Fox, "what's the point buying whole insurance which only pays for half—"

"We just explained," Milly got irritated. "insurance is so you can buy new things when old are killed and don't work anymore."

"I still don't understand. You tell me that Old Lady bought the whole insurance. Why would whole insurance only pay for half of air conditioner? Seems to me," sighed Fox, "that you got scammed. Your insurance is like Big Gray Wolf: best not to have any business whatsoever with it."

"Anyway," declared Zip, "enough about air conditioner halves, since Old Lady had it repaired already. What I cannot count is the door. FEMA only pays everything that's level with my nose, and that is less than half the door."

"Say what? Didn't you say that the door was

pushed in, ripped right off its hinges? That means one side was for sure in the water."

"Yes," confirmed Zip, "At first it swam up to me and Milly, then it sank. Got dragged to the farther wall and leaned along the . . . the door is a difficult question."

"Leaned against what?" was interested Theo.

"The farthermost wall, behind the fireplace, by the end of what used to be . . . Actually, I am not sure what it used to be. It's now all one large room."

Zip emitted a prolonged sigh and his jaw tightened, "One of the Contractors said we need to mount supporting partitions, or else the upper floor collapses."

"He's right," Fox nodded energetically, "We never dig our burrow this wide. Unless it's under a big tree root or supported by a rock. Or else it may collapse and kits would die, crushed or suffocated. Dangerous!"

"The staircase too. Old Lady said we need it quick. It's an *emergency*."

"I still can't get it," Theo knotted his eyebrows together, thinking, "Where does one get so many . . . five and five . . . last season Whitepaw and I had five . . . fluffy, beautiful, healthy . . . but I will be honest, my Whitepaw will not part with even one, not for all the doors in the world.

Theo closed his eyes and rhapsodized,

"When the kits are tiny, they squeak so tenderly . . . Then they grow up a bit and start yapping . . . Four weeks later, and they already squeal, quarrel between themselves, constantly hungry. I hunt for their food day and night. They need more and more food, and get louder and louder. I get no sleep or rest and my paws don't stop hurting—"

Bright yellow eyes with vertical slit of a pupil flung open,

"I think I'd give them all up for your door—assuming those who take them feed them. Like Freckle on her golf course. How's the feeding? Who's taking them? Besides, Whitepaw will sure be against it. I have to ask. Plus, you need another five and two."

Theo sat flat on his back, exhausted by the enormous decision.

"Theo, you misunderstand," Zip said quietly. "Not five kits. It's dollars. Five thousand dollars."

"Ah, right," said Fox slowly, pretending to understand. Curiosity won, and he asked: "What do they look like? Those five thousand dollars. Have you seen them?"

"No, never seen them," admitted Zip.

Fox would not sooth down, "If you've never seen them, how do you know all that?"

"Read. In the computer. While Old Lady was asleep," confessed Zip.

"That's illegal," interjected Milly, butting in out of nowhere and immediately pressing her opinion.

Zip did not yield.

"Nonsense! We are one family. Parents are allowed to control their children's reading and—"

"Good point," nodded Fox. "Can you *send* her an email though? If you both know how to read and email, I have a message for her."

And before the dogs could answer, Fox Theo took a firm stance and howled the message.

Old Lady, be warned
Wicked tongues are calling you too old for—

"That's no news," Milly snorted, offended for Old Lady, "She is *Old Lady*."

Fox sat back down and explained:

"There's talk. She is . . . well . . . not as good . . . remembering . . . she might be . . . not all there? It's just talk," stumbled Fox.

Zip threw a questioning glance at Milly. Then rounded on Fox,

"You saying she is batty?"

"*I* do not think that way . . . that she forgets . . . apologies . . . but she needs *warning* that the *others* say—"

"What *otherrrrrrrs*?" asked Milly, and rose up, indicating that the audience was over.

Fox smiled bitterly and walked backwards, showing off white fangs, and muttering: "Worth a try. Only trying to help. I share confidential intelligence . . . from Freckle— Almost forgot: Freckle—"

But Milly lost all her hospitable demeanor.

"More gossipy muck about Old Lady? I thank you not to share!"

Fox halted his retreat and, now from a respectable distance, enunciated ceremoniously.

"Freckle asked me to deliver—

Dear Milly—

or rather,

Dear Zip and Milly, Freckle requests the pleasure of your company for a Meeting."

"An invitation for a Meeting?" exclaimed Zip and Milly in unison.

"Yes, a Meeting," calmly reiterated Theo, and switched to his ceremonial tone again:

At the Open Terrace of the Private Residence.
Take ten fox jumps left from the Restaurant at the Golf Club
Assigned Seats are in the Jasmine Bush.

"I'll get back with you about the time," he added in a normal voice. And he was gone.

❧

Having abandoned all hope at sniffing out Old Lady's banking passwords and accessing her savings account balances, Zip turned his search to Old Lady's e-mailbox.

Using financial search terms such as *account balance, monthly statement, bank, brokerage* and *checking,* he arduously reviewed every piece of possibly relevant e-mail.

But all for nothing. Old Lady never emailed anybody about how much money she had. *We must have lots of money,* decided Zip—*or none at all.*

Either way, e-mails revealed that Old Lady was not worried about the money. Old Lady was busy worrying about something else entirely. She was looking for a lawyer.

But that was no news to Spaniels.

Old Lady complained to neighbor Susan that "It seems impossible to get a good lawyer to sue these FEMA rats."

"Everything's for sale," assured Susan, a true lawyer's daughter. "Lawyers too."

Old Lady nodded her concurrence, but days passed and no lawyer agreeable to sue the nasty FEMA rats in Federal Court.

Not for lack of Old Lady's trying.

Old Lady called, emailed, Skyped, FaceTimed, and even UberConferenced. She scheduled appointments and paid for initial consultations. That part Zip could tell for sure because her credit card provider was diligent about sending an email for every charge. After each consultation, Old Lady's credit card confirmed the consultation fee payment; soon enough, the lawyers confirmed their refusal to take the case.

Lawyer's refusals came in different shapes.

RickyRich Law reacted with an envelope with two gold-glowing embossed letters R, entangled in an unthinkable manner. The letter, typed on heavy, expensive bond paper engraved to match the letterhead proclaimed that although *RickyRich*'s lawyers were ecstatic to be considered for Old Lady's case, they were simply too *engaged* with other clients' to spare the time.

"Too busy to be bothered with our little case," explained Old Lady, as she shredded the *RickyRich*'s letter into pretty confetti highlighted with gold specks.

Tanin, Manin and Garfunkel responded with a shorter, thinner letter on much cheaper paper.

Their excuse was that they lacked "an appropriate specialist in the relevant field of the law."

"Too dumb for our tricky case," summed up Old Lady.

Good riddance, snorted Zip.

After a few more responses from the town lawyers, Milly grew skeptical.

"Zippy, what does that mean that they *lackaspecialist*? They don't have enough Humans? And why was Tanin&Manin's letter signed by only one Human—and he is neither Tanin nor Manin? Not even Garfunkel!

"I am suspicious," admitted Milly hot-headedly. Perhaps this is not a matter of money? Old Lady has the money, right? What do you think, Zippy? Did you find out?"

"Could not figure out if we have—if Old Lady has—money. All I figure is that nobody wants to fight for us, not for any money."

"Why?" probed Milly.

"It may be what the Agent said: nobody fights against FEMA because FEMA does not see the *down-side* when it is sued."

"What does that mean?"

"I still don't know. But I will ferret it out."

15

HOW FRECKLE GOT HER NAME

Even before she earned fame under the name "Freckle," this fox kit was a noteworthy free thinker.

The rest of her siblings were content playing the same mundane fox kit games that's been in Fox Theo's family for countless generations. The dried quail paw game was the favorite; featuring a slobbered, straggly quail paw trophy that was passed—supposedly "chased"—from one fox kit to another.

After a couple of jumps, Freckle saw right through the sham: the quail paw showed no initiative. Her siblings pushed and shoved the paw, but the hapless paw had no independent drive. It did not push back or try to escape. Freckle passed, concluding that the paw had insufficient *game* to warrant her continued attention.

What she wanted for Christmas was a real toy. And she had the toy picked out.

A golf ball!

White, light, plucky, shiny, adventurous.

Golf balls had flair! They were round. They rolled unpredictably after their long flight through the air. They were bred around the Scared Hare Golf Club, by Golf Club Humans.

❧

Soon enough the fox kit learned the ways of Golf Club Humans. She loved them right away. They were a mild breed, the Golf Club Humans.

They did not hunt. Most of the day, they walked around with big bags of sticks, but the sticks did not shoot.

Their men either busied themselves using the sticks to push golf balls into small round burrows, or stood around in groups of two or three, then pumped hands or patted each other on the shoulders.

Pumping hands was the game they loved the best.

They always smiled after a hand pumping, and sometimes would even sing a little bit.

Patting on the shoulder was a game they hated, but kept playing for some reason. The human who received the pat often stayed behind, his head retracted between the shoulders, like a shy turtle, with a sour long face.

There were women who used the sticks too. They tried to hit the balls just as hard, but the women were not as strong as the men.

Another thing the fox kit learned was that there were always plenty of golf balls.

Not at all like the game with the withered quail paw where the whole litter had to fight each other just for a chance to kick the pathetic toy a couple of times. The fox kit hated that—aggressively pushing aside her smaller siblings was distasteful. And bigger siblings bit her.

No, the Humans at the Golf Club got it right. Everybody had plenty of balls—and plenty of sticks. And when one of them played with the ball, the others politely stood and watched. In short, the fox kit approved of the Golf Club rules. And she especially approved of the golf balls themselves.

Hunting a golf ball for herself proved to be easy, too. There were scores of almost new, white, firm balls hiding everywhere—in the bushes, in the sand, in the shallow end of the puddles.

Playing with a golf ball was a blast—hit it with the paw on one side, catch it, roll it in the opposite direction, make it rush downhill . . . so much more delight than the stupid quail paw.

❧

Like most foxes who lived around the golf club, Freckle was not afraid of Humans.

She did not bolt away in panic when Humans drove down their gravel paths in their stinky carts with bright blue tents. Of course, she stepped out of the way, but only just as far as respect demanded. Most golf club foxes would nervously slink off into the woods when human voices were heard nearby, but Freckle did not timidly retreat. Instead, she stood and watched longingly as Humans drove away towards the pole that marked the location of the next round burrow.

Now that the Freckle had mastered the golf ball game, her ambitions did not stop.

She moved on, instead, to the next challenge.

Freckle had Big Dreams, the biggest of which was to gain access to the area where huge, deliciously smelling cans and packages were put out nightly: the garbage disposal area at the rear of the Scared Hare Golf Club's restaurant.

But gaining access to that dreamland of delicious smells was no easy task. And it had nothing at all to do with the Humans. The problem was . . . the foxes.

❧

The territory of the Scared Hare Golf and Country Club was controlled by fox kit's distant relatives—known simply as Rich Relatives. And they were not at all friendly.

No way, they would not share.

Indeed, one of our fox kit's brothers, two litters before her, had made a failed attempt to penetrate their defense of the forbidden territory. That little fox got nothing for his troubles but a tooth hole in his hide and a ragged tear in his ear, the latter of which yielded a derogatory nickname. *Ragged Ear.*

Fox Kit was sympathetic to Ragged Ear, but confident that she would avoid his infamous fate.

Twice, Freckle managed to sneak her way to the cherished cans. But, both times, Rich Relatives had detected her intrusion and menacingly chased her out, pursuing her all the way to the Golf Club borders. By the second time, Fox Kit was no longer a child; she already had grown stronger and faster—swift enough that she managed to escape the capture and reprisal that befell hapless Ragged Ear. Still, the humiliating retreat hurt. And she lamented the lost time and wasted energy.

But Freckle did not give in.

Her Big Dream was to settle down on the Scared hare Golf Course clearing, the one nearest to the restaurant, and to then divide her days between playing with the golf balls and feeding from the garbage cans at the back of the Club Restaurant. That was her dream, what she wanted. And she would get that life. Whatever it took.

She would not yield.

Some in the fox community laughed, said that her Big Dream was stupid, but the Fox Kit knew that their ridicule was baseless: there are no stupid dreams, there are only lazy foxes.

❧

Every day, Freckle got a little closer to the Golf Club Humans. After a while, she began to think that Golf Club Humans recognized her. Some of them greeted her with a breezy wave, and some veteran golfers even used their golf sticks to point her out to newcomers. She was definitely getting famous.

Everybody knows that foxes are destined to live on golf clubs, she thought. *Plenty of golf clubs are even named after foxes. That's common knowledge. Any time now, she would be selected this club's mascot.* She was sure of it.

But every success attracts its haters, and the Fox Kit's relentless climb to the top attracted the unfriendly attention of the competing foxes.

Rich Relatives, who claimed the woods neighboring the golf club as their own exclusive territory, started to grumble.

"How much longer are we going to suffer this jester?" they agitated.

"She is out of bounds! Impertinent pauper pup!"

"Those poor relatives from the other side of the Sneaky Creek have no shame!"

"Just yesterday, she snatched up an almost untouched muffin, right under my nose!"

"Take away her hunting license!"

"Chase her out! Cleanse the Golf Club!"

"Unite!"

So, it was decided. Rich Relatives united, and

Operation Cleanse Scared Hare Golf Club was quickly designed.

The plan was cunningly precise and likely deadly for any unwary outlander fox that it ensnared.

First, Rich Relatives divided themselves into operational teams.

The first team's mission was to initiate the capture: *"that intruder"* was to be located, surrounded, and frustrated from using any and all of the escape tricks and evasive ploys in the Fox Playbook.

Once *that intruder* was helplessly surrounded inside a furry tight ring of Rich Relatives, the foxes would then put into operation a *punishment gauntlet run*—a relay chase over a known route, down an agreed path, where fresh foxes on the reserve team would lay in wait and spring, relieving tired member from the capturing squad.

❧

It was agreed.

They would chase, chase, chase.

Chase *that intruder,* squeezing her onto the path along the border of the Golf Club. Successive teams of nipping, harassing, bullying Rich Relative foxes, would chase along the only possible route, leading to the remotest border of the Golf Course, along the route that ended over the steep, precipitous, murderous cliff.

Rich Relatives yipped. *Operation Cleanse Scared Hare Golf Club* was put in motion.

They made swift work of it. In no time, *imposter* Freckle was located, caught, surrounded . . . and *chased*. Chased in well-choreographed trot, herding her toward pre-planned and deadly route. They caught her off guard. It was a devilishly brilliant strategy, sufficiently clever to incapacitate any young and inexperienced fox, to bring her to an untimely end. But Fox Kit Freckle did not yield so easily.

When it occurred to her what was happening—when she saw that she was being chased down the predetermined corridor, onwards to a certain death at the cliff—something happened that nobody expected. The Fox Kit's innate obstinance, her very nonconformism, the very stubbornness that caused her to spurn those childhood quail paw games and dream her golf ball dream, her independent spirit—all that flared and flamed into a *rage*.

The little fox would not be *herded. She did not take*

direction from the pack. Never! Not in her life, and certainly not in death.

It happened in split second. As was pre-planned between the killer foxes, fresh pair of Rich Relative jumped from behind the Red Buckle bush, relieving tired pair. As predators switched shifts, the deadly relay race had slowed imperceptibly—by a split second, by just a wink. But wink was all that Freckle needed—and Freckle made her move.

She soared up high, twisting in the air at right angle—a twist away from safety of her home woods, straight into open Human-dominated danger of the Golf Club green. The fearless Fox Kit spread her whole body in the air, stretching her tail as far back as it reached and, falling into frenzied sprint, raced straight towards the Humans' land.

That was a desperate move. No calm-thinking fox would ever seek protection out on the wide-open golf course, amidst the humans walking with their sticks—and in the brightest light of day!

Freckle's predators knew: the only protection for a wild fox charging into groups of golfers would be posthumous—protection once transformed into a stuffed curiosity mounted in the Golf Club Museum. The identifying metal plaque would say, "Crazed fox shot while launching her attack on the 16th Hole"!

Not daring to follow Freckles' reckless flight—into the Golf Club! in broad daylight!—Rich Fox Relatives called of the Deadly Relay.

Loud chorus of frustrated howls and yelps announced the abortive end of *Operation Cleanse Golf Club.*

16

FRECKLE'S HUMAN

The Human did not look anything like a golfer.

No sticks, no funny head wear, no twisty, posing stands.

His eyes were shielded from the sun by nothing more than an improvised visor formed by a cupped, untanned hand.

Squinting under his palm, he had been watching Freckles and her pursuers intently. The pack of grown foxes in their prime were all united against one fox kit—a spirited but not quite yet full-grown fox. The Human was not young himself, and knew the ending of this unhappy tale. Or, rather, he had no illusions about the ending.

Mature foxes kept their alternating pace. They

slowed down a notch, as if to give their prey a rest, but soon as victim slowed down, the chasers sped it up two notches. The Human sighed. The persecutors, too, were sure of the end, and took great pleasure in the process. The Human did not share in their pleasure, but he did watch. The deadly cliff was in his sight. The chase was almost finished. The only play remaining—the final move—belonged to the chased prey. What will the fox kit choose—will she turn back for final fight? Or final, desperate escape attempt—a fatal plunge over the cliff?

How will she die?

But wait! What's this?

The Fox Kit soared into the air, and, still afloat, her body twisted rapidly—as though pushing off invisible support— and turned at a straight angle *away* from woods, *towards* the startled Human.

A graceful, unexpected spring and spin.

The hunter foxes froze, stunned—and fell aback. The Human stepped in closer.

The fox kit's fearless change-of-direction escape maneuver, one that started with such admirable grace, concluded with a clumsy, wipeout landing—as though the Earth had risen up and smacked the little fox in the stomach. The fox looked dazedly around and, dragging one front paw down the open golf green, limped as fast as it could straight towards the Human Stranger.

Her enemies had followed, but only to the edge of their woods. At the beginning of the golf course, they stood, not daring to move any further, into Human Territory. They formed into a red furry semi-circle, and, their forces tightened, froze gawking as their prey escaped Fox Justice, ambling blindly towards the Stranger Human.

Then, as though following an unheard order, a unison of red-flaming tails swooshed victoriously, and departed from the scene of battle.

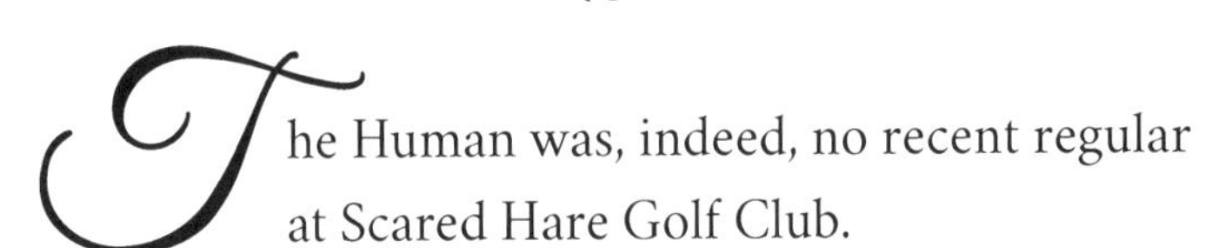

The Human was, indeed, no recent regular at Scared Hare Golf Club.

That morning, his intention was merely a meandering walk, which he did not care to spoil by following the holes in the grass. Nor had he seen this fox before, despite her status of a "regular." And, of course, the Human had no way of knowing about Freckle's ambitions.

Nevertheless, the Human understood what was happening the minute he laid his eyes on the chase. The Human had been around enough to know that every time a young kit tries to make its way in the world, there's always a pack of entrenched Rich Relatives who hate to share.

This much was obvious. What was not so obvious was what he should try to do about it.

The Human watched without moving a muscle as Freckles, having shaken off her chasers, hobbled cross the fairway and settled by his feet, head down. He was pretty sure that he knew a canine "help-me" posture when he saw one, so he made a snap decision. Warily, without taking his eyes off the animal, he stripped off his expensive shirt, tied its sleeves together to forge a make-shift knapsack, and then lowered the resulting contraption to the grass. With a leather sole of his Berluti shoe—footwear exceptionally ill-suited for either golf or the handling of wild animals—the Human slowly and carefully rolled stunned Freckles onto his shirt. Then, handling the wild animal with utmost care, Strange Human hoisted his bundle up and gingerly carried the fox away.

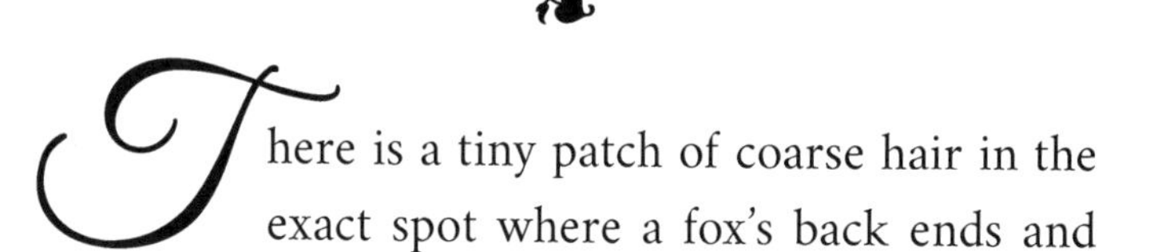

There is a tiny patch of coarse hair in the exact spot where a fox's back ends and its tail begins. The coarseness of the hair assures the smooth shape of transition between the fox and its tail.

This tiny patch is important. It has no fluffy undercoat, not like the rest of the fox's fur. It is almost all guard hairs.

Those who understand foxes, know to look at this small patch of coarse hair, because no matter how sly the fox, and how much the fox might feign indifference, that patch at the end of the back will betray every fox emotion. Akin to human who cannot help her fidgety feet or fingers despite successfully arranging facial expression into a mask of perfect nonchalance, a fox cannot help movements of that small coarse patch. When a fox gets agitated, the guard hairs of her back stand up.

Strange Human was no stranger to the foxes. He saw at once that Freckle was only pretending to be calm. In fact, the Fox Kit was on the edge of full despair: her coarse patch was swaying like rye swept by a wind.

The Fox Kit's tell-tale coarse patch was bright red. Unusual. Most foxes were dark-colored there.

"You are bright-red! I used to be a red-head too, when I was a very young boy," observed the Human, carefully studying the Fox Kit.

"By the time my playmates stopped teasing me about it, I got darker. And look at me now—grizzled, salt and pepper."

Because the tone of the voice was calm and warm, the young fox relaxed and accepted the Human's attentions. Not that the fox would stoop to being petted or touched with any familiarity, but when the perceptive Human offered her some water, the she did not say no. The water extinguished the raspy fire in her throat. Even the fiery pain in her front paw subsided—so long as she did not step on the paw. Exhausted after the chase, she started to doze off.

"By the way, my name is Matthew," went on Strange Human in his steady, certain voice, "what's yours?"

Freckle was accustomed enough to the sound of human speech so that it did not scare her. She was already half-asleep and made no objection when the Human went on to tag her with a name.

"I'm Matthew . . . never call me Matt. Is it OK with you if I call you Freckle?"

Half-asleep, Freckle wondered to herself at how the distinctive spot on her muzzle made everyone—first her father, Fox Theo, then the rest of her extended fox family, and finally this "Matthew"

Human—call her by the very same name, each of them in the language of their own species. *Odd, but certainly OK, more than OK.*

❧

In the Forest, the news spread with the speed of a frightened rabbit's flight. And even faster among the foxes—with the speed of Fox's gallop.

Motivated by morbid curiosity, and not wishing Freckles good luck, a few of the former pursuers lurked watchfully in the underbrush at the edge of the golf course.

It took only a few gallops of only a few foxes to spread the scandalous news:

Freckle is no more!

Captured!

And probably killed!

Fate unknown!

Perished!

Carried off by a Strange Human!

Days passed.

Freckle had not heard any of the frenzied rumors about her and was too zonked to care even if she had.

Matthew, who happened to be Freckle's safe harbor, turned out to be an understanding, unobtrusive sort of fellow. Although he was much older than the fox kit, his own position in life was very much the same: in a bit of a tailspin after making a sharp twist in the path of his life.

"Used to be a lawyer," he responded, should anybody ask about his job. For the past ten years, he worked in the Paris office of a large, important, and obscenely profitable American law firm—the kind of law firm that has its presence all over the world and holds its lawyers tight with "gold handcuffs," a promise of even bigger riches at a later day.

A few weeks ago, Matthew had cashed out and left, abandoning his gold handcuffs to dangle at his now empty desk: *Adieu, messieurs-dames.*

"Crocked," was his terse and cryptic explanation should anybody ask.

All Matthew's frenemies and colleagues had been

slack-jawed to see him bail out after ten years of ninety-hour workweeks—and when he was so close—only inches from The Prize, a coveted partnership in the law firm. Freckle did no understand exactly what The Prize entailed, but it was Human version scavenging from the humungous kitchen garbage bins.

Yes, Freckle's predicament was quite plain to the no longer Strange Human now known as Matthew.

Like Freckle, Matthew quit the Human chase mid-jump.

He boarded Brussels Airlines in *Aéroport de Bruxelles-National,* made a short stop in *Munich Airport,* changed planes in Washington, and jumped commuter into the *Tri-Cities Airport* in Bristol, Tennessee. From there, it was a middling-length but familiar drive in a rental car.

A few hours later, giddy, he was looking down the familiar phlox-flanked highway that ran straight into Ducklingburg, South Duck—his native town.

Rose-colored phloxes gave way to white, then pink, then white again, and at long last, the windows were rolled down, the better to breath in the familiar scents and chirps.

Matthew parked his rental by the *Hungry Leopard*—the most respected pub in town. There, a handful of childhood friends, forewarned by the chirping of text messages, were eagerly awaiting his arrival.

After three straight hours of imbibing local brew and reminiscing about the joys of their salad days—how they played hunters along the creeks of Ducklingburg ravines, back then pristinely clean; how they all dispersed around the country for their share of Socratic Method studies—a hateful way to teach, they all agreed: the gang was ready for a sit-down dinner.

The Scared Hare Country Club obliged.

Off to the Scared Hare!

Familiar grounds. Growing up, Matthew had been a regular: his father then an active member the Club's Board, now still hung on as honorable bit of ballast. At any rate, Matthew's family name was emblazoned on the roster of the Club and long established among the innermost circle of the Board and owners.

At dinner, more childhood memories were washed down with expensive wines and a drop or two of sentimental tears.

Tears dried, the childhood friends turned right to the business part of the reunion.

The small but proud Ducklingburg municipality was growing, some luxury high-rises already on the dirt and many more in drawings. A childhood buddy, Dreamer Steve, wanted Matthew and his law firm cash-out money as partners in something obscurely called "urban development."

Matthew did not want to decide on the spot.

For now, he accepted an invitation to be a Country Club boarder. One of the guest cottages was available, and he took it. Here, overlooking the golf course, he settled for the week . . . or longer, if he liked it here.

And now Matthew's golf-side cottage and its immediate surroundings became the home habitat to red fox Freckle too.

❧

She was a wild fox and proud of it.

Freckle and Matthew were no bosom buddies, make no mistake about it.

She was a *wild animal,* and not going to be "a tame fox." Never! Her dad Theo had often told her cautionary tales about "tame foxes."

In Theo's stories, Siberian Silver Foxes agreed as Theo put it, to "be scientific." They lived and bred in a Scientific Institute, with Humans. They were *tame*.

Theo's stories ended horribly.

Tame foxes lost their fur.

A hairless fox! The horror! What lack of dignity! No, Freckle had no desire to be tamed. She was perfectly prepared to push back against any move on Matthew's part if he became familiar.

But days flew by, and Freckle's Human made no such move. He kept to himself.

The two settled into a comfortable life—side by side, but each minding their own business.

He stayed somewhat aloof. She was as wild as ever. Nevertheless, there were benefits from the perception, in the minds of the club staff, that Freckle was a "rescue fox," under the protection of an influential member. Freckle still did not have full use of her injured paw. But, she made excellent use of her new connections with the Kitchen Staff. She even acquired *her usual*—the Prosciutto with Melon, from the brunch appetizer menu. For the member diners, the Country Club waiters liked to pair this dish with an Australian Moscato, which could be easily upcharged to twenty-seven dollars a glass. Freckle did not fall for the fad and took her luncheon paired simply with a splash of Evian water, served chilled, in a bowl, neat. The water was still not as cold and fresh as from the Spring in the ravine, but clean and clear and always handy in "the fox bowl."

Freckle could not wait to share her news with the Forest.

Just watch their muzzles drop and tails twitch!

She liked to re-live in her head the fateful mid-jump turn. *Wow! She really stuck it to those Rich Relatives!* She now got connections in places so high that the Forest Fox population did not even know they existed—all the way to the *Head Mistress of Putting Food into The Huge Garbage Can.*

Freckle's future looked bright and happy, bouncy like balls on a golf course, filled with new friends and adventure.

Matthew, on his end, avoided re-living in his mind his own leap.

The life he left behind always seemed to him made up, like something from a bland romantic comedy . . . and now it was getting hazier each passing day. The pressures of his former job were forgotten. The charm of his centuries-old river-side property with a real running watermill, just steps from Angoulême—bought because a woman fancied it—was also becoming a distant memory. Even the multi-thousands of euros in unpaid taxes owed on the Angoulême property to the French government were now no more than a fleeting worry.

Matthew had almost taught himself to exorcise regrets about Mrs. Matthew, the woman who chose not to follow him home. She stayed behind in Angoulême Mill House to "take care of affairs and settle the bills," or so she said. But they both knew that Mrs. Matthew was in love with the Mill House much more than with its master.

Matthew shooed away the memory. He tried to look to the future, but the future looked even more hazy than the past—and so he settled in the present, where days came and went like the water of Sneaky Creek, flowing leisurely along its meandering path though the golf course.

Before long, the Fox Kit regained full use of all four of her paws, and settled back into her native ways.

As any self-respecting Fox, Freckle had her priorities straight: hunting first, then stockpiling.

Hunting was defined extensively and included all

manner of food acquisition—whether procured by chase or by scavenge. Mice hunt was a classic, an old favorite, but garbage bin hunting was very definitely a hot new selection on the young fox's do-list. There was more thrill involved in dumpster-diving than met the eye at first—the heavy lid of back door kitchen bin could fall at any time, trapping the intrepid fox.

Freckle made good strides in caching the food that she "hunted" from the food discarded by the Humans. At least a dozen eggs were scatter-cached in the nearby field, most of them solidified into what, only a long time afterwards, Freckle learned were called "hard boiled" eggs. Odd though they seemed at first, hard-boiled eggs proved to be an easily acquired taste; Freckle quickly learned to like them better than the natural raw eggs that so often appeared on the menu at home when she was a little kit.

Freckle was already making plans for a house-warming party, to show off her new life-style to her family. Not her whole extended family, of course—she had not stockpiled that much food. Just small group. Mom and Dad. Her old man Theodore, was to be the Fox of Honor.

Theodore was a good father, supportive and

attentive and by a wide margin the most intelligent of the foxes in the whole Ducklingburg locale.

Theo never tormented Freckle with any of the hackneyed fox-parent nags like "Listen to your elders," "A bird in the paw is worth two in the bush," "Sniff before you leap," or "I told you so."

Freckle had an inkling that her Old Man Theo was a touch of a gossip who liked to portray himself in the Forest community as an "insider" able to share the latest Human news. Especially when the Human news had to do with *construction*.

Oh yes, *Construction*. Human proneness to start *Construction* in the most unexpected and obnoxious places was a bane of the wildlife's existence.

Foxes are happy to settle not far from Humans—there's always good loot. On the other paw, a separate fox territory is critical. Foxes work hard on finding just the right balance, but Humans always encroach.

Fox Theo would say:

Construction is just an excuse to chip away at foxes' territory.

Foxes love their freedom. Spouting off about the glories of life in the wild is a favorite topic of her father.

Freckle urged her dad to take a wider view. Freedom, sure! But with a close eye on the garbage bins, filled to their brims with tasty leftovers. Enough food in the bins for a life free from the constant anxiety, but the nearby woods and the hills could still belong to the foxes. *What could be better, daddy?*

Still, Daddy Theo would ask if there were *construction plans*. And Freckle never missed a chance to stretch out nearby and listen in when her Human Matthew entertained his friends. There were only two friends, Steve and Paul, who were regular visitors at Matthew's cottage.

Freckle did not have to listen in for long.

Construction was the single topic that dominated every conversation. Construction and their houses. They discussed cleaning their houses, remodeling their houses, buying, selling, and even constructing completely new houses. They talked and talked and talked endlessly about houses, their own houses, their neighbors' houses, even the houses of complete strangers and houses that didn't exist yet.

Even though Human Matthew did not own a house in America, they also talked about "Matthew's new house." Indeed, "Matthew's new house," was all Human Steve wanted to talk about.

Freckle did not mind their visits, so long as the rules were obeyed: Freckle's place was by Matthew's chair, and everything the humans did not eat escheated to the fox. Enough for a square meal and to supplement the provisions.

"Matthew, you can't keep living in this measly cottage," insisted Steve with an air of assuredness.

"Why not?" replied Matthew nonchalantly.

"Because," interjected Paul, "the cottages are designed for guests and staff. You are a co-owner, a stockholding Member of the Club now."

"We like it here, don't we, Freckle?" Matthew nudged the fox's side with a slight shove of the edge of his soft-leathered boot. They had an understanding, Matthew and the fox. No dog-like familiarity. No petting of the fur, no scratching of the head, no fawning sentimentality. The rules of respectful companionship had been worked out starting from the first minutes when they met. Sitting by Matthew's chair, accepting a light shove with his soft leather shoe along her side—these were the outer limits of their familiarity.

But, still, they came to depend upon each other in subtle ways, neither of them fully aware of the extent of that growing dependency.

So, Freckle did not move away. Instead, she pressed herself tighter into Matthew's ankle, feeling safe with the familiar smell of his leather boots and the odor of the *Frosch Waschmittel* detergent emanating from his jeans. Perhaps the fox liked the scent of the Frosch detergent partly because she had noted how the odor originated from powder in a container emblazoned with the brand's trademark, a picture of a fat, tasty looking green frog.

"There, guys, my fox agrees," smiled Matthew.

"Listen to her," snapped Steve, "she does not want to move. The lazy vixen does not even bother to hunt much anymore. The field mice have gnawed holes all over Northern field. All on her watch."

"She's a typical welfare recipient," sneered Paul. "Don't pay any attention to what the dumb beast wants. You need a house that's appropriate for a Ducklingburger of your wealth and station in life."

"We'll consider it," promised Matthew, and nudged the fox again, sinking the tip of his boot in her rich fur, "won't we, Freckle?"

"Consider quicker," urged Steve, "the opportunity won't last forever."

"If you don't want it, we'll just scrap the whole project," agreed Paul.

"Quite," barked Steve, "it's not the sort of venture that one lets strangers know about."

"Strangers? If anyone gets a wind of what's afoot,

I'm out," declared Paul and actually searched around with his eyes to ascertain that nobody was listening.

"Old Lady's house will soon be up for bid, and you better be ready," insisted Steve.

Freckle listened closely and disagreed completely.

Old Lady's house is too close to the Sneaky Creek. Living in fear of water every time it so much as drizzles—what sort of life is that? Even the poorest of my relatives, the most desperate for territory, would not dare dig a burrow in the path of water. Madness!

"Fine, we'll think about it," repeated Matthew.

Freckle made a soft rumbling noise in her throat.

"What's your welfare fox advising?" chuckled Paul.

"She disapproves," Matthew confidently and correctly translated from Fox.

Freckle was at that moment reflecting on the stupidity of Humans.

Even silly rabbits, too dumb to keep track of their own kids, would not drop their newborns there at the bottom of the ravine. Stupid! Of course, Old Lady herself was not planning any kits, but Human Matthew seems young enough. Matthew's kits in the house where water comes—no, I definitely do not approve of that "friendly project."

17

IN HER FULL GLORY

The wildlife's Meeting at the Scared Hare Country Club was perfect in every respect.

It was scheduled for the most opportune hour—around eight thirty. In the last light of the waning Summer evening, late supper time. This was the hour when all the dining terraces of Freckle's country club were, at long last, emptying of the swarming crowd of younger boys.

Freckle actually favored the small boys, and, to be perfectly forthright, she enjoyed entertaining them by jumping over golf clubs. It's a good thing that she did enjoy it, because her golf club jumping tricks were the key to her acceptance by the Human members of the Scared Hare Country Club.

There was one of her fans waiting now, a boy of about kindergarten age with tousled red hair. He was holding a golf club at shoulder height, which was about as high as he could manage and still maintain the club's shaft in horizontal position.

Full of ardor, the little fox took wing straight from the ground, with no running start, arched her back only slightly, and cleared the golf club with conspicuous ease. Then, she landed softly, two front paws catching ground first, the hind paws after, all four soft and light. The plume of her tail floated gracefully behind her.

A perfect 10.0 for style.

"Jump, jump, jump," egged on the boys, and she jumped, jumped, jumped—higher and higher. If necessary, Freckle could jump as high as the top of Matthew's head, but the boys were unable to hold sticks that high.

Her own grace and power excited her, the hairs at the base of her tail rose on ends, and Freckle let out sharp, clarion yaps.

Glances of admiration, words of praise all around her! At long last, Freckle was at the center of attention!

"Such a tame, clever, little fox," cooed little boys' mothers. Some uncouth Human might try to pet the "clever fox." Freckle resented Human familiarity but, not wanting to appear unfriendly, she compromised. She accepted offerings from open palms, her earnings from a job, and a job very well done.

❧

Finally, Freckle's audience of human boys dwindled as the youngsters were escorted homeward by parents or by nannies. Conveniently, the time of Mathew's Meeting was set to start on his torchlit patio right after nightfall. Since Freckles' entertainer job was over by that hour, the Meeting's timing left her free to play the hostess to her own friends if she so desired. And she did: she invited a few very special guests—Theo, Zip, and Milly—to a show-off party sited at the edge of the Humans' get-together. It would be an opportunity for Freckle, in her role as a proud hostess, to show off to her father and his Spaniel friends the impressive fruits of her own wit and initiative.

By the time her own private party guests arrived, Freckle had cooled down her paws in the fountain by the tennis courts and, using her left hind paw, brushed, fluffed and air-dried the fur behind her ears and under her chin. She was ready to assume her role as Matthew's cabin hostess, calm, well-coiffed and proud.

And Freckle had a lot to be proud about. The station in life she now occupied was reached through hard work, higher jumps and, let's be honest about it, by taking some grave risks. As a convivial companion of a powerful Human and a respected and well compensated entertainer, she earned her own comfortable living. Earned, not given.

As Freckle greeted her friends in her new lair, pride of accomplishment was shining in her every brushed hair.

Her guests—Theo, Zip and Milly—settled cozily in the shade of the Confederate Jasmine, just off Matthew's patio. All three were in great spirits.

Milly—because on their way to the Meeting, they circumvented the Bridge and she was spared the wretched memory of altercation with the Coyote Brothers.

Zip had never been to a Meeting before and, always an eager learner, anticipated a new and interesting experience.

Old Fox Theo was of the view that the Meeting, and especially the leftover-sourced refreshments, was an excellent occasion to repay the dogs' hospitality. And, of course, he was anxious to show off his youngest Freckle in all her glory of an accomplished hospitable hostess.

Freckle had pre-hunted four plump scallops, a dish featured on the day's Appetizer Menu. She had stealthily snagged the the treat from a momentarily unattended busboy cleanup cart where the unwanted scallops had arrived courtesy of some luncheon diner's lack of appetite. Theo's only reservation was that the waiters were stingy with the sweet garlic butter sauce, shirked their duty to properly drench the fox-bound leftovers.

The seating arrangement among the Jasmine Vines was well-suited for eavesdropping, tested lots of times by Freckle herself. She used to lounge here, back before she was fully established in her right to nap by Matthew's boot, and later, when rowdy conversations disturbed her after-dinner naps.

"Welcome! I've heard so much about y'all," Freckle bowed to the Spaniels and gave Theo a quick sniff, "You look quite distinguished, Dad."

The Spaniels, in turn, exchanged the customary new-acquaintance niceties with Freckle. The ease of their interchange caused Zip, not for the first time, to reflect on how effortlessly Dogs and Foxes can communicate with each other.

I suppose that it's because our species are branches

from the same tree, the "canines." Cats are quite a different thing, although some people think that Foxes look like Cats. Anyway, that's what I learned somehow, I can't remember where.

"Brilliant. Outstanding. Everything on track and ready-to-go," announced Freckle. "Get yourselves settled because the Meeting is about to start."

The Humans—Matthew, Steve and Paul—were getting comfortable around their own table, which, as dictated by the old-fashioned, almost hundred-year-old custom of the Country Club, was covered with a bright-white tablecloth starched to cardboard stiffness.

The wait staff, in identical white linen jackets and matching slacks and shoes, moved inconspicuously and lightly around the table, noiselessly putting finishing touches on table appointments.

"Matthew and I selected the menu ahead of time," boasted Freckle.

The Humans were exchanging smiles, greetings, pats and shakes.

"They act like siblings, from the same litter," was Theo's first observation. He asked, peering in closer, "Same litter? It's hard to tell with Human age."

"Actually," his daughter corrected him tactfully, "they are not even related, Dad."

"Why do they carry on that way, then?" Milly shook her head.

"Their families are long-standing members of the Country Club," explained Freckle, and clarified, "My Human, Matthew, and Paul are co-owners of this Club. They are, actually, the *voting* owners."

If it were not for her house hostess duty to monitor the flow of the Meeting, Freckle would definitely have launched into a boastful tale that *her Matthew* was the most important of the three. She would have liked to go into the story of *her Matthew's* share that was part of his early inheritance from his Dad, who in turn inherited it from his own. His buddy Paul was "only" the second generation.

"That Paul, I think that maybe I know his name from somewhere else," said Zip.

As to the third Human at the table, Theo definitely recognized his face—it was Cheap Steve, the guy with all the hare-brained ideas on moving Sneaky Creak and with no money even to pay for proper cleaning of the Forest which he had recently come to own.

A few weeks ago, Cheap Steve appeared in the Forest leading a handful of tripod-carrying workmen. Over the next couple of days, those tripod devices were seen in operation hither and yon around the hills and valleys of the Forest, sowing worried speculation among the local wildlife.

A yellow canary bird was the one who started the gossip. Pet canaries occupy an unusually authoritative niche in the system of avian gossip because, although their freedom of movement is severely constrained, a canary cage has enormous locational advantages as an eavesdropping post for Human conversation.

"The lady of my house mentioned . . . Steve wants to straighten the Creek and the Ravine."

A red-hatted woodpecker, not stricken with the canary's yellow outfit, did not even give her nod as a source of information, but drummed out the rumor forest-wide: "Cheap Steve has ordered a survey of the Forest! Cheap Steve is planning to straighten the Creek!"

The mockingbirds quit mocking for a minute, choked up and out of breath.

A ruffed grouse hen flew in alarm: will there be

impact on nesting? What if the straightened line ran though the overgrowth where, for many seasons now, she'd been accustomed to tend the small mound of her darling eggs?

The panic was afoot, but then, one particularly bold mockingbird, voiced its derision, louder than the rest.

"Cheap Steve!"

Inspired, the rest of the mockingbirds, one by one, showed off their skill at mimicry by rendering the same message in a bewildering variety of wildlife sounds, ranging from the cawing of crows to the croaking of frogs.

"Steve Cheap! Steve cheap! Cheep! Out of family money!" they jeered in crow, frog, fox and even owl. The comedy made all forgot the fear.

❧

Birds' memories are short, and once the Tripod Humans cleared out, all of the Forest inhabitants returned to their daily grind. There were no apparent changes afoot that affected the Forest, and the flurry of activity by Cheap Steve and his minions was soon forgotten.

Like the rest of the Forest inhabitants, Theo did

not think too highly of his Human, but Steve was nevertheless Theo's Human by right of ownership of the Forest where the whole Fox community lived and hunted. It would be shameful to share his opinion with his Spaniel friends, and especially with his daughter. That would be humiliating for her, too.

Fox Theo sighed deeply and took the easy way out: he pretended that he did not know Steve.

After all, Steve was not even a co-owner of the Club.

❧

"Co-owners," repeated Zip under his breath, trying to make sense of the prefix. "Decidedly, I don't get it."

"They own the club *together*," whispered Theo.

"That's what I do not get," Zip cocked his head and asked, "How do they do that? Milly and I only have one owner, The Old Lady."

"*Co—*" repeated Zip, trying to imagine what would happen if there were Three Old Ladies, all his owners. But Milly did not let him finish the thought.

"I cannot hear over you," hissed Milly.

Freckle came to the rescue.

"Don't worry, Milly. There's nothing to hear yet, they will eat first," explained Freckle patiently.

Fox Theo stretched out, hid his muzzle into front paws, "Then I have time for a quick nap!"

"Don't even think about snoring or baying," warned Zip, and turned around so that the smells from the Human table could more easily reach his nose.

The Humans settled around the table and unfolded heavy leather-bound embossed folios with page after page of long lists. Zip could not read any of it from his vantage point.

"*Bordeaux Rouge*," said Steve, "last time, we tried this one—"

"No, we start with seared scallops and crab legs," Matthew shook his head in dissent and suggested, "*Viognier* to start?"

"Too much fruit. *Spirit Lab, 46%*," said Steve and caused a chuckle around the Human Table.

"Just *Evian* for me," confided Paul to the waiting waiter.

"*Latour*," said Steve and all three laughed.

"*Domaine Nicolas Boudeau 2015*, two bottles," concluded Paul, and that pleased everybody.

Zip inclined his head right and left, trying to

understand, but could not penetrate the strange incantations.

"There are three parts to every meeting," explained Freckle, waking up Theo who was starting to softly howl in his sleep.

"First there's Sports and Food Talk—Did you want to say something, Zip?"

"It was just a sneeze," said Zip, although in truth he'd farted.

"—after Food talk, the Humans reminisce about their childhood," Freckle resumed, discreetly turning her nose, "and then they are ready for Business."

And, as if the Humans were actors on Freckle's live show, they turned to memories of their past.

"I've been meaning to ask something—" Matthew covered his crystal wine flute under the cupped palm, warding off the waiter who was about to refill his glass.

"I've got this," Steve interrupted and seized the bottle.

The three friends followed the wait staff's retreating back with their eyes, and, with the nosy help out of hearing distance, Matthew lifted his hand and leaned in.

"Paul, whose bright idea was to move the Creek?

And, Steve, I've changed my mind. I'll actually take a sip of that."

Paul sensed more irony than genuine interest in the tone of Matthew's question.

"Don't look at me, I'm still in service of the Gods of Justice, moving bad guys off the streets. Though honestly, it's pushing paper more than anything. Moving rivers—that's Steve's sphere."

"Not hardly . . . moving rivers," Steve chortled, getting pink with pleasure and crumpling his starched napkin. "More like pushing off a little bitty creek. But you are right. People like us, we did move up in the world enough so we can prevail over a little bit of water."

Steve's eyes got misty, probably owing to an overzealous application of the content of the bottle that he was managing. Basking in the story, he moved his gaze from Paul to Matthew and chuckled importantly,

"I always reckoned that this zigzag part of Sneaky Creek above the Bridge, is just godawful *wrong*."

"Of course you did," reminded Matthew, "You

dropped your Daddy's favorite shotgun there, smack dab in that zigzaggy stretch of water."

"But I was the best shot," Steve claimed heatedly.

Steve was gesticulating hotly, badly wanting everyone to have fun. It was as though he was their leader again, like back when they were kids, traipsing up and down the zigzags of Sneaky Creek.

"I fell in, bloodied my knee on a underwater stone, got soaked to my shirt collar. Mother grounded me for two weeks!" Paul reminisced smilingly.

Zip, who was listening intently, thought to himself that he understood Paul's words, but something was puzzling about their meaning. *Why do full-grown Human males so often smile while they are recalling bad things that happened to them during their puppy year? I don't see anything to smile about! Milly certainly never smiles when she remembers her embarrassing Bridge Fiasco. Or even if someone else remembers it.*

Steve screwed up his face unpleasantly because the conversation had taken a bad turn, had reminded him that his leadership ended when they left the Forest.

Paul and Matthew both grew up as legacy lawyers. Family tradition. But the grownup years had been much less kind to Steve. Actually, Steve's occupation was rather unclear to both Paul and Matthew. Not that they cared to know; indeed, both men felt that they were probably better off not being privy to all of Steve's activities. Still, whatever their acquired differences, childhood friendship would not let them turn their backs on the one whose Daddy's shotgun had famously been "eaten" by Sneaky Creek, who in fact had been the best shot—and who, just maybe, was also the long-ago leader of their boyhood pack.

"I did not catch," Theodore yawned widely, "what happened to that gun: was it recovered?" The Fox got up on all four paws, curved his back and started shaking off.

"Are you going off somewhere?" asked Milly, "Theodore, surely you are not going looking for that gun?"

"A gun abandoned in the Forest, that's very dangerous. My present litter's in a most risky age, pre-adolescent."

"Be quiet! People don't abandon firearms!" growled Zip menacingly, "Silence!"

"Matthew, have you made up your mind," Steve started pressing.

"About the proposed construction," weighed in

Paul, in a clear and sober voice, his lawyerly negotiation voice. Paul never actually drank at Meetings, but made it a point to keep his glasses full. "Have you decided, Matt?"

Freckle, who had disappeared from the Jasmine Vine Patio to claim the leftovers, popped up by Milly's side.

"Can you hear OK?" she whispered, spitting out a piece of crab leg, "The important part of the Meeting is starting!"

Matthew bottomed his wineglass, pushed away his plate, and leaned back into his chair, "You mean to build myself a house," he clarified, "I'm getting there. It's tempting—to build my own home, my own taste, with room for all my—"

"He's about to be a dad?" asked Theo, who had just reawakened and was still a bit confused.

"No," hissed Freckle, "don't interrupt, I can't—"

"Eavesdrop?" Zip finished her sentence.

"—listen in," corrected Freckle.

"Mind your manners. We are guests here," Milly scolded, giving Zip's cheek a not-so-gentle jab.

"Quiet, they'll hear!"

But Matthew kept droning on, with no regard whatsoever for the commotion of in the Jasmine bushes.

18

NOBODY'S BORED

"I like the plan to build my own house. But," Matthew carried on wistfully, "not sure I like that land where Steve plans to unbend the Creek. The Old Lady's place. I know that part of town very well. Ravine behind her house always . . . there's a spring."

"Say *what*?!" Zip leaped up, and digging all four paws into the grassy ground, growled toothily.

"Build *where*?" Milly almost choked in anger.

"Our house? What about our house?" barked Zip, stupefied with anger.

"Simmer down, Zip," interjected Freckle, "and let me explain their plan . . . They said Old Lady's Land was designed . . . designed to hold the flood . . . the dirty water, and so—"

Zip got more and more agitated, and did not take notice where his paws had carried him. He jumped squarely on a decorative boulder by a small flower bed, and discharged a hateful triple bark in the direction of the administrative building of the Scared Hare Country Club.

"Quiet, quiet," invoked Freckle, "I can explain! They think because Big Water comes into Old Lady's House regularly, they can condemn, and then—"

"So what if there's Water, Old Lady can wash the House," objected Milly, "she is handy with a bucket—"

"—then—" Freckle was determined to not allow herself to be interrupted for the third time, "they can *take away Old Lady's house. Make her sell it. Or worse.*"

Zip's head felt like a dozen bumblebees flew into his right ear and were buzzing through his brain trying to find their way out through the other ear. Theo's daughter's gloomy revelations made him so confused that he didn't know what to say or do next. Inside his head, Zip had a hundred of questions, but he could not find the right words for any of them.

What "they" were able to just take our house?

Where would "they" take it?

Would Zip and Milly have to live in the yard, like a dog on a TV show they once watched?

Zip whined a little, because he immediately felt lonely; he would not want to sleep away from the Old Lady—*wait*—

Where would Old Lady live if "they" took the House? In the yard with Zip and Milly?

Freckle went on, "they want to take the House and put Old Lady in the *Home*."

"Whose *Home*?" interjected Milly.

"What's *the Home*?" whispered Zip.

Theo had previously been fully briefed by Freckle about the intelligence she had gathered by listening in at earlier Meetings, but now he had intelligence of his own to contribute, information that he had personally. He lowered his tail and his voice, reluctantly disclosing a wretched secret, "*Home.* Special sort of home. And it's *bad*."

"Why," managed Milly.

"The smell. And worse yet," Theo stopped because he hated to hurt the Spaniels with what was coming next. But he decided that Zip and Milly would rather get it over with and know, so he went on, "there are *no dogs allowed* in the *Home*."

In absolute stunned silence, where one could hear saliva dropping off the dogs' tongues, Theodore repeated, to make sure that his friends had no illusions: "no dogs allowed."

Zip's jaw opened in dismay,

"It's impossible! Old Lady won't—" Milly rumbled in anger again.

Fox Theo hotly whispered, "Be quiet, or we will be found out and shooed away."

"Silence, all of you! You are not at home. This is a Meeting." Freckle was very protective of the honor of her home and nipped in the bud her Father's buddies' attempt to commence an unseemly commotion.

The Humans, paying no attention to the brief animal kerfuffle, were deep into making their plans.

❧

To the beat of Paul's periodic nods of tacit approbation, Steve ranted hotly and disjointedly about the glory of Constructing on Old Lady's land—*Prime Luxury Ten-Unit . . . no, Twenty-Unit Condos . . . we can charge a million per unit. For total of ten million . . . no, twenty million . . . minus builder's expenses, of course . . . huge money.*

He, Steve, had already planned and organized the whole thing. According to Steve, his "connections" and "influence" had ensured that "the fix is in, everything's already rigged with the City's politicians." Steve's friends understandably never pressed him too thoroughly about the details of the connections and influence that had been brought to bear.

Steve proceeded to review the steps in his scheme.

First, Steve-the-City-Benefactor donates a small part of his Forest Land that abates the Sneaky Creek. Into this piece of land, the straightened Creek will move.

Next, the grateful City dips into its Stormwater Budget, unbends the Creek at Ducklingburg's expense, to run through Steve's Forest, and even frames the now straightened Creek with "Greenway"—a splendid new place for the walking, jogging, picnicking, and other assorted pleasures of Ducklingburg's taxpayers. Steve's overgrown disaster of a Forest now becomes a tax-deductible "Greenway."

Steve's "gift" has been approved already but, of course, without any public disclosure.

Meanwhile, The City's Zoning and Stormwater

were hard at work on their plan to move Old Lady off her "unsafe" land, the very land that housed the very loop of Creek . . . which would soon be moved to Steve's . . . but has not yet.

"Zoning, flood safety, public interest, environmental protection, senility" spat out Steve confidently, "they'll all be used to justify putting Old Lady's *unsafe* land on sale for peanuts."

"That's when *you* snatch the land, Matthew, while it's still *unsafe*. And the very next week my gift and City's generosity will dispose of the flooding Creek," finished Steve.

"And formerly *unsafe* land is now safe?" understood Matthew.

"Perfectly. The Creek will be on my Forest land," Steve smiled generously.

"Old Lady's Land made safe by your generous gift . . . just shortly after she is forced in fire sale . . . cause by un-safety?"

"Such is Old Lady's bad luck!" said Paul firmly. "Bad timing happens."

"So, I'm your Straw Buyer guy!" smirked Matthew, "For real? I thought you were joking. But, if either of you were to buy it, people would know that enabling a construction project is the sneaky true purpose of the sale. So, you want me as your front man and part of my payoff is my nice new condo. I understand."

"Yes, we were not joking," Paul reacted staidly.

"I am completely lost," whined Milly faintly.

"How is that even possible," Theo wondered. "Greenway?! Rubbish! Our whole Forest is green!"

Zip, who'd lately got addicted to Politico website, managed only to squeeze out hoarsely that "America is a free country."

"Quiet! It's not over," commanded Freckle.

❧

"My only hesitation," went on Matthew, "is the owner. The Old Lady—" he leaned in, inviting his two friends to join their heads with his, which was, of course, a fruitless measure in case of dogs and even more so in against foxes.

The foursome behind the bush froze too.

Freckle was on cloud nine. The Meeting was a thrill. Nobody was bored.

"Old Lady . . . driving an 84-year old out of her house . . . yes, that's a wrinkle," replied the voice of Human Paul, a voice well-practiced in Federal

Courts. "But no worthy cause is ever quite without wrinkles!"

That observation was clearly rehearsed. Paul steepled his fingertips for balance, and went on.

"We all have older parents and there comes a time . . . sooner or later, but always does . . . when old people require full—" Paul paused, trying to find a word that would not sound official, but finding none, spat out the familiar term of art, "*Guardianship*. Let's face it, she needs a *guardianship*."

"*Guardianship*?! Guarr-rrrr?! What?" Zip unsheathed two rows of knife-sharp teeth, and shoved his head through the bushes, hairs raising along his whole spine, from neck to tail-stub.

"Wait," Milly snapped at his hind leg, "What the heck is a *guardianship*?"

Zip twisted his head back and whispered hotly, "Crazy House!"

Milly yelped, and her hind paws slipped and gave way under her. But she regained her emotional balance and licked Zip's nose, imploring "Please, we'll talk about it at home, Zip, don't be mad."

Agitated by the subject, the Humans debated up a storm.

"My sources say that Old Lady has commenced some mighty mind-blowing renovations," mused Matthew.

"Mind-blowing indeed," agreed Paul, managing to sound ironic.

With bated breath, the dogs and Humans waited for Paul to go on.

"I talked to couple of contractors. One tells me that Old Lady priced erecting a cinderblock wall around her acreage. A clear symptom of paranoia, in my opinion."

"Hah! Maybe she has delusions of being the first woman President at her own version of Camp David?" Steve mocked.

"I also have intelligence," went on Paul, "that she priced putting in ship-doors, watertight."

"Like on a submarines? Is she maybe getting *EABs* too?" Steve spent some time in the Navy and liked to show that off.

"Emergency Air Breathing Apparatus," translated Paul for Matthew's benefit, "She'll need three. Two for the dogs." That seemed funny, and all three chuckled.

"But there's more! In her garage," Paul could hardly speak for laughter, "she's ordering a mechanics lift so she can raise her car up to the ceiling when it floods."

Steve was circling a finger by his temple in the time-honored symbol for *screwy*. "The Old Lady's cuckoo," he snickered.

"Genius invention, that mechanics lift," barked Zip admiringly, "How did I miss all that?" and got cautionary bites from two sides.

"Actually, it shows an ingenious engineering mind," said Matthew, in his habitual snarky tone of half-serious-half irony.

"Depends how you look at it," cut in Paul firmly. "We take the following positions:

"To begin with, the wall-building flagrantly violates all the zoning rules. The house is in the flood plain where construction requires a special permit—which she doesn't have and would only be able to get on the day that hell freezes over.

"That's one," Paul was bending his fingers, counting the strikes against Old Lady.

"The submarine doors are sure to upset the neighbors. We call them an eyesore, a public nuisance—"

"I still think it just proves that Old Lady has good

engineering sense," argued Matthew, interrupting his friend. He was beginning to sound more and more sympathetic to Old Lady. "Besides, she had not actually installed those submarine doors yet, has she?"

"Be that as it may," disagreed Paul, "I see an opportunity here. Steve, can you get the Zoning folks working on this? Make them pounce on her with a *Notice of Proposed Findings of Violations*. Summoning her to a Zoning Board hearing will be a good start. Old Lady has a temper. If provoked by being asked the right inflammatory questions, she'll surely flare up and make herself sound like a cranky old fool."

Noticing Matthew's disagreeable eye-rolling, Paul added placatingly, "*We'll just test her good sense,* is all. Nothing extreme."

"I have one better," butted in Steve, whose addition to the flow of the information had, up to this point consisted of little more than alcohol-fueled gleeful nods and chortles. His buddies turned to him, as though surprised to find him in the room, and Steve beamed noticing their attention, "This one proves for sure that the old bird's bat-shit crazy."

"What?" Matthew and Paul both inquired impatiently.

"I have it from a good source," Steve paused for effect, his crystal with an oily bit of cognac moving up in the air, "a real doozy that will for sure prove that she has *senile dementia*."

"What? Spit it out, for heaven's sake!" roared Paul.

"It's not just what projects the Old Bat priced, it's what she's *done* already. Bat-shit."

The animal quartet in the bushes held their breath. Even though this Steve had none of his friends' power or money, maybe he might turn out to be the one with most powerful gossip. Zip tried hard to imagine what Old Lady could possibly have done to justify calling her even abnormally eccentric, let alone "bat-shit" crazy. Zip's ears moved, and nose twitched. The effort of concentration fogged his mind and closed his ears until, finally, Steve's voice penetrated mid-sentence:

"—ripped out all the sheetrock, to the studs, threw out goddamn everything."

"The whole first floor?" asked Matthew.

"It's more like a basement, actually, because the house is built into a slope," Steve explained and started drawing rough sketches on the napkins. His drawing showed how the back door of the "basement" was at ground level on the bottom end of the slope while, on a level above that, the "front entrance" of the house was through a door situated several steps above ground level on the upper side of the slope. The three men huddled over the side table, and pointed to the drawings heatedly, amid excited muttering.

"Water only half way up the walls . . . but she ripped out sheetrock to the ceiling . . . and the ceiling . . . wooden studs too . . . threw out everything . . . to the stone . . . nothing left. An effing disaster site is what it is."

"Some of my boys say that she completely lost it because her dogs got hurt," added Steve, his voice oozing with contempt. "So, what did I tell you? You put her on the stand in any court and she come across as craz—"

"Paul, don't," Matthew stopped his buddy Steve with a gesture, "Paul, let's don't ruin the old bird."

Paul shook his head politely, "I was not aiming at that, m'man. Not ruin at all. Just . . . the Judge will appoint *a friend of Court* to handle her affairs. For her own good."

Paul lingered as though he needed time to gather his thoughts together, then lowered his voice almost to whisper, "a *Guardian*? . . . No, a *Receiver*. Receiver'd take over the house and—"

None of the animals could bear to listen to the rest of Paul's plan because their tempers flared.

"*Receiver*?" growled Zip.

"To live with *us*?" yelped Milly, "Which bedroom?"

"He's going to give orders to us? And to Old Lady?" This Zip could not believe and, finding nothing else available upon which to vent his consternation, tried to bite the air.

Oblivious to the yelps and groans in the Jasmine bushes, Paul went on:

"Any Receiver worth his salt will sweet-talk Old Lady into *selling*. There is no harm in that. A good Receiver has a silver tongue. Matthew, what do you say?"

Uncharacteristically, Matthew's own tongue got tied; the situation hit uncomfortably close to home.

He had planned a come-to-Jesus meeting in the near future with his own father. His Daddy was an elderly man who, in Matthew's view, was unnecessarily delaying surrendering the reins of family power to Matthew's younger grip. In the past few years, Daddy's eccentricities, always there to some extent, had begun to verge on the arguably worrisome. A psychologist friend had once told Matthew that, rather than undergoing personality changes, most otherwise healthy senior citizens "just become more like they are than they ever were before."

Would I ever want my own Daddy to suffer the humiliation of having his mental competency questioned in a court of law? The implications for Old Lady's situation were clear, and Matthew was at a loss for how to continue the discussion.

"I . . . drifted away," he brushed off his friends, "let's call it a night and postpone this business."

❧

The guests departed, the night having ended on a sour note for humans and animals alike.

On their way to the Club's parking lot, Paul and Steve exchanged gripes that Matthew, an essential linchpin of their scheme, "doesn't seem to be totally on board."

Matthew himself was confused and grumpy as well. He had prepared a whole list of arguments to persuade the Old Man that his 84th birthday was high time to move over. None of the arguments seemed that persuasive now. They seemed cynical, almost cruel.

Milly told Zip that she so badly wanted to get

home, with Old Lady, that she did not even care if they used the shortcut under the terrible Bridge.

"It's unfortunate that your Spaniel guests got into kind of a huff about what they heard the Humans planning tonight," Theo told Freckle. "But your own success shone through for sure: *nobody was bored.*"

19

THE CONSPIRACY

Not to be outdone by some fox kit, Milly fancied calling a Meeting of her own.

She dreamed of sending invitations to Theodore's daughter Freckle, of directing her first-time guest to her proper place with a cheerful "*Please follow me, the mulch is softest on that side, and freshest as well,*" and "*Can you hear OK from there?*"

Milly craved the role of a *hostess*. She dreamed of *receiving guests, setting the tone,* informing the animals of today's *agenda*. She envisioned herself deftly moving the conversation among the guests along the pre-planned path, of using a judicious nip to stop an occasional indecorous bark or growl, and making sure that everybody got to speak in turn.

Old Lady's backyard—by the Fire Pit—afforded

Milly with a perfect venue. There were undeniable locational advantages. Close to the ravine, and far enough from Old Lady's eyes. At the first hint of any intervention by Old Lady from the house, the Spaniels would have time to effectively cover up the existence of the Meeting. If necessary, there would be ample opportunity to rouse Fox Theo from his nap, then watch him stretch, shake off, and retire noiselessly into the woods. And there'd still be time left to make pretense that they only just heard Old Lady calling. Moreover, the Magnolia tree provided shade, and the mulched cannas flower bed was soft and fragrant.

Yes, Milly had the perfect venue. That much was obvious.

However, setting a suitable Business agenda for convening a Meeting, that posed a problem for a while. But she knew her day would come.

The opportunity for Milly's First Meeting soon presented itself. But as so often happens when life grants one's wishes, Milly barely enjoyed it.

The occasion was, as Zip called it, the "Conspiracy Against Our House."

"ippy, what does it mean—*conspiracy*?"

"That's my biggest headache now."

"Where does it hurt you?"

"My whole head is heavy even thinking about it."

"There will be four of us at the Meeting—you, Theodore, me and Freckle. We'll share. Your head will only get one quarter of the weight, Zippy."

Milly leaned her head on Zip's shoulder and affectionately nibbled on the end of his ear, "I'll set it all up."

All arrangements fell together beautifully. Old Lady and her friend Lariska left for the Shopping Mall. Milly dragged to the fire pit the paper bag with leftover pill food. *Nobody's going to eat that stuff,* she figured, *so we can start with the Business session almost right away.*

The meeting started out languidly. Nobody wanted to be the first speaker.

"Human's thinking has no grounding in any reasonable wildlife rules," said Theodore with a faint grin, "I am not sure we can find a way out of this *Conspiracy Against Your House*. I have not the faintest which way to run. Let Zip tell us."

"No, thanks," Zip declined, glumly.

This is my golden moment to steer the conversation in the right direction, realized Milly, and said:

"My suggestion is: let's don't decide what to do. In Our House, the decider is Old Lady. Let's just hear a report from Freckle—what else she managed to eavesdrop. Um, sorry, what intelligence she managed to compile."

Freckle was no longer waffling about where her loyalties lie. She was firmly disposed to defend Matthew's side in any controversy. However, since Matthew had not determined his position yet, Freckle's own stance was unclear.

"On one paw," Freckle shone a friendly smile at the hostess, "Humans want to drown Old Lady's House."

"Say what?" yelped an outraged Milly.

Freckle shot a nervous sidelong glance at Milly, but continued her report,

"On the other paw, Humans plan to mount an attack to prove Old Lady's old."

"What's there to prove, Old Lady's 84," inter-jected Milly, "Everybody knows that, it's common knowledge."

Freckle swept her tail lightly, "prove that Old Lady's old," she repeated, "and crazy or not, she cannot live *unsupervised* where there can be Big Water any moment."

"That's how," joined in Fox Theo, "we . . . meaning . . . *you* . . .," Theo bowed towards the Spaniels, "and Old Lady are targets of a *two-sided conspiracy*."

"I vote we discuss that in order," declared Milly in a strict voice.

Theo nodded and plowed onward with his revelation of the gossip that he and Freckle had accumulated.

"Scared Hare's fairway for the fifth hole starts right beyond the Bridge, downstream from the Old Lady."

"And?"

"And when the rain is strong enough, Sneaky Creek used to spread out beyond the Bridge and flood part of the fifth hole's fairway."

"What's the problem?" Milly asked. "They can't play in the rain anyway!"

"Rusty dust is the problem," explained the foxes. "Rusty dust from Sneaky Creek gets left behind even after the Creek leaves." Ducklingburg's iron-rich soil had a characteristic rusty red color—and rusty red dirt, when it dries out, produces rusty dust.

"So what? It's just on thc grass and, even then, the

next little rainshower will wash the dust back down to the ground where it came from," Zip strained to understand why the dust could be a serious problem.

"It's not *just* on the grass," explained Fox Theo, "The rusty dust floats around and sticks to the Humans—settles on their white shoes and their white slacks and on their golf sticks, on their white leather gloves (Theo wrinkled his nose). What's more, it's my understanding that the rusty dust sometimes does not come completely off in the wash."

"We get that dust too," remembered Zip, "it's no biggie."

"Goes away in a few days," confirmed Milly. "Old Lady washed the yard, sprayed with the hose, and sometimes gives a good touch-up scrubbing with a brush."

"Yeah," agreed Zip, "I don't believe they would form a *Conspiracy* for just that."

"It's not just that," sighed the Fox, "They say that the dust has pathogens—Hep A, Hep B, Hep C, Hep D . . . not sure what all the names mean, but I know that they mean something bad," the fox looked at his paws and licked the left one.

Useful information, noted Milly privately. And, though her Meeting agenda turned out to be unpleasant, speaking strictly as the hostess, she was a huge success. Her Meeting was flowing well. Well organized and good participation. Nobody was asleep.

"The rusty dust gets in the air, and in the Humans' noses . . . and they are very persnickety, those Golf Club Humans. It got so—" went on the Fox Theo, determined to spill every last bean now, "so . . . that last time, when Sneaky Creek overflowed onto the golf course, the Club was closed for a week. Everybody was out of work—the caddies, the golf pros, the shop, the kitchen . . . especially the kitchen suffered." Fox licked his nose, thinking of all the goodies that could be *rescued* from the trash bags put out by the Country Club's kitchen.

"So, they want to plug the hole, so to speak, to restrict the maximum possible flow of water under the Bridge. During a flood, the water will collect *above* the Bridge, in Old Lady's low-lying property, then seep down slowly enough so that it won't need to spill over onto the golf course. They say that Old Lady's property would make a good *storm-water holding pond,* whatever that is.

"I hate to say it, but that's what the Country Club Humans are doing, they're plotting to fashion Old

Lady's property into their *storm-water holding pond.* Eventually, that will drown your House!"

Theodore was finished with the story and sat, nose to the ground, waiting for somebody to break the stunned silence. One could tell that it had hurt him to bring his friends such bad news.

Both Spaniels stayed in shock for a minute, mulling over the horrible predicament just revealed.

"Freckle, dear, what is your take on this," whispered Milly.

"They definitely have a plan to do away with your House."

"They can't," Zip barked so loudly that the neighbor's housekeeper looked out of the window and both foxes had to dive into the firepit ash, head first.

"*All clear,*" Zip reported after a few minutes of pretending that he was just barking up the passing FedEx delivery van.

"They have a plan," said Freckle, only the tip of her wiggling tail visible from the Fire Pit, "to dub Old Lady crazy. They have a doctor who will say she is *forgetful,* engages in *strange* behavior, and needs to live in a ho—"

"That's way too personal, we're not discussing that," interrupted Milly, exercising what she deemed her rights as the presiding hostess. "Old Lady's *smart*, and she remembers *everything*."

Having put the foxes in proper place, Milly turned to her older brother pleadingly and asked: "How can they take our House? They cannot take our House. Can they? Zip?"

Zip turned around to look. The House stood there, just as huge and sturdy as before. The Foxes must've got it wrong. All those wood creatures and their over-active imaginations.

"Nobody can *take* the House, Milly. It's too big to steal. And there is not even a mortgage on it."

"What's mortgage?" asked Milly.

"Exactly," Zip responded hastily, even if not responsively to Milly's question. Zip was not sure what "mortgage" was either, but he knew Old Lady was mighty proud that there was not one.

"My Human, Matthew," Freckled started out again, "always teaches me get to the root of problem, determine what's inside. Why are they doing what they are doing?"

"Exactly, why?" nodded Milly, "Who'd want to have Old Lady's House drowned?"

"If it's at risk of getting drowned," rapped out Freckle, "the House is worthless. Or, almost worthless, anyway. It's dangerous for Old Lady to live like that . . . at her age—"

"Don't talk about that," pleaded Milly.

"—So, then the House and land could be bought cheaply. And after a respectable time passing," Freckle paused to illustrate the passing of the time, "the City will dry out the land, redirect the water flow to Steve's forest. The City has huge resources, and—"

"Redirect it where?" asked Theo.

"To your Forest, Daddy."

"What resources? Did you see them, Freckle?"

"Me personally, no," started Freckle, but was interrupted by Old Lady's loud voice:

"March home immediately! The pair of you!"

The Hostess first and foremost, Milly hastily barked a formal dismissal over her shoulder, "Our Meeting is adjourned," and both Spaniels sprinted for the house.

The shopping bags lay strewn at the Old Lady's feet. In her hand, she held a green-and-white striped envelope. Zip knew immediately that they were in trouble. Old Lady already tore open the wrapper and was studying intently the little white paper that fell out of the green-and-white envelope of gloom.

Zip read it as soon as Old Lady put the letter down on the kitchen table.

FROM: Flood Water Mitigation Department
1 Chicken Coup Street
Ducklingburg, South Duck

Madame Property Owner:

Our condolences on your harrowing experience of the Big Water event this past Summer.

Always looking out for the wellbeing of its citizens, The City of Ducklingburg has made safety changes.

To serve your household better, the City has revised the FloodPlaneLines.

Under the new FloodPlaneLines, your yard and parts of your house (see attached schema) are in violation.

Specifically, the parts marked in red on the map are no longer on grade.

You have until the year-end to resolve the violations and bring your house and yard into conformity with the on grade positions.

If your violation persists after January 1 of next year,

you will be fined not less than $20 per day, each and every day. If you do not comply, the City may seek a Court Order to have the violations mitigated at your expense.

Sincerely,

Montague Dinkle,

Administrator

There was a second sheet of paper in the letter. It showed a silhouette of Old Lady's House, divided by an ominous dotted line. Italicized letters to the left of the line said "on grade," in green. That part of the House was safe.

To the right of the ominous line, the silhouette of the House was shaded red, and an ominous arrow directed the reader to the warning scribbled in Administrator Dinkle's slightly shaky hand-lettering: "*NOT ON GRADE*."

The "Not On Grade" parts included:

- the Fire-Pit and the Spaniels' favorite path from the house to the Fire-Pit;
- most of Old Lady's bedroom, and
- the part of the kitchen where Old Lady kept Zip and Milly's food bowls and the refrigerator.

In short, all of the Spaniels' favorite spots apparently did not measure up to the City's "grade" standard of approval. Zip made a mental note to move all food bowls to the "safe" part of the kitchen and wondered whether Old Lady would be moving the refrigerator and her bed.

But she didn't move one single thing.

The fridge stood exactly where it did before. She did not even visit the bed. Instead, she fired up the computer, and started printing papers.

"We are going to appeal to the Zoning Committee," explained Old Lady to Zip, who was watching her flurry of activity with mixed angst and optimism, "Montague Dinkle, the Administrator, will not win so easily."

"Little does he know that I spent most of my career battling *Old Country* bureaucrats. Dinkle wouldn't even qualify to be an office-boy in the kinds of really byzantine bureaucracies that I've dealt with Across The Pond."

Zip sighed heavily. The animals did not cover the Bureaucracy attack angle at the Meeting on *Two-Sided Conspiracy Against the House*.

"This is conspiracy from a third side," hotly whispered Milly in Zip's ear.

"It comes from Steve!" Zip's eyes widened with realization, "Remember?"

"What?"

"He said he'd *activate* his Zoning Committee buddies."

Milly cocked her head, and took a light bight out of the woolen kitchen rug to help her memory,

"I remember! Paul ordered this attack," Milly's eyes narrowed, and she issued a lamenting shrilling whine, with which Zip joined.

"It's rigged! This Zoning thing is rigged!"

"Go for a walk?" Old Lady misunderstood the cause of the Spaniels' outcry.

20

THE ZONING COMMITTEE

The meeting with the Zoning Committee was of the worst possible kind—the kind where "no dogs allowed."

But before Zip had the time to figure out whom to bribe for a detailed report, he caught a break: Old Lady's email hiccuped and spat out an avalanche of pages titled

> Transcript of Hearing before Ducklingburg Zoning Board
>
> in the case of
>
> *Zoning Board v. Old Lady,*
>
> special proceeding #17-211,

reported by Henrietta Harris, registered Court Reporter & Notary Public.

Neither Zip nor Milly had ever even heard most of these words.

The pages was accompanied by a movie. Zip hit the button to watch.

And Voilà!

Behind a long gray plastic table covered, instead of a tablecloth, with a clutter of scattered papers and rubberbands, a whole crew of Humans huddled irritably. They all jammed themselves on one side, and all stared irritably across. Although the Humans were of various breeds, ages and sizes, they all shared an identical look of combined disgust and hostility. Zip immediately felt intense dislike for each of them individually and for the whole lot together.

Again, Paul's words flew into Zip's mind: *"Steve, can you activate the Zoning folks, make them pounce on her?"*

This is the "pounce" about to happen!

Zip moved his nose closer to the computer screen and growled under his breath, warning the enemy.

"Is this a Meeting? Where's the food? They all look hungry!" whispered Milly.

"Shh, don't interrupt," Zip pushed Milly's nose away from the computer screen, "Now I have to start again."

He was counting the heads, "One, two, three, four . . . seven . . .."

Zip could count very easily to seven, with some difficulty to ten, and eleven was his absolute record.

Fortunately, the Human count stopped at nine.

Six regular Humans, without titles on their name plates, plus three Humans with nameplates that ended with "attorney": Senior Assistant City Attorney, Assistant City Attorney, and Environmental City Attorney.

The camera angle shifted, and both Spaniels took a step forward and cocked their heads expectantly.

On the opposite side from the nine strange Humans, stood a tiny table with two hard chairs. Old Lady was sitting in one. The second chair behind her table was empty. She was all alone—absolutely nobody to advise her.

"Not one lawyer in the whole Ducklingburg agreed to take us on!" muttered Zip bitterly.

"That's Our Old Lady!" yelped Milly.

The camera jerked and moved again, now to the farthest wall of the room, where a lanky looking Human with a comb-over was pointing at a very strange-looking map, filled with parallel squiggly lines, like a tree stump.

"As an Administrator," was presenting the Comb-Over, "I must protect the residents of Ducklingburg from flood waters, and it simply is no longer safe to live on the site of Old Lady's house."

Comb-over gave Old Lady a fakey smile, and pulled his palm to his chest,

"I give you my heartfelt assurance, Ma'am, that this is for your own safety."

"Mr. Chairman, I have a question for Administrator *Montague Dinkle*," announced Old Lady, her voice shaking only just a smidgeon.

"Go ahead," boomed the Human sitting in the middle of the Big Table.

"There were other houses in Ducklingburg that flooded?"

"Oh yes," beamed the Administrator, "at least a hundred houses."

"All hundred got a letter like you sent me? All hundred are no longer *on grade*?"

"No," smirked Administrator, "not all hundred."

"How many?'

"I don't have the numbers with me."

"Less than half?"

"I think so."

"Less than ten?"

"Probably."

"I am the only one, am I not?"

"Well, yes—"

"This '*safety*' concern of yours that aims to turn me out of my own house—what is this really about, Mr. Dinkle?" smiled Old Lady, as though she was inviting Administrator Dinkle to share a slightly embarrassing secret.

"I—" began Dinkle, but he was interrupted. The biggest of the Humans, seated in the middle and tagged Senior Assistant Attorney, realized what was afoot, leapt to his feet and bellowed:

"OBJECTION! THAT IS IRRELEVANT. I am warning you, Old Lady, if you keep talking about irrelevant things, the Committee—"

Zip could never manage to quite understand what the Committee was going to do. Each time Zip rewound to watch that part of the video again, he could not suppress the impulse to start barking so loudly that there was no way to hear the nasty Human through his own bark.

By the time Zip cooled down, the video already showed Old Lady talking.

"I have a solution that will put a stop to the entire problem," said Old Lady, apparently unafraid of the

Nine Humans, "Unplug the Bridge. That should make my house safe."

"OBJECTION! IRRELEVANT! I warned you, Ma'am! Did I not warn you?!" bellowed the Senior Assistant Attorney again, "You will not talk about the Bridge! The Bridge belongs to the Department of Transportation. Do you see anybody here from Department of Transportation?!" he queried in a menacing voice while pointed his sweeping finger at the row of nameplates on the table. His cheeks turned a beet-red color, exactly like the very tasty soup that Old Lady sometimes liked to cook in the winter.

"I do not believe you know where you are, do you?" he peered intently forward, and Humans on his right and left vigorously nodded their agreement.

Old Lady just opened her mouth, when Senior Assistant Attorney motioned at her, commanding silence, and demanded,

"Can you explain your bizarre actions after flood? Why did you rip out all the drywall, all walls between the rooms on ground floor?"

And before Old Lady could respond, Senior Assistant Attorney added,

"She ripped out all supporting walls"

All Humans at the table nodded eagerly again.

"Why did you order the lower part of the stairs ripped out? Why did you have drywall ripped off the ceiling? Were you aware of your actions? At the time?"

"She'd done it to herself!" chimed in Administrator Dinkle, his accusatory finger stretched toward Old Lady, "She made her own Home uninhabitable!"

The rest of the Humans nodded in accusatory concert—all of them, even the stenographer.

"And last but certainly not least, the City must also take into consideration," Dinkle's index finger rose up and all the Humans at the table leaned forward with bated breaths. . .

Milly could no longer stand it. She emitted a shrieking yelp and angrily pushed her nose into the video screen. The screen reacted to this unaccustomed abuse by freezing for a few seconds, then went out completely.

Zip did not begrudge Milly's interruption because he had already seen enough.

There was no doubt: all nine Humans on the other side were aligned against Old Lady. Nobody took her side, everybody was on the attack. That much was clear to the Spaniels.

But, try as they might, the Spaniels could not figure out what the whole quarrel was about. What was that "*grade*" that Old Lady had to find, and what was she was supposed to do with this *grade* once she found it?

I'll have to watch this again later, decided Zip.

❧

Zip spent two full evenings watching the video, straining to wrap his mind around what it was those Zoning Committee Humans were talking about, but did not come one step closer to understanding.

If only Zip could understand the words. If only somebody would explain their meaning in plain English . . ..

Why did that beetroot-colored man have the power to freeze everybody by yelling OBJECTION?

Was it a curse?

It had to be, and this red-cheeked Senior Assistant Attorney must not've been very proficient if it cost him so much effort.

And, most importantly, who could teach Old Lady a counter-curse?

After two days of angst, the answer presented to Zip fully and clearly and, as it often is the case with genius solutions, the answer was so simple that Zip could not fathom how he did not get it all along.

"Eureka!" Zip jumped up, "Milly, I got it! We need an EXPERT."

"Expert?!"

"*Legal* Expert. Somebody who speaks *Legalese*. Somebody who can explain the meaning of all these . . . *words*."

"Let's have a Meeting," barked Milly, jumping up on the wall of the Fire Pit to quickly survey the venue.

"We call the meeting and select the Expert." Milly's bark was about two octaves higher than usual, like she was announcing a squirrel in the neighborhood. She was excited by the prospect of playing hostess again.

"Fine," grunted Fox Theo, appearing noiselessly from the side of the ravine, "we'll have a Meeting." Milly was a bit startled, wondering how long Theo had lurked nearby unheard and unseen, but she continued unhesitatingly.

"Let's set a time acceptable for all participants—" Milly ordered in her official Meeting-presider voice.

"We'll start tomorrow," countered Theo, ignoring ceremony and speaking in his usual voice.

"At the time convenient for all pa—" declared Milly.

"We start as soon as I'm back," proclaimed the

Fox. "And now I should go. There's a lot to do. There will be many applicants to be an Expert. We need to consider all the applicants. I am leaving, and I will start considering . . .." Theo's voice was trailing off as he retreated toward Sneaky Creek and, before Milly could announce the official close of today's Meeting, he was gone.

"Typical Theo for you," Milly twitched her tail stub to the left, "No respect for protocol."

"A wild animal, what do you expect?" agreed Zip.

"On the other paw, decided Milly, "he is our faithful friend."

21

EXPERT SELECTIONS

Faithful Friend Theodore arrived for the Expert Selection unusually early. The sun had not even thrown its first rays at the rosebushes by the garage.

"The Meeting Is In Session," declared Milly in her newly adopted ceremonious tone, shrill and somewhat fidgety.

"We got the quorum," Zip supported his sister, "so, let's review the Street Talent."

Zip had prepared conscientiously and well for his lead role in the talent review.

A recent discovery had helped him.

After the Big Water Scare, Zip became concerned with Milly's safety and subscribed Old Lady to the *Register Your Pet* section of the *Neighborhood Network*.

Under Old Lady's unclaimed profile on the page, Zip chose the "PETS" category and typed in:

NAME: *Milly*

DESCRIPTION: *English Springer Spaniel, purebred, red roan. Purebred.*

He uploaded two pictures—front and back.

Zip had no plans of telling Milly she was now "registered," but in case it came out, he made sure that the most flattering photos were used. That was all Milly truly cared about anyway.

Ostensibly, the neighborhood watch was efficient when a pet got lost. Seeing an unaccompanied dog wandering along White Goose Lane, local Humans hastened to consult the *Pet Registry,* and in no time at all, the owner's phone started ringing with calls from concerned neighbors.

Zip did have reservation about the project: Old Lady despised social networks. But, in the end, Milly's safety trumped Old Lady's stand-offishness.

Now, his interest in *Pet Registry* came unexpectedly handy for their Expert research. For the whole night before the Meeting, he moved furtively between Old Lady's computer and the downstairs color printer to produce print-out of every canine in his and two adjacent neighborhoods. He was exhausted, but pleased and proud.

"We'll review each dog and her skills," said Zip. "Somebody is bound to have background in litigation."

"Or his," corrected Milly. "Hers or *his*." She was obviously thinking about the possibility of a good looking young dog from a litigation family.

Zip sighed, but nodded resignedly.

"Whole neighborhood? No, that will take forever," disagreed Theo, then he shuffled around, and looked in the direction of Old Lady's house, "I have not had my breakfast yet."

The hint was obvious: the cunning fox was trying to mix business and pleasure.

Milly picked up on the trickery, but, never slipping out of character of proficient hostess, offered a hospitable snack.

"Would you like some of Zip's leftovers from yesterday, Theo? . . . Zip, you don't mind if I take the liberty?"

"'Course not," barked Zip heartily, "I think Theo could use some of *your* leftovers too."

After both sets of leftovers were devoured, Theo rubbed his nose on the Fire Pit to clean off a stray piece of dill, and said:

"Why'd you want to check the whole neighborhood? That'll take too long. I still have errands in the morning—"

"Are you here for the Meeting or for our breakfast?!" scolded an annoyed Milly. "Zip, why are we checking the whole neighborhood again?"

"The dearth of talent," explained Zip quickly. "And this job wants Highest Qualifications. Look here." Zip opened his prepared printout of the DOGS section of the *Neighborhood Watch Registry*. The registry had all the pertinent information:

PHOTO.

ADDRESS.

AGE.

MONICKER.

OCCUPATION OF THE HUMANS.

It was *The Who's Who of Neighborhood Canines*.

"That's worthwhile," unexpectedly yielded Theo, "high time I case the joints. Avoid ambushes." As per usual, the Fox was only looking as far as his next meal, but, in this instance, their interests were aligned and the Meeting opened.

"Spaniel Zip will proceed with his presentation of the Available Talent," announced Milly, jumped off the Fire Pit wall, and leaned against Zip to see the photos in his printouts.

All three muzzles peering at the colored stack, and Zip paged onward to the first candidate,

SAM the GOLDEN RETRIEVER

Sam was shown in his owner's yard, contemplating the tree with his hind paw about to shoot in the air.

Milly whined softly,

"Zip, Zip, we should consider him. Golden Retrievers . . . they are . . . he is . . . so impressive looking. . .."

Zip scratched the sand by the Fire Pit to calm down a little, but parried in a calm voice.

"Milly. First off, this Retriever's Human turned you out of his yard just weeks ago, don't you remember?"

Theo snickered.

"Besides," continued Zip, biting his lip from embarrassment—*attacks on his own sister, in front of the Wild Life, what was he thinking?* "—Besides, who is this Retriever? His background is a *joke*. His family is as far from legal field as it gets."

Zip indicated the OCCUPATION OF THE HUMANS column on the page, leaving half an imprint of his wet nose along with a few grains of sand, "Sam's family reports their business as *general contractor*. And, frankly, all I ever seen them build is picket fences. NEXT!"

"—These two yappy dogs?" asked Theo, pointing down at the next page, "Says here, BELLA AND LUCKY? They have this *j'ai ne sais qua*. Reminiscent of foxes."

"Anesthesiology," chorused the Spaniels.

Zip explained, "Medical. Their Human works in surgery . . . *Anesthesiology,* to switch off the brain during surgery."

"Definitely not a match," agreed Theo. "We need maximum brain function for this. We can go to sleep later."

Zip turned over another page and his eye brows played up,

"There's MARLA, she's a BERNESE MOUNTAIN DOG."

"Fi," Milly bit her bottom lip, "Marla's Human sells airspace for phone towers. *Airspace*. Head's up in the air. They have no notion of ravines."

"How about him?"

Zip pointed to a photo of a peculiar-looking dog, a mix of poodle and a labrador, fluffy like a lovechild of a sheep and a cloud.

"He's still a puppy," said Theo.

Milly chuckled, "LABRADOODLE. I heard Old Lady call him *bummer dude*. His Human paints. Pictures, not walls"

"Freckle wants her portrait, for the Country Club," Theo was suddenly on alert.

"Nah," barked Zip, "I've seen her art. Landscapes, and colors so bleak she cannot even make her mortgage."

"NEXT," ordered Theo with a ting of hunger in his voice. Spaniels' leftovers were not exactly a full meal.

"Two BASSETS. The Human is a housewife."

. . . .

They pawed at the printouts for a long time, wading through more surgeons, real estate folks, a cardiologist, a wedding planner and a gynecologist. Milly asked what that meant, but Zip said she did not need to know that yet. They quickly rejected several bankers and a real estate broker.

"Let's study the adjacent neighborhood," announced Zip.

But Theo balked.

"I never hunt that far. Can't. Not my territory."

"What do we do now?" panicked Milly.

"I have the solution," said Theo. "But you're not gonna like it."

"We are open-minded," exaggerated Zip.

They really weren't, but Theo was in a hurry, so he blurted out,

"Simple solution. CATS."

The two Spaniels turned towards each other, their tails full-mast, muzzles half-opened, frozen.

Zip spoke first.

"I second Fox's motion," he said with effort, "We consider *cats*. We must be inclusive, and merit based."

They did not even need to adjourn until Zip could provide information from the CATS section of the Registry; the leading candidate was obvious.

"Rosie," admitted Milly, has extensive legal background. "Lives right across the street. But I must vote against her."

Rosie was a sleek, ebony-colored pussycat who liked to hunt for sport. The headless chipmunks were strewn across the road on multiple occasions.

Theo, who had no scruples whatsoever about eating other animals' kill, licked his nose and opined in favor of Rosie. "She never eats her chipmunks. I vote her in."

"She's mean and boastful, not a dependable friend," objected Milly angrily.

The discussion was getting heated.

Rosie was a subject of considerable envy on the

Street. She had two sets of Humans in two houses, was unfaithful to both houses, and actually flaunted her two-timing situation.

Rosie's original family—two fierce litigators, Husband and Wife— were good providers of material comforts for a cat, but they were emotionally unavailable. If they were not physically away in court, they were too busy preparing for court or too somber writing their appeals to be present in Rosie's life. Her food bowl was always plentifully filled, but her Humans neglected their duty to scratch behind their cat's ears. And worse, as soon as Rosie made herself comfortable on her Human's lap or by a knee, they inconsiderately moved. Once she even got a little shove! The subject of their conversations was always the law. It was as if the Humans were completely unaware that they were in a Cat's presence.

Rosie's adopted family lived across the street from the Spaniels. It was, Zip revealed to Theo, "Suzy."

"Suzy and?" asked Theo.

"Just Suzy."

Suzy had oodles of leisure time, and was prepared to scratch behind Rosie's ear for as long as the cat deemed necessary and proper. Moreover,

Suzy understood her obligation to render unto the Feline all of the veneration to which it was entitled. Rosie accepted Suzy's affection disdainfully, as was a cat's rightful entitlement.

Suzy's own occupation was a bit unclear, but her father used to be a lawyer—and no ordinary one. Indeed, a picture in an old, dirty wooden frame hung over Suzy's mantelpiece as a reminder of her father's legal prowess. So skillful and successful was Suzy's dad that he had even scored, as a retainer for his labors, a painting by the renowned portraitist F. Gilbert McKnight.

"The artist is long dead now," explained Zip to Theo, "it's from the XVIIIth century."

Suzy was always eager to boastfully retell the story: her father's client was so grateful for staying out of jail that, when he could not pay her father's retainer in cash, he offered his most precious possession—that valuable XVIIIth century painting.

Zip and Milly were not much impressed.

"What does she see in this bunch of muddy colors?" Zip wondered.

Of course, to be fair, the paint might've darkened over the years. Or maybe peering through Suzy's entrance door glass did not give the Spaniels the best view of the painting. After all, Suzy's cleaning lady was not too dutiful, and the entrance door glass had not been properly cleaned since the move-in day.

"Let's consider Rosie's *pros* and *cons*," decided Zip. "Pro: legal background all around."

"She's an Independent," added Fox. "Lives in two houses. No alliance with either. Unbiased."

"Lack of bias is useful in an expert," agreed Zip.

"She's so unbiased she could be a Federal Judge," Theo laid it on thick.

"*Con*," interjected Milly, "Cat Rosie is a feline. And we are all canines." Milly looked askance at Theo, and added, "Foxes are relatives of dogs."

"Heard this smear before," grumbled Fox Theo, who did not like to be with lumped with the domestic servants.

"But this reminds me of an issue. We all communicate among ourselves in Canine. I can hardly understand anything in Feline. Isn't that a showstopper problem?"

"I've had many excellent interchanges with Rosie," Zip reassured. "Rosie is remarkably fluent in Canine, although, of course, with a strong Feline accent."

Anyway, you speak Canine with a pretty strong accent yourself, thought Theo but was too polite to comment aloud.

In truth, the Spaniels and the Foxes each believed that their own breed communicated in the purest, most authentic Canine while the others, although perfectly understandable, sounded rather peculiar.

"Zip, if you vouch for Rosie's communication skills, that's good enough for me," Theo responded as he anxiously checked the position of the sun in the sky.

"It's getting late, I have to leave. I vote Rosie. She may be sloppy in her hunting, but she never preys on ill and sickly. Beheaded chipmunks were all fat and —" Theo licked his nose again, "Anyway, Rosie gets my vote. Gotta run now."

"I agree. Rosie," grumped Zip reluctantly. Zip disliked Rosie and, other things being equal, would support Milly's opposition. But Old Lady needed help, and Rosie was the most qualified candidate to be their Expert. Meritocracy was important.

"Then, our majority decision is official," yelped Milly, and, addressing Theo's back that was rapidly disappearing in the bushes, announced

"MEETING ADJOURNED!"

22

LEGAL ROSIE

Rosie, who was well-known in the neighborhood to never stand upon ceremony, accepted her Expert Designation right away.

In all humility, she was the one and only adequate choice, far and away the most superbly qualified Expert available—at least in the Neighborhood and quite possibly in all of Ducklingburg. Not only that, but she understood how the principle of *noblesse oblige* requires those in privileged positions to render assistance to the less fortunate.

And, she thought privately, *there is the relief from the ennui, the boredom that has set in since Big Water decimated the supply of huntable chipmunks and field mice.*

"Request granted," she purred with laconic simplicity. "I'll be your Expurrrt. I work *prrroo bono*. Meaning you do not have to pay, but I do not have any rrrrresponsibility."

Before the Spaniels could react, the Cat explained,

"I don't need your pay, I'm already immensely rich. I do not want for anything, there's plenty of food and attention.

"The Humans in my First Family feed me twice. Neither knows that the other fed me. They work so hard that they don't have the time to coordinate. They rely on this stupid two-sided sign.

One side says:

CAT IS FED

The other side:

FEED THE CAT

They never figured out that, with one swipe of my paw, I can beat that system, turn the sign around to any way I want it."

Both Spaniels salivated in acknowledgment, and the Cat went on.

"And Suzy in my second home shares everything she has with me. She tries to think of new ways to earn my approval. So . . .," the Cat arched her back and stretched out her tail so it appeared longer than she was, "So, I will work purrr . . . *pro bono*. Meaning free," she said once again, with the patronizing tone of a teacher explaining basic vocabulary to dim-witted repeaters.

"And since it is *pro bono*," (*meaning free*, mouthed the dogs silently) "you three will please control your expectations."

"Meaning what?" asked Milly.

"Meaning," said the cat arrogantly, "I am a Legal Expert, not a miracle worker. No warranties of a successful result. If your Principal, the Old Lady, is unsatisfied with my advice, no claims against my insurance."

"You are insured for bad legal advice?" Milly was incredulous.

"It's called malpractice coverage," corrected Cat Rosie, evading answering the question. "And, what's more, if your Matter comes to an appeal, my name is never mentioned as your counsel. We lawyers call that being *not of record*. Purr-fectly clear? . . . Agreed?"

Both Spaniels and the Fox only half-understood

Cat's conditions, but, as usually happens in these circumstances, all three pressed their right paw to the ground and declared compliantly:

"We do hereby Agree."

"OK then," said the Cat, jumping on the fig tree and pinning a terrified bird against the trunk. The bird fluttered and screeched something that was probably a promise to never steal one measly fig again, so long as his feathery family and their progeny lived on the Old Lady's land. Rosie discarded the lifeless body at the base of the tree.

Milly shook her dangling ears, sending sand and hairs in the air, and sprang to all four paws, "Our First Meeting will open—"

"—Tomorrow at sunrise, by your Fire Pit," injected Rosie in a peremptory tone that would entertain no disagreement. "I wake up wicked early."

"One more thing," hastily announced Theo, directing his attention to Rosie. "If nobody else wants that bird—"

❧

At sunrise the next morning, the weather was dark and gloomy. Rain had been drizzling all night.

"Bad weather. We need an Inclement Weather Plan," said Milly.

"In—Cle-where?" Zip pretended not to understand.

"The Cat will cancel," predicted Milly, biting her lower lip and wrinkling the left part of her nose in contempt. "Cats are afraid of water."

Contrary to Milly's prediction, the Cat did come.

She carried her own laptop and a black, golf-sized umbrella that was big enough to cover the entire Fire-Pit.

"My He-Human is out of town, so I pinched a golf umbrella. He won't need it, it's probably not raining where he's at," explained the Cat, then began busily unpacking her laptop, muttering, "That's my personal. We'll need two screens for this exercise."

Rosie's Huge Umbrella was inserted by the Cannas flowerbed; both hers and dogs' laptops were fired up.

Milly tried in vain to reassert her role of hostess. "Can everybody see OK?" she asked, but nobody responded with the hoped-for polite "Thank you, yes."

All eyes were already spellbound on Rosie, who chose a position with the best Cannas flowers as her background, the better to show off her ebony-black coat against the bubblegum-pink hues of the blossoms. As her pointer, the cat produced a colorful bird feather. The other attendees of the Meeting knew where the feather came from.

Theo was smitten on the spot.

"Such good hunting skills, that Cat, a regular Amazon," he murmured under his nose, "captured the bird and kept the feather for a trophy—such a great prop, makes her whiskers *pop*!"

Basking in the obvious adulation of her audience, Rosie launched confidently into her spiel.

"Before you watch the video of the Hearing, you need to learn the language," Rosie lectured.

Zip issued a soft, approving bark. He'd been watching the darn video on repeat over and over, and none of the unfamiliar words made any sense.

"Knowledge of *Legalese* is important," purred Rosie, "Start with the basics."

First word to know. Using the feather pointer to write, Cat traced on wet ashes:

OBJECTION!

"I've heard Old Lady say that!" blurted out Zip. "A lot!"

"Well, yes, she should have," acknowledged Rosie, "because

OBJECTION

means

JUDGE, MAKE HIM SHUT UP!"

Cat's upper lip spread in a conspiratorial smile before she went on with the air of one who is disclosing a key professional secret. "That's the most important word for every litigator, their absolute favorite."

"Old Lady *objectioned* an awful lot," whispered Zip, mostly to himself.

"Is that like a challenge?" asked Milly, "Do they bare their claws and duel?"

"No," explained the Cat, "After one person says *OBJECTION!*, (meaning JUDGE, MAKE HIM SHUT UP! mouthed the Spaniels) the Judge usually says

OVERRULED!"

Zip's tail stub wiggled, and his jaws spread into a happy smile,

"That's exactly like the video! Old Lady said OBJECTION!, and the Head Human at the other table kept barking *OVERRULED!*"

"OVERRULED

means

NO, YOU SHUT-UP YOURSELF,"

said the Cat firmly, "That's not good, means Old Lady was not winning."

"No, you shut-up?"

"That's what it means. But more politely," confirmed Rosie, "Can we return to the lesson?"

Without waiting for the nod, the Cat plunged on, "But sometimes the Judge says

SUSTAINED!

which means

YOU'RE RIGHT. HE WILL SHUT UP."

"Old Lady was SUSTAINED once," said Zip sadly.

"A good thing Your Old Lady said OBJECTION. If you say OBJECTION, then you can go on and appeal to a higher court. Tell them the law was not followed."

"Old Lady said *OBJECTION!* a lot," confirmed Milly.

"Like I said, a lawyer who does not even bother to mew . . . I mean woof . . . I mean make OBJECTION . . . that lawyer's stupid. The higher court will not even listen to him; the lawyer blew it!"

❧

The Cat went on lecturing, clearly repeating parts of speeches she'd overheard many times before.

"Of course, the Judge dislikes lawyers who purr-sue . . . I mean woof . . . I mean make OBJECTIONS, but *you do not come to court to make friends*. You come to court to win!" And punching her feather into the screen, Cat almost howled, "Never be demure in court!"

"Old Lady was not demure," whispered Milly shyly.

"No, she certainly was not," grinned Rosie. "Look here, at these examples in the video recording."

Rosie then gave an impressive demonstration of her thorough preparation for her Expert duties. In rapid-fire order, she fast-forwarded and paused the video a number of times, in each instance to play a short scene exemplifying what Rosie called Old Lady's "making a *proper record* for appeal."

You say that I violated your zoning rules.

I asked for your evidence, again and again.

The City of Ducklingburg never showed any evidence.

What did I even violate? What?

"Good job, Old Lady! She is not a lawyer, is she? She could be," Rosie delivered her highest compliment. The dogs shook heads in unison, and Zip made a mental note to sign up Old Lady for some law school course. There were plenty of them advertising in her e-mail.

Meanwhile, Rosie kept on using scenes from the video to illustrate Old Lady's objections.

I should be allowed to know what I violated!

"She's smart, your Old Lady," approved Rosie. "Not a lawyer herself? Sure?"

The Spaniels shifted from paw to paw, pleased with the compliment. Even the normally reserved Fox Theo was visibly exalted by the praise.

Rosie went on. "These City folks are digging themselves into a deep hole," she opined pompously. "Look at that idiot in black suit with white shirt-front! Just listen to what this dimwit barks!"

And Rosie thereupon showed the scene where the Assistant City Attorney shouted, with a hardline, belligerent inner city accent:

"The rules of evidence don't always apply. Actually."

The Cat plopped on the ground and rolled around, faking a laugh.

"HA! HA! HA! *Don't always apply*. Does this cocky dude really think that he can pick and choose when the rules apply and when they don't apply? What a blooper! HA!"

"What's *evidence*?" asked Milly.

The Cat jumped up on all four paws, twisting in the air, and stood stiffly.

"Did I not explain everything?" she asked in a tone that meant, without a doubt, that whoever did not understand her explanation was a simpleton.

"You did," agreed Milly meekly, not wishing to self-identify as a simpleton.

"But we need to wrap our heads around all that,"

admitted Zip, who was never ashamed of asking questions or worried about looking slow. Zip was very comfortable in his own fur, justifiably confident that he was a super-intelligent Spaniel. Throughout Cat's lecture, he tilted his head to let the funny words ease their way under the earflaps, but now that all these words made it inside, Zip found it all too much to digest all at once.

"Let's call it a day," he said, politely turning his muzzle away from the Cat.

"Yeah, regroup a little," agreed Milly, remembering that there was some food still left behind Zip's bowl.

"In court we call this a *recess*," said the Cat, and ordered: "Come back here tomorrow. Let's hope the weather favors." And, with that, she heaped her laptop and the notes together, and floated away under her black umbrella.

Lost in thought about the implications of Rosie's presentation, Zip uncharacteristically forgot to offer his help carrying Cat's load.

23

WHO'S YOUR ENEMY?

The next morning came with the sun shining warmly and giddily, in colors that only reveal themselves in Ducklingburg when the Southerners quit griping about *the heat* and welcome the end of a rainy spell. Everybody was happy to see the sun. Even the weeds, those unwanted intruders that encroached relentlessly on the flowerbeds, now looked oddly green, pretty and bright, washed fresh by the recent rains.

Everybody woke up jubilant, delighted to celebrate life in such wonderfully exciting times.

Milly was the only one who managed to stay grumpy, as though taking no notice whatsoever of the light, the chirping birds and the greenery.

Milly was stressed.

Her Hostess duties included taking attendance, and that could not be done yet because of *that red-coated traitor*. Millie tended to exaggerate the peccadilloes when she became annoyed at someone. It was quite true though that Fox Theo was nowhere to be seen. Either he was running late, or was not going to show up at all.

Rosie, though, had glided in right on time, carrying a stack of notes covered with indecipherable cat hieroglyphics. Rosie proceeded to attach the notes to the adjacent Magnolia Tree in two parallel lines, from top down, flowing in a cascading fashion. It became clear that the Cat was prepping for a Speech, and her DIY teleprompter was at the ready.

Milly was not prepared for this turn of events. This is not how a Meeting should run. Milly envisioned that Zip and Fox would take assigned seats by the Fire Pit. That she, Milly, would formally introduce "the Speaker of the Morning, Cat Rosie." Then Rosie would give her presentation and, finally, the audience would ask their questions during a *Q&A Session* emceed by Milly.

Without Fox Theo, the audience was embarrassingly inadequate. Milly was nervous and biting her hind paw fitfully, as if chasing an imaginary flea.

Zip came to his sister's rescue.

"Rosie," he said with the solemn politeness required by the occasion, "We all look forward to your Speech, but to warm up, could we begin with a *Q&A Session* about your fine presentation yesterday morning?"

"How do you mean, Zip?" Rosie frowned and wrapped her tail around her. She'd worked on her speech all night, and it contained a few jokes that she'd been dying to try out on a live audience. She knew that the jokes were funny in Feline, but sad experienced warned her that something was often lost in the translation to Canine.

"It's just that there are parts I don't understand," Zip smiled disarmingly, "I've been reading the transcript all night too, and I have *Questions*. Perhaps you have *Answers*."

"It's a good idea," confirmed Milly, "I don't get it either."

Outnumbered, the Cat yielded graciously. She jumped off her improvised lectern, the high ground on the Fire Pit wall, shook her front paws to clean off a few imaginary grains of sand, and announced that she'd do her best to clear things up.

"I'm listening, Spaniels."

Zip jumped right into it.

"The Cocky Gentleman in black suit with white

shirtfront said that the Fire Pit and the path are *incorrect,* and *not on grade,* need to be demolished," Zip twisted his neck and looked under his paws at the path, trying to establish what was incorrect about it. The path ran solidly from the House to the Fire Pit and showed no sign of being *incorrect.*

"It's all this talk about *GRADE,* Rosie, I just don't get it," Zip opened transcript on his computer screen and scrolled to page 110.

"Here. Look at LINE 5.

"The cocky Human in black suit with white shirtfront keeps talking about GRADE,"

Old Lady's House is not ON GRADE

....

The Fire Pit and path are entirely not ON GRADE

Zip searched around with his eyes, and declared with persuasion: "I think we better find this *GRADE,* or else Old Lady is in trouble," said Zip.

Milly, whose reading was a lot slower than her thinking, and whose thinking was often overly concerned with appearances, perked up.

"Fire Pit? Where are we going to receive our guests if there's trouble with the Fire Pit?"

"Where will we *live*?" Zip cut to the chase.

"What's the trouble with the *grade,* exactly?" asked Rosie matter-of-factly, as though she had spent years discussing grades.

In truth, the whole thing made no sense to the Cat either. However, as is so often the case with experts, she was not willing to come clean about the limits of her expertise.

"That's what I don't get," confessed Zip, and started scrolling furiously up and down the screen.

"Here!"

Three noses moved in together and three pairs of eyes squinted at the page.

It read:

Approved hydraulic models will be submitted to the Administrator.

The Administrator will determine if the construction activity is on grade.

"I see the trouble," Rosie pointed to the words with her feather pointer. "The Administrator thinks Old Lady's activity not *on grade*. He ordered to take it out."

"Take out the activity?" a bewildered Milly asked.

"The consequences of the activity," explained Rosie patiently, "whatever Old Lady had built."

The Cat looked around the yard and up to the house, and added bluntly, "In fact, *most* of what Old Lady built has gotta go."

Both Spaniels jumped up and set their tail stubs in the air, growling, "We disagrrrreee! We built nothing! We bought it readymade. Everything was already here!"

"Old Lady disagrees as well," noted Rosie. "She is *objecting,* demanding that these Zoning folk show her where exactly this grade lies—and at least what this grade looks like."

"Rosie," admitted Zip, "Fox Theo and I looked for this *grade* all yesterday afternoon. Until sunset, we dug around. Even dug *under* the path, looking for it."

Zip nodded at the fresh tunnel, at least two foxes in diameter, which started near the Fire Pit and ended in a large hole, closer to the Ravine.

"It's *not there*. Unless it's even deeper," asserted Zip.

"You two dug for it?" smirked the Cat.

"I asked Theo's help looking for the grade because Old Lady said she could not find it. She demanded that the Zoning people tell her where exactly the grade was."

"Give me a few moments to fire up that video

again," said Rosie. "I'll review with you some of the important parts of the Hearing."

The video was running and noses glued to the screen.

On the screen, Old Lady was getting a bit rowdy:

Where is it?

How do you define it?

You don't have a definition!

Your Administrator simply draws a line in people's yards, and calls it grade!

"Well, the Administrator *is* entitled to a bit of discretion," sneered one of the Zoning people crowd.

After that, the altercation between Old Lady and the City worsened.

Old Lady kept asking where the Zoning People hid the *grade*.

The Zoning People did not want to talk about the *grade* at all, but steered the inquisition to one single side issue: the reasonableness of Old Lady's clean-up after the flood.

"You could have dried out everything and re-used it," they insisted.

"You ever smelled dried-out flood water?!" snapped Old Lady in retort.

"I'm curious," mocked a deep man's baritone, "You're so sensitive about the smells. If food goes bad in your kitchen, you throw it out together with the pot?"

Zip looked up from the screen, lost and furious.

"I still can't figure it out," he said. "Why does this White Ruff fellow ask Old Lady what she does with rancid food? Here, listen to him again," Zip poked laptop keys with the stub of his recently trimmed claw, "Would you listen to this, dear Expert Rosie . . . Milly, be quiet a sec," Zip pushed another key, and all the animals froze, afraid to move.

A man's baritone went on mockingly, "How do you react to rancid food in your kitchen? You must tear out the ceiling? Or sheetrock off all the walls?"

"What are you talking about? What rancid food?" blurted out Old Lady.

Milly went on the attack, "We don't *have* any rancid food. Our food never goes bad; we eat it right away, or share with Theo."

"She's right," sounded an energetic voice. The Cannas swayed, giving way to Fox Theo. "The Spaniels have never offered any ill-smelling food. And you can be sure that we Foxes have superior sense of smell!"

"Theodore, dear," mumbled Milly, "you are welcome, love."

Milly's head was spinning a little, "We learned so much—"

"So, what was the result of the Zoning Hearing?" asked Theo business-like. "Do you understand?"

Zip did not. By page 150 of the Transcript, he got sick to his stomach. "I got so nervous that I still can't quite calm down," he confessed.

Rosie interjected to explain: "Your Old Lady has until the end of year to dig up everything that's not *ON GRADE*. After that, the City'll start fining her."

"When will they stop?" asked Milly pleadingly.

"They'll fine every day."

"Every day until when," asked Fox with unexpectedly zesty inquisitiveness.

"Indefinitely," responded the Cat, obviously enjoying the long word. "Until the fine is so big that they can take the house for non-payment, most likely."

Zip's jaw dropped in horror. Milly whined, then yelped, "I see it, the *GRADE* is right over there!" and leaped two steps along the path.

By the time Zip hastened up to her, Milly was already lying on her stomach in the sand, covering an empty spot with her front paw.

"No, Zip," admitted Milly, glancing along the path melancholically, "False alarm. I don't see that grade lying on the path either. Must've been tears in my eyes."

❧

Always the pragmatist, Cat Rosie produced a long yellow pad and a black pencil adorned with an outline of a cat and a pumpkin, and coughed out a fur ball for Spaniel's attention, "Zip and Milly, I need to ask you a question."

"I'm being interviewed as well?" Fox invited himself.

"Nobody's asking you anything," hissed Rosie, "You were tardy for my lecture."

"What's the question, Cat?" snapped Zip.

The Cat was knowledgeable, but he was beginning to dislike her snippy attitude toward Theo.

"The question is . . .," the Cat spoke slowly and solemnly, "who'd want to do this? Do you two have enemies? Anyone upset with you enough to want you ousted from your home?"

The siblings looked askance at Rosie, then at each other and, slowly, shook their heads.

Zip usually kept to himself, and Milly was too

sweet to everybody to ever ruffle any feathers. Who would be nasty enough to try and turn two inoffensive Spaniels out of their beloved home?

The Cat kept holding up her feather and asked insistently "Are you absolutely sure that there's nobody you might've offended lately?"

The Spaniels considered the issue again, but yet again hit a blank wall. Nobody was that nasty and mean-spirited. And besides, even the frogs in the yard loved them.

"I was ordered to keep my *sss-sss-silence*," Fox imitated Rosie's hiss, and added his own shrill Fox note of distaste, "*Yu-ya-ya*! But I'll speak up! This is about my friends—"

"As well as free food," interjected Rosie, cynically. She arched her back and bared her claws at Theo's impudence.

"Meeting time is almost over," declared Milly. At that moment, her thoughts about her Meeting were a mixture of pride and alarm.

My Meeting has ended up being even more engaging than Freckle's. It was not boring at Freckle's, but my guests are engaged almost to the point of scrimmage. Involving this Expert may yet end up costing a scratched-out eye or half an ear.

"I just learned from Freckle," panted Theo, also

smelling a possible beginning of a tussle and so jumping straight into delivery of the rumor.

"What?" sighed Milly.

"Freckle's Human had another Meeting with the two Human buddies, Paul and Steve. Freckle overheard them *planning*. Old Lady's House will be auctioned off. She'll owe debt to Ducklingburg, bigger than her House."

"How do they know that?" asked Zip.

"Never mind how they know, I think we now know who wants you out of the House," hissed the Cat, triumphantly. To her credit, she did not say "I told you so!"

"This means that Freckle's Human made up his mind?!" yelped Milly, finally understanding, "He wants to take away our home?"

None of the animals responded.

The Cat shrugged and started collecting her supplies. "So, now you know," she said, "and I believe my job is done here."

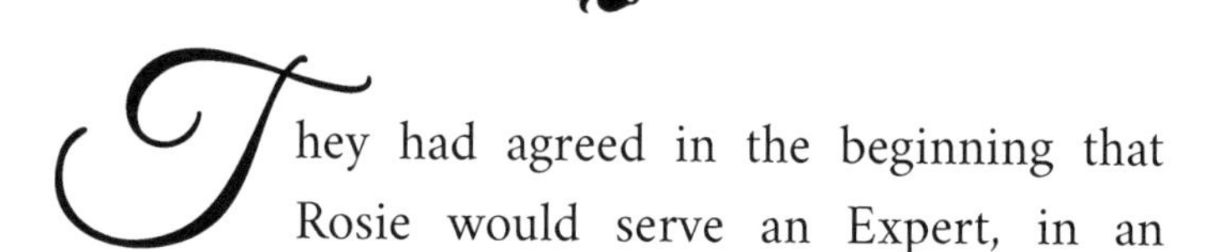

They had agreed in the beginning that Rosie would serve an Expert, in an educational capacity. The education was complete: both dogs were wizened up about the circumstances.

"We thank you for your Expert input," started Milly, but her lips were trembling and drooling too much to go on. The role of hostess weighed heavily on her shoulders right then.

"Your case is shit," Rosie delivered her summary. "Allow me one unsolicited advice. As your friend . . . as your neighbor . . . I am telling you:

GET A LAWYER!

And a good, vicious lawyer preferably. NOT pro bono."

And with that, she started homeward.

This time, despite the crushing finale to their Meeting, Zip as a gentledog had the good grace to take over carrying Cat's props.

In retrospect that night, he would recall his courtesy to Rosie as the only aspect of the day that gave him any pleasure.

24

GETTING A LAWYER

Chez Clochette's curtilage was just barely wide enough for the string of twelve round cast-iron outdoor tables. Every evening after five, the place grew posh. The tables were dressed up with white linens and the cast-iron chairs covered with plump red-and-white cushions embroidered with sheep and bells. The wine came in flights.

Lariska raised her face to the sky.

Ducklingburg has such a high, happy sky. At the moment, it was partly cloudy with only a whisper of sunset—two fluffy blobs of cloud floating in flamingo-streaked blue.

Lariska sighed: she had not thought about the sky in a long time.

And, just like that, a decision came.

She will be happy. Divorce that palling husband. No hesitation. She was ready.

The only real question was the means: a good lawyer. Ruthless. Honest. And one that would not ask too many questions.

Where to find one like that?

Lariska took in the view.

Chez Clochette offered a strategic position on *Phantom Plaza*—one of Ducklingburg's most beautiful promenades. The foot traffic had to flow past *Chez Clochette*'s front tables to get from the South end of the *Phantom Plaza* (where the attractions were: the Wish Fountain in front of the *Sleepy Leopard Inn,* the bronze statue of an elephant climbing a slippery ball half his size) to the North End of the *Phantom Plaza* (*Canard Movie Theater,* a pastry shop, a spa, an upscale oyster establishment, a hip sushi dive and two competing diamond dealers unoriginally named "*Forever*" and "*Together*").

Whatever part of the Plaza invited one's fancy, one had to stroll through the part of the promenade that housed *Chez Clochette* and its open-air front table that Lariska called "hers."

Milly was the first to spot Lariska.

"I don't like her."

"Behave," snarled back Zip, as he forced a welcoming smile, "there will be delicious bread basket," and pulled his leash tight, careening expectantly toward Lariska's table.

"She always shares from our bread basket without invitation."

"Smile!"

Lariska was waving at them already, "Here!"

Old Lady shortened the leashes, "Behave, both of you! Sit!"

From under the table, where Zip and Milly were shown, the view was not bad either.

Lariska's shoes shared the under-table space with them, her bare heels resting on the polished quartz side of a decorative herb planter.

"Smells like childhood," murmured Lariska, and four heads—two Human and two canine—turned towards the fragrant herbs. Lariska leaned in to pick up her shoe, but changed her mind mid-way. Instead, she reached for the planter, pulling a few fragrant needles off the trailing rosemary bush. She rubbed them in her fingers and inhaled the smell,

"Smells like Grandma's forest—pine and camphor."

"It's *your* forest now," corrected Old Lady.

"Can't think of it that way, still. And miss my Grandma. She was a great Old—" Lariska broke off. Grandma was Old Lady's contemporary.

One would never guess looking at her, mused Lariska for the umpteenth time, and surreptitiously surveyed her friend with an exacting professional eye, appraising Old Lady with the skill of one trained for the final fittings of custom-tailored gowns, of one skilled in identifying the smallest imperfection. Lariska noted with displeasure that there were no signs of imperceptibly sagging mouth corners, no hint of bulldog cheeks. Gravity was powerless over Old Lady. All that the eye could see was radiant skin, healthy skin with pinkish undertones that reminded Lariska of ripening Summer apples.

The waiter interrupted the awkward pause.

"Bread time!" said Zip, and shuffled closer to Old Lady.

"With cheese sticks!" echoed Milly.

Distracted by anticipation of the real Human food, both dogs forgot to listen to the women's chatter.

Old Lady thanked Lariska for supplying two consignments of amber.

"Oh yes, both orders arrived safely, in Spain and Belgium. Much obliged. Exactly what was needed."

Lariska thanked Old Lady for the payment.

"You are such a prompt business lady! I have a gift for you," Lariska dug into her purse and slid a ring-sized paper box towards Old Lady. Inside, there was a brooch with dark amber from Grandma's . . . now Lariska's amber mine.

Lariska and Old Lady smiled at each other, each satisfied.

Lariska had gainfully unloaded the defective homespun handiwork of some nameless Avossian craftsman.

In turn, Old Lady acquired another chunk of that rare type of amber, the dark Avossian only produced by a handful of soils. Indispensable material for her experiment. Neither Russian nor Polish, nor African amber would suit.

The bread arrived—in a warm, aromatic basket covered with a bright cotton napkin.

"Another basket," Old Lady added to her order, "for my Spaniels."

The waiter's feet departed. The two dogs

stretched out their noses and licked them simultaneously. The conversation above the table had started out on a tedious tack. Old Lady and Lariska discussed new outfits. Old Lady now wanted Lariska's help with fitting blouses and scouting scarves.

"No more dresses? Could you be broadening your business?" was curious Lariska, "preparing for business meetings? Would those be morning meetings or evening meetings? Cocktail attire for the parties?"

"No parties. Nothing flashy." Old Lady paused, screwed up her face, and added hastily, "for my appearances in the Federal Court."

The dogs stirred, swallowed the drool, and pricked up their ears.

"Chew slower; take it easy with the chomping," said Zip.

"You should talk," snapped Milly.

Old Lady's warm hand reached down to Milly and offered a bite dipped on one end into the greenish olive oil.

"Shush, shhh, Milly!," hissed Zip, "I want to hear this!"

"You'll tell me in detail later," reacted Milly lackadaisically, as she lifted her upper lip and inclined her muzzle slightly to gently accept the proffered bread without touching Old Lady's palm.

But, for a while, Zip listened in vain for anything further of interest. Above the table, the only sound was light clicking of the forks and knives. The candles for the table came out and Lariska said she'd like more wine.

She was in no haste to go back home. Nobody was. There was never any haste at Chez Clochette. That's where you came to be still and let the world wash through you. The evening set, the waiters buzzed bringing in wine by the flights,—and waves of beautiful people drifted past the wine lovers, so close that if you got drunk enough to reach your hand out into the foot traffic, you could touch the silk and linen on the passing bodies.

And the foot traffic was only one part of the attraction. Even more exciting was the narrow—barely one lane—pebbled auto drag. There, luxury cars circled very slowly, the drivers pausing completely to accept handshakes and kisses from the pedestrian traffic. Showing off the glimmer of its wax, each car acted as though it were starring in its own, private luxury automobile commercial.

❧

The conversation did not resume until the teaspoons clanged in teacups.

"What do you think about divorce?" Lariska blurted out.

Old Lady did not hesitate a bit: "Why not? If you don't love your husband? Easy."

Old Lady fluently supported conversations on any topic, but never spoke about her own life. Among the very few things that Lariska knew about Old Lady was that she herself would not rely on a man for happiness, and that her approach to marital problems was same as to all problems—on the surgical side. *Cut. Cut wide and deep. Don't let the gangrene spread.*

"You said yourself," Old Lady strained for the idiom Lariska had just used describing their surroundings: "You saw fishes."

"A lot of fish in the sea," agreed Lariska.

"The fish here are pretty," Old Lady switched back to Russian. "Sounds like your fish at home stinks. So, look for better fish."

Lariska did not answer.

"Why not?" inquired Old Lady conversationally.

"He told me he'll destroy me if I leave," explained Lariska frankly.

"Destroy?" Old Lady paused, considering the meaning of it. "That's love? He wants you as his wife or nobody has you?"

"Mostly, he wants me dead," said Lariska.

Not taken aback, Old Lady gave her verdict, "Divorce the stinky goat."

And nodding almost imperceptibly toward the traffic washing over the Plaza, she added, "Look! Your fish!"

And there sure was fishing in progress at Phantom Plaza.

Tonight, there were sightings of a Lamborghini slowly making a circle around the drag, then pausing at the Wish Fountain, where it caused a stir from the outdoor seats of Sleepy Leopard Inn patrons, circled again, and finally snatched a prime parking space by the entrance of *Chez Clochette,* came to rest, and raised its scissor doors. The prime parking spaces for the luxury cars were so close that front tables could feel the heat of the engines when the cars pulled in.

Of course, unlike in New York or Chicago, circling around for parking was not a necessity in Ducklingburg. One could just as easily park a hundred yards away, where the architects of *Phantom Plaza* conceived two complimentary three-story-stacked parking lots. The free parking was straight behind the shops, only a one-minute walk to *Chez Clochette,* even in high heels. But if one invested a small fortune in a showcase car, what would be the use of parking out of sight?

Besides, cruising was part of the Plaza's attraction. The convertibles lingered so close to the tables that the wine drinkers could lean in to give the driver a hug without leaving their seats. Still beautiful second-, third-, and fourth- time bachelorettes flocked to the Plaza from all over Ducklingburg to evaluate their motoring options. Some of the motorists were not in the first bloom youth either. But the cars themselves were all in the very best condition.

Both Zip and Milly were perplexed by this ostentatious display of automobiles.

"What is it Humans see in it?" wondered Zip. "All cars smell the same on the outside, like gasoline fumes. I read somewhere that car exhaust is just as bad for you as flood water."

"Really?" Milly retreated a little deeper under the table and opined that "the view from here is just as good and much healthier as far as fumes are concerned."

"Anyway, on the inside, the cars smell differently.

Leather or synthetics. Or, sometimes, stale cigarette smoke."

Neither of the Spaniels thought it worthwhile to devote any further attention to the topic of showy automobiles.

Together with evening cool, the Southern thick darkness fell.

"Another day escaped," uttered Lariska lazily. Privately, she switched her watching gaze from the Plaza crowd to Old Lady, again.

Why does she keep instructing me "Lariska, dear, dress me like a Lady, even if I'm old"?

I've seen my share of old in dressing rooms. She hides her figure, but I've noticed: her back is neither crooked as a hook, nor stiff like an ossified stick. No extra sagging under arms, no podgy rolls. Her shoulders . . . arms . . . I'd kill to look like that right now, let alone at her age. And not a word about her past.

Bored, Milly buried her nose in the soft needles of rosemary bush, lapsed into a snooze, and whistled slightly as she began to snore. Zip, just the opposite, crawled out further to better see the Human faces in the twilight of thickening evening. He knew for sure that it was the time of day when Human spoke in soft, mysterious voices of things that mattered. And he was right. Lariska was not in the mood for any more relaxed chit-chat,

"You ever hired a lawyer? How does one pick a good one?"

"I have a theory," Old Lady said, only answering the last question. She was never too keen on talking about her business.

"I have no use for theories," Lariska said vehemently.

Zip growled impatiently. Lariska was full of shortcomings.

Always "I." Always talks and talks about herself.

And always nips the bread from our basket. 'Mind if I borrow from dog's basket?'

And table manners?! NONE! Chews and swallows just like Theo after a bummed hunt.

"I interviewed a dozen firms, at least," Lariska rattled off. "Same story, every time.

"First hour they waste on puffery: they are the best, they'll fight the hardest.

"They call themselves *Attorneys of the Year* . . . or is it *of the Month*? Every one of them.

"After blowing smoke, they all demand retainer—at a minimum ten thousand.

"And that's even the ones without a real office, the rent-a-room-by-the-hour. I can see it's not their office, can't I? Nothing on the walls. The license in frame a propped up on the desk. . . . And frames with photos of their happy family, spread around the bookshelf behind them. I'm there to get divorced, not to get their happy familyness rubbed in my face!"

Old Lady did not respond, taking in her friend's rant.

"How good could they be," went on Lariska, "renting rooms by an hour . . . like—"

Lariska caught her breath. "One time, I swear it, I even spotted that "Super-Lawyers-of the Year" clearing out of "his" office *minutes* after our interview ended. Frames and puffery certificates tucked under his arm. He had to clear the place for the next "Super-lawyer," just as "talented," I'm sure."

Old Lady did not make a sound for the duration of her friend's rant, sitting back and half-smiling mildly.

Lariska was panting now and—Zip could sniff it — had worked herself into despair,

"So how do you choose a lawyer? A *theory* you said?"

"I read a book this year," Old Lady answered quietly. A local lawyer wrote it. Funny title. Something like "*Stiff Your Divorce Lawyer.*"

"Stupid. I have no intention of stiffing. Stiffing??

Like I'd provide you amber, but you wire nothing to my Spain account? Or I dress you, but you—" Lariska stopped herself, and stuttered, "I'm only saying . . . that's an imaginary example."

"The book is mostly not about stiffing, but about how to tell a good lawyer from the bad ones."

"How?" asked Lariska quickly.

"It's over 400 pages. You'd have to read."

"Who did you say wrote it?"

"Portia Porter. She's a local lawyer."

"You know her? I don't think I'll read that book. I detest con-artists."

It checks out, concluded Zip, *I knew it! Lariska cannot read. She was not born here, in America. She can speak. But reading is harder; lots of unfamiliar words.*

"Where is Portia's office?"

"Nowhere. Out of her house. A condo, actually . . . and no need to snort, Lariska. You don't have an amber business office or a couturier name for your dressmaker business. Still—we *know* you are the best. You've got real talent, Lariska."

"You been to that condo?"

"Not yet."

"Why are you pushing for that Portia then?"

"I liked her book. She spots weak links a mile away."

I get it, nodded Zip, *that Portia knows when to yell objection! And why she has to yell it. She's ready right away to complain to the Judge's boss. Demand her rights. The Judge knows it too. She will protest to higher courts!*

"She writes her own appeals," Old Lady bent her pinky.

Exactly like I thought! Zip noted proudly.

"She does not lie," Old Lady bent her ring finger.

That's not necessarily a helpful habit, thought Zip dolefully.

"That's not always an advantage," Lariska echoed Spaniel's thought. "According to TV shows, the lawyers' only job is bamboozling. Bamboozle the judge, the jury, the other lawyers, everybody. Besides, who needs the truth?"

"She is afraid of nothing," kept bending fingers Old Lady.

"Doesn't know enough to be afraid? A little stupid?" clarified Larisa.

"Not exactly. She's a fearless fighter when the law is on her side. But, if the fight is both expensive and futile, she's not afraid to tell her client to fold."

"What's there to be afraid of?" Lariska asked.

Not a tactics pro, concluded Zip. *Can't make much money off telling clients they should fold.*

Cat Rosie taught the Spaniels well and they remembered firmly:

For litigators, the money's in the fight.

"She's not afraid to piss off her clients," kept listing Old Lady. A client might misunderstand, conclude she won't or can't fight—when, in fact, she just can't go against the law."

"Sure," agreed Lariska, "that would be a waste of clients' money."

Lariska took pride in her own professional integrity—she would rather forgo her commission than foist off a dress that did not flatter a figure. "I get it."

Explains Portia's law firm being headquartered in a condo, thought Zip.

"She's not connected," said Old Lady without chagrin.

"She's no good then. Who you know is *everything*." Lariska's voice trailed off hesitantly.

"Don't be hasty, Larisochka. Connections are complex. Suppose you hire a connected Lawyer X, best buddies with the Judge's cousin. A powerful connection. But if that Judge's Cousin is also besties with your opposition . . . well, Lawyer X will sell you out."

Makes sense, acknowledged Zip blushing a little. *Take me and Theodore. Suppose I knew that Theo pirated some hens. I got my obligations to the humans, of course, but . . . What am I gonna do—set neighbors' dogs on him —Max, Bella, Lucky, or that little mitten of a dog from across the street?*

But never!!!

I'll look the other way.

To hell with justice!

Theodore's my friend. To hell with all the hens, together with their fresh eggs.

"Plus," Old Lady bent her final left-hand finger, "this Portia is an extremely *arrogant* young person."

Arr-arr-arrogant, Zip quietly tried on, sinking his teeth into the double-r sounds. *Don't get that one.*

"Arrogant? How so? Which way?" demanded Lariska.

Old Lady was silent.

Gotta Google that Portia first chance I get, decided Zip.

"That can go either way," Old Lady said rather cryptically.

Turn all the internet upside down to research that Portia, committed himself Zip.

"I'm getting the divorce whatever it takes," decided Lariska, "it's so much beauty, everywhere you look. Especially in the evening. And, quite honestly, I wouldn't mind a bit of trolling for the fish that swim here."

Lariska was right.

After dusk, the festival of lights wrapped around every tree and fixture, strung from every building corner, lent a bit a charm to every passerby, even to faces that in harsh daylight were worn and shabby. Warm, inviting, lights.

Old Lady tugged on the leashes. Milly half-opened her eyes, stretched into the downward-facing dog position, then up-facing dog, her eyes opening wider, at the lights smiling at her everywhere.

"It's already Christmas?!" she whined merrily.

Milly was perfectly right. Every night was Christmas at *Chez Clochette*.

25

SLEEPLESS NIGHT

The night before the depositions was sleepless and interminable.

Old Lady had determined that they'd all retire early and put in a good night's sleep. But that was not in the cards.

To begin with, the moon, which was round and self-important that night, plopped down on the bamboo floor of Old Lady's bedroom and lit every corner and crevice with a preternatural aura. There was not one nook left unlit, not one of the cozy shadows that the Spaniels used for lurking while they waited for Old Lady to slip into dreams and steady her breathing—enough that the Spaniels' path into her bed was clear.

Not one tiny shadow.

The fiery ball of the moon hung resolutely high in the far sky, above Fox Forest. You could count the spots on Zip's nose in the light.

"Don't even think about climbing into her bed until the moon's gone," warned Zip.

"'Course not," submitted Milly, then reminisced, "It's not like in Big Water days anymore. No way we'd climb into Old Lady's bed while she's still awake."

"There are two sides to every coin," sighed Zip.

"Ever since Big Water came, the dark side of the coin is larger," retorted Milly and settled for the night right beside the bedroom door. She carefully calculated the positioning of her ears and paws to avoid Old Lady's step and stumble if she should happen to saunter around the house for a midnight constitutional.

Zip snapped at a nonexistent fly and shook his whole body, flapping ears and cheeks. He was worried about the next day's events even more than his mistress.

Zip just did not feel prepared.

Milly and Zip had gotten almost no advance notice, plainly not enough to educate themselves adequately about the looming event.

"Zip," Milly stretched out, her nose reaching into

a bright beam of moonlight and glittering in places where it caught the ray, "What's a *deposition?*"

Zip's google search had produced incoherent ramblings that only jumbled his straightforward dog's mind. There was talk about a *court reporter*—and a picture of a harassed-looking woman who had to type down every word that everybody in the room had said. To Zip's thinking, that just did not seem possible to do at all.

Zip had tried to turn to the resident legal expert, Rosie, but the Cat was nowhere to be found: she had not spent a night at Suzy's for the past three days, and there was no response to Zip's barking and scratching at the front door of Rosie's other home, the one with the two lawyers. Such aloof behavior was not unusual for cats, but its ordinariness was hardly a consolation when one had an urgent need.

Zip panted.

The purpose of a *deposition* remained uncomfortably murky.

"It's like a Meeting, but with questions instead of food," he answered slowly.

"Questions?"

"Some Humans will ask questions, other Humans will answer," elaborated Zip, himself pleasantly surprised at how well he actually understood the process.

To seem humble, he added, "That's about all I could figure out."

"That does not sound like a Meeting at all," disliked Milly. "And no food at all? Not even treats?"

"There is a court reporter taking down every word," added Zip, and unexpectedly for himself, he made a connection: "and she cannot work if there's loud chewing. Or talking at once."

"No treats and no free participation," summed up Milly. "What sort of unfriendly, repressive court proceeding is that?!"

"Good time for a nap, if you are quiet, Milly," Zip suggested.

The uneasiness that he always got when puzzled had subsided and Zip thought that he now might be able successfully to fall asleep. He stationed himself alongside of the bedroom door, calculating his position so that Old Lady would miss him as long as she walked a reasonably straight line. Of course, if she were to sneak out of her bedroom and edge along the wall, she'd kick him squarely. But that trajectory had never happened before and wasn't worth worrying about. Zip closed his eyes, and almost succeeded in keeping the faint smell of Big Water out of his nostrils.

"Zip, are you awake?" That was Milly.

"No."

"You said the Humans will ask questions?"

"Yes."

"What will they ask, you think?" Milly's head was off her front paws, and the little lights inside her eyes flickered brightly in the moonlight.

"Go to sleep. If I knew what the questions were, I'd be Old Lady's lawyer myself," snarled Zip.

Both dogs rested their muzzles on front paws and nodded off fitfully, sentineled on either side of Old Lady's bedroom. Their snoring stopped periodically to check with a half-opened eye on the return of the shadows, so they could quietly creep into the bed.

The moon did eventually quit—turned behind the hovering corner of the neighbor's roof, and, from there, jumped behind Fox's Forest. Milly's head raised warily, but there were still no shadows.

The moon had just left Old Lady's bedroom alone when up out of nowhere came the morning star. All the shadows were chased away once again, and the whole house filled with a dim stellar light.

No shadows for the Spaniels still.

No sleep for Old Lady, either.

Old Lady had climbed into her bed before the moon started its tricks, but did not stay there for long. She got up to inspect the sky from her bedroom window, then moved to another room, where she probed the sky from a different angle. Climbed back into bed, but Spaniels heard no quieting in the breathing. In a short while, Old Lady again climbed out and shuffled to her bathroom to survey the street from the windows there.

As the night dragged on, Old Lady kept jumping in and out of the bed, floating from room to room and window to window. Her bare knees and heels and her short pajamas appeared, and sometimes reappeared, in odd rooms of the house.

"At least she stays away from the walls, or she'd for sure step on us," said Milly, backing into her wall even tighter.

Zip, who had tried following Old Lady and barely dodged an accidental kick, trotted back to Milly's side, flopped down and yawned.

"Good thing the deposition does not start too early in the morning," Zip turned on his back lazily, listening in to the sound of Old Lady rustling the window curtains.

"*They* have insomnia, too?" guessed Milly, and got up to move to a cooler part of the floor which she had not warmed up yet.

"Maybe different time-zone," Zip said and yawned again, "*They* do not live here in Duck-lingburg."

"Zip, the '*they*'—who are *they*?"

"Milly, go back to sleep. We'll know tomorrow."

"Unless Old Lady locks us in, like the last time."

"Milly, don't make a pother, and stay out of her way. Be cool, and we'll see everything."

"Zip, what if—"

"Milly, I am *sleeping*."

Until all this Big Water nonsense barged in and disrupted Old Lady's life, the days with her were pleasantly predictable. Old Lady had her routine, of which she was immensely fond.

Indeed, Old Lady's life was governed by a rule-based schedule. She woke up exactly when she felt like waking up, but usually around 7:30. She passed her time doing exactly what she felt like doing, which in the heat of summer was mostly reading. She ate exactly when she remembered that she was hungry, and cooked strictly when the Spaniels reminded her to. In short, Old Lady's life was very well organized by a simple guiding principle: there was neither downtime nor hustle nor participation in unwanted, distasteful activities at inconvenient times.

All that was out of the window now.

The early morning coolness was still hanging in the air, when the doorbell rang.

Zip and Milly, crowding each other, chased down the second floor stairs—just in time to catch the tail-end of the introductions.

A boy-man with a bouncy bright-brown forelock stretched out his hand, and smiled happily, taking no notice that Old Lady did not extend her own hand for the palm rub—the Human version of the polite butt sniff. Old Lady, did not like the palm rub, but she did not do the butt sniff either. She usually just twirled her fingers in the air instead.

The boy-man angled the finger on his unshaken hand, pointed at himself, and smiled even wider.

"You can call me Raccoon."

"Where? Raccoon where?" Zip growled with menace.

Milly sprinted and scurried to find where there might be an invading raccoon. She whizzed and circled around the odd guest, sniffed the air coming from the closing door, and smelling no danger from the outside, set off swiftly toward the kitchen.

"Not here, either," her reporting bark from the kitchen made known.

Before the dogs could investigate the rest of the house for raccoons, Old Lady caught up with their act and, working with her rather sharp and skillful knee, shoved both siblings into the windowless coat-room, a tiny square space right next to the never-used guest bathroom.

"Be quiet," she said pushing the door shut in front of their remorseful snouts.

"Didn't I warn you," snarled Zip, "It's all your fault. All the fuss!"

"You," snapped Milly, "*You* barked first! Now we're trapped here till doomsday."

"Should we try and scratch our way outta here?"

But they did not have to wait for doomsday.

Their knight in shining armor was, unexpectedly,

the very boy-man Human who had triggered their barking hullabaloo—the very traitor who was the cause of their windowless confinement in the first place. Before the dogs were even finished apportioning the blame between themselves, there was a soft scratch on the door, and they heard the doorknob turning quietly. The door was gingerly pulled open, only a sliver worth—barely enough to let out one Spaniel's muzzle.

"Doggies," came in a whisper, and a cold puff of mint chewing gum, "come here."

"Raccoon-Human! Trraitorrrr," growled Zip, and jumped, accelerating until his jaws were inches from the Human's hand, which Raccoon held out palm up —at which point Zip brought his open jaws to a stop and issued a gnawing sound, trying all the time to breathe hotly on Raccoon's trustingly outstretched fingers.

On her part, Milly made a small vibrating menacing noise without opening her mouth, a trick which she had recently picked up from the refrigerator's ice maker.

All this display was meant to warn the aggressor: *Spaniels are not to be messed with*!

We may look small, but we have enough bite force to snap apart the bone in your arm—the message was clear, albeit delivered quietly to not be caught and re-grounded. Zip even made the hairs behind his neck bristle.

But the result disappointed.

"Good doggies," praised the Raccoon-Human, clearly clueless to the animals' communiqué of murderous intent.

Undaunted, he reached inside the coatroom a little farther, pushing his shoulder in, and groped vigorously in the dark. When his hand bumped into Zip's jaws of threat, he flicked his wrist around the dog and scratched gently under Zip's collar. Which was very pleasant.

"Good doggies," repeated Raccoon-Human, and masterfully inserted his second hand to pet Milly, adding wistfully under his breath, "My grandpa gave me a pup when I was six. Looked just like you."

"Zip," whispered Milly, "we have to background check this guy. What did he do to that puppy, who looked like me?"

"You see a computer here anywhere," Zip cut her off snidely, but then remembered they were hunting dogs, and could background-check the old-fashioned, traditional Spaniel way.

Zip took a deep inhale, struggling through the

cold minty chewing gum cover, and sniffed in Raccoon's smell:

"He does not smell sick," reported Zip, "I sniff . . . Human fur wash—two kinds . . . make that three kinds. He's an omnivore. I smell pizza, but it's faint. Non-smoker. I smell paper. Smell ink. I do not smell a threat, Milly. But all the same, we should check out his Facebook account. Just to be safe."

There were now additional strange voices in the kitchen, and a new, quietly insistent voice, called out,

"RACCOON, we are starting."

"Sorry, doggies, gotta run," whispered Raccoon-Human, and started backing out. He left the door slightly ajar, just enough space for two eager Spaniel snouts to push through. And, like two pieces of quicksilver, Zip and Milly were free.

"Quietly," whispered the Raccoon-Human, bending down, his face close to the Spaniels' noses, "Quiet-ly!"

Zip calmed down his tail, and Raccoon-Human asked him, "Friends?"

Before either dog could answer, their new friend jerked open the door of the adjoining guest bathroom, and disappeared inside, noisily flushing the toilet and briefly running water in the sink. Then the bright brown forelock bounced out and they heard their new friend whisper,

"Should anybody ask, you tell them I got lost on my way to the washroom and let you out accidentally." He winked.

"RACCOON," the same low voice persisted, "we're live."

The depositions started.

"Keep your head down," turned Zip to his sister "don't make waves . . . hide under the dining table . . . duck!"

"But I can't see *anything* from here," whined Milly.

26

FRECKLE'S CHOICE

Of all the buddies of her Humans, the one whom Freckle despised the most was Cheap Steve, who wanted to be called Builder Steve.

Every conversation with Builder Steve started and ended with the same topic: Old Lady's House. Specifically, how Steve wanted to "smoke her out" of her house. And then Cheap Steve'd blabber about "striking it rich." How rich they'd all "strike" when they'd "build up" on Old Lady's land.

Which, if I understand this correctly, Freckle thought, *sounds a lot like a plan of plopping a noisy housing development right across the Forest. Thoroughly obnoxious!*

"Rich, rich, rich! . . .Build, build, build!"

All talk, scoffed Freckle. Cheap Steve did not smell like a rich builder in the least.

Freckle seriously considered stealing Steve's shoe and peeing in it as an expression of her distaste. She postponed it only not to disappoint Matthew.

As measured by the Fox community's Code of Ethics, Freckle had ample justification to despise Steve's plan.

For starters, no honorable fox is ever going to try and seize a neighbor's burrow. That's just bad form. A pirate who'd try such a stunt would earn himself nothing but a fairly well torn fur.

But even if, by some miracle, one *could* succeed with this lowlife move and manage to turn out the legitimate owner and squat in somebody else's burrow, that would not be the end of it. The offender's reputation would be mud with the whole neighborhood, to be forever shunned by one and all. *Heck,* thought Freckle, *for certain even one's own relatives would shun the guile and perfidy.*

But even aside from the moral side of the matter . . . Old Lady's land was *on the wrong side of the Bridge*! That's just rotten real estate sense.

Freckle's father Theo, painstakingly taught every litter good sense of Forest real estate.

Location.

Location.

Location.

The best and roomiest burrow under the best and sturdiest of the oaks is not a good location if it does not stay dry when the weather turns foul.

Old Lady's House sat right by the Ravine, and Sneaky Creek was out of control these last couple years. The smallest drizzle—and Sneaky Creek would jump up and out of its banks. No straight-thinking fox would live there, not for any treats.

Even Freckle's poorest relatives—and there were some really poor foxes in Freckle's extended family —avoided those parts of the woods that bordered the Ravine on *that* side of the Bridge.

The tastiest chipmunks and mice never made homes in those parts where Sneaky Creek was sure to flood.

Let's face it, Freckle reasoned with herself, *Old Lady's House is in an undesirable part of town. Why would we move to that bad part?*

Especially since Freckle and her Human Matthew already lived in the very best part of town!?

Madness!

Freckled adored the golf course and worshipped

the grounds of the Scared Hare Country Club. And who knows what sort of food Freckle would get if they moved away from Scared Hare Country Club and its plentiful kitchen? Freckle's dad Theo gossiped that Old Lady occasionally stooped to serving the dry pills food for dinner. The pills make a pelting noise when they fall into the feeding bowl and, when you eat them, there's neither good smell nor pleasant taste. They just make your stomach heavy.

No, the Country Club feeding was much healthier.

Let's be fair to Steve, noted Freckle, *on this one issue they did see eye-to-eye: the contaminated water must stay away from the Golf Club's golf courses.*

The game of golf must go on!

The games, the fancy feasts, the festive frolics, all that must go on, must be protected above all. If turning the Bridge into a dam was what it took to protect this life, so be it. So what if the contaminated water floods upstream from the Bridge? Why should Freckle care?

On this point, Freckle sided with the lot who run around the green and swing their special sticks. *We do not care what occurs upstream! Survival of the fittest,* Freckle reminded herself. *The Greater Good is served.*

That notion was drilled into her head since Fox

Kit School. Although, they also taught that nobody wins going against the pack, no matter how fit the deserter might be.

And they were sure a fit pack—her human Matthew and his friends Paul and Steve. They walked and talked and play-attacked each other just like a pack.

Old Lady's fall was just a matter of time, the way Freckle worked it out thinking logically. But in her heart, Freckle could not shake off a small voice that disagreed with logic: even though Old Lady could not win against a pack, what if she was sly enough to twist her way out of danger?

After all, Freckle was herself an outlier: Freckle did not make *her* fortune by following the pack.

No, Freckle was not a conformist.

She had gone against the pack's wisdom early on.

She had refused to play the soul-sucking game of dead quail paw. She dared to climb up the social lift and look for a Golf Club career. She ducked, and twisted, and shook off the murderous chase of her spiteful Rich Relatives . . . And look at Freckle now! Under the sponsorship of her influential Human, she has become the mistress of the entire golf course. All the golf balls hidden in every crook and cranny and bush and valley were hers to play with.

And the feeding! Country Club food had all of the vitamins a fox could need. But more than mere nutrition, it was aroma therapy.

Yes, proper food is so much more than just a means to survival! Proper food is a path to higher station in life. No more wasting away, digging for mice and compromising one's morals and safety in engineering and execution of underground passages for chicken coop robbery. Instead, a Country Club Fox walks proudly along the life's path, always well-fed and, thus, able to afford to be well-mannered and kind to those less fortunate.

At the Country Club, life floated along in the lap of luxury; every visitor to the Club cared for as lovingly as Freckle's mother, Whitepaw, looked after her fox kits. Every guest here fed as plentifully as the kits feasted that memorable weekend when Theo's hunting fell into a good streak and he returned home with that enormous snow-white hen.

Endless, boundless feast of a lifetime. Everyday life at the Country Club was a fairytale.

What cause would one have to move away from this dignified way of living, only to huddle in a strange new burrow on the bad side of the ravine with no apparent food supply?

That was madness! Steve was bonkers, plain and simple.

And what was more, the Country Club was not just Freckle's feed and shelter. It was Freckle's *career*. Matthew's pack-member Paul had taunted Freckle, calling her a welfare-moocher, but Freckle knew that he was wrong; she made an honest living, working as the Country Club Celebrity.

Celebrity success did not come to the lazy ones. Sure, the rewards were high, but it was a lot of work. And Freckle did not shy away from hard work. She diligently jumped every golf club put in front of her. She posed and twirled her beauty of a tail, and she made sure that everyone was pleased to see her. She lifted Spirits. Chased away the Worry. She earned her chicken dinners fair and square. And she earned the melon pieces too.

In a short time since she'd started her employment, Freckle had become quite indispensable at the Club. Any time now, they'll formalize her role and get around to renaming the Scared Hare Club to the Red Fox Country Club. Freckle heard a rumor that somebody had already prepared the petition for that renaming. Freckle hoped that her renown would redound to the benefit of the life of every fox in all the surrounding Forest.

The business of "smoking out" Old Lady was the sole pestilent fly in the ointment of Freckle's otherwise dreamy life. Worst of all, she could not really decide which way she leaned. Was she against Old Lady or on Old Lady's side?

Freckle's confusion was deepened by Matthew's noncommittal stance. Despite strong propaganda from his pack, Freckle's Human was teetering. He did not say *no* to the pack's plan of "smoking out," "building up" and "striking rich," but he was in no hurry to open the hunting season on Old Lady.

Because Freckle's Human was indecisive, the little fox chose to hedge her bets by acting as an *undercover blabbermouth*. She would eavesdrop on her Human's pack but refrain from betraying any plans directly. However, she would also blabbermouth everything to her Daddy. After all, what dutiful daughter could withhold juicy gossip from a parent? And Theo, everybody knew, would promptly leak every single secret to Old Lady's Spaniels. Against all reason, this course of action seemed right and just to Freckle.

The balance of information is preserved, which evens out the forces while my Matthew hesitates between the camps, Freckle thought. *Plus, Daddy Theodore will be happy and seem important with his friends.*

"What's new?" Daddy Theodore announced his presence. He had strolled up the golf course with such confidence as though his daughter owned the place.

Theo was quite right to feel safe around the Scared Hare Club.

The staff Humans all had seen Freckle and knew about her "privileged" arrangement with the very important Human Matthew. Theo rightly suspected that most of non-hunting Humans were too clueless to tell one fox from another. The Club staff would just assume that any fox wandering the Club's property with such confidence must be Freckle.

Besides, Theo flattered himself, *my daughter looks a lot like me. Celebrity is in the blood and beauty in the fur.*

Freckle issued a quiet yelp of greeting and danced on the spot, waiting for Theo to approach.

"Supper, Daddy?"

"Don't mind if I do," smiled Theo, letting himself be ushered down the path towards a heap of food that Freckle saved in expectation of his visit.

"Our cook keeps over-peppering the stew, but the figs are tastier than they've been in years," said Freckle as she introduced the menu. She then added with a gardener's pride, "I personally scared off the birds from the fig tree. What do you think?"

Theo, his muzzle overstuffed with figs, managed a muffled "Eewiii oood," but wasted no time discussing the fine points of food.

"What's with your Human?" Theo jerked his head towards Matthews's open French doors, "Is he going through with *the invasion on Our Old Lady*?"

Freckle did not answer right away. The role of eavesdropper got foisted on her gradually, and she did not much like it. But she was too far along the treacherous path to start denying it now.

All because she wanted to impress her Dad.

Theo never said so out loud, but Freckle knew that he at first was not happy about her career in the Club. However, now that Freckle had worked her way up to an advisory capacity to one of Club's most important Humans, Theo was no longer embarrassed for her career choices.

"So, what's your Human thinking'?" repeated Theo, surveying the still uneaten food even as he chewed, to make sure there was enough.

The food for little ones would have to be swallowed with almost no chewing, so it stayed more flavorful when he bought it home and coughed it back out for them.

There were five mouths to feed at home, but Theo was not worried: Freckle easily provided for everybody. Her mother and her young siblings were getting positively fat.

Indeed, Theo discovered that his little daughter had completely transformed his life. He no longer had to rely on hunting. The daily stress of feeding all his young had nearly killed him. How could he not have noticed it before?! For the first time in his life, he stopped waking up with a jolt every night, worried about where the next dinner was coming from. His paw pads were no longer cracked from hours of hunting in all kinds of weather, and he even had time to play with the kits.

But there was more! Theo's social circle broadened. The Spaniels at Old Lady's house now hung on every word that Theo brought from Freckle. Theo loved the power of having information. Well-fed and powerful—what could be better?!

"Is Our Old Lady safe?" Theo repeated his question.

Freckle pushed back, unexpectedly for both of the foxes: "*Our* Old Lady?"

She twitched the end of her tail dismissively, "Since when are *we* on Old Lady's side? Are you a fan of her tasteless dog-pills now?"

“She does not always serve the dog-pills, they have chicken on the ration most d—” defended Theo, then cut himself off.

“I have not chosen a side,” said Freckle simply, “not yet,” but her tail kept twitching and she started jumping a little on one spot, to calm her nerves. Theo joined her in performing their family’s traditional relaxation exercises.

The two foxes practiced nose-down diving jumps until the tension was eased, then laid themselves down side by side under the sweet pepper bush.

“Your jumping has improved, kid,” said Theo with parental pride. Jumping—or, to be more exact, *pouncing*—was a big thing with Theo. Freckle’s mother had insisted that he bring home live vermin for kits to learn. Even in the leaner days, when the possible escape of a fat mouse was a big hit for the family larder, Freckle’s mother was a stickler for education and counted its cost as one of the necessities of a fox’s proper upbringing.

Give your kit a mouse, and you are a good parent.
Teach your kits to catch a nimble mouse, and they are good grown foxes.

“Newest litter pups must be growing up. You

started live prey training already?" asked Freckle conversationally.

Unfortunately, that innocent comment hit a sore spot with Theo. Freckle's mother had been on his tail for a week now, nagging him to bring a live capture for pounce-training purposes. But Theo had been out of practice for so long . . . Theo frowned.

"Actually, I need a favor, kid."

Freckle was about to dutifully howl "Name it, Daddy," when they were interrupted by a noise coming from Matthew's house.

"They're just about to have a Meeting," leaked Freckle, the dutiful daughter, "and it's going to be about Old Lady's House again."

"I'll run and get the Spaniels?" jumped up to his feet Theo, enjoying the thought of issuing *Invitations*.

But Freckle shook her head.

"No way, Daddy. Last time your friends were so noisy that we almost were found. And plus, I cannot hear a word over Milly's constant questions and Zip's snarky comments. And the barking? And the farting! I missed a lot what the buddy Humans said, what with my hostess duties. And my Human Matthew, he relies on me for counsel. No, I need to stay sharp."

"What are you saying?" Theo could not believe it, "You do not want me here either?"

"I need to keep my place by Matthew's boot and listen in closely," said Freckle bashfully. "Daddy, don't be upset. I won't be distracted, and we'll all understand the situation better," went on Freckle euphemistically. She did not want to say she'd *spy* better or to define who the *all* were that would *understand better*.

Puffing, Theo scrambled on his paws and started rounding up the leftover food to take home with him.

"What was the favor you wanted, Daddy," asked Freckle, hoping to repair the damage of her inhospitality.

"Oh, yes," brightened Theo, "the cook here still has the quail coop, does he?"

"Yes, of course, it's because Madam B orders quail egg omelets," said Freckle, proud to be in the know about Country Club Restaurant comings and goings. "I saved a dozen eggs for emergencies, would you like some?" Freckle stood up and was ready to usher Theo towards her emergency hiding place, but he did not move.

"Not the eggs, kid."

Freckle scratched her left armpit with her right

back paw, which contortion was an agility exercise she took to doing now when she needed to calm herself down.

"Freckle, your brothers and sisters are grown enough for pounce schooling now—" Theo paused, and Freckle understood his meaning perfectly, but stood dumbstruck, waiting for the problem to unfold in full, unignorable fashion.

Freckle hoped feverishly that she was wrong, misunderstood the situation. She even threw a wistful look toward Matthew's house, hoping for Human intervention in what promised to be a horrible position. But—just her luck—the Humans hurried inside and closed the French doors.

Father and daughter were alone, and Freckle realized that Theo had already finished talking, and she was expected to answer. The question was hanging in the air, and she repeated it from short term memory:

"—bring a live quail from the coop and so I can teach your siblings to hunt it?"

Theo was studying Freckle's horrified expression.

"Well," he said, "It will be easy enough for you to get a live quail, won't it? You are friends with the cook? We only need the one for class," Theo's eyes glistened with suspicion, "You did not turn *domesticated* and switch alliances, did you?" he hissed. "We are still foxes!"

Freckle swallowed the response she was about to give: she'd sworn to Matthew and the cook to never hunt the kitchen quail. Well, maybe not sworn in so many words, but she had understood that certain forbearances were *part of the deal* whereby she was accorded special privileges at the Club.

"You are still a wild fox, are you not?!" taunted Theo.

"Dad," Freckle pushed back, getting irritated, "can't you do it someplace away from my Club? Isn't it *your* job to educate the litter?"

She was immediately sorry for disrespecting Theo, who took umbrage.

"*YOUR* club? *MY* job?!" snarled Theo, spitting out half-chewed bite of fried egg on toast. "You're suggesting that I'm shirking my job, after all I've done for you? Have you forgotten—"

Theo choked on his retort.

How dare the little ingrate?

The fame must've gone to her head!

Has she forgotten how I'd beat my paws to bleeding, hunting and stalking and scrounging, all for her, when she was too small to even stand up on her own?

Has she forgotten her place?

Just like her mother—always eager to saddle Old Theo with a job until he stretches out all four paws and dies!

Freckle read the anger in Daddy Theo's bright yellow eyes, and lowered her nose.

"All I'm saying, Dad—"

But Theo was too smart to burn bridges with his daughter. None of the tirade that flashed through his hot minds escaped to be said out-loud.

"It's not that I don't know it's *my* job," Theo lied. "It so happens that I am out of pocket this week, a hunting injury."

Freckle bolted up her muzzle towards Daddy Theo and inhaled with full nose. There was no smell of blood or inflammation.

"What's wrong, Daddy?"

"Yellowjackets," sighed Theo, turning around so that his lush and healthy hind quarters came in full view of Freckle. There was nothing out of the ordinary with Theo's behind. It smelled healthy, too. But he continued the plaint, slowly turning back to face Freckle, as he spoke.

"I made a little blunder. Was going to wait for quail coop to go to sleep, mind you. Stumbled smack into the midst of the nest. The nasty insects must've built their nest in the ground while I was not watching.

The blasted beasts attacked me, I must've suffered thousands of stings. And you know yellow jackets, they will not let up. Stung me under the tail. Could not shake them off. I retreated rather quickly, but they would not cease their attack. Carried hundreds of the blasted soldier yellowjackets on my tail for miles. Had to sit in the Creek half the night to deal with the swelling," he moaned, "Horribly injured," concluded Theo.

"You did not seat on your tail?" asked Freckle to say something.

"Freckle, only an ignorant kit would sit around on a tail. Did I not teach you anything?! Your tail is pride and flag—" and Theo launched into a detailed spiel about importance of tail care for a fox.

Freckle half-listened, rotating her ears gently in indication of attention, but something about Theo's yellow jacket attack story did not sit quite right with her.

"Daddy, this quail coop you were casing to hunt. Where was it?"

"Doesn't matter now, those stingers know my scent, I am not going back there."

"Dad, you weren't sniffing round the *Club* quail coop, were you?"

"What if I were?" snapped Theo hot-heatedly.

"In the first place, there are no yellowjackets for miles around," said Freckle. Club patrons would not stand for it.

Yellowjackets on the Club property were relentlessly exterminated by the Grounds crew.

"What are you saying?" Theo got defensive, "there was a fresh nest, and I know it," he lied stubbornly.

"Dad, I asked you not to hunt at my Club, we'll all get in trouble. Why spoil a good thing?"

Theo threw an angered glance at Freckle. *Here he had shared with her a grievous and embarrassing injury, and all she cares about is her precious career.* Theo shook his tail and could almost feel the memory of a thousand stings. Of course, he invented the whole story, but Theo's curse was his over-active imagination. He was a Method Actor who set out to play an injured fox and got so much in character that he could not snap out.

"Dad, please stop!" Freckle leaped up in the air, arching her back, and plunged down, nose forward, like a child throwing a tantrum at the perceived unfairness.

"Dad! I implore you! You should not even be seen slinking and sniffing around the quail coop. I'll get canned."

The thought of returning back to a humdrum wild life made Freckle's left eye twitch.

Worse, Matthew would assume that she was complicit, had allowed the crime. Or worse still, that she did it herself. Freckle's heart felt constricted. She could not bear the thought that Matthew would think she had betrayed his trust.

"Daddy, please don't," pleaded Freckle.

Feeling his power, Theo fluffed his tail, and leaned back—a negotiator knowing he was dealing from a position of power. Theo knew the art of the deal.

"I don't have to mess with that one quail coup, if it is dear to you," he said.

Freckle exhaled. "Thank you, daddy."

"But your siblings need a live catch, and they need it this week."

"But Daddy!—"

"—I am worried, Freckle, that you are acting *domesticated*. This will be a good time for everyone to remember who you are. Wild foxes hunt, my kit!"

27

DEPOSITION; FOUR FEET DEEP

Milly had a point: the hiding place indeed had a shoddy view. All that the Spaniels could see were two pairs of legs.

The first, now familiar, pair belonged to their new ally, Human-Raccoon. They recognized the smell—clearly he did laundry with too much soap and skipped the rinse cycle. Raccoon's light-brown leather shoes were kicked off and scattered under the table. His black socks-clad feet were planted firmly into the floor, which was now also beginning to smell strongly of laundry detergent.

Milly chose the closest of Raccoon's shoes, rested her snout on it and got comfortable.

The second pair of legs was completely new to the Spaniels. Those legs had no pants at all—

nothing but some stretchy thin covering that smelled like the flower-scented candles which Old Lady used when she had guests.

The legs did come outfitted with shoes, though. The soles were flat leather, like Raccoon's, but the upper was much softer, in black suede. There was a floppy bow on top, and tiny golden letters peeked from under it. Milly found two "A"s.

"Look, she wears her name-tag on her shoe! Nifty," whispered Milly.

"Don't drool on those," warned Zip, "and it's not her name-tag, unless her name is Prada. And watch where you sit, or you'll get kicked."

But neither pair of legs kicked or, for that matter, moved at all. Indeed, neither of the legs betrayed any signs of life. All four legs were apparently listening intently to the voice coming out of the huge monitor that the Spaniels had glimpsed on the run under the table.

The male voice was calm, ascertained, and introduced itself lovingly,

"My name is Paul . . .." Neither Spaniel caught Paul's family name, but there was no doubt about the title. "Assistant United States Attorney, Federal Defense Civil Litigation Unit," Paul rapped out loudly and sharply.

Paul's voice sounded like the announcers for Olympic Competitions: "Stepping on the ice now . . . competing for the United States in men's singles . . ." Announcer's voice that made every competitor's name sound super-important, like they already won.

But there was more to it.

"Zip, I know that voice!"

"Shut up!"

"Listen, this guy is United States—what?" whispered Milly.

"Federal Lawyer," explained Zip, "For the United States. He represents America."

"The whole Country, all alone?" Milly opened her mouth wonderingly.

But Zip was circling back to his Sister's discovery.

"Paul . . . Federal Lawyer . . . I definitely heard this voice before," muttered Zip to himself.

"Zippy, I know—"

"Stop talking, Milly, I can't hear over your heavy breathing," complained Zip. "Federal Paul says that he will be asking questions here today."

"Asking whom?!"

Milly had a point again. Whoever could be so smart that he'd know the answers to the questions so hard that the Important Federal Paul was stumped and had to ask?

"Let's crawl out and see," suggested Milly.

"NO," snapped Zip, and bit Milly's lip to accentuate the point, "STAY!"

Meanwhile, the mysterious Answer-Human was already answering.

His was a whizzing, raspy voice. The voice was familiar, too, in an unpleasant sort of way, as if there was an old bad memory somehow attached to it. Zip caught himself beginning to bristle the hairs on his neck and told himself to stop, to get himself under control. *Must be the nerves.*

Distracted by the tiff with Milly, Zip only caught short snippet:

"I am Duly Sworn" . . . "BadNewsCleaning Project Manager" . . . "post-disaster property rehabilitation . . . I am an expert cleaner."

The rest was a raspy, creaky, whizzy blur.

Expert! realized Zip, *This Duly Sworn Answer-Human is an Expert!*

"Expert! Like our Rosie!" Zip informed his sister, "But in cleaning. Like Old Lady."

But Milly was no longer interested.

Milly gave up and flopped over on her back, all four paws in different directions, a fluffy starfish. If she had nothing to look at except legs, she was going to make the best of it.

The two pairs of legs still displayed no initiative.

Maybe these Humans are taking a nap too, Milly thought.

The voice of the Federal Paul was calming and deep—certainly relaxing enough to consider a good nap.

"It is a matter of record that your people did the cleanup on Old Lady's house," Federal Paul was saying to the *Duly Sworn Cleaning Expert,* "How deep was the water at that time?"

"Four feet deep," rasped the *Duly Sworn*.

"The Water stood taller than us both," whispered Milly, twisting awake, "about two dogs and a half."

A flashback of the struggle in the water before she docked at the neighbor's magnolia flooded over her, and Milly's head spun. "It felt like it was *miles* deep," she mumbled feebly.

"He means four *human* feet, Milly," said Zip.

Both Spaniels stared at the human feet under the table. The pair in suede Prada with a big bow was a little smaller and daintier than the pair that belonged to their new friend Raccoon.

"Your testimony is that only four feet deep was under water," repeated Federal Paul.

"Four," agreed the rasping voice of the Duly Sworn. "Which is why I said to Old Lady that the insurance won't pay anything above four feet."

"Why is that?" asked Federal Paul, sounding offhand.

"*Water level*," supplied Duly Sworn, "Insurance never pays above the *water level*."

"Never?" confirmed Paul.

Duly Sworn made a grunting noise, and exhaled, "Yes, never, I so advised Old Lady."

Federal Paul and Duly Sworn now sounded like a well-choreographed duet they were.

Duly Sworn was no longer raspy. He now spoke loudly and eagerly— a gunner kid who wants the teacher to mark an "Excellent" in his file.

"I told her that she needs to dry it all out and and most everything is usable."

"What did Old Lady do instead?" asked Federal Paul in an accusatory tone. Zip suddenly remembered that, when he was a puppy, he accidentally chewed up a shoe belonging to one of Old Lady's acquaintances; he had to answer a similarly accusatorily-toned question: "*Who* chewed the shoe?!"

"She chose the wrong course of action," indicted Duly Sworn.

"Which was?"

"She ripped out and threw out *everything* on the ground floor," sighed Duly Sworn, "Whole ground floor *gutted*."

"Even above the water level?"

"Yes. Even the ceiling!"

"Did she give your team orders to strip the whole place?"

"Yes, sir."

"What were her exact words?"

"She said," Duly Sworn breathed in, and his next words sounded as though he was reading off a note,

> *"Get rid of anything that was anywhere near that dirty water."*

And all of a sudden, Zip remembered. Indeed, Zip remembered Old Lady saying those exact words. And now Zip remembered this Duly Sworn.

They did meet before!

❧

It was Zip's first venture to the flooded ground floor since the mis-adventure that he euphemistically called his *Big Water Swim*.

The day was hot. A whole crew of Loud Humans wearing Moon Suits with deafeningly aggressive machines were chasing out Big Water remnants. They and their loud contraption had taken residence downstairs, roaring now directly under the sofa in the fireplace room, now right under Zip's water bowl. They'd started soon after the Big Water retreated, and for a full three days did not stop for anything. Not for sleep, nor even food.

The Moon-Suited Humans made the water jump out of the back doorway in long, dark, wet arches, streams that landed in dirty puddles in the backyard.

To chase out Big Water fumes, they set around more loud buzzing ventilators than Zip could count. Then they hustled hither and yon with brooms and cleaning sticks of every shape and kind, beating out the remains of Big Water. After the first day, the Spaniels stopped barking, and only moved to parts of floor as far away as possible from action downstairs.

That morning was graven indelibly in Zip's memory.

Old Lady woke up before sunrise and left her bedroom. Upon awakening later, Zip tried his best *come back here* bark, which usually brought Old Lady hurrying in minutes.

Not this time.

Looking for her, Zip peered around the corner and, finally, trotted downstairs a level.

And there she was.

He was relieved to see that she was not trapped under anything treacherous. Old Lady looked safe and energetic, gesticulating at somebody just out of Zip's sight.

"W-br-woof! Old Lady, come up back upstairs," whined Zip.

"Zip, I am very busy," Old Lady waved him off abruptly.

Old Lady appeared to be busy arguing with someone standing right outside the back doorway.

But before Zip could figure what the argument was all about, the Somebody shouted piercingly,

"Get your pet out of here, *RIGHT NOW*!"

Zip was about to protest the insult, but he felt danger that made him jump up and bolt back, his tail trying to get between his hind legs. There was a rumble, and the ceiling plunged down, missed Zip's tail by a few inches, and collapsed in a deadly pile on the very place where Zip had just stood.

"Zip!" Old Lady clapped her hand to her mouth, "Zippy!"

"GET THAT FRIGGIN' PET OUTTA HERE!" Zip heard as he was scurrying away.

Yes, that's when Zip had heard this raspy traitor's voice before. He was the one who sent the ceiling to attack.

And that was the morning—Zip remembered clearly—when Old Lady's usually warm voice turned to steel, and she ordered "Get rid of anything that soaked up any of the dirty water; I don't care what FEMA says!"

"Milly," hissed Zip, jolting Milly out of her shallow nap, "I know this *Duly Sworn*! He was the one who tried to kill me with the ceiling."

"Grrrr," Zip could feel his tail stiffen and his teeth glisten, chasing his lips away in a murderous smile.

"Bite his ankles!" woke up Milly.

"Let's go!" they said together.

The siblings made it to the edge of the table, when Zip noticed something moving behind them, under the table.

"Milly," he hissed, "*THE LEGS!* Look at *THE LEGS*!"

Both pairs of legs under the table had awakened and now seemed to be ready to spring into an attack.

Black velvety Prada with big bow jerked and left the floor, kicking the air, its well-worn sole revealing the fact that it had been in its owner's service for quite some time now.

"I'm Portia Porter, the attorney for Old Lady," said black Prada with big velvety bow, "My question is—"

"Yes Ma'am," said Duly Sworn.

"—about the waterline."

This Portia Porter person did not have a lawyer-like voice at all, thought Zip.

Her tone was quiet. Maybe too quiet.

But it was not placid.

"Yes, Ma'am," enthusiastically repeated Duly Sworn without waiting for any question, "It's justified that the insurance company should only pay for what was submerged *under* the waterline, *not above* it."

"Is it correct that the downstairs ceiling *fell down?*"

Duly Sworn grunted noncommittally.

"And were you there when it happened?"

Duly Sworn grunted affirmatively.

"The ceiling that collapsed had been *above* the water level?"

"Yes, ma'am."

"In its entirety?"

"Yes, ma'am."

"Never submerged at all?"

"No, ma'am, never submerged."

"In your expert opinion," pushed Portia argumentatively, "*why* did the ceiling fall?"

"It got wet, ma'am," said Duly Sworn, "but please understand that FEMA . . . that insurance . . . will only pay for loss that was s—"

"Please don't say submerged," there was a chuckle in Portia's voice and the big bows on her suede shoes bounced with suppressed excitement.

"Unfortunately, I must say it. Only what's submerged, Ma'am. The insurance allows replacement value only of what was submerged under the waterline."

"In your expert opinion, can water cause damage to objects not submerged in it?" asked Portia pointedly.

This time, the Expert's hesitation stretched awkwardly, but finally he blurted out "Yes, ma'am. Sufficient moisture is absorbed from the surface of the water."

Portia smiled and drove home the salient point: "Did I understand you to say that the mechanism involved in causing damage could be *absorption?*"

"Yes, ma'am, but only if sufficient moisture is absorbed from the surface."

Zip felt a bolt of understanding and almost shouted "Eureka," when he was distracted by his sister's an insistent nag.

"Zip," whined Milly, "The Duly Sworn said we'll be paid for everything *submerged* so we'll buy new, clean stuff? Right? We need new dog beds for the downstairs—mine is a wet stinking heap—"

"Yes, hush," Zip tried to keep everything straight in his head. "Quiet!"

"I'm quiet," lowered her voice Milly, "but what about our armchair by the fireplace?"

"What about it?" grumbled Zip. Milly had been winning the internecine war on possession of that old armchair. Old Lady had stopped shooing her off. But now a new issue had all of a sudden come into sharp focus.

"The seat was *submerged,* but the backrest was always above the water! Do you think we have to buy a new chair without a backrest?" Milly was now wide awake. "We need to protect our interests, Zip."

"I don't know," said Zip honestly. "I thought that I

knew, but now I'm not so sure. This needs pondering."

"Zip," did not quiet down Milly, "What about *us*?"

"*What* about us?"

"Zip, we were *submerged* under four feet of water. Both of us."

"So?"

"Zip, this raspy-voiced Duly Sworn said that what's *submerged* will be *replaced*. Under four feet."

"Stop interrupting, Milly."

"Zip, Zip, I am definitely . . . tip of the nose to tip of the tail . . . under four feet. Zip, do you think we are worth a lot?"

"Old Lady always says we are her favorites."

"Zip, what if Duly Sworn pays for us . . . will Old Lady buy new Spaniels?"

"Will they pay for us, though?" considered Zip philosophically. "I'll ask the Human-Raccoon. He'll know. He said we are friends now."

"What about this Portia—are we friends with her too?"

"That I'm not so sure," said Zip, "I can't hear what she's asking over your whining."

Zip was right. Portia was forging ahead with more questions. Her quiet voice vibrated. It was not a calming voice at all. There was an edge of screechy steel in it.

"When Old Lady's ceiling got damp and collapsed," asked Portia, "how did you know—" she paused, as if assembling her question out of scattered words.

Her voice and tone was so clear. There was no hint of treachery in it, and Duly Sworn leaped in to help:

"—how did I know that FEMA would not pay?"

"Yes," Portia nodded and asked innocently, "Did insurance *ever* pay *anybody* for *any* damage above the water line?"

Under the table, the agile Human-Raccoon's knees started dancing—up and down, up-down.

Duly Sworn coughed, but did not answer.

Portia made a second try.

"Have you ever known anybody who received payment for damage above the water-line—ANYBODY?" There was a pause that seemed to hang in the air. And then Portia repeated, "Anybody?" As though she personally already knew that there was an *anybody* who had been paid.

It got quiet. Very quiet. Human-Raccoon's shoes stopped tossing up his knees. Zip watched without blinking. Milly inhaled, but did not exhale. The room waited.

"Yes," exhaled Duly Sworn, "It happened once."

Both of Portia's suede shoes got sealed to the floor.

"So," one Prada shoe floated up *en pointe,* "It happens that somebody gets paid for something *not submerged.*"

"She's winning," gasped Zip.

"Objection!" The new female voice was shrill and, especially in contrast to Portia's, grating to the ears. "Representing the Federal Emergency Management Agency," the owner of the brassy voice introduced herself.

"That's FEMA," whispered Zip, and both Spaniels barely suppressed an angry bark.

"Objection," bellowed the FEMA voice once again, screeching as desperately as though denouncing an intruder invading her house.

Zip smiled. "We know what Objection is, thanks to Rosie. Means *'you shut up.'*"

The suede bows floated up, a prelude to Portia's voice ringing out in response. "Paul, may I—"

"Of course, Portia, call me Paul."

"Paul, would you explain to your FEMA colleague that there's no need to yell? And about the

Federal Rules governing proper objections at a deposition? I hope you'll agree with me, Paul, that there is no basis for a proper objection right now." She paused, and added amicably, "We are asking for a break at this point, though."

"But she was winning, why stop now?" growled Zip.

"Good call," agreed Milly, "Human-Raccoon is fidgeting, sure looks like he could use a walk."

28

LUNCH BREAK: FOX & RACCOON

The break in the deposition was announced, and all the Humans trickled into the kitchen.

Zip was pleased to be wrong: like every Human Meeting, Depositions had the food.

But none of the Humans showed any interest in it.

Old Lady, who had watched the whole thing on a separate monitor, showed Portia Porter to the couch by her side, then motioned for the Human-Raccoon with the bouncy brown hair.

"Raccoon, would you—"

"Raccoon!" boomed Zip in an alerting bark.

"Raccoon!" erupted Milly in a shrill echo.

"Raccoon," requested Old Lady politely, "would you care to walk the doggies?"

Zip gave Old Lady his most severe, hardest side-stare, but she was too busy to notice.

Doggies?! They were not invited to stay for the private meeting with this notorious Portia Porter; that alone was bad enough. Zip was still seething because she'd locked them in the dark coatroom . . . if Raccoon had not saved them . . .. And now this insulting nickname, '*doggies*'?! But Old Lady did not seem to even pay attention to the stare. And suddenly Zip was no longer mad. Now, he was worried.

❧

The walk with Human nicknamed Raccoon was quick and filled with scurrying and bustle. Milly, of course, was the biggest source of fuss. She was the first to notice Theo, and that got her ears in a knot.

Theo was waiting in the usual place—by the Fire Pit, in the Cannas flowerbed. He jerked his tail tip as a greeting but did not sit up.

"Zip, should we introduce them?" Milly jerked

her head towards the New Human, her eyes still angled at Fox Theo.

Zip did not care.

"Human-Raccoon is our new friend," muttered Milly to herself, "and as a hostess, I am in charge of introductions. But on the other paw—"

For Raccoon's benefit, she twirled around in one spot, pretending to look for a good place for *business,* while trying surreptitiously to catch Theo's eye. The Fox had gotten quite persnickety of late. Can't introduce him to just any old Human.

Milly excused herself and, making like she went off to chase a squirrel, swung around the entire yard and approached the Cannas flowerbed from the secluded side.

"Introductions," mused Fox. "Depends. What does he have to offer?"

"What is needed, Theo?" sociable Milly was taken aback.

"Well, thanks to Freckle, my family wants not for food. But there *is* something he could do," Theo peeked out from behind the Cannas, then stepped back in, shaking his head negatively and then muttering "He does not have it."

"Does not have what?" asked Milly, "Try him. He is a resourceful Human."

"He won't. I need a quail, live. To teach my kits about hunting. Or some live mice. Worst case, a toad. But something alive and wiggly. With all Big Water disaster, there's plenty of stinking dead critters—useless."

Milly stared, then surreptitiously looked around in case she'd see a live mouse she could offer.

"So your New Human," went on Theo, "Can he be of help? What's the advantage of meeting him?"

"I don't know," said Milly, a little stumped. "I'll try to investigate."

"Actually," Theodore dropped the arrogant tone of a socialite accosted by unfortunate acquaintance, "I, in fact, am here on business."

"Business?"

"Yeah, no time for new acquaintances," remembered his importance Theo, "Too much work to do." That put Theo of the mind of his to-do list, and the went on again:

"Need a live thing … at least a mouse. What am I gonna do—hunt mice? Am I gonna stoop to hunting mice again? Such a letdown! But need it for the kits. Hunting class time." Mindful of his fatherly pride, Theo puffed out his chest pompously.

Then he sighed,

"Could catch a toad, of course, but when you had

enough to eat—and you see, we always have enough to eat now—anyway, the toads taste so slimy. Will slip out of your muzzle a dozen times by the time you can run it back to the burrow. Yeah, always looking to leap out of the muzzle, those live capture toads."

Theo caught Milly's impatient glance and stopped himself.

"I digress. I'm here with some important news from Freckle."

Still sitting on his hind paws, Theo lifted his right front one and inspected it carefully, twisting the paw in every direction.

"Paw pads," he said, touching his nose to the paw, "Paw pads suffer the most—they are the weakest part in hunting, and carry the biggest load. Plus, I'm out of practice hunting, and the paw pads got soft and sensitive. Over-use a little, and look here, got a painful crack."

"Theodore," Milly had no interest in discussing foxes hunting habits and what happens to paw pads when a fox is too lazy to keep up with his hunting practice, but she did not want to be rude.

"Theodore . . . paws, right . . . but what's that message from Freckle?"

"Actually, that's why I am here," said Theo

sharply, balancing back on all four paws and giving Milly a scornful look, as though his conversational dillydallying was her fault.

But before the fox could get to it, Human-Raccoon called out,

"Doggy, time to go!"

Zip issued a trail of summoning barks: the deposition was about to resume.

"Gotta rush off," apologized Milly, "Can't be late—all the good seats will be taken."

She was not going to spend another hour reduced to staring at the legs under the table.

"See you later, Theo," and both Spaniels set off in the direction of the house, Human-Raccoon trailing in pursuit.

29

WATER PERILS

Milly was in a hurry to get back and stake out a better observation point.

Her plan was simple.

When suede bows Portia held the door open for them, both Spaniels tricked through helter-skelter. Then, in studiously assured fashion, they crossed the hallway floor and entered as though they absolutely belonged in the proceeding, no doubt about it.

"Kitchen," suggested Portia indifferently and walked away.

On her way to the kitchen, Milly veered off and stole towards an up-wind spot near the low leather couch where Old Lady was watching the proceeding on her own monitor. The monitor was one which

Human-Raccoon had cobbled together earlier out of a portable TV-set, three ravels of wires, a cigarette-pack sized metal box with wiring clips and some choice imprecations. Milly was mystified but impressed by Raccoon's cleverness.

From her new observation post, Milly could now see everything that Old Lady saw on her monitor.

Federal Paul in all the officious splendor of his starred and striped tie was already there, on the tiny screen.

Milly was quite sure now. She definitely had seen this Paul guy before. She strained her memory and, for some reason, her brain summoned up his image seated in a patio chair, wearing loafers *with no socks*.

Strange.

Behind Federal Paul, the shrill and nervous FEMA Lawyer Lady was tugging down her hiking-up skirt—too narrow when she sat down.

The chair allocated to the screechy Duly Sworn was front and center and still empty when the Spaniels arrived. A few minutes later, they watched Duly Sworn shuffle back in and arrange himself on his chair. He did not look comfortable but said that he was fine and ready.

Milly took in her surroundings and congratulated herself on choosing the best seat in the house.

She scooted in a little, freeing just enough space to accommodate Zip. The closer her brother would cozy up, the easier it would be to confab. Milly lifted her nose and located Zip—back under the table with the shoddy view of Legs.

"Come over," she whispered.

But Zip was not in the mood for Milly's chit-chat. He had to ponder his new fears:

Why was Old Lady so tense?
Can Federal Paul really declare Old Lady mad for ripping out the ceiling? Even if the ceiling had attacked Zip?!
Who was this Federal Paul, really?

Besides, the new buddy Human-Raccoon also held his interest.

"I'm fine here," Zip eased his muzzle onto Raccoon's shoe.

Meanwhile, the Duly Sworn—the same Human who had bewitched the wet ceiling to attack Zip, but in a new disguise (necktie, no respirator)—got to matters that would come to torment both Spaniels for the rest of the week.

The conversation turned somehow to the topic of *water quality*.

There were three kinds of water quality,

explained the Duly Sworn—*Clean Water, Gray Water,* and *Black Water.*

"And what we had in Old Lady's house," he explained without hesitation, "was *Black Water.*"

Yes, the Big Water that came into the House was black with dirt and peril.

"Zip," yelped Milly, making to rush over to Zip's side under the table, her teeth chattering a little, "I am scared."

Zip was not feeling well himself. For weeks now, he'd been trying to shoo away the vision that tried to sneak back in every time he closed his eyes—the monstrous smacking wave that covered and pulled him down, crashed his squiggling and struggling body into a stone wall, and stuffed him full of putrid water. That nasty foul-smelling water that seemed to linger on in his mouth, nose and ears.

Zip was not really surprised they called Big Water "*black.*" It sure was dark and *smelled* dirty. Oh, the smell! Worse than those bushes at the end of Old Lady's land after Fox Theo unexpectedly marked the territory as his. They learned the hard way that stink-wise Theo is about as bad as a skunk, worse than wolves and cats even. Milly sneezed for a fort-night after that and looked askance at the butterfly bush where Theo had done his hunting grounds marking.

To occupy his nose, and chase the memories away, Zip inhaled as deep as he could, and tried to switch to something less smelly. Like Human socks. Raccoon's socks still smelled freshly washed, of unrinsed detergent. Zip's sensitive nose tickled, he sneezed and cheered up for a minute.

But Portia Porter's questions to Duly Sworn were unnerving.

"Your terminology for flood water is *'Black Water,'* is it?"

Duly Sworn nodded affirmatively inside the TV monitor.

"Why do you call it *black*?" asked Portia and made a checkmark on a long yellow piece of paper in front of her.

"It is contaminated, Ma'am," crossed his arms in front of him Duly Sworn.

"You mean *dirty*?" asked Portia airily.

"Not just dirty," Duly Sworn was getting impatient with Portia's lightheartedness, "there are contaminants in the water. A whole list of pathogens and substances—"

Zip got lost in the rest of the explanation, overcome by a flashback. The nightmares that he had just managed to block out returned, but now the stinky scary water that whacked like a bag of bricks was also *black*. He made a very quiet whining noise and closed his eyes.

"ZIP!"

Something wet pushed against Zip's nose. Milly had crawled back under the table.

"Ziiiip," Milly's upper lip was twitching to the side, "Zip, that Water swept me away. I had to wait a long time on that magnolia tree branch, a whole night."

"I'm sorry, Milly."

"Zip, I was starving on that magnolia, and I was really thirsty, and so frightened, and so—"

Zip's remembrance of Milly's terrifying experience was so vivid and chilling that the room went spinning around him, but he managed to choke out a response,

"And *so*?" Zip lifted his ear a little to hear Milly's answer, although he knew he did not want to know.

"Zippi . . . that black water . . . I *drank it*," confessed Milly in a quiet scared whisper, and pressed her nose under Zip's ear.

Above them, Portia Porter kept asking questions.

"Care to give me an example of what you call contaminants?"

"It could be pesticides and herbicides," answered Duly Sworn, addressing his words for some reason to Federal Paul, who sat right at his runaway expert's shoulder and maintained a face of stony indifference.

"I know that I saw that Paul before. Where?" Milly strained her memory, and it hit her: that was the guy from Freckle's Meeting, the important co-owner of the Golf Club.

But there was more.

"Zippy, that's the Human who plans to drown our House and declare Old Lady crazy. But we've seen him before when we investigated. Zippy, remember the glossy picture? He was the one who jailed our Criminal, the Criminal who once owned our house. Zippy, Paul must be after everybody who owns our House! Look at him, Zippy, he is powerful!"

The right side of Milly's lip twitched double time and she bit into her left lip to prevent it from following suit. Meanwhile, above the table, the Humans were discussing what was in the water.

"It could be human waste," went on the Duly Sworn pensively, "urine . . . feces."

Milly's eyes bulged out to her forehead and assumed the shape of little white boiled eggs.

"Human waste," Portia repeated skeptically.

"It could be dead animals . . . or bodies." Duly Sworn quit looking around hesitantly and was beginning to show perverse satisfaction in exposing the grim truth. "It is not safe water."

Portia went on dispassionately to questions about the use of objects touched by Big Black Water —was there any danger in handling those objects? Zip could not get her calm, quiet voice out of his ears.

"Real danger?

Yes?

Really?

What was the danger? . . .

Really? . . . Hepatitis? . . . Is there a cure for Hepatitis? . . .

Parasites? What parasites are floating in the water? . . . Do those resolve themselves? . . . No?

Giardiasis, really? . . .

Guinea roundworm? . . .

Cyclops in the stomach . . . I see."

Portia Porter even mentioned *"river blindness,"* but Duly Sworn sniggered derisively, "No, that's mostly in Africa, not known in this country."

There were more than plenty of perils locally, though, even without *river blindness.*

Zip felt his early morning snack aggregate into a stiff ball and start making its way out.

Duly Sworn barely containing the mask of supposedly objective professionalism, assured that "We get inoculated for *Hep A and B*."

"But not *Hep C*?"

For some reason, at the mention of Hep C, the Duly Sworn grunted, his professionalism slipped and his eyes grew empty and scared.

The videographer must have been unable to bear the anguished expression on Duly Sworn Expert's face and panned the camera away, catching unaware the face of Federal Paul, who was furiously scribbling notes in his yellow pad.

Behind Paul, the FEMA lady-lawyer was caught on camera with her face momentarily askew in horror, but she quickly jolted out of her stupor and concentrated aimlessly on the stack of papers in front of her.

Meanwhile, Portia Porter's face—entirely safe from the view of the videographer who was in a different room and a different city and a different State—Portia's face assumed a jubilant expression.

Duly Sworn—the Expert hired, brought and paid by other, FEMA's side, was betraying the dirty truth that FEMA never wanted to get out, and which most people did not know. And if the water was so dirty—of course Old Lady would be sane to rip out all it touched!

And now to close the trap. Portia's face and tone did not change a bit, but Zip could smell that she was pouncing.

"With all the *Hep* and *Roundworm* and *Cyclops* hiding in black water, is it *completely safe* to use whatever water touched? Wash it out, dry it off and see what is still usable?"

"Not always," admitted the Expert, looking away from the camera.

"Would you wash and use it for your own . . . kids . . . or dogs . . . old people? Yourself" Portia paused, a little too long, looking like she needed a minute to gather her own self, then added, "in your expert opinion—"

The Expert threw up his hands and jumped to his feet, speaking assuredly for the first time,

"*NO*!

"NO! Everything the water touched should go. I would not use my bare hands to wash . . . or touch . . . or . . . anything that water touched . . .. You're better off disposing of it."

"*Disposing*," went Portia for the kill, "How?" Zip turned his head to sniff the suede bow, and smelled victory. Still, his own stomach was uneasy. Portia carried on.

"There is a protocol for disposing of certain types of waste—"

Zip stretched his long ears over his head and tried to hide under his paws, but felt a heavy breath and a bit of drool.

"Zip, Ziiiip," Milly whined wedging her nose right into his ear, "Everything that water touched . . . I . . . we . . . I think he's saying . . . he means *us*? Does he want to dispose of *us*? Is that necessary? Zip, I'd rather we were washed again, that *decontamination bath*? Even though the washing was very uncomfortable and humiliating."

Zip felt an itch in his tail, which spread up, shook him in a twitch and realized that his left eye-brow had been jumping uncontrollably. Duly Sworn Expert was droning on something about "pale diarrhea," which made Zip moan and scramble on his paws to bolt to the door. He was about to beat a retreat, away from the horrors spewing from the monitors, out of Old Lady's House, but at that moment everything went black before his eyes . . . the last thing he remembered was Human-Raccoon's shoe rapidly moving into his muzzle.

By the time Zip was conscious again, the deposition was long over and everyone was gone.

Zip's nose was still pressed into Human-Raccoon's shoe, and his new buddy was petting his head soothingly.

"Wake up, doggie," Raccoon's voice was friendly and unexpectedly happy, "Wake up, buddy, you'll be OK. We won that deposition. It will settle now."

30

THE SLEEPOVER

New girlfriends Freckle and Milly were spread out under the Confederate Jasmine Bush, basking in the shade, lulled by the pungent smells of jasmine and the freshly mowed grass of the nearby fairway.

The dog and the fox both studied the other stealthily. This was their first informal encounter. No Meetings, no families. Just the two of them.

Milly had popped by the Country Club uninvited, "for a minute." Freckle, naturally, issued an invite to "stay for such leftovers." *Noblesse oblige,* thought Freckle. Plus, she was eager to hear Freckle's account of the depositions.

For a few days after the deposition day, Milly suffered from upset stomach.

Then from memories of the stomach upset.

Then she was plagued by images of all the horrible aftereffects.

Finally, Milly resolved that she would never discuss with anybody those things that happened to her, to Zip and to Old Lady in those horrid Big Black Water days. Especially since Zip and Milly now were fairly certain that Old Lady had no intention of disposing of them into one those special disposal dumps for contaminated materials.

For that reason, responding to Freckle's inquiry about the deposition day, Milly only stretched her front paws lazily into the downward-facing dog position. (As for the use of that pose and name by Human practitioners of Yoga, Milly regarded that usage as an implicit compliment rather than as an objectionable cultural appropriation.)

"Looking back on it now, I can't quite understand the whole fuss and what the sleepless night was all about. Nobody asked Zip and me any questions. We did not have to ask anybody any questions either. Was there any point in worrying?

"And nobody had us on video either. Even Portia Porter was off camera—just a voice behind the screen.

"Old Lady and the bouncy Human-Raccoon were off screen entirely too. Hardly worth the trouble of getting all dressed up!"

Milly stretched even more, lifted her muzzle into the upward-facing dog pose, and asked lazily: "Could you spare a little clean water? We never lick the water from ravine."

"Always welcome," her girlfriend Freckle invited.

Freckle was taken by Milly's well-bred manner. And there was also the fact that Milly rubbed shoulders with the *deposition crowd* including, notably, that Portia Porter Esq. about whom Paul and his buddies kept talking.

Cold water untied Milly's tongue a little.

"First of all," recounted Milly, "Portia Porter's ankles are not nearly as narrow as yours, Freckle. You have such elegant paws, my dear friend Freckle. No mistaking: there's evidence of a fine bloodline!

"Of course, Portia Porter has no fur. Your fur is so shiny, so dreamy. Honestly, if Portia Porter had any fur on her ankles, like mine, it would be a horrid sight. Can't deny that her legs are slim and long, of course. But I doubt very much that she runs quicker. . .. Humans can never catch up with us because we move on paw tips, although, of course, the paw pads sometimes suffer."

"That's right," agreed Freckle. "In our Fox Species, the Head of Household must win bread for the entire family for several months when there is a litter of young kits. If only you could see, my sweetheart Milly, how deep were the cracks on Father Theo's paw pads."

"So sorry," Milly wagged her tail sympathetically, thinking privately that Foxes were blatantly putting on airs about their pedigree. Zip had explained to her that all six types of foxes were always classified as *Vulpes,* an unimportant branch of *Canidae,* from canine, which means *Dog Family*. In second place, below *real dogs,* like us, Zip firmly believed.

Milly, who was not burdened by passion for any skills or sciences except for the skill of survival, paid very careful attention to that classification system. Both Zip and Milly were lately noticing that, as soon as Theo shook his need for finishing dogs' leftovers, he started talking more about his Fox pedigree.

But Zip forbade Milly to disabuse Theodore of his uppity misapprehensions about the Fox breed because Theodore was a good friend and often their *guest*. At the moment, Freckle was the *hostess*, and that also stopped Milly from showing Freckle her proper place.

That's OK, thought Milly, *I'll wait until we both are somewhere in the Forest, on nobody's land, and neither guest nor hostess, and clarify it for those overly big-headed Foxes.*

Long tradition establishes that dogs have more rights in country clubs. In fact, thousands of years of history prove that dogs always have more rights to be with humans. His-to-ri-cally.

But Milly was very thirsty. And the Evian water was so cool. And it was so pleasant to be a guest in a female company. Theodore and Zip often led men's conversation for hours, with no manners in their behavior or opinions.

Freckle, a master of flattery, felt in the tip of her tail that she had pushed too far with her prattle about the *Noble Fox Bloodline* and it was ill-advised to offend her guest. And, anyway, she was anxious to find out everything about this infamous Portia Porter Esq. person.

Milly, who did not have a chance to properly examine any part of Portia Porter except her feet and shoes, was interested to know what Freckle's Human said about Portia.

And so they mutually abandoned the taxonomy talk in favor of their favorite subject—gossip.

"Freckle, I cannot tell you how important for Zip and me it is to study Portia Porter's position in Human society."

"She's a Wild Card," pronounced Freckle. And, remembering what Matthew said, added enigmatically, "*Black Horse*."

"How do you mean? What does that mean? My darling sister fox, you know everything from horses' mouths. You are so in with the in crowd," Milly wagged her tail stub at Freckle. "You're so clever. You don't just in-ves-ti-gate, you also a-na-lyze."

This little dog is flattering me . . . and laying it on so thick, thought Freckle. *Although, it's all actually true.*

Her dog's nose told simpleton Milly that she had successfully concealed her real view of Freckle, *that ill-bred parvenu*. So, Milly moved on to flagrant flattery.

"Freckle, my soul, I am so happy we are now BFFs. To be quite honest, I could not completely grasp that Portia Porter's nature. And now I'm absolutely stumped with your assessment. *A Horse*, that description quite derailed my train of thought. Would you explain, please?"

"As you quite fairly pointed out, my dear Milly," responded Freckle, "I'm only competent to tell you my own thoughts of Portia Porter and, of course, Matthew's thoughts. And his friends' thoughts."

"Speak faster, why is she a Horse? And, Black? She wore black shoes but definitely no hooves. I did not see a single hoof, just a floppy bow shoe."

"I have not even seen the shoes," acknowledged Freckle. "*Dark Horse* is just a figure of speech. Paul—"

"—Zip and I nicknamed him *Federal Paul*," interjected Milly.

"*Federal* Paul. Sounds majestic," echoed Freckle. "So where was I? . . . *Federal* Paul said that Portia Porter knows a lot about the law, but that her pedigree is . . . low. She has no network. Not connected. Sort of like a lone wolf. Nobody heard about her family, not even about any of her distant relatives. Nobody knows anything. And it sounds like she has no notion of 'who's who' in our society. *Wild Card*."

"The poor thing," compassionately pitied Milly. "If she knows a lot about the law, this means she's well-educated. That is good. . .."

"Steve thinks. . ." Freckle paused remembering,

"that, if his third wife divorces him, he will hire Portia Porter for the court battle. . . "

"But she has no connections?" was astonished Milly.

"My Human," Freckle vibrated slightly, the coarse hairs on her low back stood up. There was such love and pride in how she said *my*.

"*My* Human," repeated Freckle, and it was obvious that she liked hearing those sounds even better than the sound of her own name,

"*My Human,*" she said yet again, "Agrees with Steve."

"Why? Explain it to me," asked Milly in her most solicitous voice.

"Matthew says that worst betrayal is always by those close to you. They know too much, they are too tempted, too much seeing through the lens of personal advantage."

"Oh! Ah! So many thoughts and conclusions. I have so much to ponder! Listen, Freckle, are they afraid of her?"

"*My* Human said," Freckle delivered after a short pause, "that she's a worthy opponent. But P— *Federal* Paul is not afraid. He thinks it will *just take time*."

As is so often happens to the cleverest, Freckle

was caught in the simplest flattery and lost all caution.

"Milly, honey, I think it might be better if I introduce you to my House. In the evenings, they all gather here. We'll definitely learn something new. I'll tell you more," said Freckle touching her nose lightly to Milly's shoulder, "I came to love you terribly and I would be so interested to discuss with you my own Human's position. I can't wrap my head around it; his behavior defies analysis. Whose side's he on? What does he want? The well-being of my whole family, Theo's family, depends on that."

Now again, more about her family and pedigree, thought Milly, but quickly swallowed that fleeting irritation and spread her muzzle in sincere smile of gratitude.

"I'd love to, dear Freckle. I'll stay for dinner leftovers. With all my pleasure."

❧

"If you eavesdrop attentively," tutored Freckle, "you can learn a lot. And learning . . . meaning, acquiring information—" Freckle's voice sounded with the Lady-of-the-house self-assurance.

"No doubt," nodded Milly, "What's today's information about, anyway?"

Freckle flounced happily, and bared four sharp, fairly massive ivory cuspids. Two fangs on top, two on the bottom. Rows of short wet shiny teeth sparkled between them.

Way sharp, thought Milly, *better not cross her.* Outloud, she said something rather different.

"You, Freckle, have such an open, charming smile! And ivories, such treasure! Just like the news broadcasters on the Fox Channel.

"We don't watch the Fox Channel—neither me nor My Human. We are of the view that after all those years in litigation, we need to totally unplug."

"Totally unplug from what?" Milly did not understand, but at once decided it was better not to ask such complex questions, unrelated to Big Black Water or Old Lady.

"Speaking of information," Hostess Freckle directed the conversation into proper direction, "one never can predict for sure what Humans will discuss. They talk about their wives and other women, about the President. A lot about which friend of theirs got into what trouble. I am not interested in any of that."

"I'm interested in the information about Old Lady," admitted Milly open-heartedly.

"We can't cross-examine them," said Freckle dryly, "all we can do is eavesdrop."

The chilliness of Freckle's tone did not touch Milly. She shook her head, as though shaking off water.

"Let's listen in quickly, we have good eyes on everything from here."

They did not have to wait long. The friends were already chatting.

Freckle turned out to be totally correct. First, Steve asked Paul about Paul's wife. Next, Matthew asked about Steve's children. Then all three discussed the visit of the U.S. President to France, and reasons for not including Britain.

"The interesting part is about to start," said Freckle and edged closer to Milly.

"How did the deposition go?" asked Steve nonchalantly.

"I'm prohibited from discussing the ongoing case," retorted Paul.

"Get off it, Paul—"

But Matthew sided with Paul: "Steve, you never did respect the law—"

"—And always found somebody to pull your chestnuts out of the fire," added Paul sulkily.

"Let's not fight," said Matthew conciliatory. "Steve, the law is the law. Paul, you'll have to make your depositions public record eventually. We'll read them when you file them."

"I'm not so sure I want the Judge to see them at all," said Paul pensively, "Most likely, not."

"Why not?" got curious Matthew, "the depositions were your idea."

"That's true," acknowledged Paul, "My idea. Now I got a different idea."

"Something went wrong, Paul?" asked Matthew sympathetically.

"Screwed up again, genius?" scoffed Steve, "You and your eye-witness did not see eye-to-eye?"

Oh, no! thought Matthew. *For Paul, FEMA was an important client. The scuffle with Old Lady was supposed to be an easy win, and Paul made no secret of his hopes for this case. He needed wins to mend his stagnating career.*

"No reason to sulk," said Steve off-handedly, "You and Judge Carlson are buddies, right? Didn't you say so yourself?"

That's just the trouble, thought Matthew. *Buddies. Paul and Judge Carlson started out together after law school as lowly federal prosecutors. Their friendship was all about one-upmanship. "Neck and neck," as they say at the horse races.*

Paul slid back with his notorious prosecution of Mr. Ian Sider—the former owner of Old Lady's House. That prosecution was Paul's expected ticket to a seat up at the pinnacle of Justice. But while the entire Ducklingburg was celebrating Paul's ostensible win, the inner circles were groping with the disaster that the prosecution in truth had turned out to be.

Ian Sider was an imposter: a piffling player who presented himself as the Godfather of the scheme while real criminals puffed and disappeared in smoke. Blinded by mass media hysteria, Paul led his team down the rabbit hole of Sider's ostentatious arrest and prosecution. But when all was said and done, there was not much they could ethically pin on the guy. Worse yet, the real culprits were long gone. Mr. Sider was sent away for a few months. Paul got shuffled to the end of the line. Meanwhile, his buddy Judge Carlson was made a Magistrate, then District Court Judge. Paul was two lengths behind and fading fast.

"Why the sad face?" persisted Steve, "They aren't taking your paycheck? No? I don't get your worry."

"You won't," snapped Paul, "That paycheck does not begin to cover all my troubles."

"Don't cry poor. Hundreds of thousands. I don't get you," said Steve honestly.

No, you never will, thought Matthew privately again. The *law attracts men who want to change the world.*

"Tell me," Steve did not shut up, "tell me, what happens if you lose to that Portia?"

"I'll tell you," said Paul calmly.

Paul was not really offended by Steve's thoughtless blabber. Childhood allegiance is not corroded, even by real animosity much less by mere tactless prying. Those two were his friends since childhood and for life. They will be by his side when it matters, no matter what.

"I'll tell you," repeated Paul. "I have a feeling that my career depends on this win. No, Steve, of course, they will not sack me. But this will be my final step on the ladder. I'll die an Assistant US Attorney.

"What's so important about this case?" asked Matthew with professional tightness in his voice, "Is there precedent involved? The actual money stakes seem to be quite small."

"You got it. FEMA does not like surrendering its *we only pay up to waterline* gimmick. Sure, it's a gimmick that Judges mixed in half the Districts. But not in ours.

"*Not a dime for damage above the waterline* is technically still the law here, and nobody at FEMA expected a suit to challenge it. Not in the landlocked South Duck.

"It's not that FEMA never gets sued, but almost never by a single homeowner. No lawyer in his right mind would take a case with just one house. Litigation costs will eat up all gains from winning. If there's a win."

"I'll tell you why," Paul responded to Steve's puzzled gesture.

"FEMA's insurance program is deep under government protection. It is above the law.

"All private insurance companies run scared about *wrongfully denying coverage*. They worry about getting stuck with punitive damages, including interest and attorneys' fees.

"But FEMA never has to pay any of that. The most it'll pay the homeowner is what it was supposed to pay in the first place. And usually not even that.

"FEMA wrote that into the law.

"So look here. There's no way this Portia's fees get paid by FEMA, even if she wins. Not a penny, that much I can tell you for sure. FEMA never is required to pay homeowners' attorney fees—however badly it might lose. And those fees are no pittance—a hundred thousand dollars at the least. Who'll pay Portia then? The Old Lady? Huh!"

"Phew," responded Steve.

"Yep," Paul nodded, "And this Portia gal knows it full well. I sensed it about her right off: she did not take this case for money . . . not entirely for money anyway."

Paul paused. Steve and Matthew waited, silently but expectantly.

"I knew it, right off," Paul continued with irritation now, "but underestimated. And this daft cow . . . in this quiet mumble of hers . . . somehow weaseled her way into *my* witness's confidence. And made my witness crack.

"Black water—the pernicious danger, and right in the midst of the swanky White Goose zip code. If this bit of deposition is leaked to environment protection groups . . . with three schools and a kindergarten steps away—"

Paul's voice descended into mumble.

"—Your career is caput!" Steve completed Paul's sentence with unexpected bluntness and looked around uncomfortably, surprised and a bit embarrassed at his own outburst.

The three friends grew silent.

Milly touched her nose delicately to Freckle's whiskers and said, "Freckle, dear. I am not sure I understood it all, but I sure heard an earful."

Freckle was wishing bitterly she had not asked this silly dog to stay. *Perhaps the revelation went over her Spaniel head? Freckle surely was not going to make it easier.*

"I'll explain later, Milly. After I discuss it with my Human."

"What if it is too late by then?"

"Be quiet, please. They are not finished yet."

Steve took his pensive gaze off the sweating beer mug which he'd been clutching impatiently in his large palm since the topic of the deposition came up. He took a long gulp, straightened in his chair, and assumed the childhood role of the pack's leader. He had some news from the real world that'd sure cheer up his lawyer-friends.

"A person with knowledge but wishing, for obvious reasons, to remain anonymous," Steve mimicked a broadcaster with frozen upper part of his face, "a reliable anonymous source reports that

Old Lady's Land deal is worth more than three million dollars. Three million!"

"What?" Milly's lower jaw dropped in horror, "they put three million on Old Lady's head? They want to kill her? What is he saying?"

"What are you saying?" Matthew repeated Milly's question.

"Now you are interested, Litigants. Money does not smell . . . Everybody loves money!" Steve dropped his mock TV-show style.

"Getting back to business: FEMA is prepared to pay the City of Ducklingburg up to three million dollars to eliminate the *repeat flooding* that affects Old Lady's Land."

"Means we get three million dollars!" Milly laughed with joy.

"Listen," Freckle hushed her.

"And so," offered Matthew slowly, "the City will accept three million dollars and agree to remove the concrete that had been put under the bridge? Perhaps with supervision from Department of Transportation? What's the process? They'll come with sledge hammers? Or blow up the whole thing? How much to build a whole new bridge?"

"Nobody is blowing up anything," assured Steve.

"The plan is simple. Actually, there are three plans, all simple.

"Plan A, Plan B, Plan C. For all occasions.

"Plan A. FEMA insurance refuses to pay Old Lady anything for the damage—"

"But, didn't you just say that FEMA would pay three million to fix the flooding on Old Lady's land?" asked Matthew, somewhat a surprised.

"I did not say FEMA will pay three million to Old Lady. The money will be transferred to the City. The Mayor has approved appropriation of the funds to buy six acres of land for a Greenway project, to build a promenade. Old Lady's Land will be sold to us and we will build the townhouses.

"What about the Bridge?" Matthew asked.

"Bridge stays," Steve answered, starting to get somewhat irritated by Matthew's suspicious manner. "Bridge stays. We keep playing golf."

"Well-well," sighed Matthew, "And what's the Mayor's cut?"

"Might be none," responded Paul quickly. "His predecessor got caught red-handed in the act of accepting bribery. Instead of bribe money, he got full room and board in a Federal prison."

"How fascinating!" exclaimed Matthew. "And,

Steve, you came out unscathed? Water off a duck's back?"

"Had nothing to do with that one," cut off Steve, "The Mayor pulled those chestnuts personally."

All three burst out laughing.

"Plans A, B, and C all amount to same thing in the end," Steve's face grew serious. "We get plugged in to the deal after the formal part is over. We buy Old Lady's land from City for pennies. All we need to do is make sure that Old Lady and Portia Porter do not make a fuss."

"Steve, why do you want me?" asked Matthew.

"You are a private person who'll buy the land and ill-fated house—"

"So my foxy and I are stuck scooping out the water," guffawed Matthew.

"What sort of plan is that? That's eyewash! Does Steve think My Human is stupid?" sneered Freckle.

Milly only moaned.

"Quit whining," cut off Freckle, "It's not over yet. Not the first day they are discussing this plan."

"Not the first day," repeated Milly sadly. Privately, she assessed her position with growing pessimism:

Against Old Lady, there were: Cheap Steve, the City, the whole Golf Club, and now three million dollars. On

Old Lady's side—just Portia Porter and Raccoon. Freckle has sharp teeth, but she's not the decider. Her Matthew has a wide smile and good even teeth without gaps. I wonder what he really thinks about this scheming.

"Freckle, darling, why are they cajoling Matthew into throwing us and Old Lady out of our home? They have three million dollars already," begged Milly.

"Because," said Freckle glumly, "they need more money to dig more Human burrows . . . sorry . . . build Human houses. They need millions to build. Steven and Paul don't have millions yet, but Matthew does. My Human is very rich. Maybe in the billions. Or trillions."

Freckle was obviously exaggerating the numbers but, in her eyes, everything about her Human was bigger than eternity.

"But what happens to *us*?" crestfallen Milly did not even have the energy to scorn the obvious puffery.

"Nobody knows. It all depends on My Human. But he, I feel, has not really decided yet. Shsh—he's speaking."

Matthew was standing, and so was Paul.

"You got it?" they said together, suddenly smiling.

"I'm not gonna lose this case," smiled Paul.

"The Mayor will get three million from FEMA. The City'll find a way to take Old Lady's land before this goes to court and FEMA risks a loss."

"My thinking exactly," agreed Paul.

"Champaign!" roared Steve. "To clients who help themselves. To heck with your respect for the law."

❧

Vermillion sunset colored the tops of magnolia trees dark orange. The shadows from the woods stretched out and grew blacker and, somehow, more menacing. The stark contrast between the top of the woods, glowing copper, and the lower underbrush that was submerged in bluish-black darkness made Milly nervous.

My head is splitting. It will soon get dark completely. And I'm afraid of the walk back through the woods. Milly's thoughts were beginning to assume a note of panic.

"Your house is so cozy, I would love nothing more than to visit for a little longer. My darling Freckle, you and I could admire the sunset together. But," Milly's voice trembled, and she felt her upper lip twitch.

Freckle silently gazed at Milly, her eyes glowing, pupils—sharp vertical slits.

"Did something happen?"

"No. Yes. I'm afraid of the dark."

"Of course," agreed Freckle, "you are not a nocturnal hunter."

Out of politeness, and because Milly was her guest, Freckle refrained from lauding the expertise of her Fox species at operating in the dark of the night.

The little fox and the Spaniel glided noiselessly along the Northern border of the fairway. Freckle-the-dutiful-hostess was looking forward to finally bidding good night to her guest and returning closer to her Human for the night. But Milly would not stop chattering.

"You know, my dear, we live upstream, over the Bridge. And I can't quite decide which route to take."

"If it were me, I'd take the woods," offered Freckle.

"That way, I'll have to—" Milly spoke slowly and agitatedly, "have to . . . run across the highway, in front of rushing traffic. Four lanes. Two one way, two the other. The road is rarely empty of the autos. If right side is clear, then on the left they are rushing bumper to bumper. Then the other way around: the left side is good, but the right side is like a rushing stream. At night, the headlights glare, the shadows shift with scary speed—"

"One could walk along the bottom of the ravine," said Freckle. "We hunted frogs there when I was little."

"You think so? I guess I'll have to. I must. There's a way there?"

"I am sure you can pass there," nodded Freckle assuredly, "Why wouldn't there be?"

"No, my dear, you really think it's possible? The passage under the Bridge is so narrow. Especially at the entrance and the exit. Not a single bush grows in concrete."

Freckle smiled at Milly's anxiety.

"There's nothing scary there. After it rains, could be a little deep. But there was no rain today."

"I am so happy that I visited with you, my dear," Milly kept on with reverence and bowing. Then, a vivid image of Coyote brothers of her BFF Coyote flashed before her eyes. Milly's head started spinning, there was noise in her ears, and she imagined vividly that the water in ravine was already rising. Then she was flooded with memories of the night she had spent desperately clutching the Magnolia tree branch—the memories she swore to herself that she'll never think about, let alone tell anyone about. *Rushing water all around. What if her paw missteps?*

Freckle was a little fox not devoid of a caring heart, not spoiled by her plentiful life. She still dutifully paid visits to Dad Theodore and her mother, who had new arrivals this year, five dark-burgundy-fluff covered kits. Impossible to even imagine how her parents could deal with that whole swarm on their own, without Freckle's help.

And as for the ravine under the Bridge, here Milly maybe had a point. There was more concrete every day, and fewer waterside bushes. It seems that even frogs who lived on different sides of the Bridge were severing all their family and business contacts.

"You're right, sweetheart," declared Freckle, "Mathew thinks so too—the under-Bridge conditions are volatile and explosive. Last week, all three of us—My Human, Paul and I, went for a walk along the bottom of the ravine.

No harm telling the Spaniels about it, decided Freckle.

Paul reminisced that as boys, they floated on their rafts under the Bridge. Playing Indians . . ..

Matthew agreed, "There used to be a lot more space, and I don't think it just seems so because we're now grown up."

Then Paul chimed in: "I've wondered for a while how long all this could last. The City grows. The concrete spreads. Rainwater pours into the ravine, and—"

"And," added Matthew, "if one happy day the water tears off the Bridge and, God forbid, some folks get killed, then both the City Mayor and the Department of Transportation will be in sea of trouble."

Matthew looked straight at Paul and continued bluntly.

"This will be a Federal Case and, in one way or another, you'll have to deal with these morons, Paul."

"True," agreed Paul. "but I'd rather not get involved with that mess. The fallout of damages could be drastic. The Country Club would suffer too because the whole golf course will get flooded. Meanwhile, neither of us wants to know exactly who it is that's creating the danger by plugging up the Bridge. Or *why*."

Both friends chuckled, but Freckle did not think they found it funny.

"The whole problem," explained Freckle to Milly, "is because humans rarely hear the arrival of Worry. But don't be fearful, Honey, because we the Vulpine Fami—"

Freckle wanted to include her friends the Spaniels in the Fox family, but realized that she and Milly already had a somewhat uncomfortable conversation about species classification. So, she quickly corrected herself.

"—you and I are pretty close relatives. And we both are quite expert at dealing with Worry. Nevertheless," added Freckle nonchalantly, "a hospitality obligation applies in this situation: you are welcome, dear, to stay here with me for a sleepover."

31

THE FRONT SEAT

Milly woke up at the sound of Human voices speaking oddly close to her. The voices were right above her head—like they were talking straight into her ears—a man and a woman.

The woman's voice most definitely belonged to her Old Lady. The man's voice was familiar too . . . Milly knew that she'd heard it before.

With a heavy effort, Milly deeply sniffed in the air and lifted one very heavy eye-lid—and she was immediately sorry. The world swirled in her eyes as if she'd just conquered the entire Ravine, climbed out from its deepest part at a breakneck speed. And this horrible pain, like someone poured gritty sand into her eyes.

Whoosh! Milly shut both eyes as tight as they'd go, panting and shivering.

But now she remembered!

The second voice—the man's voice—belonged to Freckle's Human, although he did not sound as tense as usual. It sounded like he was laughing.

"If anybody told me yesterday that I'd be shaving a Spaniel's back paw today . . . Never would believed!"

Yes, there was definitely a chuckle in Matthew's voice.

"You've got mad skills," he flattered the Old Lady, "You must've been a surgeon … or a vet?"

"Neither," Old Lady, still speaking just above Milly's head, retorted with a smile, "You, on the other hand, make an excellent surgical nurse, Matthew."

Freckle's Human chortled again, clearly pleased, but did not respond.

"Could not have done it without your help, young man. Can't remember the last time I had to hang an IV drip for a dog."

Old Lady peeled off green disposable latex gloves and pushed down her surgical mask, revealing a wide smile.

"So, thank you kindly!" she repeated and threw

the mask and gloves into a large garbage container, then lightly touched Milly's cold nose with her wrist.

"She'll be OK!"

She's talking about me, gathered Milly, *I'll be OK.*

She felt extremely sleepy all of a sudden, her panting calmed down to steady, even breaths.

Both Humans backed away from their patient, who was now on the mend and sleeping peacefully.

"Worried about your sister, Zip?" The Old Lady had bent down to pet Zip under his chin.

❧

Zip was actually surprised that his Old Lady even noticed that he'd sneaked into the room. Zip's post was in the corner, behind the door, where he determined he'd not add to the havoc. When his Old Lady had first put on the doctor's mask and gloved up, Zip had been stunned not less than Freckle's Human.

Freckle's Human bent down, balancing on his knee, and reached his hand out in reassurance, "She's okay. Your Old Lady fixed her, Zippy."

Zip sniffed the outstretched fingers of Freckle's Human, then licked his hand to say thanks. Even though Zip adored his own Human more than anything, and Old Lady was clearly the most powerful force on the Planet Earth, Zip was a fair-minded Spaniel and would give credit where credit was due: Matthew—Freckle's Human—had been *of help*. Indeed, without Matthew, there might not have been enough time to save Milly.

❧

Yes, Milly did survive her adventurous visit with Freckle, perhaps a bit the worse for wear. Zip and Old Lady lived through severe pangs of anxiety, and were still shaken.

Last night, after searching and calling unsuccessfully for Milly long after the sun had set and the evening had turned pitch dark, Zip and Old Lady both did not sleep a wink. Both listening anxiously, both hoping to hear Milly's bark and howl by the front door, both balling themselves.

As the sun rose, Zip finally fell asleep on the cold marble in the hall downstairs, his nose to the door, not to miss Milly's hoped-for return.

About an hour after dawn, the good news came by telephone. Old Lady snatched up the receiver on the first ring, and yelled *"Allo!?"*

Old Lady's face lit up and oxygen rushed back into the rooms. Zip galloped to Old Lady's side, to listen in.

There was a man's voice on the other side, of the phone. Zip could hear bits and pieces:

. . . found doggie on the front porch . . .

. . . the picture's in our neighborhood pet directory . . .

. . . you missing a dog?

. . . bring right over . . .

. . . No trouble at all, we are already in the car. . .

"Your sister's on her way," reported Old Lady, hanging up the phone.

"By the way, somebody added Milly's name to the local gossip page directory. You know anything about that, Zip? Didn't I tell you to keep low profile?"

But Old Lady was not angry.

Zip and Old Lady exhaled, smiled, and started getting ready to give the ill-behaved little red Spaniel her comeuppance, a proper scolding.

"No park walks for two whole days," threatened the Old Lady gruffly.

Zip wanted to contrive his own punishment as well.

He'd give Milly a good nip on the ear, he decided. *Or maybe even on her upper lip; that's more sensitive. But then he'd lick her nose affectionately to welcome her back. Or maybe he'd lick Milly's nose first.*

Zip could not find a place in his mind large enough to contain his happiness that Milly was *on her way home.*

The biting can wait.

Zip heard Milly's savior say, "I live just 'round the corner. I got the address . . . White Goose Lane . . . that's current?"

"We'll be waiting, thank you," said Old Lady.

The Old Lady took her trusted pistol out of her nightgown pocket and hid it back inside the bed stand—no need for *that* anymore—then walked over to the security system on the wall behind the entrance door, pushed the third button on the bottom left, and ordered forcefully "Open Gate."

The front gates that secured the entrance to the house started their slow move, and Old Lady calmed Zip who'd been twisting anxiously in one spot by the door because he felt that his heart would jump out if he did not move *somewhere.*

Wasn't he wise to add Milly to the Dog Registry, Zip congratulated himself privately. *Old Lady's wise not to scold me for that, too.*

"C'mon, Zippy, your naughty little sister is safe. Born under a lucky star. Chauffeured in a car, no less. Arriving home like a movie star, imagine that."

I bet she'd ride on the front seat, Zip was immediately jealous. *No, I am definitely going to bite her first,* **then** *lick her nose hello!*

Zip and Old Lady got situated on the top step outside their front door, watching every approaching car for signs that it carried Milly. Two cars whizzed by without slowing down, then a large car turned into their street, slowed down, drove up a little more, and paused again. The driver was obviously looking at the street numbers.

"That's her, that's our Milly," said Old Lady, and stretched out to her full height, waving both hands in the air, "We are here!" Milly's conveyance was a sleek late-model coupe, buffed to a dazzling shine and sporting lots of metal inlays. *Must be more expensive than our departed car,* noticed Zip, *our car that drowned.*

Most definitely, Zip was delivering Milly's comeuppance first. Bite her ear. For sure. But unwillingly, he started yipping a happy song,

"Milly, Milly, you were found, you are back! My Sister's safe! Woof-bark!"

Zip streaked down the front stairs so fast that his

ears almost did not catch up . . . but screeched to a halt and plopped on his tail: the Human emerged from the car holding on his outstretched hands. . ..

"What have you done to my Milly?" screamed Zip, "You—it's YOU?" At first sniff, Zip had identified the Human. It was Freckle's Human, the one who presided over the Meeting of conspirators against Old Lady, it was *HIM*!

Zip's heart scrunched and jumped sideways, like from a mighty blow to a ribcage.

"What have you done? Give Milly back, you scoundrel," Zip barked, "Give her back! NOW," Zip's voice was no longer menacing, but a panicky cry for help. "Old Lady, make him!"

Old Lady was already by Zip's side, and ordered Zip to be quiet.

Without so much as greeting to the Freckle Human, who was muttering that

. . . the doggie . . . it was fine just now . . . when we were on the phone . . . I went to the car and noticed . . . breathing . . . I checked . .

Old Lady ordered, "Let's carry the dog inside. Quickly."

Zip's jaw dropped in horror and amazement, but then he understood and almost bit his tongue.

Stiff upper lip, he realized, *one's gotta keep a stiff*

upper lip whatever life might bring you. The public image of Old Lady's house must be preserved.

Zip closed his jaws, arranged his muzzle into a respectable expression, and rushed after Milly who was getting whisked into the house by the treacherous Freckle's Human.

Adding to Zip's confusion, Milly and the Freckle's Human were being ushered to the prohibited part of the house, the Secret Room upstairs where Zip and Milly were not supposed to go.

Zip first found out that the Secret Room was off limits the hard way, when he decided to use Old Lady's dusty papers that were stored in the room to give Milly her first reading lesson. You'd think Old Lady would be grateful for Zip's initiative. But no. Both of them—the teacher and the pupil—were mercilessly thrown out, mid-lesson.

"OUT, the both of you, and don't ever even thinkaboudit," had ordered Old Lady, "never ever, both of you, run along now, go on!" She said all of that in one angry breath.

Scattering out of the Secret Room, Zip had made a mental note to sneak in back and investigate. Which he did. His second visit to the Secret Room yielded a scary and confusing history of the House's previous owner, a history that he still needed to clarify. But since that day, the door was locked and no paw had entered the Secret Room.

Until now.

Now, for reasons that Zip could not fathom, Freckle's Human was allowed in. *HIM?!*

Up the stairs, along the corridor, and into the Secret Room Old Lady hurried, Matthew on her heels, clutching barely alive Milly to his chest.

The key turned in the lock, and with a click and a swoosh, the doors were ajar. Old Lady stepped back and motioned Freckle's Human in, Milly lolling limp and lifeless in his large arms.

Zip slipped inside unnoticed, expecting to be banished any minute, but he was not willingly going to abandon his Milly. He took a position pressed inconspicuously into the wall by the door. It was a little hard to see from there. Another corner—across the floor, closer to where they put Milly—had beckoned him. But Zip chose to stay close to the exit. In case Old Lady'd decided to throw him out again, he would at least depart with dignity. A walk of shame in front of a stranger, no that was not for Zip.

But nobody threw him out. Nobody paid Zip the slightest attention.

The Secret Room turned out to be much larger than Zip remembered.

A medical-looking metal table with a shiny stick that ended in a hook was wheeled in mysteriously from around some corner alcove at the far end of the room.

In one swoop, Old Lady reached up to the top of the metal hook and mounted an ice-like bubble full of transparent liquid with narrow tubes that came flopping out of the bubble.

"We need to shave her paw for the IV," announced Old Lady. She was holding up a razor, the *Gillette Fusion* from the same pack that Zip'd seen in her bathroom before. Old Lady shaved her own legs on those rare occasions when she chose to wear a skirt instead of her usual slacks.

Milly's got much thicker fur, thought Zip distractedly.

"You're a guy, you do the shaving," delegated Old Lady, "You've got more practice."

"I do shave," agreed Matthew.

"I'll cut off the flags here, the bushy fur," Old Lady divided tasks. "You shave this bit. Super-smooth, like you'd shave before a big date. Got it?"

"Never shaved a dog before," hesitated Matthew, but his hands were already on the *Gillette*.

"Lucky for you," Old Lady regained her usual

ironic self. "Well, first time for everything. Let's make haste, I can't manage it all alone in time."

Matthew held the razor up to his eyes. "*Gillette*," he read out-loud.

"Let's do this! Quickly. Urgently! The dog may die if we don't hurry."

Zip felt his heart jolt and the room went dark gray before his eyes, like under the morning fog above the Ravine. A frightful word reverberated in his ears, "DIE."

He whined "Milly, do not not die!" and felt his jaws tingle and the room got freezing cold.

Zip heard Old Lady spit out orders:

"Stretch out the skin . . . that's right, between your index finger and your thumb . . . not like that, like on your cheeks. . . . No, you are doing it all wrong! *Against* the hair growth, not with the hair. . . YOU NEVER SHAVED BEFORE?!" Old Lady was almost shouting now.

The world came back into focus in Zip's head.

Freckle's Human is taking orders from Old Lady too . . . interesting, was the first thought that floated into Zip's mind.

Freckle's Human Matthew was now quiet, hunched over the high steel table where Milly was *maybe dying*, invisible to Zip. Her little body was almost entirely obscured by this huge Human's broad back. For an eternity, Zip could not see much —except that Freckle's Human' light-blue shirt started developing spots of a darker color. In the middle of his back, then around his armpits, where it turned dark blue, almost navy.

. . . .

"All done. Perfect shave!" commanded Old Lady. "Hold it here . . . Stretch to the right . . . Stretch harder . . . not that hard! I have to find the vein . . . wait . . .I missed it! . . . Here's the vein . . . I see it . . . hold still, I can barely feel the pulse.

"There you go, I got it! . . . Stop trembling. Don't jerk your head. Close your eyes, if you must. Can't you see I missed it . . . hold on, hold here. I'll go switch out the needle."

The room was silent, and Zip panicked and jumped up. *Why did she stop barking orders? Is Milly dead?* Zip raised his chin to the ceiling and let go of a high, screechy, miserable howl, but he was interrupted with Old Lady's happy voice.

"There you go, we did it. She'll be fine. You can open your eyes now!"

Old Lady and Freckle's Human were no longer

huddled over Milly, and Zip could see the familiar golden fur now.

"We did it!" repeated Old Lady.

Then, returning to her stiff tone, Old Lady asked, "You aren't afraid of blood, are you? No? Fine, I'll take some blood for tests." Her voice was firm and sharp, but Zip could smell that she was happy now.

Both Humans were quiet for another minute, but Zip was no longer panicking. Freckle's Human kept sweating, his shirt had almost no light blue spots left. Old Lady, on the other hand, grew much taller to Zip's eyes.

I always knew she is the most important Human of all the Humans, noted Zip, and privately congratulated himself for lucking into such a powerful protection.

Then Old Lady switched the bag with transparent fluid up on the stick to another color and, ordering Freckle's Human to watch that it dripped slowly, she disappeared again behind a low screen in the back of the room.

Zip was watching Matthew's dark-blue stained back with an odd mixture of hope and hatred. And a little gratitude.

What had Freckle's Human done to his Milly? Zip growled softly at the dark-blue back: "Don't even think of trying something funny again. Don't go shirking the watching duty now. I double-dare you. I'll bite you leg off."

He has no idea how strong my jaws really are. Of course, he's gonna kick me if I bite. But he'll miss, for sure. Or I'll duck. He'll miss. Or I'll duck, for sure.

Old Lady's only disciplinary technique for the Spaniels was *grounding,* so Zip had no personal experience with physical altercation involving a human, but he was not deterred.

I dare him to go against me, he thought.

The room grew quiet. Zip could not even hear any breathing—not Matthew's not Milly's. Zip was about to scream that they were all dead, when Old Lady shuffled back, sounding reassured.

"Young Man, where did you say the dog was found? In front of your house? You live on the golf course?"

"Yes, why," Freckle's Human was surprised.

"The dog's allergic to pendimethalin."

"Pendi—?"

"A common herbicide, they use it on golf courses," explained Old Lady with an air of irritation, like the chemical content of golf course sprays was supposed to be a common knowledge among all Humans.

"Some mammals are allergic," she added.

Our Milly is allergic to the weed killer for the golf course's grass, sighed Zip. *She is so sensitive, our Milly. But also so un-killable! Too bad she was half-dead on her ride here from the Golf Club. She'd have enjoyed the front seat if she were more . . . alive."*

"Thank you kindly, Young Man," said Old Lady, "We'll be fine from here on. May I offer you a cup of coffee?"

Great idea, thought Zip, *but Freckle's Human should better shower first. He's turned dark blue—not a spot of light blue anywhere—and smells like frogs from the Sneaky Creek Ravine.*

32

COFFEE AND PARIS

Everything about Old Lady's home was gleaming with warmth and jubilation. The spirits of the Humans and the Canines alike soared with the *memento mori* satisfaction that descends when a family member whose life had teetered on the brink of the grave had passed the crisis and is clearly on the mend.

Milly, sporting a shaved hind paw, was stretched out comfortably on the freshly washed dog bed, topped with freshly laundered sheets, positioned in the place of honor—on the oriental rug in front of the fireplace. Of course, the Summer months in Ducklingburg are too hot for building a welcoming fire in the fireplace, but the celebratory candles were lit on the hearth, their warm glow cast on Milly's golden fur.

Old Lady and Matthew-the-Freckle's-Human were celebrating together at the Old Lady's dining table, a table whose size could have easily accommodated another dozen guests. Settled close together at one end of this humungous table, the two Humans sipped coffee laced with cognac. They had been chatting leisurely for hours now.

Zip was the only one nervous, pacing around, not sure where to pitch his camp. He had tried lying under the table, but it was too far from Milly's bed. Yet, the Old Lady badly needed his protection too. *Old Lady must be warned about Matthew's real essence, and Zip was the dog for it.*

Zip knew all about Freckle's Human and the greedy conspiracy that he and his buddies had hatched.

And that also made him pace. On one paw, Zip's knowledge of Matthew's role in the plot made Zip loath to host a pleasant chat with such a disgusting snake. On the other paw, Matthew was the one who saved Milly. Matthew found her and brought her home. Matthew shaved Milly's paw, even though he was so nervous that he sweated through his shirt. Also, Old Lady did say that she would not have had enough time without Matthew's help. Zip was torn.

In the end, he decided that the important thing was that Milly was safely back home and went to see about making her aware how wonderful it was to have her back with her family.

"Milly, sweetheart," Zip licked Milly's nose carefully. The nose was cold and wet, so she was clearly recovered.

"Milly," started Zip again with passion, "we all, I mean Old Lady and me, we are all so happy that you are well."

Zip held a pause a little longer than was conversationally necessary.

"But can you tell me . . . what were you doing on the Golf Course? All by yourself? Without us? At night?"

Milly lifted herself on her front paws and twisted her head back to examine her rear, shaved paw.

"Zip, do you think my flags will grow back quickly? So I could be seen again, in public?"

"Milly, don't change the subject. What were you doing there?" pressed Zip.

"Oh, spying," said Milly airily, still twisting her neck and squinting to better examine the shaved leg, which was still just as bald as a minute ago.

"I suspected as much," sighed Zip, and locked his eyes on Milly's face, "AND? What's the intelligence gathered? What did you find out?"

Speaking as though she was repeating a phrase she'd heard, Milly uttered in monotone,

"Following a systematic listening in and having carefully analyzed the information, Freckle had concluded that—" Milly interrupted herself to let out the frustration.

"Zippy, take a sniff of that talk! Freckle's *deep analysis* my paw! Freckle has forgotten her place on the ancestry tree . . . what was that tree . . . ."

"Genealogical," prompted Zip.

"Right. *That* tree, where foxes are not as important a branch in our canine family—"

Zip growled grumpily.

He did not approve of fox penchant for one-upsfoxship, but did not want to appear unnecessarily judgmental. Especially since, as it was rapidly becoming clear, everybody was spying on everybody else.

"Freckle's getting big-headed," Zip agreed reluctantly, "But tell me, what did the Humans say? Think carefully and try to remember word for word. Please, Milly. It's important."

"Word for word . . . that is not easy, Zippy. You

know, I'm not sure I'd met those words before. Definitely do not know what they mean."

"Try, Milly."

Milly sighed, then lifted her head and gave a hopeful sidelong glance to the shaved leg.

"Let me think. Paul is afraid of the court fight. Because of what his own Expert, Duly Sworn said about black water. Although I personally do not understand how he can know who'll win before the fight started. Anyway . . . if there's no fight, then Paul's career does not go up but also does not go down.

"FEMA . . . FEMA is scary . . . what does she look like, Zip? you seen it? Paul is afraid of her himself."

Without waiting for an answer, Milly went on,

"FEMA wants to go on paying everybody only for those parts that got under water, not the parts that got damp — like that ceiling that attacked you —"

Zip's paws jerked at the memory, and he made to dodge sideways, then got ahold of himself and barked,

"I'm OK — I'm OK — Go on."

"Zippy, I don't know all the words. If there is a fight, Portia will have to fight so long . . . FEMA will never pay Portia for long fight. Zippy, I don't understand all words."

"Milly, there's no shame in missing a thing or two about FEMA. It's not because you never learned to read. Lots of people who learned to read, don't understand a thing about FEMA."

"Do you, Zippy?"

"That's a different matter," said Zip proudly.

He spread his hind paws wide, grounding himself better, and eyes half-closed, launched into a lecture.

"I'll tell you why FEMA is so especially scary. It's not your average insurance company that pays out when houses burn, get blown up by wind, beaten by hail, flooded by broken pumps or sewage. Of course, these Other Insurance Companies are not ecstatic about paying, either. They are tight-fisted too. But, they are afraid of court. The Human with a burned or blown up house calls an attorney and everybody goes to see the judge, and the judge writes an Order and makes Other Insurance Company pay for the burned or blown up house."

"That's what we are doing, Zippy."

"Listen. Other Insurance Companies fear court because the judge gets very angry with the Other Insurance Company for not paying up to begin with, voluntarily, without an Order. You understand?"

"I'm trying hard."

"The judge gets angry for having to spend his time, so he knocks the gavel very loudly and writes an Order:

> *Insurance Company will also pay for the lawyer who had to fight in order to make it pay.*
>
> *Huge money for the lawyer.*

And the Insurance Company has to write the check directly to the valiantly fighting lawyer."

"What about our Portia?"

"No. Listen, that's not all.

"*Other Insurance Company* was also supposed to pay for the hotel where the family will live until they fix the burned or blown up house, or buy a new house.

"And also, pay because the whole family was anxious and emotional and grieved and suffered because they did not get the money right away."

"Zippy, I was anxious and emotional when I got flooded away and was sitting in the tree. Will they pay me?"

"No, Milly," said Zip bitterly, "If it were any *Other Insurance Company,* they would pay for sure. And if they did not pay immediately, they'd pay many times more and for Portia, too. There's even a special name for that, impunitive . . . punishing . . . p-p-punitive," Zip spat out, "punitive damages."

"But no, Milly, *FEMA* will not pay."

"Why?"

"FEMA wrote a law, just for itself. Nobody gets a penny, ever except for what FEMA said she wants to pay.

"Nothing for *anxiety*?"

"No. And no matter how bravely the lawyer fights . . . and even if the lawyer wins . . . regardless how loudly the Judge bangs his gavel in celebration of that lawyer's win . . . FEMA will only pay . . . a pittance. Whatever it wants, actually."

"Why?"

"FEMA has its own secret arithmetic. It counts the flood damage with the magic formula that shrinks it. So everything costs less."

"How come, Zippy?"

Zip thought for a while, searching for an image that would help his sister—

"Got it! Remember when Old Lady put her pink sweater in hot dryer by mistake?"

"Yes! It looked exactly the same . . . except about *my* size."

"That's it! Milly, you are smart."

"Cant't the Judge help un-shrink FEMA's formula?"

"Nah. The Judge knows about this law, and does not even bother to bang the gavel, even if he's angry about it. What's the point of asking for something, if you'd never get it?"

"Zippy, I understand. If FEMA is not going to pay because I suffered, then it is best to just forget about that suffering right away. Anyway, I don't like remembering about how cold and wet I was sitting in the tree."

"You are a clever dog, Milly. I sometimes wake up at night, and also hate remembering how Black Water hit me."

"Zippy, if this FEMA only pays whatever it wants, whether we fight or not, then what's the advantage of having a big fight? For Portia and Raccoon? I don't understand—"

"You don't have to understand it all, just repeat what you remembered. I'll explain later."

"OK. Paul was afraid, but Steve was loud. Steve bawled! About that their whole plan to *smoke out* Old Lady from the House is ruined if there's no case with FEMA. Zip, do you understand what he means? He said they'd never get another chance that good to *smoke out* . . . and he said this word about Old Lady that made Freckle's Human screw up an ugly face . . . I tried to remember —"

"Skip it," ordered Zip.

"Steve is not afraid of a fight. Steve loves the fight. Steve *needs* the FEMA fight to *smoke out* Old Lady from Our House.

"Zippy, Steve wants Old Lady up in a loony bin. He thinks that Federal Judge will lock her up.

"So, Steve told Paul to not even think about giving up the fight. Paul started screaming back . . . actually, no, he was not *screaming,* but he took a really deep *low* voice . . . that *he is Federal Paul . . . he is still young . . . that he is certainly much smarter than Judge Carlson, who was a mediocre student in law school, and Carlson's family is not so prominent. . .*

"That's when Matthew . . . Freckle's Human," Milly corrected her unexpected fit of familiarity,

"Freckle's Human ordered STOP!

"And there was nothing else."

Zip was barely holding in the bark.

"Milly, What did they say about our Portia Porter?"

"Freckle said they always call her *Dark Horse.* I heard this Horse business twice, so I remembered, word-for-word, like you asked."

"And?"

"Paul said that Portia Porter is conceited. And that she does a lot of things *not to her profit*. She has no money.

"Zippy, what if she' like Steve—lots of vanity and no money? Only she's not in their Club of well-connected people. Paul knows for sure who has how much money because he's FEDERAL.

"Paul said Portia Porter has huge mortgage for her absolutely not stylish condo—

"But Freckle's Human said that she still could go fight, even though there's mortgage.

"Then Paul said that she also has her student debt, and it's . . . Sorry, Zippy, I did not even try to remember the number. I am not so good with arithmetic."

"Go on," urged Zip.

"Then Freckle's Human said that, in this case, it would be harder for Portia.

"That's when Paul cracked up laughing and said Portia took the case on conti . . . con-ti . . . You know what that is?"

"No."

"Steve did not know either.

"Freckle's Human smiled and called her a *brave girl*. And explained that Portia has to work for us for free. Even if she wins, she only gets a third of what we get. FEMA will never pay her legal fees, which is, they said, lots more. That's the law, which FEMA wrote for itself. Nobody can change it. Now that you explained, Zippy, I understand what the Humans meant.

"That's when Steve said Paul should drag this case another year.

"Paul said that he did not care how clever or talented Portia is, there was no chance she'd last a year, she'd go bankrupt.

"Steve was ecstatic about Portia being bankrupt. Then started bellowing at Paul again that Paul shouldn't even think about getting Portia bankrupt until Old Lady . . . until the Judge . . . puts Old Lady in a loony bin.

"Steve screamed at Paul. *Judge Carlson is your buddy, get him to sign a Receiver Order . . . a Guardian Order . . . whatever it takes.*"

"Milly, what about Freckle's Human? What did he say, do you remember?"

"He just shook his head and smiled funny."

"And Freckle? She said anything?"

"Oh, she had a heap of things to say," responded Milly, sounding agitated. "Freckle says . . . Her Human is on the hedge about joining forces with the other two. He still can't decide if he wants to take away Our House."

Zip could feel an indignant roar rising in his chest and swelling in a huge knot but remembered that Freckle's Human did save Milly. So, he choked down the roar, sniffed scornfully instead, and stayed sprawled out on the oriental, moving his misty gleaming eyes from Milly to the Freckle's Human and back to Milly.

"No, Zippy," whispered Milly hotly, "He is not that bad, he is not like the other Intruders. But he has an *interest*. His *interest* it to protect the golf club. They can't have Black Water spoiling the green, or else they will all lose money. They'll all be poor."

"I get it," responded Zip cynically, "Freckle and Theo will have to fend for their own food in that case."

"Seems that way . . . Yes, I'm sure," agreed Milly, "Freckle said that the Intruders Steve and Paul inspected the concrete under the Bridge and were overjoyed. Said they were gleeful about it. But don't forget, Zippy, Matthew . . . Freckle's Human . . . did save me."

"Or did he? His real purpose maybe was to infiltrate our home, to sniff around? I might have have to bite him, after all."

"No, Zippy, please!" Milly loathed anything to detract from the peace and perfection of her recovery day. "Let's eavesdrop instead. What are they talking about? Let's find out!"

"Nothing to eavesdrop, I got it already. They've been talking about Paris landmarks. Comparing their notes on the Luxembourg Garden."

"Paris? Did we live there, Zippy?" Milly closed her eyes, trying to reach for puppy memories as far back as she could, "I don't remember that she took me to that garden when I was little. What else?"

Zip consulted the reflection in the fireplace marble mantelpiece and jumped up.

"He's standing up to leave, time to go home!"

"You think she'll rub his palm now that he saved me?"

"No way! Bet you anything. Old Lady can sniff out a rotten Human as well as you and me. As well as Theodore sniffs out Worry."

"But he *saved* me," started Milly, and she was right. Before the Spaniels' widening eyes, Old Lady let the Freckle's Human step in, open his arms, and give her a brief hug.

"Bite him," growled Zip under his breath, "just let me catch this snake alone. Milly? Milly!"

"Sorry," said Milly, shaking off a bout of drowsiness.

"Milly, wake up, we need to get upstairs, to check out the Secret Room. Old Lady may have left the door unlocked. It needs to be investigated."

But Milly made no effort to move from her comfortable bed.

"Milly, we have to read the dusty papers. Too bad you do not read so well," Zip seized the sheet on Milly's bed and pulled.

"Why bother reading if you can get all the books on audio," retorted Milly sleepily.

"You are not listening! The Secret Room! And we should bite Freckle's Human. You distract him and I—"

But Milly did not share in her brother's investigative spirit nor in his combative ambition. There was still a festive smell in the air, and the effort of reaching her puppy past for foggy European memories exhausted Milly's small reservoir of energy. When Zip turned his head back, his sister was fast asleep, both hind paws in the frog pose, snoring lightly every third breath.

It always falls on me, thought Zip with resignation. *But no matter! The Secret Room will not stay secret even if I have to read those documents all by myself.*

Zip steeled his resolve: The stacks of papers in the Secret Room were a bit intimidating to a small Spaniel, but *somebody had to do it.*

"Milly, time's ticking away. Procrastination in not an op—"

"*Khhrrr . . .*" snored Milly, and smiled in her sleep.

I'll find a way in, swore Zip. *There must be an opportunity.*

33

BINDERS TIED WITH RIBBONS

An opportunity presented itself the very same week and came, as it had once before, in the shape of Human-Raccoon.

Raccoon had appeared in their doorway in response to Old Lady's enigmatic text messages.

Your assistance requested. OL
Today. OL
Quite urgently. OL

"Are you proficient with the scanning?" inquired Old Lady.

"I don't usu—" retorted the Raccoon, puzzled at what kind of scanning duty at Old Lady's home could possibly necessitate the urgent summoning that he had received.

In Portia Porter's office, manning the scanner was below Raccoon's pay grade.

"Hoppy usual—" started Raccoon.

"—$25 an hour," retorted Old Lady, a proposal which sharply grabbed Raccoon's attention.

"For just the *scanning*??"

"For your *confidence*," said Old Lady with an air that evoked importance.

Before Raccoon could object, he already had been led upstairs.

"May I see your phone? Your phone stays here," Old Lady pointed at a silver Champaign bucket that had been parked by the Secret Room door, and when Raccoon began to argue, Old Lady reached out her hand and firmly liberated the phone from Raccoon's astonished grip.

"C'mon in," Old Lady turned the key and stepped aside to usher in only the third Human whom The Secret Room had seen within Zip's whole memory.

One look inside—and Raccoon was sucked in by force of his overdeveloped curiosity. Old Lady followed, leaving the door ajar, just far enough for Zip to slide in quietly behind the Humans.

Old Lady had everything prepared for the work.

From a flat sealed package, she tore out seven sparkling-new flash drives.

Zip liked them instantly. Tiny, nifty, in every color of the rainbow, the flash drives would make interesting after-dinner toys. But suddenly, they looked important.

Old Lady had freed up a folding table right off the entrance to the Secret Room and set the flash drives in a line on the clean table surface.

"In rainbow order," Old Lady directed, "red, then orange, then yellow.

Zip watched intently. After yellow came green, followed by blue, and then indigo. Violet came last.

"Start with the red, and then follow the rainbow scheme," she ordered.

Raccoon pushed a large lock of bright brown hair off his forehead, which meant that he was thinking hard. His sense of decorum was clashing with his loyalty to client. Stalling for time, he picked up the torn packaging and lifted it to his eyes, examining.

"4GB each? Identical capacity? Why in that order?"

"Rainbow."

Apparently that was the only explanation he'd get and it was clearly wiser to stop asking.

While Old Lady was busy directing Raccoon, Zip stealthily covered the perimeter of the room and took an observation point in the corner opposite the entrance door, his place secured between two towering bookshelves. Something told Zip that he would be safe this time, not be violently turned out.

His hunch proved right very quickly. Old Lady's gaze paused on the dog, and she gave a slight affirmative nod.

I'm approved, realized Zip, and stretched out both front paws, resting his head on top to watch the show comfortably. From what he'd seen so far, it was promising to be a lengthy job for Raccoon.

Having ascertained that everybody was in position, Old Lady disappeared behind tall bookshelves and returned clutching safely to her chest a large dust-colored binder. The binder looked like it had survived each kind of assault known to paper—it had been bent, twisted, folded and stuffed in spaces obviously too small to fit it.

The sides of the binder were tied together with an equally battered ribbon, frayed and fringed at the ends, its color faded to indiscernible.

Old Lady placed the binder on the table as though it was part of a museum collection and carefully untied the indiscernible color ribbons, which then hung limply at the sides.

Old Lady stepped away from the folding table and made a sweeping invite for Raccoon to start. "Try not to mix up the pages. Never mind, you are the professional here."

Raccoon surveyed the field, separated the top page and lifted it with the practiced deftness of an office worker—his two hands supporting the page lightly, barely touching it from the top and at the bottom. His gaze peered curiously at the page and he looked up, bewildered.

Old Lady forced the smile off her face, "Can you tell the top from the bottom here?"

"Is this Latin? No, Greek?" ventured Raccoon.

"Close enough," smiled The Old Lady, "Cyrillic."

"Nifty," smirked Zip, "Old Lady made sure Raccoon does not understand what he is scanning. Clever!"

His own job, Zip decided, was to make sure that not one sheet of paper left the room. Raccoon was a friend, but the interests of the Family commanded the highest priority.

Raccoon looked up from his assignment,

guessing the dog's thoughts, "You're here for extra protection? Yes, doggy? Don't blame you."

And so they started.

❧

Watching Raccoon work was a pleasure.

First, he moved the rainbow of flash drives out of the way, to the top right corner of the table, preserving their order of succession, and clearing enough table space to situate the original in two piles—the scanned and the to-be scanned—so that not even a hair of one pile touched the other.

He worked unhurriedly, with no unnecessary movements.

Zip watched as page after page moved from one stack onto the other.

Raccoon—Zip could tell from looking at him—made no attempt to decipher the text, consumed with making sure that each page was centered squarely on the glass of the scanner. Raccoon's full attention was on the precision of his fingers that handled the sheets. The paper was yellow-gray, soft, and, judging by the way Raccoon's hands moved, extremely friable.

The whole scene looked very much like a documentary about a museum that Zip and Milly once caught on YouTube. Except without the white gloves.

The sheets of paper were moving from the bigger stack to the buzzing scanner, and onto the smaller stack until eventually the smaller stack grew bigger . . . Zip's tense watchfulness was mellowing with every page. His head nodded involuntarily a few times, and, to stay awake, he started pondering the papers.

Cyrillic, she had said, *Russian. So, should not even bother trying to read it.*

To Zip's displeasure, Old Lady had ignored all his hints at teaching him to read. He had struggled with learning English all by himself, but eventually he'd managed. Russian was much harder and Zip stayed illiterate in Russian, to his continued chagrin.

Can't read it. At all. Don't even know any letters except for "A" and the one that looks like a flat bug and means ZHZHZH, sighed Zip bitterly.

Then his thoughts jumped to one of the chats between Old Lady and Freckle's Human Matthew.

Human Matthew had been invited to tea, a second time since Milly was saved.

Bothersome, thought Zip. *Must be watched.*

Naturally, watching over Milly had interrupted his focus quite a bit, but Zip was eavesdropping with tenacity, and parts of conversation got stuck in his brain verbatim, waiting for a quiet point in time to be extracted and considered. Watching Raccoon's professional hands dancing over the brittle papers, Zip decided that now was the right time. He reached back into the crevices of his memory and, taking one by one the words he'd remembered from that afternoon, considered each separately and tried to give each a proper thinking over.

❧

The first thing that Zip remembered—and which etched itself sharply into Zip's memory—was how decisively his Old Lady had cut off all of Matthew's inquiries into her supposed *medical prowess*. Politely, but extremely firmly, like only Zip's Old Lady knew how.

Instead, Old Lady had deftly steered the conversation towards the talents of Freckle's Human himself and, pretty soon, she got him so engaged that he was doing most of the talking.

By the end of the evening—Zip was sure of it—Matthew's hands, which had started out being twisted together tensely in one big fist, had unfolded and relaxed. His knees stopped twitching, and he even leaned back in his chair and folded his left leg on top of his right knee at a right angle. Old Lady called him *Matthew*, and sometimes, *Young Man*. He seemed to like *Matthew* better.

As Zip kept flipping through his mind's stock of that early evening's images, however, he remembered something curious: at times, Matthew tensed up. It was as though—a revelation flared in Zip's head like a spark—as though Old Lady's questions were not aimless get-to-know-you.

Old Lady didn't just ask; she circled like a wasp around some point in Matthew's life, and her questions stung him a little, some quite tangibly.

Their chat moved on to paintings and museums.

Zip never understood the appeal of getting oneself locked up in confined spaces and wandering about with one's neck twisted up, gawking at what's in the frames. Humans were closer to the frames, of course, but they still had to twist up their necks to a crick.

And the smell! The paintings smelled like dust, old sour paints, old rugs or parched-up boards on which the paints were smeared. Nothing interesting about these paintings.

Matthew was not a fan of pointless museum walks either. He came right out: "No time. No energy. My work was exhausting and stressful sometimes."

Yes, Zip remembered that quite clearly: Matthew's lips tightened when he was talking about work, became a narrow line, then disappeared completely. But Old Lady kept buzzing and buzzing around the subject, like a housefly that can't find its way out through the glass of the window. She ascertained that Matthew's line of work did not include criminal law—what painting was stolen from which museum was not his problem. Old Lady moved on to the notorious corporate scandals, and kept asking about those, buzzing and buzzing.

"*Les Échos* wrote—" Old Lady would start.

"Fortunately, didn't catch that one," Matthew cut off that conversational opening.

"*FranceSoir* said . . . what was your impression—"

"I really did not have that many free nights," retorted Matthew, and bit his upper lip—yes, Zip was sure he saw that—as if Matthew was trying to calm himself at the mention of this subject.

"Free nights. In retrospect, I wish that I did not have any at all." And, with that, it became clear that Old Lady had finally hit the informational jackpot because Matthew blurted out an account of the root cause of his embittered unhappiness.

❧

One of those rare free nights, Matthew came home to his Angoulême watermill house unexpectedly early and found that his wife was no longer expecting his return.

She had gotten tired of her frustrated expectations.

Fell out of habit of living together was what she said. She saw their gardener more often than she saw her husband. When she did see Matthew, he was always tired and absorbed with his own thoughts.

Matthew was always too busy for her and too stressed for her. The gardener was never stressed, and always brought her flowers. Yes, the flowers were from her own garden, so what? *It takes a thought,* was how she put it. She liked a man who cared to at least *take a thought.*

She liked the gardener better now. Better than Matthew.

No, she never said she left him. She wanted to *stay back* and *sort things out.* That's how she put it. But what she really meant was that she wanted a divorce and to keep the mill house and all of the other appurtenances of their comfortable lifestyle. And, most important of all, she'd never ever follow him to South Duck.

❧

Matthew spat out that entire story in one breath, then—Zip remembered—a chilly spell shrouded the room. Humans act detached right after they'd shared a confidence. Zip never understood that. It'd seem that confidences would make them friends, show that they trusted each other. But Matthew arranged his face in a fake smile and hastened to wrap up the visit.

"Must push off now. . ..

"No, no thinks required. *You* saved Milly. All I did was shave her paw," and he guffawed at the memory. "*You* saved her, with your own competent hands!" He glanced at Old Lady's hands somewhat askance, "skillful hands, so adroit and," as he already half-rose from the sofa, he added with an unexpected familiarity, "your hands look so young!"

Old Lady's reaction was equally unusual.

Of course, she did not fuss or blush or twitch, or say "thank you for the compliment." That part was not odd. The odd part was not that she said nothing at all, but that she *stared Matthew down*. In that stare, her eyes started to resemble Theodore's—the narrow vertical slits of his fox pupils protect Theo's soul from every prying glimpse. Theo can smile with his mouth, and even say a lot of pleasant things, all while his eyes stare the Spaniels down inquisitorially.

That's how Old Lady got. Old Lady looked at Matthew, unblinking and unmoving.

Zip never remembered her giving this sort of stare to anybody else before. But that only lasted for a few moments and then Matthew hastily exited the house and drove off. The Old Lady did not rub his hands, as was her habit. And did not let him hug her, like the first time, when he saved Milly.

Abruptly emerging from his reverie about the odd Matthew's visits, Zip returned to the here and now.

The scanner was clicking off the seconds, evenly like a metronome. Under Raccoon's skilled hands, the pages from Old Lady's Secret Binder were transferred neatly between piles. The *scanned pile* had just about devoured the entire *to-be-scanned* pile. First binder was nearing the end.

When the job was done, Zip quietly slipped out of the Secret Room behind Raccoon, so deep in thought that he did not even try to freshen up their friendship by sticking his cold nose into an unsuspecting hand or by drooling on Raccoon's office pants. Even Zip's tail-wag was unenergetic, just a couple of uninspired twitches of the stub. Raccoon did not seem to notice; he was likewise looking engrossed in thoughts and puzzled. He silently accepted his payment in cash and shoved it, still folded, in his pocket, promising to stop by tomorrow after work for Portia to "start on the next color of the rainbow."

There's something odd going on. I am missing something, thought Zip.

34

FRECKLE DOMESTICATES

Freckle stood and watched as Matthew scooped up that silly Spaniel Milly with such a swift and gentle care, placed her on the front seat of his beloved HumanMobile, and whizzed away without as much as looking back.

And Freckle felt *something*.

An uncomfortable feeling in her stomach.

A pang.

Not that she was hungry. And not that she needed attention. Foxes are superior to dogs in that regard; a fox does not attach her whole life to one Human. Of course not!

It's just that Freckle got the urge to perform a doleful song,

Yap-Yap-Yap, Yurrr-Yoy
YAP-YAP-YAP, YURR, YOY

Maybe even several times; not sure how many.

"Yap-Yap . . . ."

Humans always cringe so hard when they hear this fox yelping.

But Freckle did not feel like hunting yelps. It was a sad song. Fox hunters have a name for it, a *fox melancholy.*

But why did the song come to Freckle?!

The little fox was at a loss.

What possibly could be wrong with her?

Everything about her life was peachy-keen. She had all the food she could eat; she enjoyed affections and indulgence and esteem from the scores of idle Humans who populated the Scared Hare Country Club—Freckle's present hunting grounds.

Her paw had mended, and her jumping skills had developed beyond those of any fox she'd ever known.

Where did the sad song come from??

Matthew still had not come back, so she sat outside in the gravel patch where his HumanMobile was usually parked, closed her eyes to concentrate, and started softly, "Yap-Yap. Yap. Yurrr—"

And all of a sudden, it dawned on her: she *envied* that silly Spaniel Milly. Envied the care with which Matthew had gently carried her to the car.

Freckle wanted to be *her Human's own Fox.*

Her Human should belong to her and her alone.

I want to be domesticated, thought Freckle, her jaw dropping in astonishment as that realization ricocheted within her own brain.

❧

Those words were still stewing in Freckle's mind when, hours later, Matthew's car crunched on the driveway, and he jumped out, in foaming sweat, as if he had run behind the car instead of driven it. Freckle barely looked his way; she was too busy working things out in her mind.

It was as though two different foxes were struggling inside Freckle's mind.

First fox inside her mind was outraged.

Domestication? What nonsense! Squash that sudden silly whim! I'm wild and proud!

Another fox inside Freckle's mind thought that

letting a Human stroke her luxurious red fur . . . would . . . after all . . . not be so very wrong . . ..

Freckle could not work out which path to send her sleek paws and, meanwhile, she slinked into Matthew's house and quietly observed her Human.

Unquestionably, their relationship had grown into trust: they both lived inside the other's presence, though independently. Busy doing their own things, living freely, but aware of one another.

When the weather got unbearably hot, Freckle enjoyed the cold air blowing in the Human's hall. At first, she stayed by the entrance door; then graduated to a place by the Human's foot when he was reading in the kitchen or in the living room.

And too, if it turned cold and nasty outside, her valuable fur was best preserved inside the house instead of soaking in the pouring rain.

She slept inside the house a lot.

Freckle came to the decision that she would mull over the issue just a little longer and, meanwhile, watch over her Human who right now seemed extremely worried about some unknown business. Freckle rested her pointed muzzle, dog-like, on her short paws and watched.

❧

Her Human was agitated.

Freckle sensed something akin to frenzied anger. Freckle's daddy Theo got that angry when Rich Relatives presumed to invade his hunting territory.

After careful observation, Freckle concluded that, right now was not the most favorable *domestication opportunity*.

Her Human crossed his arms, tightly gripping himself by the shoulders, and set out to wander aimlessly.

From his living room,

into the kitchen,

then back,

and to the living room again, in restless circles.

Freckle kept watching. *Surely he had to tire of this aimless circling at some point, and maybe then, she'd . . . try. Yes, wait until he ceased walking —and try!*

It took a while before Her Human settled into the armchair by the fireplace, hooking his ankle on his knee and slumping back into the chair.

Should I try it now? thought Freckle.

But at that moment, his foot began to kick, as though to try and shake off a bad feeling.

No, not a good time yet, observed Freckle.

After spending some time that way, the Human leaned down and untied his shoes, then raised his feet to rest them on the edge of the coffee table.

Now . . . or never. Now!

determined Freckle and jumped lightly on Matthew's lap.

He did not even flinch and kept staring ahead, over Freckle's head, as though gazing through the wall into the far yonder.

Maybe I was too hasty? worried Freckle and was already set to jump away—up and sideways—when Her Human's hand softly plunged into Freckle's plush fur coat. Freckled turned her head towards Her Human and studied him, unblinking. The Human kept on peering at something invisible, beyond the house walls, his hand deep inside Freckle's fur, pleasantly petting.

Perfect domestication timing, noted Freckle with satisfaction,

right time,

right place, and definitely

right Human.

She was about to purr, when Her Human started talking to himself distractedly.

❧

"What was I thinking," muttered Matthew out-loud, "I hate myself. What came over me? What could have possessed me to open up like that to Old Lady?

"Especially the humiliating part that I hired and *paid* that gardener. He was an able horticulturist, though, why shouldn't I pay him well?

"Not too young, not too old, about my age.

"He grew splendidly full flowers, steady blooms.

"He had a real knack for roses. He favored antique roses, historic, fragrant and time-tested. Profusely blooming, in every color.

"Yellow roses, white roses, dark-colored roses, almost black. He grew tea roses, climbing roses,

roses dating all the way to 15th century. Showy and vigorous, delicate and fragrant, he understood them all.

"And how he talked about those roses . . . the tales he told. His favorite was the fifteenth century *Autumn Damask,* or as he called it, *Quatre Saisons.* The emblem in the War of the Roses. The story was that *Quatre Saisones* was the first rose in history to bloom twice in a season.

"A hard working gardener, and high-spirited, and my wife favored him . . ..

"Now he is telling *her* all these same rose tales, sitting on the terrace of my house. My *former* house. Planting seeds. With my wife. *Former* wife, any minute now former."

Matthew are silent.

He looks so sad that I feel like singing my 'yap-yap song,' thought Freckle, *but we might both start crying if I do.*

Matthew had long since mourned his ancient ever-blooming roses, his picturesque river mill house and his perfidious woman. Right now, he was more furious than sad.

What possessed him to take the trip down that particular memory lane? Why would Old Lady beguile him into going there, return him to dwell on his turbulent past?

And what the devil was this left-handed compliment of his —"you have young hands"? Tactless! Old Lady was eighty-four; that he knew for certain. She was a hair older than his own mother.

Matthew kept stroking Freckle's fur, and as he did, his thoughts got sorted, and suddenly he saw it clearly: all this had nothing whatever to do with his wife.

Old Lady's stories and her interrogations about Paris, his French life, *Musee du Luxembourg*—all that unearthed painful memories . . . but not about his wife.

An entirely different woman.

❧

That woman, whom Matthew had never met, but who had destroyed his well-oiled career climb.

That woman, that lawsuit, Matthew's last case.

"In one swoop, I lost that river mill house, my wife, and my career," he said out-loud pensively.

❧

Matthew could not explain, even to himself, why he needed that meeting.

What was the reason he went looking for That Woman? *Too look her in the eye. To tell her . . .*

What was he going to tell her?

What could he ask of her?

He drove the entire way to Waterloo without once asking himself *why*. Her address was in a confidential rider to one of the very secret contracts which he was for certain not supposed to use for any selfish purpose.

The address was listed on Avenue de L'Ete, 298 kilometers from his office.

A three-hour drive.

The door was swung opened by a woman of uncertain age adorned by an impossible hat attached to her plentiful silver-gray curls. The hat was an intricate pillbox topped with a shiny bow in black silk.

In harmony with the black silk of the hat and the silvery curls, a silver-and-black scarf wrapped high around her neck, concealing the neck up to the ears. Half of the woman's face was occupied by her chin and, above, the eyes were aglow with welcoming good humor.

Her diction told Matthew that she was Flemish.

"*Kom Maar binnen.* Do come in! You wish to see the house? Still on the market."

The woman spoke plentifully and quickly. And asked no nosy questions.

"Let's start with downstairs."

Matthew made no objection.

"The former tenant. She was Russian, you know. *Russische dame.*

"Peculiar. Not classic beauty, but a striking looking Madam, she arranged a *laboratorium,* a small laboratory here. Or a study . . . I did not probe. *Russische dame* paid extremely well.

"This here used to be a garage. But she walled the door with brick. Her expense. I had no objection.

"The only trouble now, I have no clue how to get rid of this huge safe . . . and the commercial freezer. Where did she even get it? I've never seen anybody have one quite like it. What did she need it for? . . . And cameras everywhere:

"Here . . .

". . . In the gardens . . .

". . .In every room . . .

". . .Entire security system left behind . . .

"...Her desks and bookcases left behind...

"...Lots of empty plastic containers, like new... Dozens of them . . . You could store all your old sweaters in those—"

Matthew coughed unsure if he could ask to see them, but she mistook it for impatience.

"...Let's walk up to the main floor.

"The kitchen exits into the backyard garden. That was the main entrance where you came in. Glass ceiling. *Russische Dame's* office opens to...

"... All the bedrooms are all on the second floor . . . that's the stairs, up to the second-floor gallery. Master bedroom . . . that's another bedroom . . . bathroom... You do not wish to see? *I knew it!* Men never look at bedrooms, bathrooms or the kitchen . . .."

Matthew nodded agreeably and gawked around, his eyes swung wide open, allowing his loquacious guide to lead him back through the glass-ceiling hall.

"Let's go to the great room. Pardon my haste, I'm pressed a bit for time...

"... I'm proud of this room...

"... The flooring, take a look...

"... My cousin on my mother's side renovated his family Castle . . . actually, *our* great grandfather's Castle. My great grandfather too. My cousin switched to all new, *con-tem-po-rary*," The Flemish Madam puckered her lips, scoffing, "such faceless stuff!

"We *reclaimed* the flooring. Antique, from the great hall. Of course, we had to polish it."

Nothing special, decided Matthew. *Gray, weathered, typical old wood. With holes left by old nails. Creeks and squeaks like nobody's business.*

"*Je comprends,*" agreed Matthew.

"And, of course, the fireplace. You see the etching? Three triangles meet in the center, inside a circle. This—" The Flemish Madam sustained a meaningful, well-rehearsed pause and then dramatically shared:

"This is *Mason's Sign.*"

Exactly like the 'Radiation Danger' sign, thought Matthew privately.

"My great grandpa was an aristocrat." the Flemish lifted her index finger, touching her nose to indicate distinction.

"*Mais oui,*" agreed Matthew.

"What else would you like to know?" The Flemish Madam, concluded her tour and surveyed her domain, smiling at her duties well discharged.

Taken aback with the unexpected question, Matthew spat out:

"Where did the *Russian Madam* go?"

"Oh! The elbows sprang to her waist and her palms flew up in the air by her shoulders, "I thought you want the *house*? That she did not tell me. I don't know. A lot of people came asking for her . . .

"A memorable sort of Madam.

"At first blush, nothing to her at all, nothing flashy . . .

"Big forehead . . .

"Barely any eyebrows . . .

"No make-up.

"The eyes . . .blue eyes . . . the *usual* blue.

"Nose? . . . Normal nose, *nothing special* . . .too short.

"The lips? . . . N*ormal lips* . . . No special contour.

"Hair? Smooth. Fair.

Neck . . . Chin . . . No, I do not understand the fuss.

"Everybody and their brother searching and asking for her. But I do not know anything. . . .

"But you know, there *was* something about her! . . . And she is not even tall. A little shorter than I am.

The jovial eyes were squared on Matthew now.

"And who is she to you? You're the *vriendjie*? Boyfriend?"

"No."

"You knew her?"

"No."

"You—"

"I tried to buy her," answered Matthew simply.

At once, the Flemish Madam swallowed all her eloquence. Still, Matthew could tell that she had not exaggerated when she boasted of her aristocratic family. She had a clear understanding of business etiquette and knew how to conclude an uncomfortable meeting.

"Ah, as I had mentioned, I'm in a bit of a hurry. *Veel geluk!* I wish you good fortune."

Back in the present, Freckle shifted in Matthew's lap.

Matthew murmured "Freckle, are you asleep? Freckle?"

Freckle did not want to move. The Human held her in his lap, and all sad songs of yesterday sprang out of her head. Matthew's hand tickled her neck lightly.

So that's what it is like to be domesticated, concluded Freckle, and summed up her experience,

I like it! I like it a lot!

The Human's glance grew less distant; it was as though Matthew's eyes which had momentarily lost focus now regained their grasp on the world.

"Aha, you woke up. Let's go for a walk then. Now that you are my *domesticated* Fox."

35

LONG DAY ON FRIDAY

By long-established tradition, Friday at Noon marked the end of the hard-working workweek for all the Ducklingburg law offices, the beginning of the weekend break for both the lawyers and the support staff.

It was a glorious hour: the week's work was finished and two whole days of leisure stretched ahead to spend with family and friends.

To send an email, fax or courier to an opposing counsel after 12 Noon on a Friday was about as gracious as putting a brick through the other lawyer's window.

Receiving correspondence that demanded a response was rightly taken as a personal affront. Few mavericks dared to behave that imprudently. There were, of course, newcomers from the North who challenged this established etiquette through ignorance of local custom. But these newcomers usually assimilated soon enough into the Southern work rhythm and learned the joy of *early weekend.*

❧

Raccoon, it could be said, was plunged into the deepest measure of personal assault on the weekend respite rule: he had been working till midnight on Friday for second week straight.

Raccoon was assisted by Zip, who dutifully stood guard over the work.

Old Lady would only stick her nose through the doors occasionally, *to check on the progress,* which progress Raccoon described in colors—*Orange.*

Or *yellow.*

Or, as it happened to be today, *green.* The fourth flash drive and the fourth binder with tassels were nearing completion. The current batch of paper was somewhat less frail, but still demanded museum-like care. The work was neither challenging nor interesting. Any dull assignment palled quickly for Raccoon and was, in the usual course of business at the Portia

Porter Law Offices, unloaded on Hoppy, his office buddy, side-kick and best friend.

Hoppy earns his bread fair and square, realized Raccoon, who was beginning to become uneasily conscious of the muscles in his neck.

The sheets of paper he was scanning were now covered with writing in longhand, always the same handwriting as far as Raccoon could tell. There were a lot of drawings and charts, also executed by the same hand, untrained in drawing. It brought to memory somebody copying a school textbook in physics or maybe inorganic chemistry, Raccoon was not completely certain which. He had never mastered chemistry, and for that reason, disliked it.

Distressed by Raccoon's bad mood, Zip slipped into a fretful nap.

❧

Zip was awakened by gentle stroking on his whiskers. He half-opened one eye.

"Zip — wake up — is that you — in this picture? Wake up, doggie! Let's check."

Zip knew that his Old Lady was always absorbed with her picture-taking, forever snapping pictures.

At first, she used cameras with twist-on color

filters, later the built-in photographic capabilities of her phones. She snapped both Zip and Milly every day from every angle.

Zip did not approve of this activity, for personal reasons.

Overall, Zip was extremely proud of his breed standard conforming exterior. Zip's coat was primarily Black Onyx, highlighted by the fire-gold of a high-collar chemisette that rose to cover his throat and extended up to the bottom of his muzzle.

Two fire-gold-red spots were blazing above his eyes, like eyebrows, and made his gaze intimidating when Zip got angry. When Old Lady once got it into her head to install a cage with two yellow canaries, the poor birds did not last two days after the instance when Zip accompanied their song with his growly "Rrrr-wow-woow-aff." Zip believed in compensating for his lack of musical training with volume and enthusiasm. Terrified, both birds promptly fell off their perches to the bottom of the cage, and there they rested, two sets of unmoving claws tightly squeezed in small fists against their tiny breasts.

"There you go, Zippy," sighed the Old Lady, "You scared them into heart failure."

"All I did was look at them and do a little bit of

sing-along," objected Zip, his blazing eyebrows moving, catching devilish red sparkles from his dark brown eyes.

Zip was tremendously proud of his looks, especially in anger when he was, indeed, resplendent.

But there was one angle which Zip painstakingly concealed from prying eyes and clicking cameras. His silky black and opulent hindquarters, right under the neatly docked black tail, were dotted incongruously with a golden-yellow spot.

Insultingly yellow. For that reason Zip avoided showing his bottom at all costs, and any time he detected a camera that aimed to shoot his backside, he swung around to show one of his flanks instead. "I am not as photogenic from the back," was Zip's justification.

Prodded by Raccoon's insistence, Zip opened the second eye and viewed with dismay the photograph held in the human's hand.

Good grief, he thought, *this scoundrel Raccoon has unearthed—Lord only knows from where—a baby photo of me being held by Old Lady.*

Zip, still a puppy in the photo. Old Lady, looking seriously in the camera. Zip wrapped in her arms, Old Lady's hand supporting carefully his behind . . . and Old Lady's whole hand is sinking in this shameless, brazen, undignified bright-yellow spot that people still assume is . . . Zip did not want to be indelicate . . . as though he was not careful when doing *his business*.

"Whew, such injustice," growled Zip.

"Turn around, doggy, would you," insisted Raccoon, nosing under Zip's tail, "that's you in the photo, aren't you? And Old Lady. Yes, of course, that's you. You were a puppy then. But Zip, what year was that? . . . Hold on, this has the date."

And mercifully letting go of Zip's behind, Raccoon mouthed the caption of the photo.

Paris. Jardin du Luxembourg, 2000.

Raccoon let out a whistle, then started muttering.

"Old Lady looks the same as she looks today, not changed a hair. Of course . . . ladies. Ladies . . . they sometimes have work done on the face. Can't even tell what's what there.

"But Zippy, how old are *you now*? Two? Or 17? Do Spaniels *live* to seventeen? Never heard they live that long! Seventeen? Unbelievable! Zippy, is that you? You do not look like such an old dog, not a single grey hair in your muzzle. No older than three. No, even younger!"

And propelled by his passion for exploration, Raccoon grasped Zip's hindquarters firmly and swung him around so as to face the dog's backside.

"Assault!" squealed Zip, and growled menacingly, "Mind your own business. Let go! Get your nose from under my tail!"

"Sorry, doggy, sorry," Raccoon offered his apology, and the irritation with this long-winded, boring Friday night was gone without a trace.

Raccoon caught wind of something wicked attention-grabbing here.

What the devil was it he'd been scanning?! What do these withered time-eaten papers say? What's so precious here that Old Lady treasures so intently?

Raccoon's ardor was tantalized by his total ignorance of Russian or French. He cursed out the language instruction inadequacies of the damned American-centric education system. Old Lady was clear in her orders that not a scrap was to leave the room and personally checked that Raccoon's phone stayed sequestered downstairs in the hall, waiting powered-off in the silver bucket.

This Friday, like every time before, she said "Your phone, please," instead of a greeting and pointed with her strangely smooth index finger. Under Old Lady's sharp gaze, Raccoon took out the phone from his back packet, lingered a second, and defiantly emptied his pockets, redundantly surrendering even his set of keys on a keychain that was attached to his signature key fob, an old bronze coin etched with his totem animal— a raccoon, of course.

How he wished he could have his hands on his phone now!

Raccoon's inquisitive mind flared up with light of a thousand scanners.

How old ***is*** *this Old Lady?*

Her hair is gray all right. But her hands are smooth. Narrow, straight fingers, not one joint thickened. My mother is much younger, but keeps complaining that the joints all hurt, and paraffin wax bath don't always work.

There has to be some sort of mystery, determined Raccoon, and his feeling of self-pity and irritation with wasting another Friday afternoon on a menial job was gone without a trace.

Determined to get to the bottom of it, he soon figured out a way.

Raccoon peered deeply into the letters on the page. He was strictly forbidden to make copies, and not a shred of paper was to leave the Secret Room. But there was no proscription against looking. After all, without looking, how could he tell which way was up on each page?

There were French and Russian articles, heavily footnoted, with titles spanning miles. If only he knew which word was important . . . His memory was excellent, but not enough to hold on to three lines of senseless mumbo-jumbo—

If only somehow there was a *short* title.

That's when he saw it.

It was a single page, all handwritten. The top of the page swam in the arcana of formula—impenetrable, useless and by now as old to Raccoon, as the endless sight of waves must look to shipwreck survivors on their fifth sunrise lost floating at sea. But lo! at the edge the familiarly incomprihencible sea of arcana, Raccoon spotted a sign of life.

Two mercifully short words were scribbled in the same hand.

ZALIV

ENCERCLEMENT

Raccoon twirled the paper. It did not feel as old as others in that stack.

The back of the paper had a hand drawn map—a bean-shaped lake and circles for cities with lines and arrows around them, reminding Raccoon of old history books with battle maps. Raccoon was not a big fan of history either, but he was a big fan of Secrets. And this looked suddenly like a Treasure Map.

"Zaliv," Raccoon repeated softly. *"Encercle—* French, probably."

Zip raised his nose and sniffed the air disapprovingly.

"Don't tell on me," pleaded Raccoon, and repeated, memorizing, *"Zaliv."*

Deep Academia-net was bound to yield the answers now. And luckily, it was Friday and Raccoon had the whole weekend ahead of him to penetrate Old Lady's secrets.

"Zaliv Encerclement . . . Encirclement?? You ready to find out your Mistress's secret?!" Raccoon whispered quietly to the sulkily watchful Guard Dog.

READ NEXT EPISODE

36

ROSIE QUITS

The rain refused to stop all night. Zip woke up to Milly's sniveling.

After the depositions, Milly had developed a touch of germophobia.

She became concerned with the rainwater:

"Zippy? What if the rain is *contaminated?*"

"It's not," said Zip, "We've played in the rain before. It's just water."

"The grass will be wet. Makes me nervous now," mewled Milly.

"Don't go then," Zip tried to brush her off, "I'll play alone."

Milly threw her brother an annoyed look. She had *business* outside and rather needed his reassurance urgently.

"What about *Hep-C?*" she whined again, "you sure there's no Hep-C in the grass? That Duly Sworn at depositions said—"

The commotion was settled by Old Lady, who was in the most decisive mood that day.

"No playing outside. Do your *business* and back in the house. Get a move on!"

Old Lady held the door open and repeated, "march on!" (She actually said *marsh*, but the Spaniels did not need a Russian-English dictionary to understand that one.) Also, one thing was crystal clear without any translation: today was a day to stay out of Old Lady's way.

The morning was gray-ish, the sky was drizzly and, trotting in step, the Spaniels hurried back inside.

Milly stretched out under the dining table and Zip, giving her a lick on the nose in passing, hurried up the stairs towards the Secret Room door. Zip detested idle life, and watching Raccoon moving pieces of papers from one pile to another was an Important Business.

"Hopefully, today we can avoid reliving my puppyhood photo albums," sighed Zip and, finding a cozy spot outside the door, prepared to wait. Raccoon was running late that morning, but no matter. Both the weather and Old Lady's irritable proscription foreclosed the option of a walk and, anyhow, it was warm, quiet and cozy in the house.

Zip must have dozed off.

He did not notice Old Lady's head showing up at the top of the stairs, followed by Old Lady's shoulders and then the entire Old Lady. Still in her bathrobe and slippers, she sneaked up on the comfortably laid out spaniel.

"Wake up, guard dog!" said Old Lady sharply, inches from Zip's ear.

Zip let go of one shrill bark, intimating "*Intruder*, where is intru—" before he woke up and saw Old Lady, one hand in her pocket. Zip pricked up his ears. What's in the pocket? Does she have a gun? And, always eager to lend support to an armed human, he barked louder.

"Woke up, security detail!" mocked Old Lady. "What are you doing here, anyway? Waiting for your buddy? Raccoon is not coming today. We are now in litigation. Shoo from here. Downstairs. And step on it!"

Old Lady's hand moved in the bathrobe pocket and Zip heard the jingling of room keys. Old Lady was on her way to the Secret Room and not interested in canine company.

Zip was not going to wait for her finger to come out, emphatically pointing in the direction he was ordered to go. He yawned and stretched into the downward dog pose, emphasizing that he knew exactly what his mission was and had no need for orders. Then he turned around to touch his nose to the Old Lady's knee and, still half-asleep, missed and tangled himself in the hem of her robe.

"Go, Zippy, go," responded Old Lady gently.

An understanding was reached, the conflict was resolved, and in a trotting waddle, Zip hastened down the stairs, to wake up his sister.

"Milly, come here! We have a situation," he started calling from the bottom of the stairs. "We are in litigation. Do you know litigation?"

"Never seen it," responded Milly without a second's hesitation. "My area is more in hospitality. *Meeting* organization, *agenda* planning, making sure we stick to the agen—"

"No use in that. We need to find out . . . Can you persuade Rosie to give us more free consultations?"

"When?" Milly's eyes developed an excited sparkle, and the stub that she called her tail stood upwards and began vibrating.

"Now!"

"But Rosie is at home. What will Suzy say if we crash?"

"Suzy loves us."

Suzy lived squarely across the street. Old Lady's contact with the world began each morning with reporting that "Suzy is up—her curtains are opened! No need to stare out the window anymore."

Milly rolled her eyes, suspicious that the owner of a *cat* would have enough sense to love two *dogs* as well, but Zip's argument was solid and persuasive.

"She does. I heard it myself. Suzy was thanking Old Lady for visiting.

At my age . . . it's nice to have a visitor . . . I sleep better if I know you and your dogs are right across the road . . . should something happen . . . you are here, you know that I did wake up in the morning . . .

She must've buttered up Old Lady for half an hour."

Zip was already at the door.

"C'mon, we will be welcome."

"We could go now," agreed Milly, who had jumped up on the sofa in the living room for better view. Indeed, Suzy's curtains were open, and TV was on.

Suzy's TV screen was humungous enough to watch from Old Lady's windows, but only if one reconciled to watching without sound.

❧

Zip was right. Suzy was unmistakably glad to see them and invited both dogs in without asking any questions. Suzy's house was serviced under a contract with a cleaning company; the floors were washed each third Wednesday, whether needed or not. So, Suzy was not particularly concerned with the cleanliness of her guests' paws.

"Come on in," she invited in her warm, melodic voice. "Let me go see what I can find for your treats," and Suzy disappeared into the kitchen.

Rosie was laid out on the sofa, enjoying her program on BBC. She only twitched her tail a little to acknowledge the presence of the visitors. The guests waited politely for the end of a scene wherein a group of cheetahs missed catching one young antelope.

Milly spoke first.

"Rosie, dear. We have a situation! And, as you know, in the law sphere, you are the bestest . . .

Nobody in the whole neighborhood . . . Take Retriever Sam, for instance, all he knows is chasing the deer and getting kicked in his teeth."

Sibling Spaniels forced smiles and shifted from paw to paw in synch. Rosie's tail twitched in double time, and Milly hurriedly continued.

"Lucky and Bella are always tight on the leashes and, besides, both lack the right background . . . anesthesiology, what's the point?

"Marla? Her human's specialty is satellite poles, as far as it gets from the justice system . . . only you, my dear."

"Yes, me." Rosie eagerly ate up the shameless flattery and began to boast.

"Undeniably, I have the best legal pedigree in the area," she said. "Suzy's father was a lawyer, too. See the painting," she jabbed with her tail at the old, dark oil above the mantelpiece, "The eighteenth century masterpiece. It's a retainer from a client. The only thing of value that the client had . . . so grateful for her father's legal service."

The anecdote about the painting and its provenance was one of Rosie's favorites and she was heedless about re-telling it even to those who, like the Spaniels, had heard it many a time before. Staring at the darkened, murky square with feigned interest,

Zip had to suppress the urge to ask what it was supposed to show. That question would have been undiplomatic.

"It's so expensive that Suzy had to specially insure it. In case of fire or, you know, *flood*," boasted the cat. The word *flood* gave Milly an in.

"Rosie, dear, we have a situation. Old Lady—"

Milly gave Zip a look, and he jumped in.

"Rosie, we are in litigation."

"So?" asked the cat flatly. She was losing interest and tried to surreptitiously up the volume for her TV program.

Milly wrinkled her face, bit her left upper lip and moved her right ear back, then put the cards on the table.

"Rosie, we've never seen a litigation. We do not know what it is. You are the only one who knows."

Rosie was caught by the flattery again. She jumped off the sofa and assumed a lecturer's pose.

"*Litigation*. That's what my *other Humans* do," she looked over her back in the direction of her other Humans' house, but her gaze met only with the wall. "They do not see a flicker of daylight, bent over their desks and always filled with angst. That's *litigation*."

The cat lowered her gaze to the Spaniels who were looking at her in stupefied horror.

"I'll explain. *Litigation* happens when one or more parties—"

"What party? Will there be cake?" interrupted Milly, always hopeful.

"OK, I'll try plain English. Suppose there's a cat and a dog. They both want one chicken drumstick. And instead of sharing it, the cat and the dog start a fight."

"That happens," nodded Zip knowingly.

The cat glared at her guests and Zip shut his jaws with a clank, promising himself to never interrupt her again.

"So, this cat and dog start fighting over one chicken drumstick," repeated Rosie edifyingly, "With the unfortunate result of *mutual losses*."

The cat noticed Milly's bewildered glance and translated herself again into plain English: "The dog might get her nose scratched," it was plain that Rosie worked hard to restrain a note of species-jingoism in her voice, "And the cat might also suffer consequences," Rosie sighed, "by getting tooth-holes in her side."

The dogs nodded with understanding.

"And what's more," continued Rosie, and lowered her tone to conspiratorial whisper that a magician would use to reveal his long-cherished secret to his most-promising pupil, "What's more—the chicken drumstick most likely will be *gone* be the fight's end."

The cat basked for a second in the surprised bafflement of her audience and then explained, "either the chicken drumstick will get torn up and bitten in the fight, or some cunning animal who's passing by might swipe it while our cat and dog are busy trying to kill each other."

Rosie sighed, and finished sententiously: "*Litigation* is when Humans can't agree. Because they did not learn to share."

"We understand," said Milly, "No use in litigation. It's better to share. Or even give up the chicken drumstick if it's going to disappear anyway during the fight."

"Problem is," interjected Zip, "we are already *in litigation.*"

"Who's the plaintiff?" asked Rosie quickly, and responding to the two fireball brows that almost jumped off Zip's face, repeated in plain English, "*Who started it?*"

Zip and Milly looked at each other, and Milly fished out the name out of the crevices of her memory, "I think, her name is FEMA."

"FEMA?" Cat Rosie bolted upright, and sat stiff,

"FEMA? Old Lady's taking on FEMA? Rrrrrrrespect!"

"I thought it was the Ducklingburg Zoning Committee," said Zip.

"We think it's both," said the Spaniels in sad chorus, and their faces lengthened, "Ducklingburg Zoning too."

"Oh dear," Rosie rolled her eyes and puffed her chest, "The usual set-up."

Both Spaniels stared, flabbergasted.

"I mean that everybody is suing everybody and their brother," explained Rosie. "They call it *counter-claims* and *cross-claims* and . . . that's litigation for you.

"That's what my Masters do, and why I am so rich. *Litigation.* Everybody is suing, nobody cares how much it costs, nobody is counting their money anymore, neither cat nor dog. The only people counting the money are the lawyers. RICH," repeated Rosie pompously, then decided to take the spotlight off herself.

"By the way: does Your Old Lady have a lawyer?"

Zip and Milly nodded in unison.

"Who?" inquired Rosie.

"R-r-raccoon," blurted out Zip.

"Raccoon? I don't think Raccoon is a licensed lawyer," said the Cat.

"Portia Porter," clarified the guests.

"There you are," Rosie suddenly tightened up, "Portia Porter. The contrarian."

Rosie rose on hind paws in excitement, lost her balance and landed on her butt.

"A maverick, she is. Always going against the current." Rosie was gesticulating with her front paws, in step with her delivery, her voice sounding more in approbation than condemnation.

Zip and Milly did not move for fear of missing even half a hint.

Rosie's eyes were aglow with green lights. She stuck out the tip of her little pink tongue, panting with vivid memories.

"Brilliant mind, that Portia, but—" Rosie paused meaningfully.

Zip and Milly, who thought that they had already developed a keen understanding of litigation, wanted to know how Portia fared in an open combat.

Rosie kept silent, the end of her tail twitching slightly.

"What do you mean by *but*," barked Zip grumpily,

"Portia is a great scholar, one of the best . . . most clever in the whole Ducklingburg."

"But Zippy," interjected Milly softly, "Clever Humans do not fight."

"Not necessarily," retorted Rosie, "Human history is a history of wars."

"That's exactly what I said," agreed Milly wisely, "And how is our Portia when it comes to war? Please tell us. Dear Rosie, your opinion as an expert . . . that's why we are here. . .. Is she valiant?"

"*Too* valiant," Rosie replied evasively and privately thought, *more valiance than common sense. No grasp on local customs and realities.*

"Rosie, could you please tell us . . . what is she like in a fight—"

"—In court," interrupted Zip.

"Why not," preparing for an unhurried narration, Rosie lowered herself on all four paws.

❧

"In our Court," started Rosie smoothly, "there is an unwritten code of local custom. The judges here are not fond of writing Orders. That's the reality of life—"

"What's *'Orders,'*" interrupted Milly abruptly. "Could you elaborate, Rosie, love?"

"Yes, please elaborate," agreed Zip.

Ordinarily, Zip hated it when Milly butted in. But, this time, she had a good point. Zip was not legally educated and was not sure if it was a good thing or a bad thing when judges did not want to write Orders. "Use simple examples, please," he implored.

Rosie looked out of the window, shot a sideway glance at the TV where the cheetahs kept silently chasing their dinner, and started explaining in an energetic voice.

"Thats the whole reason Humans fight in court. The one who get the *Order* from the judge is the winner. The judge decides which Human won and gives him the Winning Certificate, and that's what they call an Order.

"This Winning Certificate . . . called Order says: there was a fight about . . . eh . . . and the winner is . . . eh . . . for instance . . . let's use simple examples.

Cat and Dog fought in court.

Cat won.

The Winning Certificate . . . the Order . . . says:

Here's what happened. Dog nipped Cat's paw.

The Cat is in the right, Dog should not've bitten him.

The Dog will pay. There vet's bills for Cat. And plus the Dog will feed the Cat until Cat's paw is mended enough for to go back to catching mice.

"You're right," yipped Zip happily, "but what if Cat scratched Dog's nose in that fight . . .

Who'd pay that Dog's vet bills and feed the dog who cannot sniff?"

"Exactly."

The Spaniels stared.

"Judge does not want to write the Order. You see, if Cat wins the Order, the Dog could go on to an even higher Court and complain about the Judge. The Higher Court could take the Dog's side because . . . for instance, the grapple was about a milk bone, which actually belonged to the Dog."

"What does Cat want with the bone?" wondered Milly. Zip pushed his nose in Milly's face, "Shh, Milly."

"I don't understand," admitted Zip.

"But that's the point!" explained Rosie, "It's hard to keep it all straight. It's hard for the Judge to figure out who wins and write a proper Order.

"But didn't you say it's why the Humans go to

Court? To get the Order. Strictly speaking, they could fight without Orders anywhere."

"Right. So, your much-vaunted Portia," Rosie smirked as though to herself, "can't get it through her head that our whole legal community chose to live *without Orders*. Everybody chose that way! Judges. Lawyers. Cats. Dogs."

Shaking as though she had trouble believing her own words, Rosie continued forlornly.

"As the court fight goes on, Judges offer *comments,* sort of like *hints,* about who is the Winner, and who's in the Wrong. Then the Judge pretends that one of the lawyers will write first draft of Order and Judge will check and sign. But lawyers never actually finish their drafts. Or, if they do finish, the Judges never sign. Of course, an Order without the Judge's signature is just a useless piece of paper, not an Order," Rosie contemptuously finished her thought.

"Then what can be done? How does one get the money for the vet?" asked Zip.

"In that case," clarified Rosie with an air of unwillingness, "the lawyer for the Cat advises his client to use the home remedies . . . self-help. And Dog's lawyer advises—"

"What about Portia," interrupted Zip rather rudely.

"Portia?" Rosie's eyes glowed with the heat of a battle, "Portia insists on Orders. Complains to the Higher Court. Says our Judges do not do their jobs.

'The Judge is shirking his responsibilities. Judge does not do his job. Make Judge write Orders.' It's called MANDAMUS," added Rosie proudly, "a complaint like that."

"Wooo-w," exclaimed Zip with admiration, "Wow, that's a real brawl and fracas!"

"What happens next?" asked Milly, delighted. "and what a rumpus! Does Portia win?" and, without waiting for an answer, turned to Zip, "I want to go see that Portia now. I only have a clear impression of her feet."

Miffed at the lack of appreciation from her audience, Rosie turned back to the TV screen.

"Go. Go see that Portia. What are you wasting my time for?"

"We don't know where she is," admitted Milly, "She always comes to us. Or sends Raccoon."

The Cat sniffed and arched her tail with disdain, muttering "If I were her, I wouldn't be advertising my office arrangements either."

"Why?" asked both Spaniel's in chorus.

"Turn left on our White Goose Lane, then first right, then seventh turn to the left.

Rosebuds Drive

You'll see a tiny condo. Second floor. They hold most meetings on the deck outside—you can see and hear perfectly."

"How do we know it's her condo?" insisted Zip who liked clarity.

"Oh, don't worry, you'll know it when you see it," snorted Rosie, and added enigmatically, "in the words of the Supreme Court."

The Spaniels hesitated. They never liked Rosie's arrogance, but on the other hand she was already a familiar old shoe, and close to home. Who knows about that Portia Porter. Plus, the drizzle outside had turned to an honest-to-goodness pouring rain.

"Rosie," started Milly, "there was a mention of asking for the court to appoint a *Guardian*; perhaps you could explain—"

"Honey," hissed Rosie, getting irritated, "My time is worth . . . if I would not've wasted . . . I would have finished watching what came out of the hunt of those quick cheetahs. Or did they go to bed hungry?" She nodded towards her enormous TV screen in an exaggerated show of grievance at her now lost-forever opportunity to learn the fate of the young cheetahs.

Rosie was almost hissing, but the dignity of the day was saved by return of her Human, Suzy, carrying the species-appropriate treats.

“Here you go, I found the dog biscuits!’ And fluffing each of her guests in turn, Suzy spread the feast.

37

AT PORTIA PORTER'S

"That Cat was right again," admitted Zip reluctantly.

There was no confusing Portia Porter's office building with any other house on the entire stretch of its posh and pompous *Rosebuds Drive*. The Spaniels did *know it* immediately when they saw it.

"How is *this* still here?" did not believe Milly.

"And it's not ashamed of itself!" admired Zip, "at all!"

"Is that why we have not been invited here?" Milly screwed up her face, "Because her place is shabby?"

The two-story red brick of a hundred-year-old construction reminded of its former glory with crumbling natural stone of the roof. The building's thrifty architectural decision caught the passerby's eye like a bloody crash splashed over the smooth surface of an interstate highway.

Barn-like, thought Milly.

Barracks, growled Zip.

The sight evoked mingled emotions. From one perspective, it aroused a contemptuous befuddlement about how this eyesore stayed *here,* smack dab in the same row with all the ostentatious entryways guarded by precious sculptures of marble owls and lions, with intricately wrought iron driveway gates protecting secure entrances into secluded underground parking places. From another perspective, though, the building induced a grudging sense of respect and plain awe: This shabbiness still stands! And does not seem to give a damn! Completely unabashed!

❧

Knotted together by the by-laws of their Condo Association, three owners inhabited the two-story edifice of the cracking red brick.

Portia Porter's law practice occupied the East half of the upper, second floor.

"Approach it from the rear and look for the enormous Christmas glow-balls above her side of the porch," Rosie had instructed.

The West half of the second floor—including the western part of the porch, divided from Portia's quarters by a short wooden partition, was the property of a merry childless couple in their early thirties ("Never home, always away on the endless project of some Summer-house remodel").

The first floor had the same set-up as the second —two units sharing a wall. On the West half, a plain young man devoid of any politics, pets, quirks, girlfriends, or bad habits whatsoever, or at least none could be ascertained from careful review of garbage cans content. That sort of neighbor was enough to make any normal person nervous. Yet, he was not the problem either.

It was the unit on the East, directly under Portia Porter, that caused her trouble. That property had changed hands a short time before and presently served as home to a plump Greek Maiden of a romantic age and disposition, who was as passionate about the "face of their condo" as the rest of Portia's neighbors were unconcerned.

Greek Maiden's purchase of a home on posh *Rosebuds Drive* was a source of great personal pride.

An equivalent of a Park Avenue address in New York, *Rosebuds Drive* address marked an ascent onto another rung up society ladder, meant an entrée into the chic circle of Ducklingburgers, possibly even opened the doors to the exclusively selective *Azalea Ball.* Impressive invitations and eligible bachelors would soon be lining up. Even receiving a piece of junk mail as a *Current Resident* at Rosebuds Drive was an event of identity . . . She made it! Greek Maiden celebrated with Champagne for three straight days after the closing. She had arrived! She was *somebody* now! A part of Ducklingburg elite.

On her fourth day as a fresh Rosebuds resident, the new member of elite was awakened to to the view of a ladder holding up two dusty torn sneakers of the handyman unapologetically defacing the brick wall above her window with a brand-new wall plaque which proclaimed the designated quarter of the condo to be

LAW OFFICE OF PORTIA PORTER, ESQ.

Greek Maiden screamed and, still wearing her two-piece red-hot pajamas and a rather see-through cover wrap, sprinted up the back stairs in search of satisfaction.

"I'm duly registered and permitted under the condo bylaws," gave no satisfaction Portia.

"You *sneaked* this on me," wailed Greek Maiden, "You waited till I bought to unearth this monstrosity," she hollered, nodding at the plaque.

Portia, who was in truth rather proud of the shiny faux-bronze plaque, calmly returned fire, complaint for complaint.

"Speaking of monstrosities, kindly cover up your silkies. You'll scare off all my clients. They'll think that my office shares quarters with a bordello."

"I *live* here," retorted the scantily clothed intruder, "I'll wear what I please."

Greek Maiden winced and retreated. Barring a full Condo Board resolution, there was no fighting Portia head on. But, Portia's snarky remark about a bordello had given her an idea of how to counterattack. She'd *embarrass* the lawyer out of business.

To that end, three sleek-looking drying racks went up on Maiden's half of the porch, each rack destined to display a slew of attention-grabbing splendor.

Greek Maiden owned undies in every fashion and every color. All designed to turn heads, there were fire-engine reds and pastel pinks with touch of shimmer; there was an engineering wonder and a black-lace construction with a legion of snaps and ties; there were coquettish jammies and lacy bottoms.

In no time at all, the back porch below Portia's law firm was presenting a strong appearance that the place housed a lingerie boutique, a wannabe *Victoria's Secret* store.

Naive Hoppy was puzzled: "Why does she have so much laundry?"

"Because," explained the more observant Raccoon, "this helps our clients find their way. The law firm where you

Enter Above the Undies.

Not gonna forget that one, will you?"

"No," agreed Hoppy, and could not resist chiming in with

Briefs Over Briefs.
Law Above the Lingerie.

"It could've been worse. She could've—" started Raccoon optimistically, but halted, failing to imagine a more embarrassing introduction for a law firm.

"It's residential, and I have the right to air-dry,"

said the Greek Maiden when Portia brought the problem to her attention—after letting matters air for the first week.

And, lifting from the rack a black, lacy garment, Greek Maiden rolled it in a ball and threw it at the feet of thoroughly bewildered Portia.

"It's war, you bitch," Greek Maiden added in an incongruously sweet, clear voice that sounded as elegant as a Reindeer bell.

"You think our clients . . . the guests . . . maybe they *won't notice*?" had hoped Hoppy.

❧

Milly noticed the underwear right away.

"Is this a poor family," she asked compassionately, "they do not have a working dryer?"

"Portia's on the second floor, those are not hers," said Zip sharply, "plus, we are early. Their Meeting has not yet started."

Milly smiled, "Good, there's time to find good seats. We are the first ones here."

"None of the neighbors are home, either," established Zip, his nose up in the air.

"You can tell by sniff?" admired Milly.

"Nah," admitted Zip, I counted the cars outside.

And so he had. It became obvious once he had pointed it out. The parking places, marked A, B, C stood empty.

The parking space marked D contained a Jeep with license plate that read enigmatically "CA IRA" and was covered in orange stickers that declared its owner a proud graduate of the University of Virginia Law. That Jeep must be Portia's, concluded Zip.

Zip recognized a well-polished red Vespa motor scooter wedged into the same space as the Jeep. "That's Raccoon's," confirmed Milly.

After a short debate, the Spaniels agreed on making a bold move. The patio belonging to the always-missing Merry Childless Couple was only half-divided by a low wooden partition, five dog-step strides from Portia Porter's outdoor round glass table.

From Merry Couple's side, the dogs would hear everything and even sneak a look through holes in the wooden partition. The problem was the Merry Couple's minimalist approach to furnishing. One small garden bench and a coffee table offered almost no cover. Spying would be risky. But, no risk—no return, decided Zip. They made a dash. Zip took cover between the wooden legs of the bench. The comfort-loving Milly jumped onto the bench's lean seat cushion.

If they were found, they agreed to passionately storm Raccoon, their proven friend, and give no explanation of how they got there or why.

Zip immediately located a wood knot hole and applied his right eye to the opening. Milly stretched out comfortably above, to better hear. Whatever she'd not see, she would ask Zip. And they could sniff everything, anyway.

❧

The dogs did not have to wait long.

A red, shorthaired head popped out without and called back inside, "Raccoon, the weather's perfect, let's meet on the porch."

"Coming, Hoppy." The answering holler from inside was followed by—the Spaniels were relieved to sniff the familiar smell of un-rinsed detergent—their friend Raccoon, stumbling backwards into the doors, carrying a stack of folders that towered higher than his bouncy hair. He dropped the folders onto the table with a plop and commenced stacking them around in even piles.

"I was right. Raccoon's the leader of this pack!" pronounced Zip.

"Can you believe they are still pressing that baseless nonsense," fumed Raccoon.

"Frivolous," agreed Hoppy.

"It's how they roll," accused Raccoon bitterly, "bullies!"

"Zip," whispered Milly, "these Hoppy and Raccoon guys, they work in unison, like us!"

Zip thought of his and Milly's intruder bark ensemble and smiled, but whispered strictly, "Be quiet, little sister!"

Milly swallowed a whimper. And just in the nick of time. The patio door swung open to let out—

"That's Portia," recognized Zip. "Jeans and sneakers today?!"

"Old Lady flat refused their stupid medical exam," Raccoon related hotly.

"Pity," said Portia, "cheaper to fold than to fight."

"Right," echoed Raccoon, and immediately lunged in contradiction.

"*Their* argument at first was that Our Old Lady's bonkers because she tore out all the sheetrock off her ground floor walls." He shrugged exaggeratedly, conveying that nothing could be more normal that a client stripping their own wall.

"We—" Raccoon threw a respectfully head jerk at Portia, "got *their* own witness to admit that it was a pretty good idea, taking off contaminated sheetrock. FEMA'S OWN EXPERT SAID SO! No crazy thinking there."

The Raccoon was getting louder and bolder at the memory of the deposition victory,

"Cheaper to get the doctor's note," repeated Portia in a soft monotone.

"But their own *expert* witness said so. Nothing crazy about removing contaminated sheetrock. . . . Responsible lawyers should've dropped the motion once it became stu—"

"Frivolous," hissed Portia, losing her calm, but making no increase in decibels, abruptly flying into an whisper-quiet fury. "But no! They won't dismiss, they even had the gall to file *one more* baseless motion," she hissed.

"I have not seen this one yet," Hoppy admitted and, after extracting the stapled pages from the pile in front of him, read the title out-loud:

DEFENDANT-FEMA'S REQUEST
FOR
PLAINTIFF-OLD LADY'S
MEDICAL

RECORDS

"So," Hoppy, leaned away from the table, "FEMA's claim is that *something* in Old Lady's medicals will prove that she is bonkers anyway? Unless Old Lady shows them a clean bill of health, they want a Guardian appointed to take over control of her life?

"FEMA's whole argument is

She's old, so must be crazy?"

"That's a fair summary," muttered Portia thoughtfully, and rounded on Raccoon,

"You got her medicals?"

Raccoon shrugged and challenged Portia insubordinately.

"Why don't you fight it? You *should* win squarely on the law, can't you?"

"Don't want to fight. Remember *Oliver v. Oliver*?"

"Crooked Judge," Raccoon deflated.

Portia spoke in a bleak monotone, like one reads a grocery list.

ONE:

The crooked Judge appoints a Guardian.

TWO:

We appeal

THREE:

Time passes . . . stinking Guardian turns out Old Lady into Loony Bin and sells the House

FOUR:

a year later, we are victorious on appeal, but

FIVE:

There is no House. We won a piece of paper. Useless.

"Unless the Judge grants us a stay that halts the Guardian until our Appeal is decided," asked Hoppy.

"As if! Appeal is useless," Raccoon conceded dolefully.

"What he said," agreed Portia democratically, "a pyrrhic victory."

"*Oliver v. Oliver*, we fought to the last drop of death and won," said Raccoon bitterly, avoiding Portia's side-eye.

"Now we know better," said Portia ignoring Raccoon's dig. "Old Lady has nothing to hide. Her mind is plenty sharp. FEMA wants the medicals—let's give it the medicals. Arrange our own doctor to examine her, need be."

"Right," agreed Raccoon, "I asked Old Lady.

Explained the situation. *Cheaper to give the records.* Tried three times."

"No luck?"

"*Some* luck. She gave me tea," offered the Raccoon, "and her Spaniels seem to like me. But medical records, that no."

"What's her objection? Verbatim?" Portia held up a sharpened pencil.

"'*Zei are not getting my medical rrrrecords, and zat is final, Young Man,*'" Raccoon imitated Old Lady's accent unconvincingly.

"And, beyond that," he continued, "she just refused to talk to me."

"I'll talk to her," said Portia.

Raccoon made a half-yelping noise and started digging in the pile of folders under his chair.

"You should actually see for yourself first. What's actually *in* her medicals," Raccoon was mumbling hotly.

"*What medicals*?" growled an outraged Milly. "Old Lady's never sick!"

"Never," hissed Zip.

"We have her bloodwork," admitted Hoppy and Raccoon in chorus, as a thin stack appeared in front of Portia. "Old Lady had the standard blood test panel drawn first year she came to Ducklingburg! You never want a judge to see this. Or anybody else!"

Face scrounged, Portia studied the print-out. On five pages of columns, the technician helpfully highlighted bad results in red. A lot of red.

"ALP . . . hemoglobin . . . platelets . . . She got *anything inside* the normal range? How *bad* are these numbers, you checked?"

Raccoon nodded and mutely pressed his finger to a chart, extracted from another folder.

"Not bad. Odd. This—" Raccoon pressed his finger into one of the red columns, "would get her dead in a few months."

"It didn't."

"Her primary had figured they got a wrong sample, e-mailed her to re-test."

"It got better?"

"That's the oddest part," burst out Hoppy, extracting more papers from the pile, "Next, her doctor's note.

Patient is pleasant . . . well-oriented. . . friendly . . . well-nourished, optimistic . . .

Refuses all further blood tests . . . hemophobia.

Means she is afraid of blood."

"I know that that m— So—Old Lady's *is* sick, that's her whole secret?" asked Portia in a deadened voice.

"No way," retorted Hoppy, "With these results she'd be long *dead*."

"Her doc thought, lab mistake," inserted Raccoon, "but—"

"—We have a theory, Portia.

Portia only shrugged.

"Thing is, we checked the internet for normal numbers . . . . all her numbers would normal for a younger woman."

"Deadly for her age," repeated Hoppy, but, "normal if she were younger."

"How much younger?"

"A li— A lot. By a few . . . decades. Six. Seven?"

"This is not twenty years young," said Portia.

"Totally not dead, though," persisted Hoppy.

"Eternal youth. I can see how that's more likely than Ducklingburg Medical Group Lab had switched her records. How did you get the records, anyway?" asked Portia, changing the subject.

"We hacked into Old Lady's own account with DuckHealthCare. Easy," boasted Hoppy, "Old Lady's password—even a child would crack it—"

And Raccoon and Hoppy sang out together, "*Zip&Milly.*"

The last bit proved too much for Milly's frayed nerves. On hearing her name, she jumped, and not knowing herself why, yelped,

"Wwooh, yeh, ohh, It's me! I'm Milly, you called my name!"

Zip could not help himself, and barked his greetings even louder, "Woof-rrr!"

"Old Lady is afraid of blood?" repeated Portia quietly, and shrugged, "Yeah, likely story."

❧

"Unlikely story," mumbled Matthew.

Old Lady . . . does not look that old, by the way . . . That's pile of horse shit in her records.

I personally shaved that Spaniel's leg and saw her working needles with my own eyes.

I held that dog, she stuck the vein.

Not on her first try, but still—she found the vein, waited for the syringe to fill with blood, and deftly connected catheter with liquids. Ably, competently, with no fear at all . . . she's not afraid of blood, impossible!

Matthew was relaxing on the terrace of his Scared Hare Country Club quarters, his bare feet resting on the spare chair, Freckly stretched out comfortably in his lap, purring as Matthew lightly petted her neck. Freckle purred like a fox. Not like a cat who rolls her purrs, *puuuuuurrrr,* but shorter and abruptly, *pu-ur, pu-ur.*

An envelope marked CONFIDENTIAL delivered from Paul's omniscient and ever-powerful office, lay tossed under the table.

Incredible stuff's happening, thought Matthew, *fox purrs, Old Lady . . . no, I saw her draw the blood myself. She figured out with astonishing speed that the dog was allergic to pendimethalin. Plus, that room was like a lab . . . there was equipment . . . sort of a study, sort of lab.*

Sort of a study . . . Sort of a lab . . . .

Matthew kept stroking the fox; his mind obligingly returned him to Waterloo.

Somehow this Old Lady reminds me . . . no, she can't remind of anything, I've never actually seen that other Lady. The emptied basement and the Flemish landlady, eager to uptalk available rental to a prospect.

How did the Flemish lady put it?

"A lab. Sort of."

Another image floated into Matthew's heated mind.

He had left that empty rental, already in his car, ignition key turned, when the Flemish landlady—

had just about pushed him out of the door—was out of the house, knocking on the driver's side window and, with a wordless gesture, asked him to crack it open. Which he promptly did.

"Glad I caught you.

"*Russische Dame* . . . the Russian Renter, she forgot this. Took everything else, mind you, nothing left behind, not a toothbrush, not old lipstick, not a scrap of garbage. Very tidy, *Russische Dame* . . . She was a good renter," the Flemish Landlady sighed. Then she shrugged and, remembering, she returned to the business at hand,

"*Ze was dit vergeten*. She left this."

The Flemish stretched out her hand through the car window, palm up. Lying in the palm was a small brooch, the kind that in olden times a woman would pin to a demure dress. An unassuming brooch, a costume jewelry, bijouterie. Shaped like a flower with dark-chocolate inside and lighter yellow petals.

"Vergeten . . . she forgot *this*," repeated the Flemish landlady, stressing the word *this* with an air of derision.

This bijou was of no value, so he could have it. Just a trifling thing, tasteless even, hardly worthy to call a decoration, "*this crad*."

Crad, a useless bling.

Matthew never could work out why he had accepted the "*crad.*" He simply reached to the stretched-out palm and grasped the brooch in his fist. He did not even mouth "*Dank u*. . . thank you," and, remarkably, the markedly ceremonious Flemish lady did not offer "*Graag gedaan*. . . you are welcome."

"What devilry and witchcraft," said Matthew outloud, waking Freckle, "those dogs, too. . .."

Matthew carefully shook Freckle off from his lap and stretched to his feet, his thoughts on *those dogs*. Spaniel Milly, all of a sudden thick as thieves with his fox Freckle. Why? And Matthew louder still, repeated,

"Those dogs are way too clever."

❧

The way-too-clever dogs had scrambled through the bushes under Portia's porch, shaking off half-rotten last winter's leaves that kept sticking to their ears.

"This Meeting made me feel completely stupefied in the head," sighed Zip.

"I just can't abide people who refuse to use their dryers in this twenty-first century," said Milly, giving a contemptuous side-eye to the first-floor Greek Lady's multicolored underpants that were still flapping like defiant flags in the breeze.

"Let's go," Zip pushed Milly's side, and swaying two short tail stubs in unison, without haste, they departed the law firm's premises.

❧

"Zippy, why aren't you asleep? What do you think, Zippy?"

"About what?"

"About that Lawyer Portia in old sneakers. The house is old, a faded flower. The partition has holes. Everything is so age-worn there."

"Except for the underwear, that's all bright and looks brand new. Who recommended her? Lariska?"

"Nope! Old Lady found her herself. I like Portia too. Although not totally. She says contradictory things."

"I think Raccoon is one who says things there. And that other, red-head. They are in charge. About Portia, I did not quite get it straight. What is she thinking?!"

"You'd know if you learned to read, Milly, do not be so lazy."

"No, Zippy, no. It's enough that you can read. And you have already read some things that Portia wrote?"

"Yep."

"And?"

"I think she's cunning. She wrote a book, called *Can You Stiff Your Divorce Lawyer?* The book uses the same contradictory style as her legal work. First hundred pages say you can totally stiff your lawyer. There's a shrewd explanation of how to outsmart a lawyer and never pay for the work done."

"What's so contradictory? She is plain dishonest. Against her own pack. Double-dealing—"

"The next hundred pages," Zip went on with some uncertainty, "explain why stiffing your own lawyer is horrible idea."

"Like I said before. A lying double-dealer," repeated Milly firmly.

"It's all not so simple," warned Zip, "She understands that justice is expensive and people are sorry for spending money fighting. She tries to coolly consider both sides of every issue—just as I think that she's doing now, in Old Lady's litigation."

"So?" yawned Milly.

"Also, when I read . . . I felt sorry for her . . . and for all those greedy sleazy lawyers."

"How come? You said yourself they're *sleazy, greedy*—"

"And most of them not all that educated . . . Don't take this the wrong way, Milly, but they remind me of you."

"What do you mean? You still love me, don't you?"

"Of course, always. But Portia Porter . . . she had this client who fired her because he did not want to pay . . . she worked hard for him, but he felt it was just too painful to part with the money that she earned."

"Client greedy too," exclaimed Milly.

"Don't interrupt. The Client hired another lawyer, and that other refused all Portia's help on the case."

"What help?"

"Portia wanted to tell new lawyer all details of the case. No charge."

"No, Zippy, she's not like me. If Old Lady stops feeding me, I do not know that I will do guard work and bark at the intruders."

"I'd still love Old Lady," said Zippy gruffly. "Even hungry. . . . The new lawyer was suspicious that Portia was going to harm the case and did not take Portia's help."

"Portia did not want to harm?"

"No. She said: If artist Michael— Michelangelo did not get paid, he would not grab a hammer and destroy his own painting in the Sistine Chapel."

"She is not Michel—whatsisname."

"She thinks of her case as a masterpiece."

"Zip, way too many long words. What's with the hammers, and where's the masterpiece?"

"The thing is, Portia never, not for any money—"

"Or for no money," interjected Milly.

"Be quiet, Milly . . . would never harm her own work to get back at a greedy Client. She works to do masterpieces. Meaning, she works very well, loves the art of lawyering."

"Zip, I don't understand a thing. She works well, without money? What does she live on? Is she crazy? Her condo is old and weather-worn. Although, it's all very clean."

"She does live in an old condo, agreed."

"Crazy, for sure. Zip, what do we need a crazy for?"

"Not crazy. Arrogant."

"How's that?"

"Conceited. She wrote in her book. Not this one . . . another one, *Beaver vs. Beaver—"*

"Beavers? They live in rivers, Zippy."

"No, those were Human beavers, wife and husband."

"Fighting each other? That's wrong, Zippy. I understand if dog and cat, but fighting your own mate—"

"Anyway, Portia wrote . . . that lawyers are all a *compulsively competitive lot*."

"What does that mean?"

"Means they fight so fierce for their clients that some of them die right there, drop dead fighting. And, anyway, there's a saying that some of them are willing to fight until the last drop of blood—their clients' blood!"

"Fight how? Like cat and dog fight? Like Rosie explained? Why did Old Lady pick Portia? I do not want that fight without a win. Do you?"

"Like I said in the beginning, I like her. Although not totally."

"You know what, Zippy, I am not going to take reading lessons yet. Maybe you can teach me how to read, but understanding all of this? I refuse."

"Then go to sleep. I have not finished reading Portia's book. There's a chapter called *The Price of Ignorance*. No, not about you."

38

OLD LADY

It was that rare sliver of time in Portia Porter's law office when punishingly onerous labors of litigation preparation were winding down for the day. Nothing any member of the team could do today would bring the coveted win any closer, and Portia had already called it quits.

"You're starting to make mistakes. Pick up tomorrow."

Raccoon and Hoppy cherished the respite and happy-houred in the kitchen. Hoppy applied himself to brewing coffee. Raccoon was expectantly holding his mug, ready to slip outside and grab the best place on back porch.

There was no set quitting time for Portia Law work days. The day was finished when they heard

Portia's order, "Done for the day. Tomorrow, we'll pick up with—"

Quitting-time only signaled a temporary reprieve; the work never ended.

"Raccoon!" called the quiet insistent voice from the front room. Raccoon replaced his still-empty mug. The reprieve was put on hold.

The office of Portia Porter sprawled to every room of her condo with the exception of her bedroom—a small room just off the kitchen which, although not covered by a specific injunction as off-limits, was always behind a firmly closed door.

The kitchen and back porch were the usual sites of strategy meetings, food breaks and rest. The remaining two rooms were the *office proper*: shelves crammed with books, folders with tabbed papers, computers, scanners and copy machines, recycle bins with shredded and always growing pile of to-be-but-yet- un-shredded papers, gray plastic folding tables and boxes of cheap copying paper. Everything was arranged for the comfort and efficiency of their work.

The clients were received here too.

The architect's interior vision for the space was open—arches between the principal living rooms and kitchen, no doors.

From the kitchen, Hoppy heard Raccoon receiving instructions from Portia.

“Mrs. NewRussian’s on the line.”

“I just got word from bodyguard she ordered,” called back Raccoon, “she can rest easy.”

“Cancel the muscle, she says.”

“Cancel? The guy had only just punched in. He’s at her gates, not even had the chance to lay his eyes on the *body* he’s supposed to *guard*.”

“She no longer feels her husband’s all that dangerous.”

“Mr. NewRussian’s mellowed. Got it.”

Hoppy, clutching two now filled coffee mugs, and Raccoon, both thumbs tapping on his phone, slid outside to the back patio.

“Disproportionately many Russian clients lately,” remarked Hoppy.

“Just the two. Old Lady and this one . . . with bodyguards. Nothing wrong with Russians . . . if they pay on time.” Raccoon’s fingers finished tapping and he announced “Done! Cancelled. Now, where’s my coffee?”

Hoppy pointed with his eyes at the mug on the patio table, “How did the Muscle take his loss of job?”

"Said he was off to binge-watch *The Americans,*" laughed Raccoon.

"Our Russians do not look like spies," Hoppy sighed.

Both grew quiet, cherishing the well-deserved rest and satisfaction of the job well-done.

Portia made a clever choice hiring these two: both youths felt unweighted by the work and executed their duties with unexamined devotion to the cause. None of them, not even Portia, had learned enough to feel the pall of daily tasks of a divorce law practice—disentangling human lives from the self-inflicted pains of clients who, having made an ill-fated choice of a domestic partner, perpetuated their own misery for lack of strength to cut the stifling ties with an appropriate degree of fairness and civility.

Hoppy stirred honey into his coffee mug and ventured into his favorite subject.

"I can't get over the Old Lady Mystery."

"Me neither," admitted Raccoon.

When they first learned about Old Lady's science-achievement based green card, Raccoon and Hoppy spent hours combing through every bit of Academy-net in search of answers.

Siberian Institute from which Old Lady hailed

was easily located on the web. It even offered an English version of its website—well, *sort of English*. Some parts were clearly lost in translation penned by the locals who learned the language without ever leaving Russia. Raccoon and Hoppy, both avid snoopers, quickly assembled piles of information. That's when it got hairy. Although easy to find, everything about Old Lady's Institute proved tough to understand. The articles penned by the Siberian scientists could be downloaded easily enough. Comprehending them was a different story. Even the titles sounded like senseless egghead jokes.

By: Vanya Volkov, Tanya Zayats:
The Genetic Web and What Gets Caught In It.

"Supposed to be funny," said Raccoon astutely.

"I don't get it," admitted Hoppy.

By: Zhukov, Bukashkina, B. Korovkina:
Determining the Sex of Insects: It's Not What We Thought It Would Be.

"Bewildering," said Hoppy.

"Do we even want to know?" retorted Raccoon.

Still, hard-working Hoppy spent many evenings

ploughing text of the articles themselves in search of elusive bits of sense. But his diligence yielded nothing: most of the pages were covered by multi-line, odd-symbols-packing formulas which he could not even read. And whatever words *were* left puddling about the sea of Greek and obscure symbols were so oddly multi-syllabic that they barely even qualified as English.

Eventually, both Hoppy and Raccoon halted the quest. But they did not give up wondering.

"Raccoon, d'you sign the non-disclosure?" Hoppy asked.

"Where?"

"For Old Lady. Did you?"

"Nope. Signed nothing. She never asked to sign. Gave my word though."

Hoppy's face blinked in a spasm, "Raccoon, you oughta tell me."

"Nothing to tell," snapped Raccoon. "She checks that nothing leaves the room—not a single copy or a piece of paper. Sequesters my phone by the front door. Each time."

"And?" pressed Hoppy.

"— *And* — I don't read in Russian, " snapped Raccoon.

"Those dogs she has . . . funny. All but can talk,"

Hoppy shot a sideway glance at his friend and pressed, ". . you *know* something."

"*Zaliv Encirclement*," blurted out Raccoon. "She is a military mastermind."

"Gossiping about Old Lady?" Portia was silhouetted in the doorway.

Raccoon resolved to not hold back.

"She—" Raccoon's fingers were clicking furiously on his phone. "Here. It was a *military* project, Portia."

Under the iridescent stock photo of empty droppers propped on a row of glistening glass vials, the lead shouted:

> *Dr. Lerusse of the Belgium Genome Defense Institute announced today . . . result of multinational collaboration effort. . .*
>
> *. . . researchers located . . .*
>
> *. . . dedicated protein molecule with ability to neutralize . . .*

"*Neutralize* . . . as in *destroy*?" raised a mocking eyebrow Portia.

"No, not exactly. I *messes* with people. In field tests . . . this *dedicated protein molecule* took out of commission a ten-thousand person army."

"Out of commission how?" asked Hoppy, visions of blood and gore swimming in his eyes.

"Which army?" asked Portia matter-of-factly.

"In Avossia—it's a small country, they—It's not what you think. This *dedicated protein molecule* . . . can work on anybody the scientist tells it to. So if the scientist tells it to go after redheads, and there's only one redhead in a crowded bus, then that's who'll get attacked by the molecule.

Those Avossian soldiers . . . the *protein molecule* was only set to go after the Avossians— they got *neutralized* by making them . . . non-soldier-like."

"Forgot how to shoot," giggled Hoppy.

"Worse. The protein molecule got released on them and out of the blue, overnight, every soldier woke up and decided he was going to be a *transgender*."

"Pardon?" said Portia.

"They all went to bed brave Avossian soldiers, in service of the Crown, business as usual. Woke up giggling and effeminate, preoccupied with panty-hose and frilly underwear competitions amongst each other. A regular sorority party. In the end, the entire ten-thousand-man army allowed to get itself surrounded by the enemy."

"Which enemy?" asked Portia.

"The Russians, I think. Avoissian Generals are still working out prisoners of war exchanges. Here's the link, this proves it. *Zaliv Encirclement.*"

"And our Old Lady had a role in this *how*?" Portia asked. "Got a link?"

"This was with her papers—" Raccoon halted. Their client Old Lady as a military mastermind sounded better before he said it outloud.

"You didn't ask her 'bout it?" ventured Hoppy.

"Course not," took offense Raccoon.

"Drop it," ordered Portia. "We're not hired to snoop into her science projects. Hired to protect from FEMA overreach. And needs some serous protection, by the way."

"Raccoon thinks Old Lady does not need our protection. She'll just turn all enemies into giggling schoolgirls," snorted Hoppy; but his joke fell flat.

"Get out, get some rest," said Portia dryly.

The usually chatty duo did not exchange a word on their way out. Raccoon's motorcycle was over-heating in the parking lot, and they geared up in synchronized silence. Neither was even roused by a sudden charge from the gloating Greek Maiden who apparently lay in wait downstairs to thrust on them a thin piece of paper and a shrill squeal,

YOU OUTTAHERE!

Your stinky law firm is out!

Condo Board finally decided!

Hoppy only jerked his neck, like a horse dismissing a pestilent fly, unthinkingly sending Maiden's papers flying, then turned back to his buddy:

"Raccoon, what do you reckon you are scanning for Old Lady?"

"No clue."

"You don't actually think it's military-grade?" whispered Hoppy, "Experiments on dogs?"

"She'd never harm those dogs. . . . Hop up, I'll tell you—" Raccoon was about to read his best friend into his suspicions of Zip's agelessness, when a shove into his motorcycle nearly toppled them. Still grinning maliciously, the Maiden pushed in her re-assembled papers:

CONSIDER YOURSELF ON NOTICE!

YOU ALL OUT!

TELL YOUR BOSS!

YOUR LAST DAY'S FRIDAY!

"Move away," muttered Hoppy, nettled, "or Portia will show you *your* last day."

"Raccoon what were you going to say ? You think Old Lady can turn Federal Paul into a giggling girl too? With those *protein molecules*?"

"Don't be a moron."

"I still think that body guard we cancelled might not stay unemployed for long."

39

CHOLESTEROL PILLS

Theodore was a fox in his physical prime and at the peak of his financial might.

Material resources, notably including a bountiful supply of food, were inexhuastible.

His new life, idle and entirely provided for by his rich daughter Freckle, had altered his disposition. Theo the fox became positively more strong-willed. No, he never took a despotic tone with family; for that he was too smart. But these days, he frequently did not consult his wife when making big decisions and Whitepaw, his love and mother of his children, would tilt her head respectfully and impress an attitude of deference upon the kits.

"Children, you heard your father!" or "No, you

can't do that, your father does not like it," or "Ask your father first!"

Whitepaw did not display any displeasure even when Theodore suggested radical changes to their usual set-up for the children's education.

"Sweetheart," cajoled Whitepaw, "it's hunt class time. We could use live rabbits, that'd be good. Or at least pick up us two-three mice, won't you?"

Theo retorted pompously, "From now on, I delegate the hunting lessons equipment to your competent jaws. Why don't you, my dear, run along and snatch live quail, or rabbit, or a little mouse. Shake a paw, my sweets! My dear, beloved wife, the mother of my children, the incomparable Whitepaw, would you not say that you're in need of cardiovascular exercise? So many weeks you are taking care of kits . . . without any romping around the forest . . . we used to train together . . . This must be taken care of at once!"

"Who'll babysit the kits, though?" asked Whitepaw, surprised.

"I'll do it," Theo nodded vehemently, "We all just had a square breakfast, we have provisions for a great dinner, so you run along, and . . . happy hunting!"

Theodore amazed himself by how smoothly he

had handled that nagging hustle of providing the live catch. His Whitepaw was no simpleton herself and she prioritized maintaining the harmony of their loving family. In a flash, she was off.

The little fox kits were frolicking around, their bellies tightly packed with breakfast. Theodore adored his kits beyond all measure and, unburdened by any other immediate duties, he turned his mood to self-congratulation.

My kits! All so fluffy, so clever! Fox closed his eyes and pondered. *So well-tended . . . so brilliant . . . they'll grow up to be . . . even this one, who's been chasing his own tail for two days now, of course he's only whirling 'round in circles—but just you look at the dedication of his circling! . . . I wonder if he might be dizzy? . . . No, a dizzying success, is what he'll be! I have no doubt he can be as brilliantly successful in their careers as my Freckle. And that is nothing compared to success of these two, they've hunted down big bug already! And look at my fattest one, he even has the gall to mount an attack on the bumblebee! Genius! What hunting lessons? His kits had no need for lessons, they were naturals. . . . But then again . . . Well, let's see what Whitepaw can hunt down on her first try. The forest wild hunting is not a simple chore.*

And then Theo's thoughts drifted to his own labors. *Back in my day, I, Theodore . . . Yes, my salad days are behind me. But I'm far from being old. A fox still in my full vigor of life.*

In the exhausting old days of rat-race and hassle to provide for his family, fox Theo was too beat to appreciate how fine a fox's life can be, how many wonderful adventures could lie ahead. He now saw the life stretching out before him as one beautiful gala of which he never wanted to see the end. All one had to do was live long, take care about one's health.

Cardio-vascular training, that's what I said to Whitepaw. But truthfully I'm not sure. Humans are big on talking about exercise. But I've known rabbits who did nothing but cardio-vascular, and that did their lifespan no good.

On the other hand, Turtle Lusha claims she was acquainted with my great great-grandfather. She is never eager for any training. Cardio or otherwise. Foxes in the wild live only a few years. Then again, sedentary foxes in the zoo live as much as twenty years.

Theo could feel the hairs at the edge of hit tail stand up and wave like grass in high wind. Theo loathed the idea of serving in a zoo. A cunning fox, stuck in four corners with bars—his whole nature rebelled against it.

A long life with no smells of the forest, no walks on the banks of the creek, no ardor of the hunt on an empty stomach, no intoxication of full meal. . .. No, that "living" was not life at all, not for him. Of course, Freckle seemed happy. The whole community watched jealously as in the twilight—the foxes' cherished hunting hour, his Freckle lackadaisically struts along the forest line, escorted by her Human. Walking side by side. The Human always tells her something, he must be needing her advice.

Even as a child, Freckle was exceptional, he remembered. *Gifted, determined, charmed. A regular child prodigy. And how determined she was, grasping luck by its evasive tail. Brave. Strong. Fearless. Hard-working. Takes grit, jumping golf clubs every day.*

Without a warning, a horrible thought had gored its way ripping through Theo's mind: *What happens if Freckle grows old?* Too old to clear every golf stick, what happens then—*to him*? To all his family? To Freckle herself? Like a bolt of lightening out of clear blue sky, despair struck Fox Theo; a surge of anguish overcame him. He desperately fought the notion that the life has limits, that a fox's life is short. It was so good to him, his life!

Theo sighed deeply, found a comfortable position in the sun, and hiding his nose under his tail, prepared for a power-nap.

"Still snoozing?" Theo was awakened by Whitepaw's question and a puff of fresh field air coming from her luxurious fur, "The quails are under too-heavy protection. Got two field mice, though, and a spunky chipmunk. Wake up and look at our children; such quick studies they all are! And what beauties!"

Theodore admired his progeny for a spell, his nose tucked behind Whitepaw's left ear, the one with several white hairs in deviation from the typical exterior in her line—such a titillating quirk, in Theo's mind. Theo was a tireless admirer of Whitepaw's beauty and never wilted from expressing his feelings.

"My sweets, the forest walk becomes you! Your eyes are dazzling bright and fur is billowing with fresh air. Relax a bit now, darling. As for me, I promised Freckle that I'd pop by. We have a matter to discuss. Yesterday, we got interrupted, so. . . Keep an eye on the kiddos, will you?"

Indeed, Theo's yesterday's discussion with Freckle did get interrupted. When she got a sniff of her Human approaching, Freckle stopped their chat mid-syllable.

"Sorry, Daddy, gotta jump. Take care of yourself and don't forget to check on your cholesterol. Also, you might want to curb your stress. Don't hunt in places where they incite guard dogs against you."

So quick, so clever, my little Freckle, Theo watched Freckle with parental pride. *So thoughtful, his daughter. Worries about his cholesterol. And the dogs. Although some dogs are friendlier than others . . . there's Zip, for instance.*

On a whim, Theo was off towards the Spaniel Land.

❧

When Theodore reached the fireplace meeting place at the far end of the Old Lady's yard, Zip was already lying in his usual spot under the Cannas, his nose almost touching the screen of his favorite iPad. The device was dressed in a bright red case engraved on the back with the words

This Property Was Stolen from Old Lady, please return for reward,

and, in the left bottom corner, Old Lady's phone number.

The birds on Magnolia Tree screamed,

announcing Theodore's arrival, and Zip unglued his head from the screen, eagerly greeting his buddy with full ceremony.

"How are you this early morning, Theodore? Come on in! Make yourself at home! Are all the foxes in your pack quite well?"

"All," said Theo, "all of the foxes are quite well."

Zip moved over, clearing a place for Theo, but the fox would not lie down, standing stiffly instead, with an air of business. It was obvious that Theo did not feel like embroidering on the canvas of inter-species pleasantries.

"Something the matter?" inquired Zip politely.

"My wife Whitepaw and I," Theo began beating around the bush, "discussed today that there may be health benefits to cardio-vascular training—"

"And?" Zip raised his right fireball eyebrow inquisitively.

"And—" Theo paused, debating whether to share the piffle of his skillful passing of the buck of child education onto his spouse. Whitepaw will now have the health benefit of early morning walks, strengthening her paw muscles and her heart and veins—and also the chance to pick up a field mouse or two along her way.

"And?" repeated Zip, as he looked down at his

own, slightly bulging, tummy. Zip was about to defend his exercise efforts by pointing out that he and Milly regularly chased the fluffy yellow ball hurled by the strong throwing arm of Old Lady, but then Theo's chat went in an unexpected direction.

"We concluded that we should watch our cholesterol. Freckle's Human swallows two whole pills each morning. For his cholesterol."

"Cholesterol pills," mused Zip, "Where does he get those?"

"From his doctor. I suppose, Old Lady has a doctor too?" inquired Fox politely, "Whitepaw and I, we thought— If she has lots of cholesterol pills, could we share? Surreptitiously?"

"Trouble is," said Zip, "Old Lady does not go to a doctor."

"Where does she get cholesterol pills then?" asked Theo impatiently. "We can share if she buys over the counter, too."

"Old Lady does not eat any pills at all, we all don't—" Zip's memory jumped unpleasantly to the Big Water night when Old Lady had gripped tightly at his jaws, forcing him to swallow the hateful pills. He was barely able to force himself away from reliving the harsh after-effects of those pills. His insides still shook violently every time he was reminded. Brrrrrrr.

"No pills at all?" Theo was taken aback, his mind obviously spinning, the inquiries pelting out of his jaws. "No pills? Like us? Like wildlife? But—how old is she? Is it not dangerous to live without cholesterol pills—what's your view, Zip?"

"I have not formed a view, just yet," said Zip somberly, "I'm still at the research stage. You see, the place where I was born does not—"

"—How do you know where you were born?" interrupted Theo.

"I have a birth certificate. I read it. It says I have a pedigree, too," added Zip proudly.

Theo sighed and confessed, "I cannot read."

Zip sniggered under his breath but did not comment.

A plan immediately ripened in Theo's head—they'd do research together.

"Zip, dear, I don't mind if we do research together. We form a study group. I'd be delighted."

Zip had been suffering of pangs of loneliness for several days now because Milly flatly refused to leave the house except for quick business until the skin-shaved hind paw regained the golden fur to match the unshaved paw. So, Zip was happy to accept the offer of Theo's company.

"It's quicker in a study group," he nodded, "twice quicker with the two of us. The internet is full of science. Old Lady has an interesting site bookmarked, I have just been reading up . . . Siberian Conference on Cell Stem Research and—"

"See if there's anything about cholesterol—" spat out Theo, pleased that he got out of the jam so skillfully.

Always a good friend, Zip started scrolling, but his mind wandered off to the nagging thought that plagued him of late.

The day Zip learned that his Old Lady refused to show her medical records and refused to check her blood, Zip started nursing a suspicion that Old Lady was concealing something. His brain was full of worrisome questions.

Suppose the Fox was right? Suppose Old Lady knew she had cholesterol? Suppose all her veins and arteries got greasy with cholesterol, and blood was stuck and could not properly reach her brain? Was there some truth to the accusation that Old Lady was not thinking quite right? Then will "they" come and take her house? Where would he live? And Milly?

The Raccoon had already tried twice to cajole

Old Lady into a trip to a doctor. He found the best doctor, so he said, the most independent.

Old Lady would not budge.

“Raccoon, may I offer you a cup of coffee,” she’d respond, “or tea perhaps? Do you suspect my cognitive abilities, Young Man?”

“Me, no!” denied Raccoon, “But if the Judge—”

“The Judge has never even met me,” Old Lady would say sharply.

Zip, who was not invited to lap any tea or coffee but was allowed to be part of conversations, listened to this repartee until he was struck with a pang of realization. Even though all four of them were friends, they all had different agendas. Milly still refused to be seen with a shaved hind leg and cared not for what was happening in the world about her. Raccoon’s single obsession was to win in court, at any cost. For his part, Zip was worried sick about the House. What was Old Lady thinking? It would be nice to know Old Lady’s thoughts. But nobody knew.

Raccoon, who knew by experience that nothing could be done for clients who refused to help themselves, nevertheless was at Old Lady’s house, to try one last desperate plea.

“We’re due in court tomorrow morning. We’ll lose and they’ll stick you in old people’s—"

He caught the expression in Old Lady’s eyes, winced, and resignedly murmured “Thanks for the tea.”

Distraught with yet another blow against his plan to make Old Lady see the light, Raccoon lingered, hands in the pockets of his slacks . . . removed his car keys and rubbed his lucky bronze coin etched with his totem animal . . . twisted the raccoon key fob nervously around his finger. Then got flustered by his own familiarity, smiled embarrassedly, and reluctantly announced, “Gotta go.”

The feeling of disconnect between Old Lady and Raccoon had begun to really bother Zip. It breathed melancholy into the air, and Zip had lost all interest in any activity.

“You know, Theodore, I feel a little under the weather today . . . Raincheck—” but before Zip could finish, a grippy human hand skillfully snatched him by the scruff of his back, and he was in the air, level with . . . *Raccoon!*

Raccoon was back, must have turned the car around. And as annoying as ever!

“So, guys, what were you two conspiring about? Where’s your friend?” asked Raccoon nosily.

Theo was nowhere to be seen.

No wonder that they call him Raccoon, thought Zip, *he's got the stealth.*

While Zip was wrapping his head around what had happened, Raccoon already had stuck his nose in the iPad, reading out-loud.

"'Some interesting pages you have here. *Siberian Science'*—I heard of Siberian Science; *'longevity and cholesterol'*—you do not say? Let's see this—"

And Raccoon, a child of the dot-com age, propped up the iPad on his knees and started clicking furiously through Zip's recent search history.

"What's *this,* Zippy?"

From a photo on the screen, Old Lady looked out at the Raccoon, a laser pointer in her hand, directed at some charts and graphs and, for some reason, pictures of a few goats and sheep. High up by the ceiling, big letters spelled out "Ninth International Symposium."

"Where did you get this, Zippy?" rejoiced Raccoon, "That may just solve some mysteries."

"It's mine," growled Zip it protest, swatting at the flapping bright-red casing of his IPad so forcefully that it flew out of Raccoon's grasp and landed in the cannas.

“Let me see,” Raccoon persisted, amused by Zip’s display.

“It’s Old Lady’s secret, rrrrrwayrrrr,” threatened Zip, his paw on the top of the screen.

“You’ll scratch it, Zippy. Move the paw, please.” Raccoon kneeled over, gently brushing at the dog’s paw but, reacting lightning-fast in an alarm, Zip pressed his paw closer to the screen and there suddenly was a sharp noise—

CLICK . . .

When, half an hour later, Old Lady set out to Zip’s favorite place by the fire pit to look for him, she did not find any living creature there. Only set of car keys, their keychain’s fob a fake antique coin etched with a raccoon, glittered where they had been dropped on the stone path. Raccoon-Human’s car sat silently, its owner nowhere to be seen. The iPad with its distinctive red cover also had disappeared, together with Spaniel Zip.

“Ah, Yuri Ivanovich!” breathed Old Lady, and in an entirely uncharacteristic gesture, slapped her hip.

40

DISREGARD IT

The morning sky above Ducklingburg flaunted its usual shade of clean radiance, aglow with marvelous luster of peace and tranquility.

Disregard it, Portia ordered herself.

Disregard this puny tactical victory engineered by her neighbor, the local outpost of *Victoria's Secret.*

Nothing irregular about that unanimous condo meeting vote. Every one of her neighbors voted to oust her law firm—as was their undeniable right. They are entitled to live their lives without bumping into a constant parade of hapless folks traumatized by an expensive quest for uncertain justice.

No problem.

Portia and her crack team can always meet with

clients in a rent-by-the-hour office. For just a couple of hours at a time, they'll rent an empty desk in some high-rise. Hoppy will spread out photo frames of ersatz loved ones, like it's *their* office. Raccoon will give out bottled water. She won't be the first local lawyer to do this.

And as to the court prep, that's no problem. No condo board can enjoin her. Behind the closed door of her current-on-rent condo unit, it will be business as usual—the copy machines spitting out pages through the night; email messages arriving, Skype and internet heating up the bandwidth—it all will work pretty much the same way it did before.

Disregard it.

And no panic that Raccoon went missing. She does not even need him for court today. There are no exhibits for Raccoon to hand her in predetermined sequence. She's got none.

If the Judge has queries for her side, she has no answers, no arguments, no supporting documents for Raccoon to quickly and unerringly place into her blindly stretched out hand.

Disregard that her 84-year old client, Old Lady—who albeit Russian-born has competent command of spoken and written English, is strikingly good-looking, and possesses not only a sound mind but also near-perfect recall—refused production to the court of easily-procured proof of her perfect cognitive abilities and extraordinary physical health. Refused to prove ability of living on her own. Would not reveal her medicals.

As is her right.

She hired Portia's law firm to represent her *wishes,* not her best *interests.*

Like every client does.

There are at least arguable, even if not correct, allegations of eccentric behavior and now it appears that we'll have no countervailing evidence to offer. She is eighty-four—and what if the court appoints a Guardian or a Receiver to take over management of her life? That's likely to be touted as "humane" even. The local government accepting care. Everything taken care of . . . thought of for her. . ..

Disregard the fact that this caretaker's first decision will be to arrange a fire-sale of her home and line the pockets of some keg in that very local government. The outlays for Old Lady's care in the "facility" for the elderly so steep, they'll say.

She's 84.

Her science achievements will inspire respect in Federal Court Judge Carlson, who'll feel his civil duty honorably discharged upon confining her to an old people's house.

Disregard that FEMA will not pay a penny to Old Lady. Instead, FEMA already earmarked a grant to the City—three million dollars supposedly for protection of the native environment along that ill-fated Ravine and Sneaky Creek. They'll sow seed for the greensward to look good come Spring, but the grass will be washed away by the first strong Autumn torrent. Judge Carlson was surely reminded by the interested parties of his duty to the native environment.

Disregard that the dreamed of settlement with FEMA will never happen. The resolution will be more to the satisfaction of powerful interested parties whose names will not be even mentioned at the hearing today.

Disregard the fact that this charming, astute Old Lady, who looks way younger than her age—and prosperous-looking at that—will surely spew the usual client poor-mouthing ploy: *that she's terribly sorry, but she has no money to pay her legal bill anytime soon, if ever.*

Disregard the fact that thirty minutes from now, she, Portia, will be obliged to nod to Hoppy, "Thanks for accompanying Old Lady here," and then offer to

Old Lady nothing more substantial than an empty smile and feeble smalltalk. "How did you sleep? You look so nice today. No need to be nervous. Nice weather, isn't it?"

Disregard the whole godforsaken thing.

It's lost already. We're just going through the motions.

Portia's *Opposition to the Motion to Appoint Receiver-Guardian* is bombed.

Licked, clobbered, slaughtered. No chance.

Judge Carlson will clear-heartedly find Old Lady incompetent and in need of . . . Receiver serves . . . a guardian . . . speedy transfer to the assisted living . . . whatever. The Judge's mind been made before he takes the bench. Disregard whatever it is he will write in his ultimate Order.

Disregard—

Portia glided to a stop for the traffic light. Federal Paul and his entourage of young clerks equipped with identical leather folders were energetically crossing the street. She was around the corner from the courthouse—only remains to make the turn and enter the spacious multilevel parking facility of the Federal Court Building.

Tell Hoppy to have the parking ticket validated. Don't

disregard that one! That'd be their only perk financed by the taxpayers, after all is said and done.

Her Jeep was parked. Time to go.

Disregard it. The whole thing. The sky's not going to fall.

Portia jerked her head up toward the high-soaring sky and, never lowering her chin, turned the corner and squeezed through the revolving door of the Courthouse's side entrance.

Without much glancing around, only politely returning bows and nods and friendly salutations, Portia trudged down the hallway toward the court-room reserved for the hearing.

She was prepared for the loss. She felt no panic, angst, or fear. She was not embarrassed. She'd seen her share of losses in her day, there's nothing to be done about that. Her team did all they could for a client that stubbornly refused to do what was neces-sary in order to win.

Disregard it, Portia admonished herself one more time, the Courtroom door-handle already in her hand.

Disregard that neither Hoppy nor Old Lady are here on time. Can it be that—

A cheerful, slightly out-of-breath "Sorry, you—

Portia?" from behind her was followed by a not-so gentle shove.

"Name's Lariska. Read this before you speak—" A thick yellow envelope plunged heavily into Portia's hands was blank except for her own name, designated as the intended recipient:

For Portia Porter

❧

The morning was sunny.

The sky was high and likewise Federal Paul's spirits.

Crossing the street before the Courthouse, Paul almost brushed against the hood of a waiting Jeep, its wheels encroaching on the zebra crossings. Paul gave a side-glance at the driver. Portia did not see him, he was sure. The somewhat forlorn expression on her face disrupted the rhythm of his morning only momentarily. It was an energetic rhythm of life which he had enjoyed the moment he accepted the command to go *all in*. Pull out all the stops. Pull whatever strings that he was capable of manipulating. It was his last and most important career move.

Steve was the one who made him see the light. His Loser Buddy Steve! How about that?!

"What is your problem?" pushed Steve. "Open your goddam eyes. Stop sitting between two chairs —make a choice. They don't appreciate you as a lawyer. So be a businessman.

Paul had only stared.

Steve was undeterred.

"Start *using* your connections instead of burning them in pointless games of *who is smarter*. The *smarter* thing," insisted Steve, "is for us all to strike it rich. Your buddy Carlson will agree," added Steve.

Amazingly, Judge Carlson was on board.

Agreed happily that the best resolution of this unimaginable case—OLD LADY v. FEMA, what when newspapers sniff it out?—was the appointment of—"*was it Receivership or a Guardian, Paul? Oh, why not do both hats . . . you draft the Order, Paul.*" Using the FEMA Federal law issue as an excuse, Carlson had taken Federal jurisdiction over the whole case involving Old Lady, including the Guardianship/Receivership request that normally would have been dealt with in State court.

It was a done deal. The fix was in. Old Lady's land was, for all practical purposes, already in the bag.

The hearing was scheduled as an emergency matter, with only twenty-four hours' notice. The court procedure that was about to start was merely perfunctory, a matter of formality.

Paul had already seen the signed copy of the Order.

In ten minutes, it will be e-filed to ECF, the Electronic Case Files system used by the Federal courts. Signed, ECF-ed, and there for everyone to see by searching Federal PACER, the national on-line document index.

Ten minutes, and it will all be done.

The justification was simple. The Land and House were in a hazardous zone. An owner whose cognitive ability and mobility could be questioned . . . Oh, let's be honest, she is not equipped to handle zone of danger, this doddering woman of 84. She nearly drowned chasing after her flooded car. She *must* require help. Paul's client, FEMA, was generously disposed to provide just such help. Call it a Receivership. Call it a Guardianship. It mattered not.

The appointed Receiver-Guardian will have full run of House and Land.

This upstart Portia, that motionless, heedless face behind the Jeep's wheel—she will not know what hit her.

Moving in concert, Paul and his legal team sped up their pace and one by one applied accustomed pushes to the heavy turnstile into Federal Court Building.

❧

The first thing Judge Carlson said was addressed squarely to Portia:

"Having benefitted from the excellent factual submissions of counsel, I am satisfied that I fully understand the merits of this case. Is there anything you wish to add before I rule?"

His Honor's eyes were glued to his private document monitor at his elbow, but his tone was pointedly polite.

"Do I see that your client is not present?"

Fighting a stupid urge to turn and search the door behind her, Portia stood up and tried to obtain a few minutes delay to ascertain the implications of the just-received mysterious envelope, no doubt from Old Lady.

"I just received *this* from my client. I was not able to contact her. May we recess—"

"Denied."

The Judge's eyes slid to the manila envelope with indifference.

"Are you entering exhibits in the record," prompted the curious Clerk in a stage whisper.

Portia nodded. She might as well not disregard what looks to be her client's last instructions.

The flap was not sealed and Portia's unnecessarily forceful tug sent the three stapled, legal-sized pages flying. Frantically following the glide path of the papers, Portia momentarily lost mental balance, her mind turning to the disregarded . . . Where *is* that Raccoon?? Left last evening to try one more time to persuade Old Lady to be reasonable, and had not been seen since!

The papers landed in the aisle for all to see.

"A real estate deed?" she mumbled, mostly to herself. Paul and his team were also eyeing the pages. They bore the unmistakable formatting of land transfer papers. Portia bent and scooped up the document and gave it a quick glance. She was flabbergasted by what she read.

On the top of the first page, a bright yellow sticky note bore handwritten instructions boldly lettered in oversized handwriting on three perfect straight lines.

- *House is Yours.*
- *Tell Judge to Stick His Guardian You Know Where.*
- *P.S. Key under the mat.*

Under the note, the top left square of the deed contained Old Lady's name and titles.

"Your Honor," Portia hurried under the Judge's inquisitive gaze, "My client has transferred her House . . . *the property at risk*, as FEMA puts it . . . . 7 White Goose Lane is no longer in my client's name."

Paul's team put two and two together a few moments before it dawned on dumbfounded Portia, but they did not interrupt her somewhat dazed address to court.

"The Quit Claim Deed was registered last night . . . the new owner of the House . . . Paul's argument of my client's cognitive impairment is now irrelevant because . . . Your Honor, Paul has no evidence that *today's* owner of 7 White Goose Lane is impaired . . . needs a Receiver . . . Much less a Guardian."

"You got the lucky name there?" asked the Judge with unexpected informality.

"Right. . . . New owner—" Portia pulled the Deed close and suddenly turned the color of the Soviet flag.

In consideration of the legal services rendered and in repayment of all heretofore outstanding invoices . . . Grantor transfers any, should any there be, interests she might have to the Law Firm of Portia . . .

"Your Honor, the new owner of the house will have no difficulty with proving her cognitive ability. There is no longer need for Guardian."

Portia swallowed, finally realizing the brilliance of Old Lady's plan to escape the clutches of Guardianship.

"New Owner is an Officer of Your Court, Judge. Move for immediate dismissal of the Guardianship Request. We 12(b)(6), Your Honor."

And rounding on Paul, Portia added a final gloss, her voice flat and glee-less, her face as impassive as when he spied her at the crossroads when she was steeling for the certain loss.

"Paul, I'm happy to pass a physical."

Lariska whirled into the courtroom without slowing her speed at the precise moment when Honorable Judge Carlson authoritatively declared the morning to be good.

Lariska got oriented easily: on the left—a swarm of agitated youngsters orbiting a funeral-colored male figure; on the right—a solitary unmoving back in morning-blue-sky colored jacket. Not a bad designer, but off the rack, noted Lariska automatically with professional accuracy.

Trying to catch her breath, Lariska leaned over the solitary back and exhaled in loud whisper:

"Sorry, you—Portia?"

Without turning back, the smoothly-brushed head lowered in a detached half-nod.

"Phew," exhaled Lariska, and leaning over the unmoving stone-like figure, smacked the delivery on the table in front of Portia—a thin manila envelope addressed in Old Lady's hand:

For Portia Porter, Esq.

"Phew," she repeated, "made it, it's done!"

Lariska straightened up, without a trace of awkwardness trotted circling Portia from the back and plopped onto the empty chair by her side, as easily as if she did belong at the table of Old Lady's counsel.

"Read this before you—" she pushed the envelope with her finger, sliding it into unmoving hands.

Lariska's delivery instructions, which she would follow to a "t," were to *observe reaction and report* to Old Lady using FrozenChat, a very private phone messenger.

Privately, Lariska had no doubt of Portia's reaction, but it still was fun to watch.

From her co-counsel place, Lariska took in the surroundings with eagerness, doing her best to keep from fidgeting and twisting—preserve the dignified posture due in court. More amused than worried that her appearance caused a hiccup, she nodded to herself as red-faced Portia informed the suddenly attentive judge:

"Your Honor . . . as I just learned . . . my client has transferred the real property at issue . . . the 7 White Goose Lane . . . out of her name. The parcel ID, for the record is 10912345."

"You have new owner's name there?" the judge was almost leaning over his bench.

"New owner . . . Your Honor . . . is Portia Law. I'm happy to get tested, but there's now no need for Guardian to help along the owner. The new owner. I . . . The court will take judicial notice: I do not require a guardian, being of young age and still quite sane," managed Portia without a trace of smirk.

Did not hesitate accepting the windfall . . . the greedy

sleazy lawyer, Lariska thought with a touch of condescension.

And, her mission in the courthouse accomplished, took lightly to her feet, and briskly exited the courtroom of Honorable Carlson, adjusting shoulder-strap of the carrier bag containing her next delivery, the second envelope.

❧

Clean brightness of the Ducklingburg morning sky was disappearing, giving way to the saturated Southern blue. Lariska lingered outside of the Courthouse entrance just long enough to get on FrozenChat and punch out:

PP accepted
On my way to Golf Club now.

41

WEATHER TODAY

"Freckle, what do you think about that cloud? Partly cloudy today? Or you think it'll rain this time?"

Freckle tilted her head to the right, then to the left, and followed her Human's gaze up to the sky disinterestedly. It remained the little fox's instinct to throw a quick glance overhead from time to time, to check for flying predators—eagles, owls. But now she mostly did it by force of habit or rather, responding to the voice of her blood. Side by side with her Human Matthew, the young fox stepped forth serenely, utterly certain that no predator could be so brazen or plain daft to make an attempt on her safety.

The high, bright-blue sky that had just developed

a small elongated wispy cloud held no interest for Freckle.

"Maybe it's not even cloudy. It could be a trace from an airplane. You didn't hear an engine hum, did you Freckle?"

Freckle pricked up. Even the most insignificant of shifts in her Human's mood threw her into an overblown whirl of turbulent passions—from self-serving worry (will she still be safe?) to a sincere concern, a wholehearted care for Matthew's good spirits.

Freckle was uncertain of her role when her Human sulked. Was she to press her side into his calf? To climb on his chair and feel his hand sinking into her fur, slightly nervous, until his fingertips ceased vibrating, quieted down? Or is it better to wait it out, sitting on a sideline, keeping a watch over his even-cadenced, wide-spaced pacing around and around in restless circles?

The boys at the country club taught her a new trick.

"Shake hands, Freckle, shake," they cried gleefully and reached out to her with open palms. Freckle obligingly covered palm with paw. And her audience laughed with happiness.

Would that trick make her Human happy too?

How was she supposed to teach him to reach out his open palm so she could put her paw on top and tilt her head—right-left? Her Human always responded to the head tilt. He started talking in a trusting, tender voice. And telling stories, long stories. Oddly, he rambled a lot about Old Lady, the woman who owns that land on the other side of the Bridge, along the Ravine.

Freckle did not much fancy the Old Lady. Freckle disapproved of this lame-brained notion of moving into Old Lady's house, a scheme that was recently being urgently promoted by Paul and Steve. Freckle's fervent hope was that they wouldn't move.

In fact, she was sure that they'd never move. She would not take her Human to be one to follow along with the schemings of Paul and Steve. She would not think her Human was the sort to rob Old Lady of her land and house. Which, just so happened, made Freckle even more upset.

You'd think that Freckle would be happy that she got to stay in the cozy little cottage on the East end of golf course, so close to her native Forest and the home of Theodore, Whitepaw, and an untold number of her siblings. Matthew would not rob Old Lady, she knew for sure, because there was something *between* her Human and Old Lady. Although it could be that her Human only imagined that there was a connection. He was not certain. It was just a feeling. And that was exactly the part which Freckle disapproved of. Freckle herself definitely had a *feeling* that Matthew had a special *feeling* about that Old Lady.

My feeling about his feeling, thought Freckle, *is that —*

But trying to complete that thought became too full of twists and turns for her brain. Freckle sneezed loudly.

She was in no mood to share her Human with anybody—not with the Steve&Paul cronies, and most certainly not with this Old Lady.

But maybe I'm imagining the whole thing? she thought. *It's so hard to wrap a fox's mind around problems that even my Human does not understand.*

Lately, her Human only very rarely talked about the Old French Millhouse and the talented gardener and those roses. Freckle knew how to fight those stories with a distraction: demand a walk—and thoughts about the Gardener and the roses almost magically went away. But the disastrous downfall of her Human's professional career in Paris was another matter altogether. Nothing helped against his thoughts about it: not the walks, not even her soft pr-pr-pr.

Proud of her own career, Freckle was crestfallen about her Human's shattered vocation. He told her all about it: his Paris career tanked because of a Lady Scientist who had escaped, complete with all her instruments and vials and the two assistants. She skipped the country on the eve of the closing day—when all those things were supposed to be transferred to the ownership of Matthew's client.

"Just before closing. You would not understand, Freckle."

But Freckle understood. It's like if the kitchen chef were to run off together with the feathered chicken and the sous chef, right before Big Dinner. That would get the restaurant manager fired in a jiffy. *That's devastating. Freckle understands.* Her Human had never actually met this *runaway,* but for some reason he thought Old Lady was her. So, he was investigating. Freckle knew the whole story and it made her nervous.

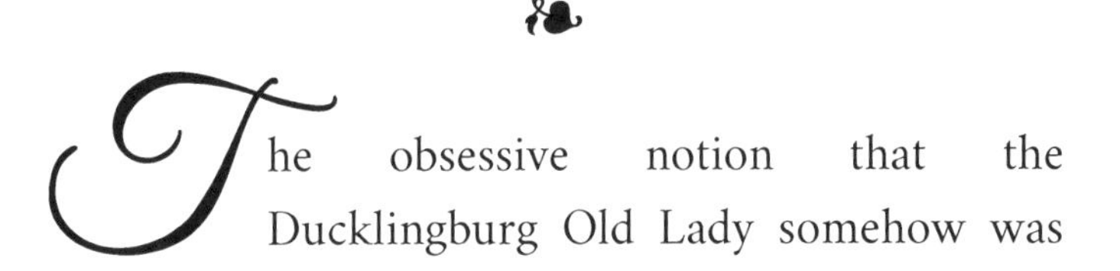

The obsessive notion that the Ducklingburg Old Lady somehow was related to that other woman—whose untimely flight was the cause of Matthew's burned out life in Europe—refused to exit Matthew's head. With the resolve so typical of hard-driving men, he determined to put his cards on Old Lady's table, so to speak. He'd solve the mystery once and for all.

His plan was to present Old Lady with the brooch, the *crad,* the bling that the Flemish landlady had foisted upon Matthew. He had kept it and it was time to play that card.

Old Lady's table soon presented itself for Matthew's cards.

Old Lady was serving tea.

They were both nearing the bottom of their second cup, poured into tiny translucent Staffordshire bone china when Matthew wordlessly extracted the brooch, from his pocket and placed it on the table, in front of her.

He managed to conceal his tension, he thought. His fingers on the brooch held still, the gesture was nonchalant.

The brooch shone quietly on the table, between them. *The ball is in your court,* thought Matthew.

Old Lady barely threw a passing glance at the brooch and, instead, settled her eyes on Matthew. Old Lady's gaze held neither fear, nor confusion, nor affectation or coquetry. Matthew was put in mind of Old Lady's expression that day he blurted out a stupid compliment about her "young looking hands."

Old Lady did not speak. Matthew waited, then understood it was for naught: Old Lady would not speak first. And Matthew smiled, sincerely apologetic for his tactless stunt. Old Lady smiled back, an open smile.

"Encore une tasse de thé?" Another cup of tea? she asked in French and Matthew's hand jolted his saucer and its tiny spoon so that they chimed.

"Natural—" Old Lady stretched out her hand and picked up the brooch.

She does have extraordinarily young-looking hands, thought Matthew. *Come to think of it, her face also looks much too young for her age, but that's no wonder. Women now have all sorts of work done on the face, all sorts of gory surgeries. And, no, she's not afraid of blood. Seen that personally.*

"They sell these brooches in New York. By exits from Battery Park, and in China town. It's real amber. From the Baltic Region, or maybe Avossian. You want me to have it?"

Not a hint of affectation or surprise.

"If you'll have it, it's yours," offered Matthew. Old Lady lowered her eyelids and lightly bowed her head in agreement.

And, just like he did not say "thank you" to the Flemish landlady back then, Old Lady did not thank him either.

The brooch, the bling, the crad—returned, Matthew marked privately.

❧

Even now, his thoughts are not really with the clouds. Taking him for a walk did not help at all, thought Freckle dolefully. And softly sang the sad fox song: ya-yap-ya-p. Twice.

"What?" responded Matthew.

Freckle licked her nose several times.

"Need water?" asked Matthew.

Freckle sharply jumped up.

"Go home then. Or march to the fountain," ordered Matthew, and the duo turned back towards their home cottage.

And just in time.

They had a visitor. Freckle spotted her from afar and gave a warning yap.

Right outside the cottage, a young, happy-looking woman stood up towards them. Freckle did not like the visit, but concealed her indisposition.

"Whew!" exhaled the Visitor, "Had a job finding you'all."

The Human looked at her inquisitively.

"To what do I owe?"

"You don't owe," replied the young woman jovially, and introduced herself,

"I'm Lariska. You are Matthew—I recognized you by the fox."

Matthew arranged a smile and nodded, inviting Lariska inside the house.

"Oh, no, thanks. No time. I'm on an errand—got message from Old Lady."

Freckle felt it right away: Matthew's stance showed high alert. But he kept silent.

"Old Lady's gone," Lariska interrupted her excavation inside her floppy shoulder bag to wave fingers happily above her head and repeated, "Flew off, left her house to Portia P-Porter . . . and left something for you, here—"

She held out an unpretentious white envelope —"a letter."

Without any show of surprise, Matthew accepted the envelope. It was unsealed and addressed with

Matthew's name only, written in the same manner as Lariska's first delivery in the courthouse earlier in the day. Mathew made to slide the letter in his pocket, but Lariska stopped him.

"No, read now," and added with unexpected emphasis, "please!"

Matthew smiled and slid out the single slip of paper, folded twice.

My dear Matthew,

I am not feeling any reason to have to apologize for what happened. But I do feel sorry.

As you know now, I left the country. I soon will need an attorney to sell my company.

Will you represent me? Think about it.

With best regards,

— O.L.

As Matthew's eyes scanned the letter, Lariska took in his expression. Freckle was watching both Lariska and her Human.

"No-no," spoke Lariska quickly, "don't respond now. We'll be in touch," and she turned on her heel and set off up the green.

EPILOGUE

After a while, Zip could no longer tell how long it'd been since his return home—or, to be precise, since the day when Raccoon hauled Zip in the stinky laundry basket back to the house which, for some reason, Old Lady had gifted away to Portia Porter.

Fox Theodore delivered the news.

"Old Lady and Milly packed lightly and left urgently," he said dolefully. And added, "my understanding is, they were chased after."

"Not captured?" asked Zip quickly.

"Don't think so," surmised Fox Theo firmly, "the Forest floated no rumors of a capture."

"That's good," said Zip quietly, and his eyes welled up with tears, acquiring resemblance with the renowned physicist Albert Einstein—sad and wise. "That's a very good thing," repeated Zip, "the only bitter part is that I—" Zip shook one feather-silky ear, "got left behind."

"I don't think so," contradicted Fox, "Milly reported that they were in a big rush and even bought open tickets."

"How's that," asked Zip.

"That's when the travelers have no clue where they want to travel. Milly mentioned Australia. Or maybe Austria. I did not remember for certain. Can't begin to think what all that means. No intelligence about it in the Forest. Even the mocking birds have no scoop."

"Sounds like," suggested Zip, "these open tickets mean that nobody yet knows where they flew."

"Nobody," Fox Theo was surprised.

"Nobody," confirmed Zip, "exactly what Portia Porter said—'*nobody has the address for Old Lady and Milly*'."

"I have a feeling," Theodore bowed his back and lowered his head contemplatively, "that Old Lady gave them the house in payment for looking after you,"

"Look after?" Zip repeated quizzically, "how do you mean?"

"She delegated them to be Your Human until her return."

"All of them?" was taken aback Zip, "the whole lot?!"

"What's the head count there?" queried Theodore.

Zip started the count.

PORTIA PORTER — ONE . . .

MANAGEMENT — TWO . . .

"—That's new," Fox interjected.

"Explain later," promised Zip.

. . . HOPPY — THREE . . .

NICK TVOROG —

. . . comes in occasionally. . .,"

Zip gave Fox Theo a quizzical side-eye.

"Count him in too," ordered Theodore, who could only freely count to five because he and Whitepaw never had more than five kits in any one litter.

In Theo's youth, tending to the kits' feeding overtook Theo's days after each new litter was born—no sleep, no rest.

No time for school either, self-justified Theodore, *but I always strained myself so that five little ones were fed.*

"These days, our table welcomes," Fox Theodore proudly switched to one of his favorite topics, "five-fold many-many times five and over of distant relatives—"

"Means you learned to count many times five?" Zip inquired.

"Not exactly," clarified Fox Theo, "Whitepaw or Freckle do their head count. But I try hard to memorize the names."

NICK TVOROG – FOUR,

Zip and Theo counted in chorus.

"Who is Nick Tvorog, exactly?" asked Theo, "I've never seen him."

"You're interrupting. I'll tell you later," shooed him off Zip.

"That's *two,*" counted Theo.

"Two what?" Zip tilted his head sideways.

"Two explanations you owe me. First—the

cholesterol. Everything about it, and how to achieve longevity. Second—the identity of Nick Tvorog."

"OK," Zip waved dismissively, "Later." Zip frowned his forehead and spots of bright yellow-orange eyebrows jumped up, "You are messing up my count —

"This NICK TVOROG, I do not know who he is — FOUR . . ."

prompted Theo importantly.

Zip shifted from paw to paw and said thoughtfully, "We counted MANAGEMENT already. I try to avoid her."

"That's new too. What's her function?" Fox asked.

"Barks orders at them all and counts their money," responded Zip.

"Count her first then," suggested Fox, "She is the most important."

"Also, there's Lariska.

LARISKA — FIVE . . .

She used to hang with Old Lady. Now she pays money to hang with Portia Porter."

"Well, I don't know about all that. How much money she got?"

"She conceals. For fear that her husband nabs half of it."

"Humans always complicate things so," Theodore shook his head and reminded,

"What about that one . . . with a Forest name . . .

. . . RACCOON?

"Last time I saw you with him, you both dissolved in the air together. First you grew gray, like shadows in a full moon, then blue like shadows in a cloudy night, then . . . I'm out of comparisons. And then you both were gone. Like a stone . . . only not in the water. In the air. No . . .."

Zip listened with intent interest.

"Go on," Zip asked, "that's interesting."

"Nothing interesting about it," disagreed Theodore, "I returned soon, but no trace of your footprints . . . sorry, slip of tongue, no trace of your paw prints . . . but foot prints too, actually . . . leading nowhere. No smell of you either. And I grew so so melancholy. . .."

Fox shook off the beginning of a howl, and declared in a certain tone:

"We count Raccoon. He has qualities that are indispensable when being chased. Where did you go, by the way?"

"Siberia," shivered Zip, "I'll explain later. Don't count Raccoon, I dislike him the most," Zip vetoed.

"Why's that?"

"Knows too much. He's dangerous."

"Cross him of our list, then," Fox agreed, "but not too many good candidates for Your Human remain."

"Old Lady was the best," sighed Zip.

"But she is gone, and you must adjust to the world around." Theo sighed too, then gave his head a shake and said.

"Your picks are limited. Two of them—Tvorog and Lariska—do not overnight at home. Even if you were to pick them, it's not clear if you'd be invited to their places. Raccoon, also known as a GHOST, is a Human of doubtful reputation.

"How about this. Who was the first you laid your eyes on at the house? Love at first sight?"

Zip concentrated and remembered.

"It was Hoppy. But there was no love."

"Hoppy," repeated Fox like an echo, "But if there's no love at first sight . . .," Fox's eyes dimmed and he pushed his muzzle into a frown. "Don't know what to say in that case. Whitepaw and I . . . everything was decided in first the instance, we did not even have to see each other . . . all I did was sniff her paw print . . .."

Theo's eyes grew wet and glistened.

Zip moved around agitatedly and let go of an short indignant roar.

"OK, Fine," agreed Fox, "love at first sight did not happen then. But then what happened?"

❧

First thing Zip saw back home was a leg. . .

He was jerked awake by a shove. A well-tanned leg covered in short stubby fair hairs leapt away from Zip's Siberian Laundry Basket, then leapt back, and Zip and his basket were smoothly rolled aside, coming to rest in the vicinity of the dishwasher.

"Hoppy, quit kicking the basket," came Raccoon's voice.

"Kitchen's no place for a dog," came another voice—without malice but unequivocal. Zip learned later that the voice belonged to Management, the all-knowing and the giver of the orders to all.

"Raccoon, why is the basket here?" asked

Management, and added in same breath, "Hoppy, remove the dog from of the kitchen."

"Leave the dog be," quietly reacted Portia's voice.

Zip yelped agreeably.

"Dog hair everywhere," contradicted Management.

"Leave Zip alone," without raising her voice or sounding annoyed Portia repeated.

Zip heard the refrigerator door slam, and jubilant Hoppy's voice declared, "uncorked bottle. Portuguese wine."

All heads turned as Hoppy mouthed slowly:

GRAHAM
40 year old
TAWNY PORT

"What's this? Anybody knows?" Hoppy asked.

Portia brushed off the query. Raccoon said, "Never tried that." The all-knowing Management then clarified.

"Good everyday alternative to Vintage Port. Keeps well a few weeks uncorked."

"How much," queried Hoppy, holding tightly to the bottle.

"Not going to bankrupt you, but not cheap either.

Two hundred dollars maybe. Personally," went on Management, "I favor thirty year Kopke, sixty bucks a bottle. Or even better, 10-year old Tawny for $16. That's my favorite."

It was at that moment that Zip realized it: *he'll never ever make peace with this know-it-all voice.*

Zip knew about PORT. Old Lady treated Matthew to lots of it after he saved Milly from the golf course poison. Old Lady and Matthew visited quietly together, speaking in soft voices, without haste, sipping the port slowly. And nobody ever mentioned how much it cost.

A Huckster, Zip christened her immediately. *Most favorite Port of my favorite Old Lady,* remembered Zip and moaned wordlessly.

Zip quieted and listened in: they were all talking prices now. And about money. And the Port.

Zip re-closed his eyes and inhaled the bouquet of delicate fruit, chocolate and slightly burned toffee . . . and Zip could almost feel Old Lady, leaning into the laundry basket, her soft hands touching Zip's head . . ..

"Everything in the house is ours now?" Hoppy's ringing jubilant voice cut into Zip's reverie.

"First floor in its entirety is for business only,"

commanded Management, who ignored Hoppy's question.

She went on assigning rooms, as Zip choked with horror. Old Lady's wooden-paneled room with oil-on-cavas Vermeer copies on the walls was relegated for Portia's "full-dress office," to impress important clients on their first-time visits.

Old Lady's library room—to house the case files.

The large dining room with its humungous dining table—for depositions. That table will house a dozen lawyers easily.

The fireplace room—for informal chats with more long-standing clients.

Old Lady's kitchen . . . the coatroom where he first met Raccoon and the adjacent washroom . . . *all was theirs now, the invaders . . ..*

"Hoppy and I want to move into the loft above the garage," almost yelled Raccoon, "that OK?"

Portia nodded affirmatively.

"The floors above, the business floor," business-like voice of Management went on assigning rooms. ". . .so that the dog doesn't get in the way. When there are visitors, the dog will be taken to the ground floor—"

Zip prepared to roar an objection, but he hadn't

the force, and so he only issued one short wheezy bark.

"The dog will be wherever he is," Portia said mildly.

"Meaning?" asked Management.

"Same as when Old Lady lived here."

❧

It'll never be the same as when Old Lady lived here, wailed Zip.

"Of course not," agreed Fox Theo calmly, "Not the same without Old Lady," then added, "otherwise, there would be no diverse experience in life." Fox Theo stayed quiet for a moment, then said pondering, "What about Hoppy? Not such a bad Human, you'll be fed and given drink under his rule. First thing he did was check the fridge, that's a good sign . . .." Theo quieted again, then asked, "Has he any money? What is it he does for work?"

"Confounding question." Zip momentarily raised the brightly glowing orange spot over his right eye. "Hoppy is incapable of settling on his final choice of occupation. *What does Hoppy want to be?* Zip repeated the question to himself. He hadn't a clue.

"Hoppy can't get oriented. When Portia's

winning, in Court, Hoppy wants to be a lawyer," said Zip.

Fox Theo nodded approvingly. "A good lawyer makes a pile of money, Rosie told me."

"She did say that," remembered Zip. "But lawyers are always so busy."

"So what? Rosie walks herself. And nobody challenges her right to freedom. She loafs around all day on Suzy's sofa."

"Watches BBC," chortled Zip.

"How often does Portia win?"

"Depends on which Honorable Judge is presiding," said Zip thoughtfully.

"Elaborate," demanded Fox. "Explain about those Honorables. Two of my kits—last season's litter—had big pow-wow with our distant relatives.

Distant Relatives insist that there's no way Portia will win against this FEMA thing since Federal Paul already picked the Honorable Judge, Paul's good friend.

Zip nodded. The news of that friendship had reached Portia's Firm a little while ago, throwing Hoppy and Raccoon into sleepwalking depression and causing Management to hiss like butter applied to red-hot frying pan,

“Cease that defeatissssst whining. Prepare to hold our own. Preparation, ten times preparashhhshn.”

“And?” asked Fox excitedly.

“And—they were up all night. I had to drag my own laundry basket into the coatroom. They all kept sleepwalking into it and kicking me. Hoppy the worst. He is the one in charge of papers among that lot. He organizes everything into order, and then glues a square to each paper that says

EXHIBIT #
and the number

“You don’t say,” marveled Fox. “So Hoppy’s the pack leader in that lot? Should we reconsider him as your Human?”

“Yes,” said Zip, then thought some more and added “Maybe.” Considered further, and decided: “Not even. I think that Portia is definitely more important. She took a brilliant deposition. So brilliant that . . .” Zip did not find a word to reflect the brilliance.

“Brilliant like a silver spoon in a sun ray?” offered Theo, “I’ve seen a magpie with one.”

“Much more brilliant,” said Zip proudly, and started on the story of the brilliant questions which

Portia asked of Expert Witness Duly Sworn. Zip used long words like *examination* and *cross-examination*, and explained them before Theo even asked.

"So deft, so brilliant that in the end, all witnesses brought by Federal Paul had to switch to Portia's side, admitting that Black Water—" but at that point bad memories overtook Zip and he became depressed.

"Get on with it, get to the bottom line," demanded Fox. "We Forest dwellers had large casualties too."

"She examined with such brilliance that all Federal Paul's experts admitted unanimously that the Water was Black, that there was no washing the sheetrock parts of the half-soaked walls, and plus the half-way flooded furnitures could be discarded, and FEMA owes for the replacements.

"Federal Paul was devastated . . . his own witnesses and experts turned out to be against him . . .." Zip considered quietly a while, then added proudly,

"Hoppy arranged it all in order, glued on all the necessary stickers . . . and the bottom line was that we were all owed a bunch of money for everything that was flooded, soaked and sodden, destroyed by

Black Water . . . in short, for *everything* that was on the ground floor.

"You do remember the ground floor? Right? The walls, the partition, the ceiling sheetrock . . . we had to replace it all . . . you do remember the state of things there?"

"Course I remember," confirmed Fox, and started listing passionately: "Doors floated, ceilings drooping, the staircase a-kilter—"

"—Enough," asked Zip, "or I'll get a headache from bad memories again."

"I won't go on, I won't," agreed Fox, and immediately changed the subject. "Cheap . . . Ch— Steve boasted that Federal Paul had a friendly judge, who would rule his way. Freckle told me. I told Whitepaw, and before we knew, the whole Forest started buzzing—"

"Please . . . don't tell me more. I get it. The Forest knows," said Zip pleadingly.

"By the way, about that fight," changed the subject Theo. "My Last Season Litter Kits are still of the view that the Honorable Judge will rule honestly. Portia should win. But Distant Relatives maintain that with the Humans, Justice never prevails . . . ."

"So?" asked Zip.

"So, in this fight for justice, both sides had casualties. One of mine lost a claw. One of theirs got a tip of his tail torn off. So, I am of the view," Theo's shiny eyes were glued to Zip unblinkingly, "we should consider Hoppy more carefully. He had good reasons to doubt victory."

"They *all* doubted victory. All and one," said Zip bitterly. "In my view, this Human court has no justice at all. Just rules and regulations."

"What's wrong with rules," ventured Theo meekly.

"I'll tell you what's wrong. These rules and regulations let the Judge ignore those brilliant depositions."

"How?"

"Judge can just ignore anything he does not like."

"How??"

"Any of these papers Hoppy numbered so carefully to bring to court. The Judge is free to say:

I'M JUST NOT GONNA LOOK

"How???"

PRETEND IT NEVER HAPPENED

Theo stared. "So, looks like my little nutty kits

tore off their claws for nothing?"

"Looks that way."

"The lawyers even have a special word for that.

EXCLUDED

"Meaning: If Judge does not like something, he puts a big black cross on it and plays make-belief that it did not even happen.

"Everybody must delete it from memory. Whoever mentions it will be punished . . . SEVERELY," finished Zip in a somber whisper.

Fox listened raptly, then snorted, "Then why do Humans go see that Judge?"

"Nowhere else to go," said Zip simply.

"What about Portia Porter, what do you think about her?" asked Fox.

"Have not decided what to think."

"What does she think of you?"

"Dunno. I need to look closer. Will start tomorrow morning, first thing."

The morning has not yet arrived.

Zip half-opened one eye. The sky had

just begun to fade around the part where Sun always came out. As Zip stretched lazily, he made out the single cloud—narrow and long, like an ash-gray cigar with fire-red making its way through the smoldering coals.

Never seen a cloud like that, thought Zip, *must describe this beauty for Milly,* he decided. But while he was searching for reflective words, the sky around the cigar-cloud faded out completely and the smoldering cigar transformed into a trace of watercolor brushstroke, of *amazing color,* but Zip was hard-pressed to tell the color's name. Another moment—and the cloud was nothing but a barely discernible wisp in pink. The sky, meanwhile, yellowed.

Zip decided he did not need to be distracted by cloud-gazing, especially since he had the job of looking into Portia, who always spoke in such a quiet voice.

Calls for increased scrutiny, decided Zip.

Up till now, Portia had not attracted the Spaniel's attention as a prospective candidate for His Human because she did not smell of food, spoke softly about extremely uninteresting topics, and spent her days on the third floor in her "not full-dress" study.

Hoppy and Raccoon intermittently visited her, and sometimes Management did too.

Zip never went; he did not see the point because Portia was not in the running for His Human.

Ofttimes, Portia moved from her room into the adjacent room where Hoppy and Raccoon had their stations. She had her own desk in their room too, with an enormous computer monitor that showed her everything that Hoppy and Raccoon were doing on their computers, and also the computer screen of a pretty lady lawyer called Aster who worked from somewhere near York, UK; and the computer screen of a thin tax lawyer who worked for her from Singapore; and of fat lawyer Mike in Alabama—and of anybody else who might participate in the job of preparing the papers against FEMA and Federal Paul.

In Zip's view, that whole setup was one huge privacy violation; but no complaints had yet been clocked in from any of them. Even quite the opposite, they apparently encouraged Portia to tune in and look at their screens.

After a few hours of *intense scrutiny,* Zip was beginning to think that there was simply nothing to learn about this dull Portia. Seeing no advantage in selecting her to be His Human, Zip peacefully snoozed on his post until the lunch break.

Everyone assembled in the room which Old Lady used to call the Fireplace Room.

Remembering that he was granted access *anywhere he wanted,* Zip pushed his laundry basket next to the fireplace, using his nose and shoulder, and flopped down beside it. Privately, Zip detested the basket because of its its jarring jumble of residual smells—including the socks and kitchen towels of its Siberian ex-owner. Nevertheless, the location of the laundry basket, was Zip's home-base. Its sturdy frame often softened the blows from Hoppy's constant air-headed stumbling over.

The conversation immediately turned to Zip's favorite topic—Old Lady. It seemed that this was the conversation that they've all had many times before.

The Fireplace Room was buzzing. Everybody was speaking at the same time, Hoppy the loudest.

"She left us everything!" squeaked Hoppy not quite on point but spiritedly, "the linens, the leather couch, the paintings . . . silverware!"

Hoppy still could not wrap his mind around the thought that Old Lady had given them her House *with everything*: including the loft above the garage where Hoppy and Raccoon were rapidly getting accustomed to living.

"Who is this Old Lady, anyway? Rich Russian—why?" asked Management, "Mob connections? Organized Crime? Human trafficking?"

"Coz not," snorted Raccoon, who detested Management for her niggardly way and constant, repressive orders, "she's a scientist."

"Have you considered," Management kept on her message pointedly "*why* this client dropped it all in your lap and skedaddled?"

"Old Lady," said Portia pensively, "I paid good money to figure out who she was."

"*After* you accepted title to her house," accused Management.

"Paid to whom? What'd you find out?" the room went wild with questions.

Portia said nothing for a second, ignoring the fuss, then said simply: "She did not at all look old. I think she tested her secret experiment on herself . . . and maybe on her Spaniels."

Three pairs of Human eyes jumped at the laundry basket—Portia, Hoppy, Management. Zip did not even move his muzzle muscle. He looked straight at Raccoon.

Zip had a feeling about Raccoon, who lately had

turned uncharacteristically taciturn and more and more often threw Zip a watchful gaze. To his upset, Zip could not quite pinpoint his own feeling that overswept him each time he sensed Raccoon's intense attention. Zip turned to face Raccoon head-on, but Raccoon looked above Zip's eyes and then simply turned away.

Zip sighed and resolved to forever cross out Raccoon's name from the list of Candidate for His Human. He should be added to the Evil Humans list, resolved Zip—those who wanted to disassemble Zip into molecules so as to ferret out Old Lady's secret of eternal youth, and then sell to their profit.

"Longevity, eternal youth and immortality!"

Out of the corner of his eye, Zip caught Management wrinkling her little nose and covering blue veins on her right hand with long, thin fingers of the left. Zip had no empathy for her, as she kept complaining that her "favorite color is now black and orange, everything in the house is now covered with black and orange dog hair, including our clothes."

"I still don't get it," Hoppy pressed on with his thought, "if she did have money, why wouldn't she—?"

"It's simple," said Management curtly. "She

refused the blood test to guard her secret. And she gave up her house not as a payment for your fees, Portia, but as an incentive for your win."

Management narrowed her eyes, again slid her palm over the blue, slightly bulging veins on the back of her other hand, and paused.

"This House is a Trojan Horse, not a gift. Old Lady's playing a Chicken game and you are the Mad Player."

I hate horses, thought Zip. *I'm not having anything to do with that Horse.*

The rest of the crew were now listening with rapt attention.

"What that has to do with us?" sounded Raccoon.

"Nothing to do with you at all," shot back Management quickly. She answered Raccoon's dislike with like coin, disapproving his baseless ambition. "Portia, on the other hand—Old Lady knew this—will fight for a paying client to the end. To the last drop of blood.

"Besides," summed up Management, "who inherits Old Lady's house, inherits the Concrete-gate troubles. Know what I mean."

Concrete, constricted bridge, flooded upstream, I'm tired of the talk about ConcreteGate, stood up Zip, trembling with irritation.

Chicken games was something new, though.

I better go ask Fox Theodore; that sounds like fox sort of business.

❧

"C*hicken* Games," repeated Fox Theodore slowly. "You sure? Never in my life seen chickens play any games. They are too dumb to even fly. Who fed you stories about those gaming chickens?"

Fox Theodore and Spaniel Zip un-hastily walked down the bank of Sneaky Creek. It had not rained for a week, and the Creek's dry bed was finally freed from even the slightest remnants of Black Water. A shallow stream zig-zagged around a tiny rock splashlessly and noiselessly, and before he even had a chance to sing the shortest tune, was gone, only leaving a wet dark-chocolate spot of mud.

"Let's turn at the fountain," suggested Theodore, "I am thirsty." And the two buddies continued on the subject of the chicken games.

"Chicken is my favorite food. Best-tasting, most succulent . . .." Fox licked his nose and gave Zip a long stare of his yellow eyes:

"You did not answer. Where did you hear about chicken playing games?"

"Hoppy and Raccoon. Said Portia is actually very good at chicken games. The Management said it's a game for suicidal maniacs, and she, Management sure hoped that Portia had enough good sense to stop playing theses chicken games."

"Now you totally confused me," was upset Theo, "I'm not even thirsty anymore. Let's go see Freckle. She'll know."

"Chicken games? Sure. I know about it," said Freckle.

"You need two cars. And two players.

"Two cars start at the opposite ends of a narrow road and race headlong on a collision course.

"First to veer off is a coward and a loser. CHICKEN. And the winner is Mad Maniac, the one who keeps on driving, even at the risk of—dead," Freckle's voice trailed.

"That's horrifying," yelped Theo. "And if nobody veers off? What then?"

"Then," scoffed Freckle, "they can share the cost of a burial plot."

Zip said nothing, as his head was getting filled with horrible visions of his life if Portia did die in a *chicken game* and Management took charge and applies herself in earnest to elimination of his red-and-black dog hairs off every surface of the house.

"Wonder if the Chickens know that the game is using their name and likeness," hackled Theo.

"Doubtful," opined Freckle importantly.

"Daddy, you smell thirsty. I stored all you can drink fresh Evian water behind my Jasmine Bush. Follow me?

"Zip, your nose just got quivery-pale. Don't worry, they do not use actual speeding cars in court. Chicken Game is a figure of speech. It's all about who gives in and accepts the other side's offer first. Portia is notoriously an unreasonable maniac who never veers off, never settles, no matter what. Better perish in the collision—I mean take a loss in court. She's known for that.

"My Human Mathew says that's why Old Lady chose her. To win a Chicken game, nothing better than the reputation for being a maniac who will not veer off. If Portia and Federal Paul go to court, they both get buried in the same grave, I mean both lose. That's what my Human Matthew said. Zip, stop shaking."

Theodore was licking water thirstily and only half-listening, but Zip was all rapt attention.

"Daddy, do not worry," continued Freckle, "Matthew says playing Chicken Game is dumbwitted—"

"—What *should* we play then?" Zip asked quickly.

"Negotiations. Entirely different game," responded Freckle confidently.

"What are the rules?" asked Zip who was generally fond of rules.

"The most important rule is to create a sound and friendly relationship with your adversary."

Theo kept lapping and started snorting louder. Freckle and Zip politely quieted down while their companion tended to his thirst—and his nervousness.

When Theodore was finished, he coughed off excess water, and proclaimed.

"Zip, you should listen to Freckle. She knows everything firsthand."

"I know she does," acknowledged Zip, irritated. N*ow the foxes will set out on their usual self-important refrain: Mathew, Freckle's Human, is beholden to Freckle's advice . . . not a step without Freckle. Freckle's always in the know . . . blah-blah-blah ad nauseam.*

"I know that Freckle knows," confirmed Zip hurriedly.

". . . Negotiation is all about relationships," said Freckle. "Friendly relationships. Complete cooperation. Let's don't threaten and bully each other. Let's don't be like those dogs who fight so hard over their pie that there's no pie left—it got all stomped over or else a raccoon stole it."

Freckle spoke benignly and persuasively.

"Don't fight. Instead of fighting, you sit together at the table, and find what the other dog wants. Inevitably, you'll find out that Dog Lucky favors pie's stuffing, and Dog Spots prefers the crunchy crust. Easy to please both with one pie.

"What if Lucky and Spots both like the same thing?" asked Zip philosophically.

"Mathew said it nearly never happens."

Fancy how much this little Fox had learned, thought Zip.

Freckle tilted her head and, directing herself at Zip, whispered confidingly,

"I'll tell you . . . I know first hand . . .."

Zip swallowed his pride and stepped toward Freckle, leaning in lower, as Freckle continued her advice.

"It is known for certain that Federal Paul plans to

invite your Portia Porter for a Meeting. At her house. On her turf. She will be surrounded by her Humans . . . Federal Paul will tell her what he wants. And she should accept.

Freckle's eyes met Zip's.

"Zip, I can tell you what Federal Paul wants. He told Matthew. They rehearsed together, many times."

Freckle went silent, waiting. Zip opened his mouth slightly and did not even sniff.

"You want to know?" Freckle asked.

Zip nodded.

"Federal Paul wants—" Freckle's voice trailed up; she was repeating a well-memorized list, "The Bridge stays exactly as is, *semi-corked*—"

"Don't interrupt her, Zip!" warned Theo.

"FEMA keeps paying everyone who floods in South Duck only *to the water-line*. No payment for the walls above the magic line. Even if their ceilings falls down from water seepage."

"Just let her finish, Zip!" inserted Theo.

"In exchange, Federal Paul gives a *heap* of money to Ol— actually, Portia's the owner now. Heap of money to Portia!"

"*Piles of money*!" repeated Freckle, half closing her eyes. "But—" the fox's eyes swung wide open and the pupils narrowed into thin gleaming slits—"it must be a *confidential settlement*."

"You understand *confidential settlement*, Zip? Means *in secret*."

Theo howled, understanding. "Nobody will know. No fame and glory for Portia, but heaps of cash. You understand?"

Zip nodded.

"She'd be a fool to not agree," summed up the foxes hotly.

"What if she *is* a fool," asked Zip?

"Then they go to court," Freckle said knowledgeably, "best case for Portia, she wins a little money. Even if she wins. Small money for Portia, but huge loss for FEMA."

Zip exhaled the air for the first time since Freckle started the lecture. The foxes misunderstood the resultant sound for confusion.

"Because before Portia, FEMA only paid South Duckers up to the waterline. If Portia wins, it will set a new precedent, a new policy in South Duck. FEMA will have to pay everybody who floods in South Duck for all the damages *above* the waterline. Lots of people flood. Lot of money FEMA will have to pay. And everybody who gets paid by FEMA will be praising Portia's name. In our South Duck, it is a *case of first impression*. Means Portia will change the law. Lots of fame."

Zip could not hold back the bark. He enjoyed praise and fame.

"*Empty* fame," persuaded Freckle, "Portia'd be a fool to go for it."

"But what about the Bridge," insisted Zip.

"What's that have to do with the Bridge," Freckle spat out curtly, "the Bridge's gonna stay like it is."

"That's not what Old Lady wants," objected Zip.

"Sue Department of Transportation, it's in charge of Bridges. FEMA is not in charge of Bridges," said Freckle quickly.

"Another lawsuit," understood Theodore, deflated. "Zip, they can't afford another lawsuit, they already feed you pill food."

"You must," Freckle flung a smile in Zip's general direction, "You must persuade your Humans to quit *playing chicken games. They should negotiate.*"

"Not my Humans," Zip whined.

"Thought we discussed *looking into* Portia," said Theo, surprised, "You did not look into her?"

"Not yet," Zip said sadly.

"But now," Freckle's voice lowered, she dropped all pretense, and was again the happy, carefree little fox, "I saved a feast. I have so many left-overs left. . . you'll be licking your vibrissae all night!"

Late that night, taking a moonlit detour to avoid The Bridge, Zip trotted home, his best friend Fox Theo at his shoulder, a bounce in their steps.

Freckle's left-over feast was, indeed, utterly delicious. The weather was delightful, the air clean, and the friends' stomachs were filled with pleasant soft heaviness.

"Negotiations are like splitting a big pie," muttered Theo in a full, thick voice, "you must advise Portia—"

Zip had not yet figured out how he would get through to Portia Porter with this new advice.

"What am I gonna do, send her a text?" Zip muttered.

Portia, Zip here.
Chicken games is so last season! :(
Negotiations games :)
That's what cool lawyers play now :)

Theodore was insisting patronizingly,

"Zip, just have faith in Freckle's words: Federal Paul will really be friendly."

Zip did not answer. He was busy computing in his head.

Whatever happened, one thing was clear now: Portia did a good job and Federal Paul was weary of the battle. Otherwise, why would Federal Paul insist on negotiating to share the pie? A big piece of pie could be had by Portia's team. Does that make Portia fit to be his Human?

"Wait until the pie's divided," Theo tuned into Zip's thoughts. "Don't be hasty. See how much money she's got, then decide."

Theo's stopped. Zip slowed his trot. They reached the moonlit meadow where rabbits were playing their midnight jumping chairs game. The pathway forked and it was time to say goodnight.

"Well," said Theodore, "that's me. I go right here. By the way, you never told me: what happened in Siberia?"

"Tell you tomorrow," promised Zip and, wagging his tail stub, set out on the left prong of the fork to what he still called his Old Lady's House.

WHAT'S NEXT FOR ZIP & MILLY?

by Fox Theodore's special request

Zip's Siberian's Adventures will be revealed. Stay tuned for the new release coming out this Winter 2018.

ZIP & MILLY: Siberian Adventures (Winter 2018)

LEGAL STUFF

MAP OF OLD LADY'S LAND

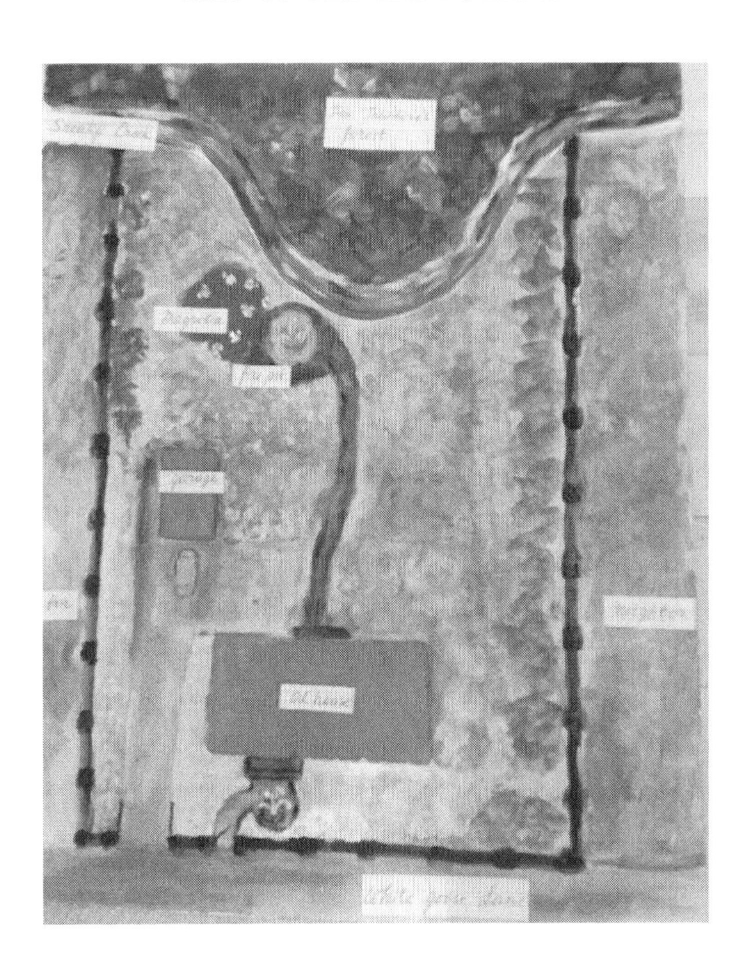

Old Lady's House, 7 White Goose Lane

The Fire Pit where Spaniels Zip&Milly

and their friend Theo the Fox gather for important *Meetings*.

Sneaky Creek loop divides Old Lady's Land and Theo's Fox Forest.

The *Garage* where Old Lady nearly drowned trying to save the late Car.

Made in the USA
Monee, IL
10 December 2020